EYES WIDE OPEN

EYES WIDE OPEN

Andrew Gross

**Doubleday Large Print
Home Library Edition**

WILLIAM MORROW

An Imprint of HarperCollins*Publishers*

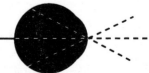

This Large Print Book carries the Seal of Approval of N.A.V.H.

To Alex Jeffrey Gross, his memory
and brief life

Is a dream a lie if it don't come true,
or is it something worse . . .

—Bruce Springsteen, "The River"

EYES WIDE OPEN

PROLOGUE

Sherry Ann Frazier knew she'd seen him somewhere before.

The gaunt, sharply cut edge of his jaw. The narrow, dimly lit eyes, staring back at her. The probing intensity of his crooked smile.

Maybe on a trip somewhere, or at an airport. You know how you pass by someone you might never see again and yet their face is permanently implanted in your mind. Or maybe she'd seen him at her shop. People were always coming in . . . She'd seen him before—that much she knew. Definitely.

She just couldn't remember where.

She was packing her groceries into her hatchback in the lot outside Reg's Market in the town of Redmond, Michigan. On Lake Superior on the Upper Peninsula. Sherry had a bakery there, a couple of blocks off the lake. Muffins, zucchini bread, brownies. And the best damn apple crisps on the UP, according to the *Redmond Crier*.

She called them Eve's Undoing—a temptation no one could resist.

He was simply staring. Leaning in the entrance to Singer's Pharmacy, next door. Looking very out of place. He never took his eyes off her. Initially, it gave her the chills, but nothing bad or creepy ever seemed to happen in Redmond. Maybe he was a workman at one of the marinas. Or a war veteran down on his luck. The town always had a few of those; they made their way up here in the summer, when the place was filled with vacationers. She always gave them a treat. Everyone has dignity, Sherry always maintained. Everyone was always loved by someone in their life.

In Redmond, the biggest worry was losing value on the Canadian "loonies" the tourists came here to spend.

Aware of him, she felt herself hurrying to fill up the car. Then she wheeled back the cart, telling herself not to make eye contact.

As she climbed in her Saab she allowed herself a final glance in the rearview mirror.

He was still watching her.

That's when she had the sense that she had seen him somewhere before.

Sherry was fifty-two, youthful, still pretty, she knew, in a bohemian sort of way. She didn't wear much makeup; she still kept her hair braided back from her days as a flower child. Still wore peasant blouses and kept herself thin. She was single again. Tom and she had divorced, though like a lot of people in her life, they remained good friends. She took art classes and yoga, studied Reiki. She fancied herself a bit of an energy healer. She even did work in Healing/Touch in the pediatric ward at the hospital in town.

Maybe that was it. Sherry brushed away her goose bumps. Maybe he just found her attractive. A lot of people did.

As soon as she pulled out of the lot and onto Kent Street, she remembered why she was there. Her daughter, Krista, was driving up from Ohio with her little four-year-old "muffin," Kayla. Sherry had closed the shop early and had brought home some carrot muffins and cinnamon buns. She picked up *Shrek Forever After* and *Finding Nemo.* She headed out of town and put the man at the market behind her.

An hour later Sherry was at the house, a converted red barn out on Route 141. Her kitchen was filled with copper pans and her famous coffee mug collection, old Beatles and Cat Stevens albums, and an RCA record player her granddaughter referred to as a "wheelie."

Along with Boomer, her old chocolate Lab.

She was up to her elbows in pie crust. Krista had called a while back and said they'd be arriving in another hour. The kitchen door was open; they were in the midst of a late summer heat wave and in this old house, she needed any breeze she could find. She was listening to NPR on the radio, a discussion about end-of-life medical treatment and how much it was costing. Sherry wasn't sure where she came down on the issue, as long as you could ease people's suffering.

Suddenly Boomer started barking.

Usually it was a car pulling up in the driveway, or maybe the UPS truck, which often came around this time. Sherry wiped her hands on her apron. Maybe Krista had surprised her and gotten there early. She was just the kind to do that.

"Boomer!" she called excitedly, hurrying to the front door.

She looked, but no one was there.

She didn't even see the dog anywhere. Not that *that* mattered—the old boy didn't go anywhere anymore. He could barely crawl onto his mat and take a nap.

Then she heard a yelp from out back.

"Boomer?"

At his age, Sherry knew a jackrabbit could scare the dog half to death. She left the front door ajar and went back into the kitchen. She wanted to have the pie done by the time the girls arrived. *Get that mama into the oven . . .*

As she got back to the table, her eyes were drawn to the floor.

"Boomer!"

The old dog was on his side, panting, unable to move. Sherry ran over and kneeled beside him. *"Poor boy . . .* Not *now,* baby,

I'm not ready for this." She stroked his face. "Krista and Kayla are on their way . . ."

She ran her hand along his neck and drew it back, startled.

Warm, sticky blood was all over her palm. **"Boomer, what in God's name happened?"**

Suddenly she heard the shuffle of footsteps from behind her. She looked up.

Someone was there.

A man was in her doorway. He just stood there, leaning on the door frame.

Her heart almost came up her throat when she realized just who it was. It was the man she had seen at Reg's Market.

A shiver of fear ricocheted through her. *What could he possibly be doing here?*

She looked at Boomer, the dog's blood on her hands, and glared back at him. *"What the hell have you done?"*

The man just stood there grinning, leaning against the door. "Hello, Sherry."

She stood up, focusing on his face, years tumbling back, like a fog lifting over the pines and the lake coming into view.

Her hand shot to her mouth. *"Mal?"*

It had been such a long time ago. More than thirty years, a part of her life she had long buried. Or thought she had. Forever. She never thought she'd see any of them again. Or have to account for what she'd done. She was just a crazy kid back then . . .

"It's been a while, huh, doll?" His dark eyes gleamed.

"What are you doing here, Mal?"

"Making amends." He winked. "Long overdue, wouldn't you say? The master of the house—you remember that, don't you, Sherry? Well, he's come home."

He was grinning, teeth twisted, that same unsettling grin she had seen at the market, tapping something in his palm.

It was a knife. A knife with blood all over it.

Boomer's blood.

Sherry's heart started to pound. Her eyes shot to her dog, whose chest had now stopped moving. A chill sliced through her, and with it, a terror she hadn't known in years.

The man stepped inside, kicking the screen door closed.

"So tell me"—he smiled, tap-tap-tapping his blade—"what've you been up to all these years, hon?"

PART I

PART 1

CHAPTER ONE

A myriad of lights flickered brightly in the distance. The whoosh of the surf cascading against the rocks was only a far-off whisper hundreds of feet below.

From up here, the lights all seemed just like candles to him. *Millions of candles!* Like the whole world had all come out and assembled before him, an endless procession at his feet.

It made him smile. He had never seen anything more beautiful in his life. He had always wondered what it would be like from up here—the gigantic mound of rock, miles and miles of coastline stretching below.

Now he knew.

You could probably see all the way to L.A., the boy imagined. He was no longer a boy really, he was twenty-one—though sometimes he still felt like one.

What are the voices saying to you now?

He stepped out closer to the ledge. "They're saying this is where I was meant to be."

He had made the climb up hours ago, before it got dark, to be alone with his thoughts. To calm the noise that was always in his head. To *see* . . . And now it was just so beautiful. And all the voices had quieted except one.

His angel, he called her. The one voice he could trust.

Have you ever seen anything more beautiful? the angel asked him.

"No, I haven't." He looked down at the lights of the small coastal town. "*Never.*"

Waves crashed against the jagged rocks below. His heart picked up excitedly. "I can see the whole world."

Yes, it's all there for you.

He hadn't taken his meds today. Usually that made him a little foggy, his thoughts jumbled. But today, maybe for the first time ever, his mind was clear. Completely clear. "I feel just like Jesus."

Maybe you are, his angel answered.

"Then maybe I should just return from where I came. Maybe God wants me back. Maybe that's what I'm feeling."

You're not meant for this world, the voice replied. *You're smarter. You were destined for greater things. You've always known that, right?*

Yes. The voice was soothing and close to his ear. His heart began to pound like the surf. *There's only one way to find out . . .*

He took another step, closer to the edge, the darkness surrounding him. The breeze brushed against his face. "That feels good. *I* feel good. I feel good about this."

Just spread your arms, his angel instructed him.

"Like wings?" He opened his arms wide. "You mean like this?"

Yes, just like that. Now think of heading home. The pain you will no longer be feeling. You see those lights? They're all so beautiful, aren't they?

"They are!"

Beneath him, a piece of the ledge broke

loose. It took several seconds until he heard the sound of it breaking apart on the craggy rocks below. He stepped back, fear springing up in him. "I'm scared."

Don't be. This is the moment it's all been leading to. All these years. You know this, don't you?

"Yes." He nodded. "I know . . ."

Then open your arms. Just let the wind caress your face. Let the darkness take you. It's easy . . .

"I feel it!" the boy said. He spread his arms. "I do."

Feel how loving its touch is. How free of pain. You've been in so much pain lately.

"I have been. Yes, I have."

It would be good to be rid of the pain, just for once. To stop the voices. To stop feeling he was letting everyone down. He knew how much of a burden he was. To his parents. To everyone who had expectations of him. The absence of pain is heaven, isn't it? *Heaven.* That would be nice. To finally be free of it.

Then just reach out, the angel said. *Let it take you. Like the wind. Just think of heading home. That's all it is. You can do that, can't you?*

"I think so," he said, nodding. "I think so."

Sucking in a breath, he stepped farther out on the edge, his pulse picking up speed. Only the cushion of darkness beneath him. The welcoming sound of the surf far below. How incredibly peaceful it all was. And those candles, so beautiful . . .

So this was it . . .

"I'm so sorry!" he shouted to the panoply of lights. To his mother and father. He knew how much this would hurt and disappoint them.

"Like an angel . . ." he said, shutting his eyes. A final cacophony built in his brain. He stretched out his arms wide, palms in the air.

"Like this . . . ?"

Yes, just like that, the angel said.

Then fly.

CHAPTER TWO

The gal in the white lace sundress was as sexy as I'd ever seen.

She had shoulder-length, sandy-blond hair, a little tangled and windswept. Eyes as blue and inviting as a Caribbean cove, the kind you could dive right into. A strap of her dress dangled loosely off her shoulder, exposing the shape of her breast, and she smiled, bashful yet unconcerned. The second I laid my eyes on her I remembered thinking, *Now there's the woman I've been waiting for all these years. The one I could live with forever.*

And as I stumbled down across the

dunes to the ocean, lugging the bottle of Veuve Clicquot and our meal, the lights from our beach house washing over her face, I said for about the millionth time in the past twenty years just how lucky I was that I had.

"Get down here," Kathy called. "There's not much time before I start to freeze my butt off and the whole thing's ruined."

"You know, a little help might do the trick," I yelled back.

I was balancing the champagne, the bowl of fresh pasta I had just topped off with truffles and butter, and my iPod speaker. The blanket was already laid out on the sand— the "table" set, the candles lit, re-creating that night from twenty years ago.

Our wedding night.

No fancy party or trip. Just us, for a change. Both of our kids were away. The truth was, we rarely even celebrated our anniversary, not since our daughter, Sophie, was born a year later on the very same day. August 28. But this year she was already at Penn and our sixteen-year-old, Max, was at fall lacrosse camp before school began.

We were at our beach house in Amagansett, basically just a cozy cape house nestled into the Hampton dunes.

"Yow, sand crab!" I yelped, hopping onto a foot and almost pitching the tray.

"You drop that bowl, mister, and you can forget about whatever you have in mind for later!" Kathy jumped up, taking the pasta from me and setting it on the blanket, where she had laid out a hand-printed menu, bamboo place mats, fluted champagne glasses, and candles. There were even little name cards.

I looked closer and noticed that they were from Annette's, up in Vermont, where we'd had our wedding.

The very *same* name cards—with the same little blue ribbons—but this time they were inscribed with the words: *"To my wonderful husband. For 20 beautiful years."*

I have to admit, my heart crumbled just a bit on that one. "Nice touch."

"Thought you'd enjoy that one. Sophie did the lettering. Not to mention letting us have the day."

"Remind me later to thank her," I said. I sat down and started to pour some champagne. *"Wait*—almost forgot!" I connected the speaker to my iPod and pushed the play arrow. "My contribution!"

Bob Seger's "We've Got Tonight" spread

over the beach. It wasn't really "our song"; it was played a lot back then when we started getting cozy with each other at college. I was never the big romantic or anything. Kathy always said she had a thirty-second window to hold my hand before I would let go.

"So happy anniversary," I said. I leaned in close to kiss her.

"Say it first," she said, keeping me at bay.

"Say *what*?"

"You know damn well what. . . ." She lifted her champagne glass with a determined glimmer in her eye. "Not like you said it back then . . . like you really mean it this time."

"You mean how you were the one I wanted to honor and take care of for the rest of our lives . . . ?"

"Yeah, *right*!" She chortled. "If only you *had* said it like that."

What I'd said, or kind of barked at her back then, going eighty on the New York Thruway—kind of a running joke all these years—after being nudged and pressed to set a wedding date, holding off until I'd finished my residency and hooked up with a job, then further delaying until Kathy was done with hers, was something a bit more like: "Okay, how about Labor Day? Does that work for you?"

"Does that work . . . ?" Kathy blinked back, either in disbelief or shock at having received about the lamest proposal ever. "Yeah, it kinda works . . ." She shrugged.

I think I drove on for another exit before I turned and noticed her pleased and satisfied smile.

"Well, it seems to have . . ." I wrapped my champagne glass around hers, looking in her eyes. "*Worked.* We're still here!"

The truth was, I'd come from a family of revolving divorces. My father, five—all with beautiful younger women. My mom, three. None of the marriages ever lasted more than a couple of years. In my family, whenever someone popped the question, it was more like code for saying that they wanted to split up.

"So then say it," Kathy said. Her gaze turned serious. "For real this time."

It was clear this wasn't her usual horsing around. And the truth was, I'd always promised I'd make it up to her if we lasted twenty years.

So I put down my glass and pushed

onto a knee. I took her hands in mine, in the way I had denied her those years before, and I fixed on those beautiful eyes and said, in a voice as true as I'd ever spoken: "If I had the chance to do it all over again—a hundred times, in a hundred different universes—I would. Each and every time. I'd spend my life with you all over again."

Kathy gave me a look—not far from the one in the car twenty years ago—one that I thought at any second might turn into, *Oh, pleeze, Jay, gimme a break.*

Until I saw her little smile.

"Well, you *have*," she said, touching her glass against mine. "Taken care of me, Jay. All of us."

I winked at her. "Now, can we eat?"

I think we both knew we would stay together from the first time we met. We were undergrads back at Cornell, and I had long, curly brown hair in those days and broad shoulders. Played midfield on the lacrosse team. We even went to the Final Four my junior year. Kathy was in veterinary science. I still kept my hair kind of long, but I'd added tortoiseshell glasses now, along with a slightly thicker waist. These days, it took a hundred sit-ups and a half hour on the treadmill every couple of days to keep me in some kind of shape.

"Yes." She started to spoon out the salad. "Now we can eat."

My cell phone sounded.

I groaned. I hadn't even realized I'd had it on me. Habit, I guess. After twenty years of being on call, the ring of the phone intruding on a potential Cialis moment was the ultimate deflating sound.

Kathy sighed. "Probably the kids. You know how they like to bust a good mood."

I looked at the screen. It wasn't the kids at all.

"It's Charlie."

My brother. Eight years older. He and his wife, Gabby, both bipolar, each with a history of drug and alcohol abuse, lived in California as wards of the state, along with Evan, their twenty-one-year-old son. We helped out with their rent, pitched in financially when they got in over their heads. Which was often. They always seemed to need something. A call from them was rarely good news.

Kathy exhaled at me. "It's our anniversary, Jay . . ."

My first thought was to let it go to voice mail, but I picked up.

"Hi, Charlie . . . ," I answered, some irritation coming through.

It wasn't him. It was Gabriella. "I'm sorry to bother you, Jay . . . ," she began, like she always began, in her gravelly, deep-throated voice and still-heavy Colombian accent. "Something terrible has happened here." Her voice was shaky and distressed. "Evan is dead."

"Dead?" My eyes immediately shot wide, finding Kathy's. Evan was their only child. He had always been troubled; he'd been diagnosed as bipolar as well. Out of school. Not working. In and out of trouble with the law. But dead? *"How?"*

"He jumped off the rock. In Morro Bay." Then she choked back a sob, any attempt at control completely unraveling. "Evan is gone, Jay. He killed himself. My son is no more."

CHAPTER THREE

I turned to Kathy, the bottom falling out of my stomach. "Evan's dead."

She looked back at me, tears forming immediately. "Oh my God, Jay, *how* . . . ?"

"He killed himself. He jumped off a cliff."

Like everything with Charlie and Gabriella—every monthly call on how they were, how Evan was doing, every veiled plea for money or to be bailed out—it spun your head.

Just a week ago we'd gotten a call that Evan was improving. That he was back on his meds. He was even thinking about going back to school. I brought my nephew's cherub-like face to mind, freckles dotting his cheekbones. That smug *Don't worry, I got it all figured out* smirk he always wore.

"Oh, Gabby, I'm so sorry. I thought he was doing well."

"Well, you know we haven't been telling you everything, Jay. It's not so easy to have to talk about your son that way."

"I know," I said, bludgeoned. "I know."

I was a surgeon. I dealt with life and death every day. But when it's someone close to you, your own . . . everything changed. They'd never had jobs or money. Or even friends that I knew. They lived on welfare, totally under the radar. Evan was their only hope. The only thing good in their own failed lives.

Now that was gone . . .

When he was younger, my nephew had shown a lot of promise. His early report cards were always A's. He was kind of a basketball whiz, his room lined with trophies. I remembered how brightly Charlie and Gabby spoke of him back then.

"How's Charlie holding up?" I asked. "Let me talk with him." Kathy inched closer and took my hand. I shook my head grimly.

"Your brother cannot come to the phone," Gabriella said. "He's a mess, Jay. He can't stop crying. He's blaming himself for the whole thing. He can't even speak."

Blame . . . My brother's life was a monument to blame. I could think of a million reasons he might be feeling that.

Charlie was my half brother, from my dad's first marriage. Eight years older than I was; I barely knew him growing up. He was raised in Miami, in the sixties, brilliant in many ways—a math whiz, early into quantum physics and Eastern religions—but just as wild. My dad's marriage to his mother had only lasted a year and a half; then he made his way up to New York; started his business, a women's apparel firm; and married my mom. He barely even acknowledged he already had a son.

Charlie was smoking pot by the time most kids were hiding beers. Then he went upward from there: speed, mushrooms, LSD. He grew his hair out, totaled his Corvette. A ranked junior in tennis, he flung his racket into the stands at the state high school championships and never went back. He always had this dream of becoming a big-time rock star. And he even produced a record once, in L.A.—the only real accomplishment in his life.

Then there were a lot of dark years . . .

First, when he was twenty-three, it was the Hartford House of the Living, where he spent three months after the cops picked him up on the streets raving that he was Jesus Christ.

Then the street scene in New Orleans, with this ragged band of drugged-out bikers and felons known as the STPs— the Stinky Toilet People—who slept on the floors in abandoned buildings, whacked out of their minds. Charlie once told me that you could wake up with a knife stuck in your chest if you simply rolled up against one of their girlfriends wrong.

And finally that commune up near Big Sur, where I'd heard about this cult of stoned-out musicians and drifters, several of whom were later convicted of a string of horrible murders, though Charlie always claimed he was hanging around there only for the chicks and the drugs.

For years, he bounced in and out of hospitals and jails. Schizophrenic and bi-polar, he'd been on lithium for thirty years, not to mention his own private pharmacy of antipsychotics and mood stabilizers. He always battled with our father, right up to the day he died.

Ultimately, he did settle down. He met Gabriella in a recovery clinic back in Miami. Together, they moved out west and lived this quiet, codependent life in a coastal California town, granted disability by the state, just enough to squeak by.

They had Evan, and they tried their best to raise him. We always pitched in, anteing up for a car when theirs broke down or paying off their debts. Charlie once said to me, "You know how ashamed it makes me, Jay, to have to take money from my little brother just to get by."

But of course they always took it. We were all that kept them from living under a bridge somewhere.

Now Evan . . .

My nephew's life was a perfect storm of things that had gone wrong. Mental instability. No money. Violence and fighting in the house. At first, everything seemed on the right track; then it all changed. Scrapes at school became brushes with the law. He started taking drugs—speed, ecstasy, OxyContin. He and my brother began to clash—just as Charlie and our father used to clash—furniture tossed, punches thrown, the police called. Evan's behavior grew increasingly erratic and withdrawn. He started hearing voices. He was placed on a daily diet of the same pills his father took—lithium, Klonopin, Thorazine—but he always seemed to be more off them than on. Finally he dropped out of school, got himself fired from a series of menial jobs. I tried my best to get him private counseling, to lure him away from their house. Once, I even begged him to come live with us and go to a junior college back east. But Charlie and Gabby never seemed prepared to let him go.

Only months ago, they'd told us that Evan had turned around. They'd said he was back on his meds, being helpful around the house. Even thinking of going back to college. Then only last week they'd left a message: He'd been taken away. He was in a state hospital. They were talking about finding him some kind of a halfway facility where they could place him under supervision. Force him to stay on his meds. We thought this was good. For the first time in years, we thought maybe there was a reason to hope.

Now this . . .

"Your brother needs you, Jay," Gabriella said. She choked back a sob. "I'm afraid for what he might do. You know we don't have anywhere else to turn."

They had no money. No jobs to focus on. No friends to help soften the pain. All they ever had was this kid. And now he was gone.

I gave her over to Kathy, who tried to comfort her, but what was there to say? In a couple of minutes she put down the phone.

"I have to go out there," I said.

She nodded.

I scrolled through my commitments for the following week—mostly things I could pass off on my partners, other than a pro- cedure I had to perform on Friday on the teenage daughter of a friend.

"I'll go Monday. I'll only stay a couple of days."

Kathy shook her head. "You can't wait until Monday, Jay. These people need you. You're all they have." She took my hand in hers. "You have to go tomorrow, Jay."

My gaze drifted to the meal spread out on the blanket, now cold. The glasses of champagne. Our little celebration. It all seemed pointless now.

I realized I hadn't seen my brother in more than five years.

"I'll go with you, you know," Kathy said, moving next to me. "I will."

"Thanks." I smiled and drew her next to me. "But this is something I ought to do alone."

"You're a good brother, Jay."

She handed me my glass. Then she took hers and we touched them lightly together. "Here's to Evan," Kathy said.

"To Evan."

We took a sip and sat, knees up, watching the waves against the shore. Then she leaned over and re-pressed the play button on the iPod.

"Like the man says . . ." She put down her drink. "We've still got tonight."

CHAPTER FOUR

The three-hour drive up the California coast on 101 to Charlie's the following day gave my mind time to wander to some old things.

It went to my brother as a long-haired eighteen-year-old who had just dropped out of college, his conversation rocketing back and forth between complex string theory, Timothy Leary, and how the Beatles' *Abbey Road* was the new gospel, in what I knew now, but not back then, was one of his uncontrolled, manic rants.

It went to how he had once visited me at Cornell—after he was released from the psychiatric home in Hartford—and how we took a weekend trip to Montreal. I recalled how we had trolled for girls along Sherbrooke Street, near McGill, and how Charlie had ended up screwing our waitress back in the hotel room after he'd convinced her he had taught Eric Clapton all he knew, and air-played her the opening riff from Cream's "Sunshine of Your Love," while I pounded the pillow over my head in the other bed, alone.

My brother could charm the birds out of the trees.

It's easy, Charlie always said, with that sly, mischievous grin. *If you ask every chick you run into if they wanna screw, now and then one of them says yes! Even when you look like me!*

Eventually, winding through the wooded canyons around Lompoc, my thoughts roamed here:

To the last time he had any kind of relationship with our dad.

It was maybe twenty years ago, Charlie's last chance at a real life before he permanently gave up.

Somehow he had persuaded my father to dispose of his old design samples by sending them down to Miami, where Charlie had set up a rack in a women's hair salon near his mother's dance studio, selling them as one-of-a-kind creations.

It was only a wobbly metal rack in the rear of this cheesy salon, crammed with colorful velour and cotton cashmere sets— my dad's particular genius. But to Charlie, it might as well have been the epicenter of the apparel world. He held court, shuttling back and forth between hair stations, his own hair bound neatly into a ponytail and dressed as cleanly as I'd ever seen him, the blue-haired women eating out of his hand. He'd mesmerize them with stories about his famous father in the rag trade, the glamorous women he screwed while in L.A., celebrity rockers he did coke with, lurid tales of his years on the road, all the while pushing oil stocks on the Canadian stock exchange.

He was turning dozens of sample sets each week at fifty to sixty bucks a pop. Real money in his pocket for the first time in his life. Living in a decent place on Biscayne Bay with Gabby and his infant son. He had an exuberance I'd never seen before—a twinkling in his eyes.

For the first time he was making it—in the real world.

And with his father, who had let him down a hundred times.

Later, he took me back to the storage room where he kept his stock. Charlie's mood shifted. He started ripping open shipping cartons, his voice accusatory and familiar. "Look at the shit he's trying to pawn off on me," he said, tearing out newly received merchandise still in plastic bags. I could see rips, flaws, mismatched color panels mixed in with legitimate samples. "You see the kind of business I've got going here. These people don't want crap. I'm selling 'one of a kinds,' not this garbage. *And look*—" He ripped an invoice out of the box. "He's fucking billing me for them! He's not even giving me terms."

Everything always came back to this: Charlie trusting himself in our father's hands, and Lenny pulling the rug out from under him again. "*I can't sell these, can I?*" He looked at me for confirmation. And, yes, there were a few seconds, the prior season's returns that had probably been in someone's stockroom forever, design prototypes with busted zippers and mismatched panels.

"It would be hard," I said, agreeing.

"He's trying to screw me again, isn't he?" Anger rushed into my brother's face. "You know what he did? He had his accountant call me up and demand payment. His accountant! *I'm his son, for Christ's sake.* He just can't stand to see me successful . . . We're selling dozens a week of these, and he doesn't want me to take his luster away from him so he's trying to shut me down."

To me, it was probably just the shipping manager throwing in the kitchen sink. My father probably didn't even know about it.

But to Charlie it was like he had personally handpicked them to ensure he would fail.

A fight ensued, and weeks later, my dad stopped shipping to him for good. There was a huge battle over payment. My dad called Charlie "an ungrateful sonovabitch." Charlie threatened to come up north and kill him.

They never spoke again.

He took Gabriella and Evan and moved out to the coast. Ten years later, when my father—drunk and down on his luck—drove his Mercedes into the waters of Shinnecock Bay, he wouldn't even come to the funeral.

I got off the freeway at Pacific Crest Drive. Pismo Beach was a quaint, sleepy beach town tucked under rolling hills of dazzling gold and green, leading down to rocky bluffs overlooking the Pacific.

Grover Beach, where my brother lived, was its seedier next-door neighbor.

I'd been out there only once before, five years ago, when I brought the family while we were vacationing in San Francisco, four hours to the north. Up to then, my kids hadn't even met my older brother. They'd only met Evan, their cousin, the couple of times we had brought him east.

Their place was a tiny two-bedroom apartment provided by the state with a single bathroom and pictures covering up cracks in the plaster in a downtrodden two-story building across from abandoned railroad tracks.

That visit, we sat around for most of a day, listening to Charlie and Evan banging on their guitars, belting out barely recognizable rock tunes in hoarse off-pitch voices, amid my brother's rants about how his father had ruined his life and how by the time he was Sophie's age, fifteen, he was already whacked out on LSD.

It was scary.

We watched them apportioning their cache of colorful medications on the kitchen counter. Gabby said how she was once a beauty queen back home and had never bargained for this kind of life, and how she might just go back to Colombia, where her family would gladly welcome her.

My kids were a little freaked out. We took them out to lunch, to a café on the main street overlooking the beach, lined with surf shops, tattoo parlors, and oyster bars. Charlie said it was the first time they'd been to a restaurant other than Denny's in years.

We left the next day.

I drove down the long hill toward the ocean and turned on Division Street. I found Charlie's building a half block down, the familiar blue Taurus I had bought for him parked beneath the carport out front. I pulled into the next space and sat for what seemed like a full five minutes.

What could I do for them here?

My mind went back to something.

The day Evan was born. Back in Miami. Kathy and I happened to be in Boca, so we went to see them at the hospital. Charlie was so different from how I'd ever seen him before. Cradling his little Evan in his arms, in his blue blanket, looking like any doting new dad, but with his wild, Jerry Garcia hair and bushy beard. He let Kathy hold the baby for a while, and he and I went down to the cafeteria.

"This is the start of something new for me," Charlie said. "I can feel it."

But as he picked up the coffee cup, something changed. "I need you to promise me something, Jay . . ."

"Sure." I was twenty-eight then, still in med school. Kathy and I weren't even married yet.

"I need you to promise me you'll take care of him. Whatever happens to me, okay? I need to know Evan'll be safe."

"Nothing's going to happen to you, Charlie. Of course he'll be safe . . ."

"No." There was something dark and brooding in his eyes, a storm massing. "I need you to promise me, Jay, that whatever happens, you'll be there for him."

I said, "Of course I'll be there, Charlie." I met his worried eyes. "You have my word."

He smiled, relieved. "I knew I could count on you, buddy. I just hope—"

Someone moved behind us on the line and he never finished. But now, all these years later, I thought I knew what he was about to say.

I only hope he doesn't have what I have.

My son. The demons in his brain.

I only pray his path is easier.

He'd asked me, not Dad. And sitting under his carport, I couldn't help but wonder: If it had all somehow worked out, back in that stupid salon . . .

If they had lived in a place without cracks in the walls . . . If their boy could have grown up proud, instead of filled with shame and anger . . .

Would his fate have been different or the same?

Even if the demons had found him, would my nephew still be alive?

CHAPTER FIVE

I went around the side through a brown, patchy courtyard, past a broken plastic kiddie car on its side. I stopped outside apartment two, wincing at what smelled like dog urine. Lurid, brightly colored graffiti spread all over the asphalt wall.

I knocked on the door.

After a short while I saw the curtains part, and the door opened. Gabriella appeared in a blue terry robe. She was normally a pretty woman with short blond hair, a nice shape, and a deep, throaty laugh, but now her cheeks were sunken and pale, her eyes raw from tears, her hair matted and unkempt. As she let me in she kind of turned away, almost unable to face me. "I'm sorry that you have to see me this way, Jay . . ."

"It's okay, Gabby, it's okay," I said. We hugged, and I felt her latch on to me. It always made me feel a bit awkward, her gratitude for me for how we helped them get by. "I'm so sorry, Gabriella."

"Oh, you don't know what it's like." She moaned, anguish etched into the lines around her eyes. "I never thought I would ever feel something as difficult as this. Never to see my son again. My heart breaks, Jay . . ."

"I know." I kept hugging her. "I know."

"Your brother is not so good." She pulled away, brushing the hair out of her eyes. "I don't know how he's going to make it, Jay. You'll see for yourself. He's old now, and Evan was all we had. I'm glad you're here."

She led me inside. The place was small. Still, it was neat and tastefully decorated, with floral pillows and pictures of her family in Colombia and even some watercolors done by Charlie's mother.

I heard a familiar voice on the stairs utter quietly, "Hi, Jay."

My brother came down. He looked grayer, older, hunched a little in the shoulders, a shadow of what I last recalled. His beard was flecked with gray now, his hair straggly and wild. Charlie always had a twinkle in his eyes and an irresistible, wiry grin. It was what always captivated the girls. But nothing seemed to be there now. He wore a pair of ragged sweatpants and a brown flannel shirt. He forced a smile. "I'm glad you came, little brother . . ."

"Of course I came, Charlie."

"C'mere . . ." He got to the bottom of the stairs and we hugged. I was surprised how natural it felt. Hugs weren't exactly the norm in our relationship. He placed his face on my shoulder and started to weep. "We're sunk, Jay. It's gone for us. I can't believe Evan is dead."

"I know. I know . . . ," I said, squeezing him back and patting his shoulder.

"We failed him, Jay. He was a good kid, in spite of everything. We didn't do right by him."

"You did your best, Charlie. He wasn't an easy kid."

We all sat down at the small table in the kitchen. Gabriella poured some coffee. She laid out the long line of medications he was taking: trazodone, Caduet, felodipine, Qua-pro, Klonopin. Sedatives, blood pressure controllers, mood stabilizers. I didn't really know much about what had happened. Only that Evan had jumped off a rock, but not how he had gotten there or why.

"Can you talk?" I asked him.

Charlie nodded, cupping a few of his pills in his hands and knocking them back. Dully, he looked up at me like, *What is there to say?*

I said, "Then tell me what happened."

CHAPTER SIX

We always took care of our son." He peeled an orange and put it on a small plate in front of him. "No matter what anyone can say, we tried to do our best. We always kept him safe."

"I know that, Charlie," I said, squeezing his arm.

Tears shone in his dark eyes. He shook his head. "I just don't know how he could do that to us . . ."

Gabriella got up and wrapped her arm around him from behind. She picked up for him. "Ten days ago . . . You know for a long time, Jay, our son had been acting really crazy . . ."

Of course I knew. Sitting around in a silent state all day in the house, no job, no school. Usually off his medications.

"Well, he'd gotten worse. He was off his meds. We no longer knew how to handle him. He would just sit there—on that couch—for twenty-four hours straight. Not a single word—just staring. Into space.

"Just a few weeks back we heard noises in the middle of the night, and we came down. He was just sitting there, talking"—Gabby pointed to what looked like a wood-burning heater in the corner— "to the furnace, Jay. My son was talking to the furnace! He told me, 'I hear voices in there, Mommy . . .' I said to him, 'Evan, you have to let us help you . . .' We didn't know what to do."

"He was always so angry at us," Charlie said. "He wouldn't take his pills. He would just hurl them at us. Then he'd just smile coyly. I couldn't fight him anymore. It was like he was torturing us, trying to make us suffer along with him."

"Two weeks ago"—Gabby took a breath to steady herself—"we found something . . ."

I took a sip of my coffee. "What?"

"This is so hard for me to tell you, Jay. It really is . . . I went through his things. Because I was scared. I was scared at some of the things he was saying to us. He called me a stupid, uneducated whore . . . a wetback scum. He called your brother a miserable kike who could never get a job. His own father . . . I wanted to see where he was learning this from. What was influencing his crazy mind? And we found something. An application . . ."

"For a job?"

Gabby laughed. "*For a job?* If only for a job! It was an application to buy a gun! A twenty-gauge shotgun. From a gun store in the next town. And for what? To kill someone, Jay. Maybe kill us. You see these stories on the news, about what people like our son can do. We said, this kid can't have a gun . . . He's mentally unstable. He's been diagnosed by the state. He has a record with the police. These people cannot sell him a gun . . ."

I screwed up my eyes in disbelief. "*How?*"

"He lied, Jay. He lied about everything on his application. That he wasn't sick; that he had no record. Maybe they would have caught it, or maybe not—but we went there. To stop them. We told the man at the shop, 'Are you out of your mind? You can't sell my son a weapon! Do you know what he might do with it?' We threw the application back in his face. We were scared . . .''

I said, "I don't blame you for being scared." I thought of my troubled nephew with a gun, with the image of Columbine or Virginia Tech vivid in my mind, with all the anger and sociopathic behavior he had shown. "You did the right thing, Gabby."

"I know we did the right thing. But then we found something else . . ." She looked at me, eyes downcast. "I can hardly even say it, Jay . . ."

"We found a kind of diary Evan was keeping," Charlie interjected. "These ramblings, crazy things . . ."

"I have to cross myself to even tell you these things," Gabriella said. "Things like, 'Better to suck the dick of the devil than to live here with these two dead people one more day . . .' That's *us,* Jay. Our son was talking about us—your brother and me!" She dabbed at her eyes, shame and grief etched deeply there. "But we didn't know what to do . . . We knew he's acting truly crazy now. Off the charts. We can no longer control him. It's clear he hates us . . . That he wants to kill us. And then himself. And who knows, maybe take other people with him . . ."

"So what did you do?"

"We showed it to him." Gabriella looked at me as if seeking dispensation. "Everything. You know what he did? He takes me by the hair, and twists me, like he wants to kill me right there, and throws me against the wall. *Look!*" She opened the top of her robe and showed me purplish marks covering her shoulder and onto her neck. "He's too big for us to fight now. Look at your brother. He's weak, old. He is no longer able to protect me. We didn't know what to do . . ."

"So what *did* you do?" I asked.

"What did we do? We called the police," Gabriella said.

Truth was, I had always pushed them to do exactly that. To put their son in custody when he assaulted them. But they never would. They never once pressed charges. *How could we?* they would say. *On our own son.* And then the excuses would start. *He's just a boy. He's ashamed of what he's done. He promises to stay on his medication.* I guess I understood. Who wanted to make that kind of choice? But by not getting Evan help, by always protecting him and shielding him from treatment, I saw the events build that could lead nowhere but to catastrophe.

"When the police came"—Gabby rubbed her forehead, shaking her head—"Evan went out of control. He looked at me. 'You do this to me, Mommy? You called the cops—on your own son!' I saw something in his eyes I had never seen before. Like an animal. I told him, *'You're sick, my son. You need some help.'* He grabbed me by the hair again and tried to beat the shit out of me. Your brother, he tried to help. But Evan threw him against the wall. He almost broke a rib. The cops saw it all. They finally got Evan in a choke hold. They came and took him away. To the hospital, in San Luis Obispo. To the mental ward. That's when I called you, Jay."

"They placed him under a suicide watch," Charlie said. "They took away his belt. And laces. Put him under twenty-four-hour observation. I've been there before. I know the drill. Apparently he told the doctor who first examined him that he wanted to kill himself. That the gun he was trying to buy was intended not for us, but for him."

He shook his head. "We failed him, Jay. They said they were going to take care of him. Help him." A mixture of grief and anger hung in his eyes. "We thought maybe we finally did the right thing. That maybe this was the best way. The social worker there told us they were going to keep him safe. That they'd watch him, for as long as they possibly could. Three weeks, they said. Then they'd find somewhere for him. I said, 'Whatever you do, you can't put this kid back on the street. You see how angry he is? He'll blow people away . . .'"

"You know the name of the doctor?" I asked, something starting to tighten in me. They had trusted the authorities to take care of Evan, and they had let them down.

"Derosa. Mitchell Derosa. But we never even spoke to him. No one would speak to us. Only the social worker there. His name was Brian something. We have it written down. And a nurse. They said for us not to worry, they were going to have several doctors observe him, and they would get him into some kind of facility."

Gabriella chortled cynically. "You know what we were thinking? We're thinking, *Maybe this is a good thing after all.* That's when I called you, Jay. You probably thought it was just for more money, but it was to tell you, maybe Evan is in a good place at last. We felt relieved."

I nodded.

"But then they call and tell us they're going to release him! This social worker. Brian. After around four days. He says Evan is stable now and they had found a place for him. *Four days?* They said three weeks! I'm telling you this kid was psycho, Jay. I said, 'Are you sure, so soon . . . ?' But they said, 'Your son is an adult, Ms. Erlich,' and that they couldn't hold him indefinitely against his will, now that he had calmed down and was no longer a threat to himself. What kind of a crazy thing is this? I said, 'You can't do that. Maybe he's an adult, but I am his mental guardian. You see the shape he was in.' But they say Evan agreed, and they're gonna put him in a good place."

"What kind of place?" I asked.

"They didn't tell us shit!" Charlie snorted. "They wouldn't even talk to us. That's what happens when you're poor and on disability in this town."

"But now they're scared," Gabby said in a haughty tone. "Now they all see what happened. It was on the TV. On the news. They know they screwed up. They're all running to cover their own asses now."

Something brushed against my leg. I looked down. A gray and white cat was nuzzling against me.

"That's Juliet," Gabby said. "Poor baby—she misses Evan too." She reached down and lifted the cat up, took her to the back door, and put her gently outside. "Get back outside. You can't be bothering us now."

The cat slinked back to the yard and jumped onto the fence.

"So where did Evan finally end up?" I asked.

"You want to know where they put him?" Gabby replied, her tone hardening. "You want to know where they threw my son, like some sack of garbage? In this unsupervised home in Morro Bay. Completely unrestricted. With a bunch of fucking old people. Alzheimer's patients. Walking around like the living dead. Evan called me. He said, 'Why did they put me in here?

Why did they put me with all these old people, Mommy?'

"The woman who's in charge there said he went to take a walk. She just let him go. Waved him out the door. They don't give a shit. They get their money. Evan was just a voucher to her. A check from the state. *That's all!* They had him on so much medication. Seroquel. Two hundred milligrams. Two hundred milligrams is enough to drop an elephant, Jay. You know this stuff. You know what it does. It makes you act like a zombie. It takes away your will. She didn't care, as long as she got paid. My son went to take a walk and never came back. This woman, Anna, she called us late that night. Two days ago. Evan was missing. Where is he, she asks. She said she thought maybe he came home to us. But you know where he was, my son . . . ? You know where Evan was? He had climbed the fucking rock there, that's where he was. He was probably already dead."

Anger flared up inside me. This just didn't wash. Every patient had a medical history. Treatment charts. Diagnoses and evaluations. They don't just dump people at will. In a place where they won't be watched.

"She just let him leave?"

"Yes. Walk out. I told you, she don't give a shit, Jay. That's the way it is here. But, believe me—she was scared when she called us. She knew she screwed up. And the next morning, my son, he turns up dead. He was up there on the rock, Jay. The whole stinking night. In the cold. Alone. Without anyone to watch over him." She started to sob again. "My boy was on the rock. I want to sue that bitch."

"You want to know what really hurts?" Charlie took her face and brought it against his shoulder. "We were watching the news that morning. Friday, I think. Or Saturday . . . I don't keep track of time so well anymore. They said some kid had jumped off Morro Bay Rock. A John Doe. No ID on him. We go, 'Thank God that's not Evan. Thank God *he* is in a safe place.' And it's our own son, Jay! They were talking about Evan. We're listening to a report about our own son . . ."

He started to sob, loud choking tremors. Gabriella held his head in her arms. "We just failed you, Evan . . . We let you die."

It was horrible. I didn't know what to do or feel, other than my hands balling into tight fists. Rich or poor, it didn't matter. There was a complete breakdown. Not only of treatment, but also of responsibility. And Evan was the victim of it. I knew in my world, this could never happen. Not without some kind of response, accountability.

"Where is he now?" I asked.

"At the coroner's," Charlie said. "They're doing their autopsy and tests. We can't even see him."

Gabriella wiped her eyes. "He called me, you know. The day before. I asked, 'Are you all right, Evan? You know I love you, don't you, my son?' And you know what he told me? He said, 'I'm gonna make the best of it, Mommy.' *Make the best* . . . Does that sound like some kid who wanted to kill himself the next day? They say it's a suicide, but it doesn't sound like that to me. You know what I think? I don't think my son would kill himself. It sounds like murder, Jay. By the state. They took my son and screwed his head up on drugs, then dropped him in a place that wasn't right for him. *They murdered him.*"

As a doctor, I was always quick to assume that the system handled things correctly. Sure, mistakes were made, but generally it did things right. But as an uncle, I couldn't disagree.

It was like murder.

We sat around in silence for a while. Charlie and Gabriella just hugged each other, helpless and crying. Then Gabriella got up. She cleared the table, put the coffee mugs in the sink, and ran the water over them. Then she turned and faced me, her palms back against the counter. "At the end, it was very, very bad, Jay. You have no idea. Our son never left the house. He would just sit there, on that couch all day, never even talk, just smile at me. You know that little smile he had, like he had the whole world figured out. Like he knew the truth and no one else did."

"I know it." I wasn't sure whether to smile or shake my head in sorrow. I smiled.

"He said to me, just last week, before he did this . . . He said, 'I think maybe I'd like to be a cop. Or an FBI agent.' He said he was talking to the police and they wanted him." She cleared her throat derisively. "*A cop?* My son barely left the house. He didn't talk to anyone, Jay. No friends. No girls. Not even us. *Only to the fucking furnace!* He was dreaming. Like he always did,

Jay—*dreaming*." She looked at me. "He might never have gotten better—I understand that. But he didn't deserve to die."

She came back to the table and sat down next to me. "We took care of our boy for twenty-one years. Then we give him to the state—for four lousy days . . . *And he's dead!* Maybe we don't deserve medals, Jay. But we damn well deserve to know why, don't we? We deserve to know why my son had to die!"

I looked back at her, my gut tightening.

Years of the differences between us peeled away.

I said, "Yes you do. You damn well do deserve that, Gabby."

CHAPTER SEVEN

My life had been easy, to this point.

I mean, we've all faced hardships and disappointments. I was no genius, but I always did well in school. I could whip a mean underhanded crank shot that got me a ride to Cornell; I married the girl of my dreams. We raised kids who seemed to be equally achieving, who were polite and self-assured and didn't seem to mind being around us.

I'd worked my butt off to get where I was: I'd put in the eighty-hour weeks and still remained on call twice a week. We had friends; we went on bike trips to Spain

and Italy. For my fortieth birthday I got myself flying lessons and now had my own
Cessna. Two years ago, when it came
time for the hospital to name a new head
for our department, the chief of staff didn't
hesitate and turned to me.

Still, I felt like I'd barely broken a sweat
in life. The world always seemed to open
up just enough for me to slip through.
But for Charlie, the world always seemed
to close at every chance and shut him
down.

I don't know if I was a good brother. I
don't know if I ever lived up to that vow I
made regarding Evan. I knew I'd always
done just enough to keep them from sinking.

Enough, but no more.

Maybe it was too late to put myself on
the line for Evan.

But I could damn well start doing it for
Charlie and Gabby now.

I checked myself into the Cliffside
Suites, the nicest of the motels perched
along a high bluff overlooking the Pacific.
My room was at the end of a long outside
corridor above the parking lot. Inside, it
was clean and large and I stepped out

through the sliding glass doors to the terrace with a panoramic view of the ocean and the steep cliffs below.

I threw myself on the bed and thought about Evan and his last visit to our house. How everyone thought he was so weird, no matter how much I tried to defend him: He was smart. The odds were stacked against him. He was my brother's son.

"He doesn't even know how to order food, Dad," Sophie had said. "He always seems a bit stoned out."

"He does spend a lot of time off in space," Kathy said. "You have to admit he's a bit weird."

I told them, "He's on medication, guys. Cut the kid some slack."

"I'm sorry, but he gives me the creeps," said Maxie. "How much longer is he going to stay?"

I spent the next couple of hours watching a baseball game and picking at a burger from room service. Around four my phone rang. I was happy to see it was Kathy.

"Hey," she said.

"Hey . . ." I exhaled wearily.

"You sound exhausted. How are they

doing? I called a little while ago, but nei- ther really wanted to talk."

"Devastated. How else could they be? You're not going to believe how it happened, Kathy."

I told her everything I'd learned. How Evan had been looking to buy a gun. How he was taken in and put in isolation after trying to beat up Gabby, and then re- leased after only a couple of days. To the care of a halfway house that let him walk out the door.

"That's just so awful, Jay."

"Someone has to get to the bottom of this for them. They're not capable. It's tear- ing them apart."

She hesitated just a bit. "Get to the bot- tom of *what,* Jay?"

We hadn't always seen eye to eye about things with my brother and Evan. Usually, it was how we were always coming to their rescue. First, for a nicer place for them to live. Then tutoring for Evan. Then when he smashed up the car. And finally bailing them out from under all that credit card debt. "When do *they* try, just a little?" Kathy would say. "Gabby can work. Our kids get summer jobs; why not Evan?"

But mostly, it was that incident with Max.

It was on Evan's last trip east. He and Maxie were playing a little one-on-one in the driveway. Something set them off. Things always seemed to cross the line with Evan.

I was in the den, flipping through some medical magazines. Suddenly I heard screams. Sophie's. From outside. "Get off, Evan. Get off! *Mom! Dad!*"

I bolted up.

Somehow Kathy, who was in the kitchen, got there ahead of me. She jumped on Evan's back, Evan's arm wrapped around Maxie's neck; Maxie was turning blue.

"Evan, let him go! Let him go!" Kathy screamed, but at six feet, close to two hundred pounds, Evan was too big for her. "You're going to kill him, Evan!"

"First he has to take it back . . ." Evan squeezed tighter. *"Right, Max?"*

Max couldn't take anything back. He was gagging.

Kathy screamed, unable to pry him away. *"Jay!"*

I got there a second later and ripped Evan off by the collar, hurling him across the lawn.

My nephew just sat there, eyes red, panting. "He called me a frigging freak!"

Max had had bronchial issues from the time he was three. He needed a respirator back then, twice a day. His face was blue and his neck was all red and twice its normal size. He was in a spasm, wheezing convulsively.

I knew immediately he had to get to the hospital. I threw him in the car and told Kathy to get in. I called ahead to the medical center. In eight minutes we were there. They immediately placed him on oxygen and epinephrine. His airway had closed. Acute respiratory distress. Five minutes more and he might have been dead.

When we got back home, Evan tried to say he was sorry.

But it didn't matter. Kathy never quite forgave him. She wanted him out of the house.

The next day I drove him to the airport and he was gone.

"I need to get to the bottom of why he was let back on the street, Kathy," I answered.

She didn't respond right away. "Look, I know I haven't always been the most supportive when it comes to this . . . You're right, they need you, Jay. Do what you can. Just promise me one thing."

"What's that?" I asked.

"Just promise me, this time, you won't let yourself get drawn in. You know how you always get when it comes to your brother."

Drawn in . . . Meaning it always ended up costing us something. I didn't want to debate it, and the truth was, she was probably right.

"Deal," I said.

CHAPTER EIGHT

The next morning, I called the county coroner's office and set up a meeting with Don Sherwood, the detective handling the case—the *only* person, Charlie and Gabby said, they could get any straight answers from.

He was the one who had knocked on their door two days earlier and asked if Evan was their son—he had ultimately been identified through fingerprints from his police record—and after asking them to sit, showed them the photos of Evan in the county morgue.

Sherwood said he'd be nearby in the

early afternoon and we could meet at the station in Pismo Beach around one P.M. I told him we'd be there.

My next call was to the psych ward at the Central Coast Medical Center. I asked for Dr. Derosa.

The nurse who answered asked who I was, and I gave her my name and told her that I was a doctor from back in New York and Evan Erlich's uncle. She kept me on hold awhile and finally she came back on saying how very sorry they all were, but that the doctor would be out all day on an outside consult and would have to get back to me.

I left my number and said that I'd be around only a few days. I figured I'd hear back in a couple of hours.

A few minutes before one, I went with Charlie and Gabby to the one-story police station on Grand Street and met Detective Sherwood in a small interrogation room there.

He seemed to be in his midfifties, ruddy complexioned, with a husky build and thick salt-and-pepper hair. He stood up when we came in, gave Charlie a shake with his thick, firm hands and Gabriella a warm hug. Charlie had said Sherwood had worked for the local PD and coroner's office for more than twenty years.

"How're you holding up?" he asked them, motioning to us to sit down at a table in the cordoned-off room.

"Not so good," Gabriella said, shrugging sadly.

Sherwood nodded empathetically. "I understand."

"This is my brother, Jay, from New York," Charlie said. "He's a doctor."

The detective sized me up—my blazer; an open, striped dress shirt; jeans my wife had picked out for me—and showed a little surprise.

"Thanks for seeing us," I said.

"No problem at all." He nodded. "Very sorry for your loss."

"My brother and sister-in-law have a few questions they'd like to ask," I said. "Not only about Evan, about what happened . . . but also about his treatment at the hospital. How he could have been released after just a few days and put in a place where he was essentially allowed to roam free. I'm sure you understand how this isn't sitting well with them."

"I know you have some issues." He looked at Charlie and Gabriella. "We've scheduled an autopsy and a toxicology lab later today. But I'm happy to fill you in on the details of what I know."

"Thank you." Gabriella nodded gratefully.

"Some time late Thursday afternoon," the detective said, opening a file, "Evan apparently left the halfway house in Morro Bay saying he was going to take a walk."

Charlie narrowed his eyes. "*A walk*? My son was medicated."

"The woman who runs the facility suggested she took it as a positive sign. His first day there, he'd been pretty withdrawn."

"They told me they were putting him in a restrictive facility," Gabby said bitterly. "That woman killed my son."

I squeezed my palm over her clenched fist to calm her. "What happened then?"

"Some time that afternoon it appears he wandered down to the rock in the bay and found a path up on the southwest face. He was probably up there a considerable time. Some time during the night, at maybe two or three A.M., it appears he fell from a large height onto the rocks below. We can approximate the time from the

body's temperature"—he turned to me—
"as I'm sure you understand."

I nodded. The lower the body temperature, the longer the body had been dead.

"He was discovered early the next morning by two clammers at seven A.M. The
coroner's finding is that your son was killed
on impact. The wounds on the top and
back of his skull are consistent with his
belief that essentially Evan did a back dive
from a height of around a hundred and
fifty feet and hit *here* . . ."

Sherwood placed his palm on the back
of his head.

"Oh, God!" Gabby's hand shot to her
mouth. She crossed herself.

Charlie just sat there numbly and shut
his eyes.

"Are you okay hearing this?" Sherwood
asked. "It'll all be in the coroner's findings
when we're done, which you can read at a
later time."

"No, we're okay," Charlie said. "Go on.
You're sure it was a suicide? He could
have just fallen, couldn't he?"

"I suppose there's always the possibility,
but there were no defensive wounds on
his hands or arms that might've come from

trying to brace an unexpected fall. The first part of him that contacted the ground was his head. He seemed to choose a location that had an unencumbered path to the rocks below. Not to mention what his motive would be in even being up there in the first place, at night. I'm sorry, but I'm not exactly sure what other ruling there would be."

Charlie fidgeted in his chair. "Did anyone see him climbing?"

The detective shrugged. "Not to my knowledge."

"The first time you saw us you said he was missing one of his sneakers?"

Sherwood nodded blankly. "That's correct. Yes."

"Did you ever find it?"

"No." The detective looked at him quizzically. "Not yet."

"So maybe he was just climbing," Charlie said, pushing, "and just slipped. He always kept his laces undone. Maybe that's what did it. Maybe he just lost his footing up there. That could be right, couldn't it?" His question had an air of desperation.

"Look, we're looking into everything," the detective said, "but we have to make a determination and given when he left the recuperation facility and the time of death, taking into account his state of mind and how long he was up there . . . I know how painful this all is. I know how tough it was not to have been notified for so long and to have seen the story on the news. Just know, we're doing everything we can."

Gabriella started to weep. She took a tissue out of her purse. "I want to see my son."

"I'm afraid that's not possible right now. They're finishing up the autopsy and toxicology findings. Anyway, the trauma was quite severe. There's going to have to be a bit of reconstructive work done . . . Maybe in a couple of days."

Gabriella put her hands in front of her face.

"Look, I'm no psychiatrist," I said, a hand on Gabby's shoulder, "but one of the things my brother and sister-in-law are trying to deal with is why Evan would have even been released from the county hospital and transferred to that facility in the first place, given that only a couple of days before he tried to purchase a weapon and had been removed from his home in a pretty violent state, put on suicide watch, and heavily sedated with a mood-altering antipsychotic. I'd like to talk to the doctor in charge of his case. I don't understand how they could make a determination to just dump him back on the street."

"They didn't dump him," the detective said. "They put him in a state-approved halfway house. Maybe not the best suited, as it turned out . . . I know where you're heading. But I've looked at the doctor's reports. He was deemed to be stable and mentally capable upon his release. He told them that he no longer harbored any desire to terminate his own life. He was over twenty-one. They're only permitted to hold him against his will for a matter of days."

"This kid could have been a hazard to *anyone,*" I said, "if he followed through on that weapon, not just to himself. You're saying all you have to do is claim that you're no longer suicidal and they can put you back on the street?"

"Not *can,* Dr. Erlich. They have a legal obligation to do so. It's the law. If they don't feel like he's an imminent threat. As I say, he'd stabilized. I didn't want to say this myself, but apparently he'd informed them there he did not wish to return back home upon release. They process thirty or forty people a week through that ward. They found a bed for him at a smaller facility, where he'd receive proper attention . . ." He turned back to Charlie and Gabriella. "I promise you, everyone is extremely sorry about what happened.

"In the meantime," he said, placing a folder on the table, "I do have some things for you . . ."

He took out a large manila envelope and pushed it across the table. "Your son had these in his possession at the time . . ."

Charlie and Gabby's eyes stretched wide.

There was a large plastic bag inside. I saw a couple of dollar bills and some loose change. A metal-link key chain with a single key attached. A crumpled candy wrapper. And something else . . .

Gabby pulled it out.

It looked like one of those cheap plastic holograms that came from a Cracker Jack box. An eye—wide open if you looked at it straight on. Then it closed, in a kind of wink, when it was shifted the other way.

"Evan was always picking up stupid stuff off the street." Charlie shook his head forlornly.

"He went around collecting recycling,"

said Gabby, eyes glistening. "For the money. He would go through people's things—their garbage. Bring things home. People's shit. You wouldn't believe what was important to my son . . ."

She picked up the bag and held it like a cashmere cloth against her cheek. "I can feel him, my Evan. I know he didn't kill himself. He would never do that to me . . ."

"You have to look into that sneaker," Charlie said, his eyes fixed on Sherwood, as if it was the missing piece of a puzzle. He jabbed his finger. "That could be the key."

"I promise, I'll do my best." The detective nodded obligingly. He stood up and caught my eye. "Got a second?"

I stood up across from him. "Of course."

He went around and opened the door and walked me outside to the hallway. "Your brother said you're a doctor?"

"Vascular surgeon. At the Westchester Medical Center. In Valhalla."

"Vascular . . ." He nodded thoughtfully. "You work on hearts?"

"Veins, predominantly. Endovascular repairs. I keep the works flowing. Guess you could call me more of a plumber than a mechanic." I smiled.

Sherwood nodded. "I'm a liver recipient myself. Going on two years now. So far so good, I guess. I'm still here."

"Good for you," I said. Liver transplants resulted either from cirrhosis from booze or from hepatitis, the C kind, the killer, but something made me suspect the first.

"Now all I got is this TMJ." He massaged his jaw. "Hurts like the devil whenever things get stirred up. In fact, I'm starting to feel it now . . . You say you're from back in New York . . ."

"Westchester." I nodded.

"I got a cousin back there. Nyack."

"That's across the river. In Rockland County."

"Well, wherever it is"—the detective looked at me directly—"trust me, Dr. Erlich, it's a whole different world out here . . . Look, I don't want to hurt anyone's feelings—I've been doing this a long time, and I know how hard it is to hear—but this kid plainly wanted out of the game. You know what I'm saying, don't you? He'd made statements that he wanted to end his own life. He claimed to the doctors that the gun he was looking to purchase was intended expressly for him. I shouldn't go into this yet, but your nephew's toxicology report came back. He was clean. Nothing in him at the time of his death—*nada*. Not even Seroquel, doc. You catching what I mean . . . ?"

I caught exactly what that meant. Evan hadn't been on his meds.

That explained how he had managed to climb all the way up there. How he still would have had the urge to follow through with it.

It pretty much explained everything.

"So how the hell did he manage to find his way all the way up there?" I asked.

"I don't know." He sighed. "But I do know how the death certificate is going to read. Death by suicide." He reopened the door and looked at me before he headed back in. "What the hell else would the kid be doing up there in the first place?"

CHAPTER NINE

After they left, Sherwood slipped back into the interrogation room, shutting the door.

He took out his cell and pressed the number for the hospital over at County, worriedly thumbing the edge of Evan Erlich's file.

Stories like his happened every day out there. Gang executions, drug ODs. Runaways. They all had mothers who wept and didn't understand. Suicide or accident? What did it really matter? The kid was dead. A tragedy was a tragedy. If it hadn't ended like this, the next time—and there would have been a next time, Sherwood knew—he would have likely taken the mother and father out too.

His job was to try to make sense of the rotten outcomes. Just not too much sense.

Tomorrow, sure as sunrise, there'd be two more.

The hospital operator answered. Sherwood placed the phone to his ear. "Dr. Derosa, please."

He knew about tragedies. And not just on the job. He thought of his son, Kyle, more than twenty years ago, and his wife, Dorrie—almost two years now. He had this new liver. A gift. From a minister. Edward J. Knightly. Now he even peed righteous, Sherwood sometimes said with a laugh. This whole new chance at life. This new lease. What the hell was it even for?

How do you make sense of others' tragedies when you can't even figure out your own?

A voice came on the line. "Dr. Derosa here."

"It's Sherwood," he said, leaning back in the chair. "I'm calling about that Erlich kid. That jumper . . ."

"Yeah . . ." The doctor sighed, as if he didn't need to be reminded. "We're all really sorry about that one here. I got a call this morning from some relative of his. A doctor."

"And how did you handle it?"

"How we always handle it, Don. You know we don't put ourselves directly involved."

"Yeah, well, maybe you ought to get a bit more directly involved in this one."

The psych ward doctor cleared his throat. "What do you mean?"

"They want a look at his medical records. They're right, of course. Funny, they want to know how the hell their son was dropkicked back on the street and a day later ended up dead. And you know what?"

"What?" The doctor sounded a little peeved.

"I can't say I really blame them on this one, Mitch. Just thought you'd want a heads-up."

"The kid was a ticking time bomb, Don. We do our best to stop 'em. This one went off."

"Well if I were you, you might want to look at it again. That it's all buttoned up."

"Buttoned up?" The doctor's tone now had an edge of irascibility to it.

"Any loose ends . . ." Sherwood stared

at the file, at the copy of Evan's medical records included there.

Ones the poor, grieving family would never see.

They didn't need anyone tugging on loose ends here. Not the family; not some pushy outsider from New York. The problem with loose ends was, once pulled, you just never knew what would tumble out.

"I think you know what I mean."

CHAPTER TEN

I tried the hospital again as soon as we got back to the apartment.

Again, no luck.

The doctor in charge, Derosa, still hadn't called me back. Which was starting to piss me off, since several hours had passed, and it was professional courtesy to receive a reply. A secretary at his office said he was still at an outside consult.

Even a call to Brian, the mental health social worker there, went straight to his voice mail.

I was beginning to feel like a wall of silence was being erected, and the doctor and his staff were bricks in it.

Finally I got fed up. I was losing valuable time. I tried the nurse's station at the psych ward. I got to a Janie Middleton, who identified herself as the chief nurse on the ward. "I'm told you wanted some information on Evan Erlich?"

"Nurse Middleton"—I softened my tone—"my name is Jay Erlich. I'm a surgeon in vascular medicine at the Westchester Medical Center back east in New York. Evan was my nephew . . ."

"Oh," she said, betraying some nerves, "I assisted him while he was here. He seemed like a nice boy to me. We're all so, so sorry for what took place . . ."

"I appreciate that," I said. "Look, Janie, I know Dr. Derosa isn't around . . ."

"He's—" For a second I thought she was about to say *He's right here*. Then she seemed to catch herself. "I was told he might not be back for the day, but the first step in any patient inquiry is to request the doctor's report. The next of kin is entitled to it, of course . . ."

"Of course." Everyone was hiding behind

the damned report. I just wanted to speak to somebody . . .

"Janie . . ." I took a breath, trying to hide my frustration. "Are you a parent?"

"Yes," she said, her reserve softening as well. "I am."

"Then you'll understand. My brother and sister-in-law have just lost their only child. They want an answer."

How Evan went from being on suicide watch to being released, after just days. How he was placed in an unrestricted facility and a day later he was dead. "You can understand that. They're feeling— they were making the responsible deci- sion to put their son in the hands of the county when he got out of control. And no one's giving them any information on how this happened."

"Of course I can understand," the nurse replied. "Look, just petition the medical records. *Off the record . . .* then the doctor has to officially respond to your questions. I honestly think that's the best way." She lowered her voice. "I hope you understand what I'm saying . . ."

Was there some kind of cover-up going on? Was that why no one was willing to get on the phone with me? What was the hospital hiding?

"I hear you," I said, sighing. "So how long does that generally take?"

"Four or five business days, I think."

"Four or five days!" I wouldn't even be there then.

"Ask for the medical reports," she said again. "That's about the best I can say. We're just all so sorry . . ."

Frustrated, I thanked her for her time.

"See, now you're starting to see what shits they are out here," my brother chortled, as if in vindication. "How no one lifts a finger for you if you're poor. You're just not used to that, little brother."

"I'm not done."

I called the hospital one last time and asked for the head of the Psych Department, a Dr. Emil Contreras. I explained to his assistant who I was. She told me Dr. Contreras was at a conference in New Orleans and wouldn't be back until Thursday.

Thursday I'd be going back home.

"When he checks in, if you can please have him give me a call. It concerns Evan Erlich. It's urgent."

I left my cell number. I wanted to slam down the phone.

It was only two. And I wasn't sure exactly what I had accomplished. "What's next . . . ?"

"I think I need to see it," Gabby said.

"See what?"

"Where it happened."

Charlie looked at her warily. "You're sure?"

Detective Sherwood had given us detailed directions to the spot where they found Evan. Underneath the rock.

"Yes. I have to see it." Gabriella nodded. "I have to see the place my son died."

CHAPTER ELEVEN

It rose, gigantic and majestic. A single mound of volcanic rock dominating the coastline, six hundred feet high.

We could see it from miles away, before we even reached the quaint coastal town. I couldn't take my eyes off it. Partly because of its vast size. And partly because of what happened there.

"This is crazy," Gabriella said, hiding her face in her hands and glancing toward Charlie. "I can't believe I'm actually doing this. Going to the spot where my son died."

The massive rock was situated on a narrow strip of land, overlooking the tiny fishing bay. Sherwood had said to drive all the way to the parking lot along the south side of the rock, then go through a chain-link gate and across the shoals. A narrow path snaked up the rock face there. He said to look for a ledge about a hundred feet up, above the jagged rocks.

The place where a couple of early-morning clammers had found Evan.

My heart poured out, thinking of Evan being drawn to the site as he walked there, alone and confused, voices clashing in his head.

"Now you see, you see what my poor boy climbed?" Gabby turned to me. "In the fucking dark. You have to be crazy to do that, right?"

I didn't answer, but there was nothing in me that disagreed.

We parked the car and walked out onto the rocky shoals in the shadow of the mountain. A handful of people were milling around. Fishermen tossing out lines, tourists snapping photos, a few makeshift souvenir stands. The breeze picked up, and Charlie and Gabriella seemed to waver.

My brother said, "Maybe he went up there

to see God. Evan was like that. Maybe that's what he wanted to do."

I had heard about as much of this "Evan was Jesus" stuff as I could bear. "The kid was disturbed, Charlie. He wasn't looking for God. He was sick." I heard myself echoing Sherwood. "What the hell do you think he was doing up there anyway?"

"I don't know if I can do this," Gabby said, suddenly white as a ghost.

I went over and put my arm around her. "You don't have to, Gabby. We can go back."

"No, I *do.* I do have to." She brushed back her hair and fortified herself with a breath. "Let's go."

We walked, Charlie trailing, until we found the chain-link fence Sherwood spoke of. There was a gate to walk through, but also a sign: NO VISITORS PERMITTED PAST THIS POINT.

There was no park ranger around, no one stopping us. Sherwood had said to keep going as far as we could walk.

"I think it's over here!" I shielded my eyes and looked up. A craggy overhang protruded high up the cliff face, nothing in its way to break a fall to the rocks below. I noticed a loose path winding up the face and another sign that cautioned against climbing.

Gabriella looked up, tears massing in her eyes. "I can't believe this, Charlie, I really can't. I can't believe our boy would do this."

Charlie leaned against me, his long hair whipped by the wind. "He didn't kill himself. I know it. Don't you see, that's why they never found the other sneaker. He slipped somehow, climbing up. Maybe it lodged in the rock. It's up there somewhere. He wouldn't have jumped. I have to believe that, Jay, you understand?"

I wanted so much to tell him, *Stop it, Charlie, just stop. Evan's dead.* Like Sherwood said, accident or suicide, what did it even matter now? Instead, I just squeezed his shoulder and nodded. "I understand."

Gulls cawed, flapping in the breeze. We stood there for a while with my arms around both of them, solemnly staring at the place where Evan had fallen. Pain was etched in their drawn, anguished faces as they relived the image of their son's backward descent, picturing him landing hard onto the unforgiving rocks. They had seen the photos: the blood on his face, his spine shattered.

Having to think of him lying there all night. The surf washing against him. Gulls picking over his body.

I remembered Gabby's words: *Your brother feels responsible, Jay.*

Of course he feels responsible. Evan had become him. Charlie had passed his legacy of disease and blame onto him. Fanned it, like a brush fire, with their anger and how they lived, pointing the finger at everyone for what had gone wrong in their failed lives.

And not to mention they were the ones who had called the police and sent him away.

Gabriella shook her head in frustration and balled her fists. "Oh, Jay, you don't know how tough this is. I held him in my arms. That first day. Every parent has a dream for their child. I told my son, 'You are going to make us proud. You are going to live the life we've never led.' A child is supposed to go farther than their parent. That's how it's supposed to happen, right? That's the law of nature. *Not this . . .*"

I gazed up at that ledge and knew whatever hope they still harbored that their son had simply slipped was just another of their delusions. Why would anyone have climbed all this way, other than to jump? Why would he have remained up there through the night? And, ultimately, like Sherwood grimly said, why did it matter? Evan was dead. No one would ever tell us what was in his mind.

Suddenly Gabriella picked up a stone and flung it against the rocks. Then another, freeing her pent-up rage. "*You bastard!*" she yelled into the wind. "Damn you!"

Damn you.

I didn't know if she meant Evan or God, or maybe even the giant rock.

She yelled, "I want to know why my son had to die! I know we're poor. I know we don't matter. But I deserve that, don't I, Jay? Evan deserves that."

She was right—this wasn't the ending that had to be. It was the ending Evan received, because the system looked the other way.

We all did, in our own way.

Gabby hurled another stone against the rocks.

Yes, Evan deserves that, I answered her in my mind. *That's the least he deserves.*

Watching her, I knew why I was there.

CHAPTER TWELVE

The Harbor View Recuperation Center was a converted white Victorian house with a large front porch and a green awning on a quiet street, a few blocks from the town's touristy center.

If Gabby wanted answers, this was the place to begin.

"You're sure you want to go in?" I asked Charlie and Gabby as we pulled up across the street.

"This woman killed our son!" Gabriella declared bitterly. "She let him leave—when he was supposed to be in the care of people who would watch over him."

"Okay," I said. We parked the car and headed in.

A couple of Adirondack-type chairs with chipped paint sat on the porch. The lawn was thick and a bit overgrown, in need of trimming. Inside, we found a couple of elderly people milling about, just as Evan had described. I didn't see any guards or orderlies around.

"Look at this place," Gabriella said, her eyes flashing with barely controlled rage. "I can't believe they dumped my son in this shit hole."

I knocked on an office door and a squat, pleasant-looking woman in black pants and a floral blouse glanced up from her desk. She appeared Filipino.

"My name's Dr. Jay Erlich," I said, introducing myself. "Evan was my nephew."

Anna Aquino's almond eyes grew wide. "*Oh . . .*" She jumped up, came around the desk, and took my hand. "I am so, so sorry about what happened. I've run this facility for eight years. We've never had anything like that happen here before."

"These are Evan's parents . . ."

Instead of being defensive, Anna Aquino took Gabriella's hands warmly in hers and gave her a compassionate hug. "I spoke with you the night he disappeared. When he didn't come back, I was so worried. He seemed like such a good kid, your son. If I knew he was in such a state, I never ever would have allowed him to be admitted."

Gabriella pulled away. "What do you mean, if you knew he was in such a state? You let our boy just walk out of here. We trusted you to take care of him and now . . ." She glared at the woman with reproach.

Over the years, I've seen my share of indifference when it came to caregivers. Nurses just going through the motions, care facilities doing the minimum, bilking the insurance companies. But Anna Aquino wasn't like that at all.

"Ms. Erlich," she said, "I know how you must feel, but look around . . . This is an open facility. We don't keep people here against their will. We're not set up for that sort of thing here. We can't even force our patients to keep on their medications. It's strictly voluntary.

"That first day, your son was like a zombie here. He was totally snowed on so much Seroquel he could barely talk. He wouldn't even eat. But by the afternoon of the next day, he seemed so much better. I know he called you—"

"Yes," Gabriella said, "he said he wanted to make the best of it here, but . . ."

"That afternoon, he came up to me and told me he was going to go for a walk. I was actually excited to hear it. I thought he was coming back to life. He said he was just going to walk around the town. When he didn't come back, of course, we were worried, and that's when we called . . ."

"I think what my brother and sister-in-law would like to know," I asked plainly, "is just how a violent, bipolar kid on suicide watch just a couple of days before could simply be allowed to walk out the door."

Anna looked into my eyes and shook her head. "Because no one ever informed us of that, Dr. Erlich."

I squinted, not sure I'd heard her properly. "*What?*"

"No one told us your nephew had been suicidal. Or about any of his behavioral history. I had no record on him at all, other than he was bipolar and had spent time at County and was placed on a high dosage of Seroquel. Believe me, if I thought he was a danger to anyone—or to himself—

there's no way I would have ever admitted him here. You can see for yourself we're not equipped for that sort of thing."

"You're telling me you received no patient history?"

"No." Anna shook her head. "Zero. They just drop them here. Like baggage. With a two-line diagnosis and a medication chart. When they saw I had an open bed, they brought him here. I'm a state-funded facility, Mr. and Mrs. Erlich, so I can't simply refuse. This is my biggest frustration. They never give me any history. You see my patients here . . . We specialize in dementia and Alzheimer's care. Believe me, if I knew your son was schizophrenic—not to mention *suicidal!*—I would never have let him stay here even for a night. Poor kid, I'm heartbroken over this . . ."

My anger was increasing. No history. Not even a medical report from the hospital. They might as well have pushed him off that ledge themselves. What was the hospital hiding? "Do you mind if I see his charts?"

"Not at all," Anna Aquino said. "I have them right here." She went around the back of her desk and came back with Evan's file.

A two-page transfer form from the Central Coast Medical Center read, "History of bipolar behavior." It listed his medication, Seroquel, and the dosage, two hundred milligrams. A hundred milligrams was normally the prescribed dose. A drop-dead maniac would be turned into a zombie on that! The form said the patient had been released from care and was being transferred to the Harbor View Recuperation Center on a strictly voluntary basis.

It was signed *Brian Smith, Social Worker.* And cosigned *Mitchell Derosa, MD.*

My blood stiffened. I saw that Evan had signed it too.

I had to restrain myself from crumpling it into a ball and hurling it against the wall.

There was no history of his previous psychological behavior. Not a single word about the nature of his treatment in the hospital. Nothing on the violent actions he had manifested when the cops took him away. Or his attempt to purchase a firearm.

Not even a mention of his urge to kill himself.

They had basically just thrown him here!

As soon as a bed opened up. Like Anna Aquino said—*baggage*.

What had happened to the restrictive facility they had promised Charlie and Gabriella? Where their son would receive monitoring and attention? They were right—everything just fell between the cracks because no one felt they mattered.

"Can I have a copy of this?" I asked, handing Anna back the forms.

She shrugged. "I don't see why not."

"Look," I said, "I don't know how we're going to handle this . . . But would you go on the record on any of this? What you just told us. To the head of the hospital, or even to an attorney? It would be helpful if we could count on your support."

"I've been on record on this for years," Anna Aquino replied. "Just look at the people who are here. They're not threats to anyone . . . Look at our staff. We couldn't even restrain someone like your son. It's almost criminal . . ."

Yes, it was. It *was* almost criminal!

She turned to Gabriella and, almost with tears in her eyes, said, "I'm so sorry . . . I thought I was doing the right thing . . ."

Charlie looked at me as if to be saying, *Now you see, you see what it's like to be poor. You see what it's like to be in a place where no one cares . . .*

I checked my watch. It was four now. No one from the hospital had called me.

But at this point, I was no longer giving a shit about procedures.

CHAPTER THIRTEEN

Charlie and Gabriella had mentioned a local television station where they had first seen the story of the Morro Bay jumper, then a John Doe, three days before.

"You've got to be careful, Jay," Charlie said, cautioning me. For twenty years they had lived under the radar, afraid that the state would cut them back. "You can't just stir up trouble for us here. It's not like with you. We live off the state. We can't make waves."

"Sometimes you have to make waves!" Gabby said. "This about our son, Charlie. We need to do this."

I looked up the number for KSLN and asked for the news department. For the reporter who had handled the segment on the Morro Bay jumper. I gave my name, identifying myself as an uncle of the dead boy.

It took a couple of minutes, but finally a woman came back on. "This is Katie Kershaw. I'm an assistant producer in the newsroom."

"Katie, hi. My name is Jay Erlich. I'm a doctor from back in New York, and I'm the uncle of Evan Erlich. Your station did a story on him."

"Yes, of course. That was terrible." She knew who he was immediately. "We would have followed up, but it's a policy here, for family reasons, we generally don't report on suicides."

"I guess I can understand that," I said. "But listen, Ms. Kershaw . . . I think your station is missing the real story behind what happened with Evan."

Two hours later a reporter named Rosalyn Rodriguez and a colleague with a hand-held camera knocked on Charlie and Gabby's door.

Gabby seemed lifted. She had changed, washed her face, and applied a little makeup for the first time since I'd been there. Finally someone was going to take their side.

Charlie seemed a bit edgy. "Are you sure this is the right thing?"

"You always want to do nothing," she said to him. "You're always afraid the state will find us. They'll discover your brother is helping us with the rent. Our disability will be cut. Yes, I want to do this. *It's for our son, Charlie!*"

When the reporter arrived, we all sat in the small living room. Her questions closely followed the narrative I had given their producer on the phone.

How did you first find out what happened to your son? What do you feel about what happened? Do you think the doctors at the hospital bore any responsibility? Do you think your son belonged in a more restrictive facility?

"That's what they promised us." Gabby nodded. "Yes."

Charlie just sat there, not saying much.

Gabby started with Evan's being released from the county psychiatric ward after just three days. Three days after having attempted to acquire a gun. How they were being stonewalled from getting even the simplest answers to their queries. How the Harbor View facility didn't even have a clue what kind of patient they were dealing with.

I jumped in and said, *"The police . . .* they just seem to have washed their hands of all this. They want to get rid of the case as quickly as they can. Maybe it's because my brother and sister-in-law aren't important here. They live on welfare. To be frank, they're concerned that because they draw their income from the state, everyone's just stonewalling them in the hope it will all just go away. They're convinced they have no right to look into their son's death."

The reporter glanced at her cameraman, basically asking, *You getting this?*

"Look, I'm a doctor, for God's sake," I said. "Wouldn't you want to know how a twenty-one-year-old kid goes from twenty-four-hour suicide watch in a locked cell to an unprotected halfway facility in just a matter of days—and then ends up at the bottom of a six-hundred-foot cliff?"

At this point, I no longer cared whose feet I was stepping on.

"All they're getting from everyone is just, *We're so sorry. That's tragic.* Well, *sorry* simply isn't enough. They want someone to take responsibility. They want some answers. You'd want that if it was your family, wouldn't you, Ms. Rodriguez?"

"Yes, I *would* want that." The reporter nodded, the cameraman shifting to get her reaction. I could see it was affecting her too.

She asked us for names. And we gave them to her.

The doctor, Derosa, who was clearly ducking my calls. And Anna Aquino, who ran the care facility Evan had been dumped in.

And Detective Sherwood.

She promised she would contact the hospital and speak with officials there.

"God bless you." Gabby wrapped her arms around her and thanked her. "For whatever you can do."

"I want them to know they can't just shit on us," Gabby said after they left, coming up and giving me a grateful hug. "We may be poor, but our son deserves some answers too."

Charlie sat there, distracted, unconvinced. He picked up his guitar and strummed a few chords. "You're going to go home, Jay, but we're still here. These people own us. Maybe we just should have let it lie."

CHAPTER FOURTEEN

That night, Gabby asked me over for dinner.

I came up with maybe a dozen reasons why she shouldn't go to the trouble, but she insisted.

"You are here, Jay, and I'm allowed to invite you to our house. Maybe it'll take my mind off everything."

Sherwood had called earlier, saying we could come and look at Evan's body tomorrow, which didn't exactly elevate the mood.

In spite of it all, she threw together a pretty good meal.

A paella of chicken, sausage, and shrimp on a bed of yellow rice. I bought a local sauvignon blanc from a store called Scolari's Market.

"What the hell," Gabriella chortled, pouring a glass for herself as well. "I think tonight God will forgive me if I drink a little too."

We ate and polished off the wine, and despite all that was going on, the mood managed to stay upbeat and light. We talked about Kathy and my kids. How adult they had become. I always tried not to build them up too much. Sophie and Max, who took AP courses, played on the lacrosse and field hockey teams, volunteered at food banks, went to the Bahamas on spring break. Even in their most ordinary moments, they had more to show than Evan had accomplished in his life.

Sooner or later, as it always did, the conversation came around to our dad.

Leonard the Good and *Lenny the Louse,* as he always referred to himself.

You never quite knew which one you would get.

No one could charm a room like my father. No one could be warmer or more captivating.

And no one could cast you out as quickly when he suddenly felt betrayed.

He always surrounded himself with a constantly shifting circle of wealthy, influential people: models, Wall Streeters, retail executives, movie producers, not to mention his inner circle of rakes and hangers-on, who eventually sucked him dry.

Dad's charisma was boundless, but his temper was even larger. And it always seemed to rear up after a couple of scotches. He would elevate brand-new acquaintances as his closest friends in the world—true geniuses, movers and shakers, even those who it was clear only wanted something from him.

The same people down the line who when the tide eventually turned—and it always did—were banished from his sight.

His biggest customers—not just lowly buyers but upper management, even store presidents—loudly thrown out of his showroom and told to never come back. His panicked salesmen scurrying after them, feverishly apologizing. They even came up with a brand that poked fun at his legendary outbursts: Lenny Didn't Mean It, it was called.

He would introduce me to his pals as the "Remarkable Dr. Jay," even as a kid. And I had to admit it always made me feel like the most important person in the world. Growing up, he would take me out for dinners with his drop-dead girlfriends at Gino's or to sit at the bar with his Irish bookies at PJ Clarke's.

Then he wouldn't call for weeks, completely forget important events. Disappoint me terribly.

I never understood what was behind my father's rage. The truth was, if he were diagnosed today, maybe we would know. He ran away from Brooklyn in the forties and headed out to Hollywood, where he took up with starlets and ingenues and managed to become the right-hand man of Louis B. Mayer, the head of MGM. His homes were always filled with bikinied beauties in the pool and glamorous people dropping by. Opera blasted over the beach on the stereo.

He made millions over the years—and gave back every penny.

At the end, his business partners grew shadier and shadier, as the glamour crowd wanted nothing to do with him. The Wall Street honchos became shiftier and the retail bigwigs turned into low-priced dis-counters.

There was the suspicious fire in his ware-house in Brooklyn. The SEC was on his back over cash that had disappeared from the firm, as well as the IRS over back taxes.

He became sort of a sad figure, driving around in his ten-year-old Mercedes, scrounging around the city's flea markets, arriving unexpectedly at the house with some bizarre new "find": paintings no one wanted or retro board games for the kids missing the key pieces. *"Lenny Presents!"* they grew to call him.

We managed to become close in those years.

Ten years ago, he downed his usual two Rob Roys at a local watering hole in the Hamptons, where he still had a small house near the beach. The bartender re-membered him going on about some new idea. A couple of women were at the bar, but they didn't want to be bothered by him. He threw a twenty on the table and waved good-bye.

The next morning they found his car at the bottom of Shinnecock Bay.

After dinner, we sat around the living room, Charlie strumming on the guitar. "Evan was getting pretty good himself," he said with pride. "Even better than me!" He picked through versions of "Get Back" by the Beatles, the Byrds' "Mr. Tambourine Man," "White Room" by Cream, Rod Stewart's "Maggie Mae."

"*Jay . . .*" His eyes lit up. "You remember this?" He sang, "*Just when you say your last good-bye / Just when you calm my worried fears . . .*"

I did recognize it. It was the song he had recorded back in L.A. More than thirty years ago. "One Last Thing."

"Just when the dawn is breaking / There's always one last thing . . ."

He always played the same two verses. Only them. To this day, I wasn't sure I'd ever heard the whole thing through.

Charlie cooed, happily. "*Ooooh, girl, it's always one last thing . . .*"

He put down his guitar. "You know it got to number twenty-nine on the charts," he said with his ground-down grin. "In 1973.

Of course I was crazy as a loon back then. Not to mention I was popping LSD like vitamins. I got to thinking my record company was trying to screw me. Hell, I thought *everybody* was trying to screw me then . . ." He cackled, a glimmer in his eye.

"Hey, check this out, Jay!" He went over to the chest against the wall and came back with a bulging photo album. It was stuffed with artifacts from his past: pictures of him, of him and Dad in happier days at his beach house. Charlie growing up in Miami in the sixties, before his crazy hair and wild eyes.

He laughed, "I was so deluded on acid I told them I would burn down their fucking building if they didn't send me out on tour. And you know what they did? *They pulled the record!* Right off the airwaves." He snapped his fingers. "Just like that! And you know what? I could hardly blame them. Who would put a nut job like me out on the road?

"But you know what, Jay? Maybe if I hadn't been off my rocker back then, you might be sitting here with Rod Stewart. *You wear it well . . .* In a mansion in Brentwood, not this shit hole here, right? *Look . . ."*

He opened the album and pushed it over to me, a soft smile lighting his eyes.

It was a clipping from an old *Billboard* magazine. Yellowed, dog-eared, protected in a plastic liner. Top Singles for the week.

I noticed the date: October 1973.

At number one was "Angie" by the Rolling Stones. Midway down, I saw a red, drawn-in arrow marking number twenty-nine:

"One Last Thing." Charlie Earl.

"Hey!" I grinned. I'd never seen this before. I never even knew if I truly believed him, all the times he talked about it.

Charlie winked. "Not bad from your loony older brother, huh?" Then his grin seemed to wane. "Hell, who's kidding who, right? Biggest moment of my life, and I fucked up the whole damn thing. Guess that's where all our similarities end, right, Jay?"

He picked up his guitar again.

"Charlie, what do you want me to do?" I asked him. I came over and sat across from him. "About Evan. You want me to find you a lawyer? You want to try and make a case against the hospital? You know I'm going to have to go back in a couple of days."

My brother nodded, scratching his scruffy

beard, pushing his graying hair from his eyes. "We don't want a lawyer, Jay. People like us can't make waves. You go. Gabby and I, we appreciate what you've done. You just being here."

I patted him on the shoulder and got up. "I'm going to make a call."

I went outside and stood against the building in the cool night air. Their apartment faced a grassy courtyard. Beyond it was a darkened street. The light from a single streetlight cast a glow.

People were arguing loudly in an apartment across the courtyard.

I called the house.

"Hey, how's it going?" Kathy answered, happy to hear my voice. "How are Charlie and Gabriella?"

"The poor kid should never have been released." I exhaled. "You should see where they put him." I took her through my day, my frustrations. "All the doctors here are just stonewalling us."

"You're going to be coming home in a couple of days. What are you going to do, Jay?"

"All they want is an answer, Kath. Someone has to take responsibility. That's what

I'm doing." I told her about visiting the rock and the halfway house. Then the TV station.

"I warned you, didn't I," Kathy said, a little in jest, but a little in truth too, "you'd get drawn in."

I was about to tell her she was wrong. This time I wasn't being sucked in. I just had to help get them through some things.

That's when I noticed something out on the street.

A car, black, or dark blue maybe, parked beneath a tree. A VW or a Kia or something. A hatchback.

And someone sitting in the driver's seat. The person's face was hidden under a cap. I couldn't even tell if it was a man or a woman, but the window was cracked slightly and the person was smoking.

And they seemed to be watching me.
"Jay . . . ?"

Kathy's voice brought me back. "Sorry . . ." I said, ducking back under the carport.

"I said that Maxie's coming back tomorrow. I'm picking him up at school. And Sophie said she texted you . . . She'll call them later today."

"Okay . . ."

I heard an engine start up and glanced

back and saw it was the car I'd been watching.

The headlights flashed, momentarily blinding me. I was about to turn away when the driver's window rolled down and the person behind the wheel, eyes still seemingly fixed my way, flicked their cigarette onto the street.

In my direction.

Then they rolled up the window and drove away.

The whole thing had the feel of some kind of strange warning.

"Jay, have you even been hearing me?" Kathy sighed, frustration in her tone. "You know, you're not going to change them. You know that, don't you?"

"Yeah, I know that, Kathy."

I stepped out from under the carport and watched the car drive away down Division Street. "But what happened to Evan was wrong, Kathy. And when I get back on that plane Thursday, what the hell else have they got?"

CHAPTER FIFTEEN

That was nice," Gabby called from the kitchen after Jay had left, finishing cleaning up.

Charlie had picked up his guitar again. "Yes." He strummed a few chords distractedly. "It was nice."

"Here, do something . . . ," Gabby said to him. "You're always in your own world. Make yourself useful." She bundled up a bag of trash and handed it to him to take out.

"All right." He put down the guitar and, without objecting, took the bag outside to the plastic trash bins on the side of their apartment.

She was right, of course, he decided—it was nice to have Jay out here. To feel they were close again. Like time had taken them back to a simpler and better day. *Even if . . .* Suddenly the reason Jay was there came back to him.

Even if it was because Evan had died.

He lifted the plastic trash cover and was about to drop in the bag when . . .

He barely noticed it at first.

It was just lying there, on top of yesterday's trash. Staring back at him—as if alive.

And in a way it *was* alive!

"Gabby!" he tried to scream. *"Gabby!"* dropping the trash bag, but nothing came out.

Only a tsunami of shock and overwhelming confusion swept through him.

It was a black Nike sneaker.

His heart came to a stop. *Evan's sneaker.*

The one he'd been wearing up on the rock the day he died.

The one they never found.

Hands tingling, Charlie gingerly picked it out of the trash bin. Yes, he was right—he was sure!

It was Evan's sneaker.

What could it possibly be doing here?

At first his heart almost exploded. Overcome with joy. This proved it, didn't it? What he'd felt all along? That Evan wouldn't have killed himself.

He turned to shout: *Look! Look what I found.*

Gabby!

But then he stopped. The elation throughout his body shifted to fear. He scanned around, expecting someone to rush out of the shadows at any moment. But no one was there.

He held the sneaker like a priceless relic, tears welling in his eyes.

He knew he couldn't tell anyone. Not Gabby—poor Gabby—who would die herself just to see this.

Not even Jay.

No, no one could see this. Because he knew who had put it there. The past had brought it. Just as he always feared.

The past.

That's what it meant.

That the past had found him.

And there was nothing he could do about it. Nothing he could do to stop it now.

CHAPTER SIXTEEN

I took Charlie and Gabby to view Evan's body the next day, and it was one of the toughest things I ever had to do.

He had a deep gash in the back of his head. Some reconstructive work had been needed. He had a calm look on his face, that same little smirk, like he knew more than the rest of us, seeming finally at peace.

Gabby kissed him all over his face and hands and said her good-byes. Charlie seemed almost wary, saying once with his eyes wet, "I forgive you, son."

The decision was made to cremate him later that afternoon.

It was a long, quiet ride back to Grover Beach, and Gabby spent much of it in the back weeping. Charlie just sat there with her, holding her hand. I got off the freeway and drove down the hill to drop them back at their apartment.

A thick manila envelope was leaning against the front door. It was from the county hospital.

Evan's doctor's report.

I didn't know if it was pressure from the TV station or from Janie, the nurse I had spoken with. I was just happy to see it there.

I asked to read it over first and Charlie and Gabby agreed. I took it back to the hotel, but instead of going to my room, I ordered a beer at the bar and took it out to the grounds in back that ran along the bluffs overlooking the ocean. People were always milling around, observing the gulls and pelicans that congregated on the cliff, scanning the waves for a meal. I'd sat out there to clear my head a couple of times before.

I found a bench and took out the thick report. Central Coast Medical Center. Patient: *Erlich, Evan. Patient #3233A32.*

It began with his admitting evaluation. *August 23.* It stated that the patient had attempted to purchase a gun and that his parents had called the police. That Evan had demonstrated violent behavior toward them. There was a box with various courses of action:

Intent to harm self and *Intent to harm someone else* were both checked.

The report went on to say that "the patient was admitted in a hostile and agitated state and had exhibited extreme physical behavior toward his parents and resistance to officers on scene and was unresponsive to efforts to calm him." He was sedated: Risperdal, Klonopin, and Ativan. He was placed in a treatment cell and put under full observation.

Day two, Evan was still a mess: "Patient appears calmer, responsive, but remains agitated and depressed. Admits to depression, feelings of isolation, hostility toward family, but has not taken his medicine in weeks. He feels the need to get a gun to protect himself from them." There were further observations with comments like "agitated" and "anxious." "Still having thoughts of suicide." "Protective watch continued."

As well as the heavy doses of sedatives and benzodiazepines.

I put it down, my gaze drifting out to the congregation of gulls and pelicans on the rocks.

"Hey, friend, got a buck for an Iraq War vet?"

A panhandler had wandered up to me in disheveled clothes and carrying a hand-scrawled cardboard sign. IRAQ WAR VET. NEED FOOD.

"Any chance you can help me out, chief? It's Veterans Day tomorrow. Can you spare me something for a meal?"

I looked up at him. "Veterans Day's in November, chief. Nice try."

"Dude, every day is Veterans Day." The guy grinned. "When you're looking for something to eat."

Our eyes met and the spark of humor in his eyes along with his gaunt, haggard ap-pearance made my resistance soften. I thought of Charlie, who had been down and out for many years himself. I reached into my pocket and came out with a five, and handed it to him. "Here. You take it easy, man."

"*Dude!*" His steel-gray eyes were suddenly bright and he cocked a hand at me and pointed, as if aiming a gun, making me wonder if he had ever served a day. But I wasn't caring. He backed down the path with a grin, his oversize pants brushing the pavement, and waved back at me. "You have a good day now, chief."

I gave him a wave in return, reflecting that the contrast in this town was startling. Beautiful homes, a stunning coastline. But also a kind of refuge for the down-and-out, whom life had passed by.

I smiled as the guy walked away, waving at me one last time. "See ya around."

I went back to Evan's report. I wasn't sure what I was looking to find, but in the next two days there were pages and pages detailing how Evan had gradually become more responsive. Seroquel was added to his treatment, two hundred milligrams, a massive dose. By the third day it seemed to have done its trick and blunted his rage. "Patient now denies any real anger toward his parents." "Now admits the gun was meant for him."

No kidding. He was a zombie, Anna Aquino said. Completely snowed.

On his last day, he had even begun to

express remorse. "Patient indicates a desire not to return home as it is a volatile situation. It is suggested an intermediary living situation might be located."

That made me angry. Anyone professional had to know the demons that were still lurking inside.

In the final pages, the report went on to note how Evan understood that he had to stay on his meds and even expressed a desire to get better. "Patient feels that the current environment at home may not be compatible with that goal. Social services is looking for an appropriate outside environment."

Evan's scrawled, semilegible signature was on the release form, along with Mitchell Derosa, Supervising MDs.

Maybe Sherwood was right. Suicide or accident, Evan was dead. I was leaving in the morning. What did it even matter if the system had let him down?

The kid was crazy, delusional. *He was talking to the furnace, for Christ's sake.*

The die was really cast the day he was born.

CHAPTER SEVENTEEN

That Wednesday night, I stopped off at Charlie's to drop off the report and say good-bye.

To my surprise, they had a couple of people over. Two of Evan's friends: One was Pam, a cashier from the store where Evan had bagged groceries for a while. She had a row of hoops in her ear and wore one of those gold-plated necklaces with her name in large script.

The other was a friend from Evan's high school days, Miguel, a heavyset Latino kid with a shaved head and baggy denim shorts down to his knees, accompanied by his mom.

Both of the friends seemed to be genuinely sorrowed by Evan's death. They traded stories of him at the store and at school. How he was always the smart one. "Always knew how to do things, you know, bro," Miguel said brightly. How he used to dazzle everyone on the court. "That boy had game."

"Yes, my son had a chance to really be something." Gabby nodded, her eyes glistening.

While they chatted, I excused myself and went out with Charlie to the tiny, fenced-in backyard. "Here . . ." I handed him back the medical report. "I made a copy at the front desk. I'll take it back with me if you don't mind."

His long, unruly hair was clipped back in a beret. "What does it say?"

"It says he was sick, Charlie. That he needed to stay on his meds and be in a place he could be observed. *The rest . . .*" I shrugged and held myself back. "I think they treated him with the intent to make him better. He just needed a lot more than three days in a county ward."

"I understand." He nodded. We sat down on his lawn chairs. "You're leaving tomorrow?"

"In the morning. Look, you have to let me know what you want me to do, Charlie. If you want me to find you a lawyer. If you want, I'll make some inquiries for you. But you ought to talk to someone. A social worker or a grief counselor. I'm not gonna be here for you."

My brother shrugged, a cast of inevitability clouding his face. "I told you before, we can't make waves, Jay. We have to accept who we are. Anyway, what does it matter for Gabby and me? It's all over for us now. It would just be nice to get some answers."

"I wish I could have done that for you, Charlie."

"You did, Jay. You have any idea how much it means to us, you coming out here like you did? You did everything."

He reached forward and put his hand on mine and squeezed. In that moment, he was no longer my crazy, wayward brother whose life had spun out of control, but someone who was every bit my equal yet was powerless and needed me. Whose life would never be the same.

I pulled him to me with a hug. "I truly wish it could have been different, Charlie. And I don't just mean with Evan. I mean with all of it. Dad. You and me. Our lives."

His grip tightened. "I wish that too, Jay." I suddenly felt tears dampen my shoulder. "I love you, buddy. You're all I have . . ."

"I love you too, Charlie."

"You go back to that beautiful family of yours . . ."

"I will. Unless something changes, right?" I patted him warmly on the back and pulled away.

"Anyway what ever changes with us"—he smiled—"right?"

We went back inside. Pam and Miguel and his mom had stood up to leave. "I'm really sorry for your loss." Miguel put out his hand to me.

"Thanks," I said. I asked what he was doing with himself.

"Trying to get back into school. I've had some setbacks, you know. But I'm getting it back together. I start Cuesta in the spring." Cuesta was the local junior college where Evan had gone for a semester.

"That's good." I walked him outside to

the carport, where his mom and Gabby were saying good-bye. "Keep it together."

He shook his head confoundedly. "You know, things could have been really different with Evan, man. The dude was smart. He used to show me how to do my math. Like it was nothing to him. He had a way out of this place. Not like the rest of us . . ."

He took a step toward his mom's van, then turned back around. "You know, it was like with that cop. The one who was always looking for him . . ."

"What cop?"

"That old dude. He came around to the courts a few times, looking for Evan. First, maybe a month ago . . . Evan wasn't around. Then he was back, a couple of weeks ago . . ."

I stared. "This cop was looking for Evan?"

"Yeah. I rang Evan up and he came down. Two weeks ago. That was the last time I ever saw him. We were all jiving him: 'What do you got going on, dude? You thinkin' 'bout becoming a snitch?' My boy just laughed and said how the guy was only showing an interest in him. Said he was trying to get him to take the test."

"What test?" I asked, my heart suddenly jumping a beat.

"You know," said Miguel, "the test to become a cop."

It was like a switch was flicked, everything inside me brought to an immediate stop. I flashed back to what Gabby had told me that first day. Evan staring at the furnace, hearing voices coming from it. *They want me to become a cop.*

My son was sick, Gabby had said. *He was always dreaming.*

You'll see, Evan had said with that all-knowing smirk of his.

"You know his name?" I asked Miguel, my pulse picking up again. "This cop? It's important, Miguel."

He shook his head. "Nah. Just some older dude. Maybe fifty, sixty. White hair. Not from around here, though. He showed us his badge. From somewhere down south. Santa Barbara, I think he said. I'm sorry, mister."

"That's okay."

It might be nothing, I realized. Just another one of Evan's ramblings. *His stupid dreams,* as Gabby said. One that happened to be connected to the thinnest thread of truth.

This cop, who wanted him to take the test.

Or maybe it did mean something.

I started after Miguel, who'd opened the van door. "You remember anything else about him? That cop. Other than he had white hair and said he wasn't from around here."

"I don't know, man . . ." He scratched his shaved head. "He had kind of a limp. And, oh yeah, he did have something on his face. Like a birthmark, you know? This red blotch. On his cheek. *Here*." He touched the left side of his face.

"Thanks, Miguel," I said.

They backed out and I watched them drive away. I reminded myself I was leaving. Come morning, I was going to be in my car, on the way back to LAX. Then on a plane. Home.

I had things pulling me back.

But I couldn't suppress the weirdest feeling, like the world had suddenly shifted.

Something just changed.

And a thought wormed into my brain, ever so slightly: *What if Evan wasn't quite as crazy as everyone thought?*

CHAPTER EIGHTEEN

I barely slept that night.

I tossed and turned for most of it, my blood racing. The echo of what Miguel had told me going back and forth in my mind.

They want me to take the test to become a cop . . .

I kept thinking, *What if Evan's ramblings might not have been total delusions after all, but were twisted with a thread of truth? Reality.*

Why did an old detective need to find him? What could he have been caught up in? I kept hearing my brother's voice: *What if he had gone up to that ledge just to think? My son would never have killed himself.*

I rose up. What if that stupid missing sneaker did actually mean something?

At two, I tossed off the covers and stepped out on the terrace, letting the breeze from the ocean cool my face. Listening to the whoosh of the dark sea against the rocks.

Did any of this make the hospital less responsible? No. They still bungled it. It didn't change much. It wasn't going to bring Evan back. Or alter my brother's grief.

You've got to be on a plane in the morning, Jay.

My wake-up call shook me out of a deep sleep at just before seven. I had a one P.M. flight out of LAX and it was about a three-hour ride. Stacey Gold was being admitted that afternoon. I called in and told my secretary I'd be ready to scrub in at six A.M. tomorrow. I checked that everything was set for her operation.

Stacey was seventeen and was starting at Boston College that fall. The surgery had forced her to push back her start date. Though two years younger than Sophie, they had been in a dance class together a few years back, and in the summers, she worked the refreshment cart that drove around the course at our golf club.

A month ago, she started experiencing a throbbing in her right thigh near the groin and felt pressure on the pelvic nerves. An MRI discovered an aneurysm leading into the iliac artery. I had to feed a stent through the femoral artery. It wasn't a big deal, but it was the only way to relieve the pressure; otherwise there was the risk of it bursting.

I turned on the *Today* show and hopped into the shower. Afterward, I stood in my towel shaving. On the tube, they were talking about a missing toddler in Tennessee and then they switched to the local news.

"A retired Santa Barbara detective is found murdered in his Santa Maria home . . ."

It took a moment, until the words "Santa Barbara detective" slammed me head-on and I ran to the screen.

They had the victim's photo there. In his early sixties. A hard, square jaw, wrinkles around deep-set eyes.

What had Miguel told me? The cop was around sixty. White hair.

"Walter Zorn," the news report began,

"who for the past ten years had lived in the Five Cities area . . ."

Then they showed another photo of him—this time in uniform, receiving some kind of commendation.

Just like Miguel had said, there was the blotch of reddish pigment on his left cheek.

My eyes went wide.

Zorn. There couldn't be any doubt. He was the cop who'd been looking for Evan.

And now he was dead.

He had been stabbed in his home during the night. In Santa Maria, fifteen miles down the coast. A neighbor had called the cops after hearing a scuffle. There were no immediate suspects. He hadn't seen the perpetrator.

Something truly horrifying took shape in my mind:

Zorn had just been murdered, and Evan had died suspiciously the week before. They'd been in contact with each other.

Could their deaths be connected?

Then, my whole body crashing to a stop: *What if my nephew didn't kill himself after all?*

I dressed, finished packing in a daze,

my hands and chest tingling with something I couldn't figure out.

I had a plane to catch.

I zipped my bag and headed for the door. Suddenly I heard the lead-in for a different story:

"Could a tragic local suicide possibly have been prevented? News Eight's Rosalyn Rodriguez reports on this disturbing case when we come back in a minute."

Evan's.

The report came on and it was mostly fair, bouncing back and forth between Evan's psychological issues and the suggestion that the hospital might have wrongly sped him through the system. They showed Gabby, a mother's heartbreak etched in her face, and then flashed to me: *"The police seemed to have just washed their hands of it . . ."*

I didn't remember even saying that, but there I was . . .

They also managed to get a statement from a Dr. Vargas, the medical center's chief of staff, who supposedly had been away.

But there he was. "We delivered a full report of Evan's stay in the hospital to the family today. There are guidelines for privacy and disclosure we have to abide by, and despite this tragic ending, we feel the state-sponsored home he was assigned to, as well as his treatment here, met all established benchmarks of professionalism and care. The hearts of everyone here go out to the family."

Established benchmarks of professionalism and care, my ass!

I hurried downstairs and threw my bags in my car. I paid the bill, said good-bye to the Cliffside Suites, and headed up to the freeway.

I had five hours to my flight. I should be at LAX in three, with time to spare. I pulled onto the freeway south, my gut still throbbing with something I couldn't put aside.

Evan. Zorn.

I told myself I had to put it behind me now. What could I do? What did Charlie even want me to do? Evan had climbed up there in the dark. He had gone off his meds. Anything could have happened. A couple of days before, he'd been in a raging, almost homicidal state. He tried to buy a gun.

What the hell else for?

This retired detective, whoever he was, he was a completely different person. Who happened to intersect with Evan. His death probably had nothing to do with him.

Maybe I'll become a cop. They want me to take the test . . .

C'mon, Jay. I focused back on the road. *He was talking to the fucking furnace when he said that!*

I thought of what was on my plate back home. What I had committed to in the morning. Stacey.

Here, there was only grief. And questions that would never have answers. That no one wanted answers to.

The kid was dead, Sherwood said. *Next time he would have taken his parents with him. What did it even matter?*

It damn well did matter.

Zorn and Evan. Something connected them. And I was the only one who saw it.

I brought to mind Evan's face at the mortuary. Gabby's tears. Then Charlie—the day his son was born. Promise me, Jay, that whatever happens, you'll be there for him. *Promise me, you'll take care of him, Jay.*

Promise me.

You have my word, Charlie.

I felt this sense building inside me that I was about to do something completely crazy.

I made it as far as the next exit and turned the car around.

Two minutes later I was back at the exit where I'd just gotten on and wound down the hill to Charlie's apartment. I left the car under the carport and ran across the courtyard. It was barely seven thirty A.M. They normally didn't get out of bed until around eleven. I banged on the front door.

"Charlie! Gabby, let me in!"

"All right, all right . . ." I finally heard my brother's voice. "Who's there?"

He opened the door, standing in a T-shirt and boxers, his hair loose and wild. He looked at me, befuddled. "Thought you were heading home, Jay."

"Do you know the name Walter Zorn?" I asked him.

He shook his head, scratching at his beard. "Should I? No."

"He was a retired detective. From down in Santa Barbara. He was killed last night. *Here*."

He blinked back at me. "What does he have to do with us?"

I thought I saw something in his eyes. Maybe there was something in my question, some new conviction jolting him out of his ruined life, the ever-present grief he hid in.

But I just looked back at him, like a man who had finally accepted his vow. "Something just changed."

PART II

CHAPTER NINETEEN

My first call was to my office.

To Lev Avital, one of the other surgeons in the practice, who'd been part of our group for the past eight years. I caught him at his desk during a consult. "Jay, what's up? How is it out there?"

"Avi, I need a huge favor," I said. "Can you handle an iliac stent for me in the morning tomorrow? The patient's the daughter of a friend of mine from our club. I'd planned to be back, but I really need another day or two out here. I promise, it's a layup, Avi."

"Let me check." He took a look through his schedule and came back to say he was free. He only had a couple of consults to juggle around. "You know we were all so sad to hear about your nephew, Jay."

"Thanks. I owe you big-time, guy," I said in relief. "I hope to be back next week."

"I'll remind you about this at Thanksgiving. I'm on call this year."

I gave him some background on the case and how it was all pretty much totally routine. Just inserting a stent through the femoral artery and bypassing the aneurysm. Avi was an ex–Israeli tank commander. He'd seen action in Lebanon. He'd studied at the Hebrew University in Jerusalem and at Harvard, and could probably do an iliac bypass in his sleep. Probably even better than I could.

"You'll be out by lunch," I promised. I said I'd have my secretary e-mail over the MRIs with Stacey's file. "Call me if you need to discuss. And, Avi . . ."

"Don't even mention it," he said. "I'm hoping things go well for you and your family out there."

"No—I meant, call me as soon as you're done and let me know how it went," I said. "But thanks. *Thanks a bunch*."

I told him I'd alert the family to the change.

My next call was to Kathy.

My stomach clenched a bit at the thought of having to explain this to her. It was eight fifteen in California. Eleven fifteen back home. I dialed her on her cell and she picked up, from one of the examining rooms.

"Hey," she answered brightly, "I'm in with a very unhappy Lab named Sadie who's got a big blister on her paw. I got your message last night. You at the airport yet?"

"Don't be mad," I said, sucking in a breath. "I can't make it back today."

"You can't . . . ?" Her voice sank with disappointment. Maybe an edge of exasperation too.

"Look, I know what you're thinking, but something's come up. I just need another day or two, that's all, to see something through. You trust me, don't you?"

"See something through? I thought you had a procedure Friday, Jay. On Marv and Susie Gold's daughter."

"I just got Avi to cover it."

"Avi? And we had the Hochmans coming tomorrow night. *All right . . ."* She sighed frostily, not even attempting to conceal her frustration. "Jay, I know better than anyone

how much you want to do something for them, but—"

"Don't even go there, Kath. It's not even about Charlie and Gabby, or what you might think. I just have to see something through. Related to Evan. I'll explain it all later. I promise."

There was a pause, one of those moments when it's pretty obvious no one wants to say what they're really thinking.

"Look, I have to get back to my patient," she said, exhaling. "She's very impatient. She's starting to growl at me. We can discuss this later, okay?"

"Okay."

Then, almost as a good-bye: "And of course I trust you, Jay."

CHAPTER TWENTY

The county coroner's office was located twenty minutes away near the sheriff's department in San Luis Obispo. It was on a remote road a few minutes out of town, tucked dramatically at the base of one of those high, protruding mesas, not exactly your standard police setting.

A sign on the outside walkway read DE-TECTIVES UNIT.

It was strange, but I felt there was only one person I could trust.

I went up to the front desk. A pleasant-looking woman seated behind a computer asked if she could help me. I said, "Detective Sherwood, please."

He was out of the office. The woman glanced at the clock on the wall and said it might be a couple of hours. There was a bench in the room outside. I told her I'd wait.

It took close to two and a half hours, and maybe a dozen calls from me, for the detective to finally return.

"Hey, Carol," he said, waving to the woman I had spoken to, coming in through a rear entrance off the parking lot. "Calls for me?"

The secretary pointed to me and he saw me stand, his demeanor shifting. He glanced at his watch, as if he was late for something, then stepped up to me, clearly the last person he was looking to see. "Thought you were on your way home, doc. What brings you all the way out here?"

"I'm not sure Evan killed himself," I said.

The detective blinked, as if he'd taken one to the face, and released a long, philosophical sigh. "Killed himself. Fell off a ledge while climbing—like I said, what does it really matter, Dr. Erlich? I have a death certificate to make out and it has to say something. You come up with any better ideas about what he might have been doing up there?"

I looked at him. "What if someone else was responsible for his death?"

"You mean as in maybe the medical staff at County. Or even the police?" His gaze didn't have anything friendly in it. "How did you phrase it . . . That we were *'washing our hands of it*?'"

I remembered the news report on Evan and how that must have sounded. "No, not the medical staff at all. Someone else. Just hear me out."

"Someone else now . . . ?" Sherwood nodded patronizingly. He glanced at his watch again, then forced a barely accommodating smile. "Well, you might as well come on back. You've driven all the way out here. Carol, hold any calls for a couple of minutes."

I grabbed my blazer. "Thanks."

He led me down a long hallway to his office, a small cubicle workstation separated by gray fabric dividers from the workstations of three other detectives, with a view of the rolling hills.

"Hey, Joe." He nodded to one as he

stepped in. He took off his sport coat and draped it over a divider. "Don't get comfortable." His desktop was cluttered and piled with bulging files. There was a credenza behind his chair, more files stacked on it.

Along with a couple of photos. An attractive, middle-aged woman, who I assumed had to be his wife. And a younger woman, in her twenties maybe. A daughter.

He sank into the chair and nodded for me to take a seat.

"You don't mess around, doc, do you? A couple of days back, you're stirring things up about how your nephew had been criminally neglected and that the county was responsible for his death. Then you rouse up the local press that there's some kind of big conspiracy going on here. How we're not doing our jobs. You go out to that halfway house in Morro Bay and suggest maybe you'll bring a lawyer in. And now you're saying *what*?" He ran his thick hand through his salt-and-pepper hair. "That the kid's death may not have been suicide at all? Or even an accident? That leaves us exactly where, doc? *Foul play*?"

My heart was pumping. "This retired detective who was killed last night in Santa

Maria . . . I think his name was Zorn. You happen to see it on the news?"

"I saw it." He snorted derisively. "You know, homicides are kind of a hobby with me, doc." He leaned back, propping his foot up on an open desk drawer. "The floor's all yours . . ."

"This detective, Zorn, apparently he was in touch with Evan. Twice in the past few weeks." I told him how one of Evan's friends had seen him asking around for Evan at the playgrounds. The last time less than two weeks before he had died. How Zorn had had some reason to contact him and had shown an interest in Evan.

"You're suggesting *what* now . . ." Sherwood smiled, a bit deferentially. "That these cases are somehow related?"

"Two people end up dead, who just days before are seen talking. One of them clearly *was* murdered. The other, Evan, at the very least, there are some open questions . . ."

"The kid jumped off a cliff, doc! Who are you now, the Amazing Kreskin?" He put his palm on the top of the tall stack of files. "*See these?* I've got four gang killings, a hit-and-run, and two likely drug ODs to process." He pulled out a red one

from on top. "See *this* one? The son of a prominent builder in town. Tight end on the high school football team. OxyContin OD. Everyone's all over me . . . And *these . . ."* He wheeled around to the other stack of files sitting on the credenza. "These are all disposed of, awaiting my final sign-off. If I can *get* to them." He picked one from near the top. *"Your nephew."*

"I know there's some kind of connection between the two cases."

"I'm sorry, doc, but I don't work for you."

It was clear that the comments on the news had cost me what little equity I had with him. It was also clear the hospital wasn't exactly going to be an ally now, not that they ever were.

"Look," I said, "I'm sorry about that interview. We were all a little frustrated the other day. My nephew died. No one was returning our calls. I was leaving town. I was just trying to do whatever I could to get them some attention."

"Attention? What the hell have I been devoting to it, doc—*spare time*?" He drilled a look of displeasure at me. Finally he let out a breath. *"Gimme a name."*

"A name?"

"The name of your nephew's friend," he answered impatiently. "The one who conveniently spotted the two of them together."

"Miguel," I said. "Miguel Estrada. Apparently, he and Evan were basketball buddies. According to him, Zorn was asking around for Evan at the courts."

"Asking around . . ." He twisted in his chair and punched Miguel's name into his computer. He waited a few seconds, putting on thick black reading glasses, then sort of smiled cynically as he shifted the screen around to me. "You talking *this* Miguel Estrada?"

There was a photo of Miguel, shaved head, tattoos and all. A mug shot. Along with a police record that stretched down the entire page. *I've had some setbacks . . .*

My heart sank.

Sherwood ticked them off: "Sale of banned substances, sale of prescription drugs, failure to show up for court hearings. Falsifying doctor's prescriptions. *Shall I go on?* We're not kids here, doc. Before we jump to any conclusions, you think perhaps we ought to consider the source?"

"He told me this early last night," I said. "Before the Zorn story even broke."

"He gave you Zorn's name?" The detective's eyes widened and I saw where he was heading. An ex-cop was dead. Maybe this Estrada kid was involved.

"He didn't know the guy's name," I said, defending him. "He just described him to me. Fifty or sixty. White hair. From Santa Barbara. Slight limp. Birthmark on his cheek. This morning, as I was about to leave, I saw the news."

"Well, you should've just kept on going!" The detective glared at me. *"Look"*—he pulled the monitor back around, shrugging— "even if this kid *is* somehow on the level and they did talk, so what? Why are you so sure there's a connection?"

"Because two people who had contact with each other just a few days ago are dead. And one of them was clearly murdered; *the other . . ."* I didn't say that maybe Evan's death wasn't quite as clear as everyone thought. "If this wasn't about some welfare kid who was half off his rocker, you would look further—"

"Half?" The detective held back a smile, a tiny crease of his lips. "No one's even agreeing that they *were* in contact, doc."

"Look, I'm sorry I made things difficult

for you. Please, I'm just asking you to take a look. I know you'll find something."

He took off his reading glasses and folded them on his desk. Then he blew out a long breath, friendlier now. "Look, why not go back home, doc? You're wasting your time trying to rake things up here. You're a sensible guy . . . You deal in facts, right? And I know you can see how your nephew may have done your brother and his wife kind of a cockeyed favor. We both know—next month, next year—the next time he went unhinged, we'd be cleaning up a whole different level of mess here. You understanding what I'm saying, doc?"

"There are other police, you know. Homicide. Someone would be interested in this."

"Oh, yeah." Sherwood's grin radiated with amusement. "And after yesterday, they're all just dying to team up with you, doc. You be sure and give 'em my best."

"I'm not leaving," I said. I got up. "Not now. Not until I find out what Zorn may have wanted with Evan."

Sherwood sighed. He picked up his phone, the friendliness melting into resignation. I watched him punch in a number, and I was about to say something I'd regret when he suddenly raised his eyes back up to me, as if to say, *You're still here?*

"Did your brother know this detective? This guy who was killed?"

"He said no. He'd never heard of him before."

The person Sherwood was calling came on the line, but he placed his hand over the mouthpiece, only the tiniest softening of his gaze, his irritation morphing into something that, if you knew him better, might have almost looked like a smile.

"Don't wait by the phone."

CHAPTER TWENTY-ONE

Charlie sat at the kitchen table in his T-shirt and shorts, sipping his morning coffee.

He didn't know how the detective who'd been killed might've figured in with Evan. Only that, with the sneaker he had found, it gave him the slightest spark of hope that what he knew in his heart was true: that his son hadn't jumped off that rock on his own. He would never have hurt them in that way.

To him, this was just another rung on the long ladder of how he'd been screwed over in his life. Beginning with his father. To the doctors Charlie had seen, who never truly understood him. Who had put him on brain-numbing meds for thirty years. To the state—how they barely gave him and Gabby enough to squeeze by. How they had placed Evan with all his young promise in that crap hole of a school, filled with future meth heads and gang members. Who chewed his son up and spit him out, and started him on his decline.

"You see, Gabby, you see!" Charlie said, his pulse pounding. If it wasn't clear to that stupid detective what had happened, it was clear to him. "He didn't kill himself after all. I know the truth. Evan's sneaker. They never even made an attempt to find it. You know what that means, don't you? His sneaker, Gabby, I'm telling you, that's the key."

"You have to calm down, Charlie," Gabby said. "You're in a rant. Jay will handle it for us. Here . . ."

She doled out his pills—trazodone to calm him down, felodipine and Caduet for his blood pressure, Quapro for the kidneys, Klonopin to calm his shakes. Six or seven others. She laid them out in a long line on the counter. The blue one was lithium. He'd taken it for thirty years, and now his kidneys were starting to break down.

"Here, Charlie," she said, shuffling up in her robe, putting them into a small dish, and giving him a glass of orange juice.

He swallowed them in one gulp.

"Good boy, my husband," she said, petting him on his shoulder. Then she sat down in the chair next to him, strain etched in her face. And grief—grief no one should have to bear. Today was no different than it would be every day. Every day for the rest of their lives. He could see she was an inch from tears.

"Jay says they'll have to reopen the investigation," he said, upbeat, trying to make her happy. He squeezed her hand.

"I always thought my boy was crazy," Gabby said. "Talking to that thing over there." She looked at the furnace. "But now I don't know. Maybe we didn't do the right thing, Charlie. Did we kill our own son?"

He had to hold back tears himself. "I think we did, Gabby. I don't know . . ."

He switched on the TV, the local news station, taking his coffee to the couch to hear the news. "Maybe there'll be something further on Evan . . ."

Then he remembered they hadn't picked up the mail. In days. Not that there was ever anything there. Only bills. And catalogs with merchandise they couldn't afford.

Still, it gave him something to do besides drive himself crazy. He got up. Went to the door in his shorts. "I'll be right back."

He stepped out, if only to get some air, if only to get out of their cramped, tiny tomb of an apartment filled with so many painful memories.

This shit hole where they lived that filled him with disgust. That hadn't been painted in years. That stank like piss. The grass in the courtyard hadn't been cut in weeks. Look at where they forced him to bring up his son.

I've been talking to the police, the boy had said. *They want me to take the test . . .*

Yes, they did drive him away, Charlie realized. They killed their own son.

He shuffled out to the carport in front where the mailbox was. Several days of mail, stuffed in, tumbled into his hands. He flipped through the stack: California Power and Light, the pharmacy, the cable company. All he did was pass the bills along to Gabby.

At the bottom of the stack, one large envelope was addressed to him. In an unfamiliar handwritten scrawl. It didn't appear to be junk mail or a bill. He didn't get much personal mail these days.

He flipped it over. No return address. Trudging back to the apartment, he put the rest of the mail under his arm and opened this large one, slowly easing the contents out.

There were photos. Several of them. Black and white.

He stopped.

The photos were of a woman. Her eyes open; her face twisted in a horrible expression. Bloodied and cut up. Red marks disfiguring her.

What the hell was he looking at?

The woman wasn't young, but she was naked on top. Her nipples were bloodied, the tips cut off. A dark red slit circled the bottom of her neck, and blood was pooled off to the side. She had other slash marks under her eyes that ran down to the top of her cheekbones like a trail of tears.

He cringed. Who would send these to him? Was it some kind of cruel joke? Someone who knew what had happened to them and wanted to hurt them further?

He stared in revulsion at the disfigured face, the eyes wide open, the victim's mouth parted, the mole on her cheek . . .

Her braided long blond hair.

Suddenly Charlie's stomach climbed up his throat.

He realized he knew her.

He felt stabbed in his chest, spun back in time, like in one of those low-budget sci-fi movies, hurtling back through the vortex of time.

They had been together for only a short while. Months, maybe. Years ago. They had traveled around for a time. Back in the day. Then gone their separate ways. Who had sent this? How would anyone even have known? Or even put them together?

It had only been a short time, but in it they had shared the biggest secret of their lives.

Sherry?

He brought her pretty face to mind. It had been more than thirty years.

The other envelopes fell out from under his arm, scattering on the walkway, as his legs grew weak and an even greater dread took hold of him, bringing with it a fear that reverberated through him like the first frost of fall.

Who even knew that he was there?

CHAPTER TWENTY-TWO

Truth was, Sherwood sighed, stepping out of his car, he didn't buy a word of what the doc had told him.

He didn't believe the murdered ex-detective and boy who jumped off that rock had even the slightest connection. He didn't believe this Miguel Estrada kid was on the level. Or that he had ever even seen the two of them together.

Not for a second.

What he *did* believe was that it was far more likely Miguel had something to do with Walter Zorn's death.

And since one of the cases he was handling happened to be from Santa Maria, fifteen miles down the freeway, he had a perfectly valid reason to stop in at the local police station there.

So after meeting with the grief-stricken family of the sixteen-year-old Pequillos member who'd been tossed in the woods behind the Grover Beach tracks, he made the drive and parked in the lot on Cook Street.

Larry Velez was one of the two homicide detectives stationed there.

"Keeping busy?" Sherwood knocked on the door. He and Larry had worked together at times over the years. Velez had started out as a detective in Pismo before moving down the freeway.

"Never the problem." Velez sighed. Santa Maria was a town of only ten thousand, but the total lack of jobs there, the shit-ass education system, and the control of the local gangs gave it the highest rate of violent crime in the area.

"Don't say I never gave you anything . . ." Sherwood dropped his findings on the Pequillos killing on the detective's desk.

"*Surprise*—coroner's ruling it a homicide. I passed it over to McWilliams." Dave Mc-Williams was head of the homicide detail in Pismo Beach.

Velez put the file on top of three others. "Nice of you to bring it down."

"So how's it going on that retired detective?" Sherwood took a chair and asked. "What was his name, Zorn? Anything further?"

Velez shrugged. "Only prints we found were from him and a housekeeper who came once a week. A neighbor saw a dark van parked on the street that night and heard some noises inside. Word is, the guy kept a bunch of money in the house. We found a desk rifled through. A metal lockbox opened. We're checking any day laborers in the area who didn't show up for work today."

Sherwood nodded. "I didn't catch a COD on the news." Cause of death.

"Not a coincidence," the Santa Maria detective said. "The guy was strangled."

"Strangled?"

"With an asterisk," Larry Velez added.

Sherwood looked at him, a little confused,

and pulled his chair closer. "Listen, Larry, I know this isn't procedure, but you mind if I take a quick look?"

The homicide detective hesitated. He and Sherwood were friends and all, but they generally didn't open their cases like that. His chief wouldn't go for it. Velez scrunched his brow. "And what's the reason, Don?"

"A case I'm working on. Kind of a long shot. There's a chance this might tie in. You remember that jumper in Morro Bay?"

Velez chuckled. "I heard there was someone stirring things up on that. That they even got one of the TV stations involved. Perokis down your throat on this?"

Perokis was Sherwood's boss.

Sherwood shook his head. "Just so I can cross it off my list. C'mon, Larry, what do you say you just go grab yourself a coffee, and I'll just wait for you here?"

Velez seemed to ponder it a second and then stood up. He pulled a blue folder from his slotted file and dropped it in front of Sherwood. "Light or dark?"

"Dark," Sherwood said with an appreciative smile. "Thanks, partner."

"Be back in five . . ." Velez left, shutting

the office door. Sherwood took out his reading glasses and picked up the blue file.

Walter Zorn. A series of crime scene photos. The white hair, the red blotchy birthmark the doc had mentioned.

The first document he found was the 10-05, the report filed by the responding officers at the scene.

There were signs of a struggle. The lamp cord wrapped around his neck. Body found at the couch in front of the TV. Apparently the old guy stuck mostly to himself. Before moving up, he'd spent twenty years on the Santa Barbara force. Worked a couple of high-profile cases back in the day. Retired with the rank of inspector, senior grade.

It was a small community and Sherwood had never seen him around at any of the bars or cafés where cops generally hung out.

What the hell would Zorn possibly have wanted with Evan?

Sherwood leafed through the crime scene photos. The victim's eyes were bulging. He looked like he'd put up quite a fight. Just run out of strength. Zorn was a big guy and not one who would go down easy.

Robbery did seem likely.

Satisfied, Sherwood tapped the photos back into a pile. He'd done what he'd promised. He told the doc he'd take a look, and he had. He saw nothing that connected the old cop to Evan. This kid Miguel was probably just trying to make some hay. To be safe, he'd mention to Velez he ought to run Estrada's prints anyway.

And that if Evan's name ever happened to come up to let him know.

As he was putting the crime scene photos back in the file, another dropped out. It had been taken during Zorn's autopsy.

Sherwood picked it up and looked at it, almost randomly. It was a close-up of what appeared to be cut marks on the victim.

Cut marks, Sherwood saw, staring closer, on what appeared to be the underside of the dead detective's tongue.

An asterisk, Velez had mentioned.

It appeared to be kind of a circle with a red dot in the center of it, enclosed in two irregular curved lines.

Even a traffic cop knew no burglar left a mark like that.

Suddenly his heart came to a stop. He adjusted his glasses and looked closer.

No fucking way, Sherwood said to himself. *Can't be . . .*

He blinked, bringing the photograph close to his eyes. Looking at it one way, it appeared to be nothing—simply random, unconnected cut marks.

But if you turned it another way, and he did—and stared at it from another angle—there it was, plain as fucking day. Staring right back at him.

An eye.

"Sonovafuckingbitch," Sherwood muttered, taking off his glasses.

An *open* eye.

CHAPTER TWENTY-THREE

The six o'clock news carried an update on the Zorn murder.

A pretty Asian reporter stood in front of an undistinguished, white ranch house, explaining that the retired Santa Barbara detective had been strangled in his home, in what the police were describing as an apparent robbery. She said how Zorn's drawers and closets had been rifled through and a locked metal box in his desk was pried open and emptied.

I was on the bed in my hotel room, hoping that Sherwood might call me back, when the news report came on.

The reporter said Zorn had lived quietly in the area for almost ten years after he retired from the Santa Barbara force. For a while he had volunteered in local youth programs. Then he pretty much just kept to himself, battling some health issues.

In his hometown of Santa Barbara, the woman reported, Zorn had been a decorated policeman and a respected detective. He had even worked some high-profile homicide cases going all the way back to the 1960s. There was the Veronica Verklin murder, which had made national headlines, in which a celebrated porn star was believed to have been beaten to death by her convict ex-husband, but eventually it turned out to be her boyfriend/director.

And Zorn had also been involved in the investigation of the Houvnanian murders, in which a charismatic cult figure and four followers committed a series of drug-induced ritual killings of affluent residents in the Santa Barbara hills. This was back in 1973, and it had created national headlines.

The group lived in a commune on a ranch up near Big Sur once owned by Paul Riorden, one of the victims. The perpetrators were all convicted of several counts of murder and were serving life sentences.

The mention struck a chord with me. The Riorden Ranch. I was pretty sure Charlie had lived there for a while. Back in the early seventies. Well before the killings.

The reporter closed by saying the police were appealing to the local residents for any leads.

I sat there for a while, the idea of this vague connection knotting my stomach. Charlie had always distanced himself from the terrible things that had happened on the ranch, always shrugging it off by saying he left long before then and only hung around there "for the drugs and the girls." It was all part of the lore that made his past so captivating.

I watched the news through the sports, then I decided to call him. He answered with a kind of a downtrodden tone. "Hi, Jay . . ." I'd spoken to him twice already that day, and both times, he sounded sullen and kind of medicated. "Did they find any connection between Evan and that cop?"

"No, not yet," I said. "But tell me about Russell Houvnanian."

He paused, the delay clearly letting me know I had taken him by surprise. "Why do you want to know about that?" he asked me.

I didn't want to fully divulge why. Right now I didn't have anything—only this vague, decades-old connection that probably wasn't a connection at all. Plus, I knew how Charlie's mind operated and didn't want him to get all worked up over things that might lead nowhere.

"You lived there for a while," I said. "Didn't I always hear you knew him?"

Charlie's past was always so vague, so clouded by his many retellings, not to mention the drugs, that it was hard to know what was actually the truth and what wasn't.

"I was only there for a couple of months." His tone was halting, as if he were still trying to figure out where I was headed. "I was long gone before anything took place. You know how stuff like that always gets built up. Dad always liked to tell it that way. Like when he was trying to bang some chick and needed to wow her with one of his stories."

I kept on him. "But you were there." Years before, he had told me about the Rasputin-like effect Houvnanian had on his followers.

The cultlike mix of religion, music, sex, and drugs. "You met the guy, right?"

"Yeah, I met him," Charlie said. He didn't follow up for a moment, but when he did, it almost knocked the phone out of my hand.

"You met him too, Jay."

CHAPTER TWENTY-FOUR

I drove right over and we sat on the lawn chairs in back. My brother recounted an episode that for years was buried in the most remote corner of my mind because I had never given it the slightest significance.

I was around fourteen, visiting my father in L.A. He had moved out there after selling his first business and had bought a sprawling ranch home high in the Hollywood Hills.

He wasn't working at that time and his girlfriend then was a waitress at the Playboy Club. She and a couple of her equally mind-boggling friends were hanging out in the pool, which I remember had most of my attention. A buddy of my dad's was there as well, a goateed so-called real estate entrepreneur named Phil Stella, who I later found out was an ex-con and whose main role then was pretty much as a supplier of hot chicks whom he referred to as his "wards," but who I eventually realized were actually working for him.

That afternoon, Charlie and a couple of his friends dropped in. One was a blond surfer type in a Hawaiian shirt, whom Charlie introduced as a record producer or something, and the other a thin, dark-featured guy in an embroidered blue caftan with long black hair and these intense, deep-set eyes.

All I remembered was the three of them animatedly trying to pitch my dad—who clearly wanted nothing to do with it—on the idea of anteing up several thousand dollars to help Charlie produce a record.

After the thousands he had spent on hospitals and lawyers bailing Charlie out of jails, Lenny wasn't biting.

"You remember what he did?" Charlie asked me, as if the scene had happened yesterday and was still vivid in his mind.

"You mean the guy you were with?" I asked, to get him to clarify.

"No. Dad," Charlie said with an edge. "You remember the rest of the story?"

What I did remember was my dad and Phil looking at each other amusedly and Phil shrugging. "I don't know, I'm a little intrigued. Why don't you go out to my Jag in the driveway?" Phil said. "There's an envelope in the glove compartment with a bunch of cash in it. Bring it in."

Charlie and his Hawaiian-shirt pal got all excited, their legs spinning like in the cartoons as they dashed out to the driveway. A minute later they returned, empty-handed and humiliated, faces flush with anger. Phil was cackling like a bully who'd just tripped a naïve freshman in front of a group of girls. My father told Charlie and his loser friends to get the hell out. "*What are you, fucking crazy?*" he exclaimed. The surfer dude was seething. Charlie, veins popping, jabbed his finger at my dad—"*You've fucking shat on me for the last time!*"

The longhair in the blue caftan just stood up with this cryptic half smile. He told Charlie to let it go, that they'd find the money somewhere else. That it wasn't right to treat your father with disrespect. He thanked Lenny for his time, casting a thin smile toward Phil, who sat there shaking his head as if they were the biggest rubes on the planet. The guy in the caftan said he was very sorry to bother them all. Then they all left. Afterward, my father and Phil just sat there laughing.

"That was Russell Houvnanian?" I said to Charlie in shock. I looked at him and conjured the scene I'd buried in my mind for more than thirty years. I don't think I even saw Charlie again for years after that. It was one of a thousand such moments. I'd never had another reason to bring it to mind.

"Yes." Charlie nodded dully. "That was him."

"And when did all the bad stuff happen?"

"The bad stuff . . . ?" Charlie said with a smile. "The bad stuff always happened, Jay. But if it's the Riorden murders you mean— six months, maybe a year later.

"Anyway," Charlie said, "it's all a little foggy to me too. It's been thirty-five years, not to mention a couple of hundred hits of LSD . . ." He looked at me. "Why is all this so important now?"

I told him the murdered detective, Zorn, was one of the original detectives on the Houvnanian case.

"Oh." I heard Charlie draw a breath and was expecting him to come back with, *So what does this have to do with Evan and me?*

Instead he said, "Listen, Jay, you've done what you can, maybe you oughta just head back home tomorrow . . ."

I already planned to pick up with Sherwood again in the morning. Maybe Zorn knew about Charlie's past and wanted to contact him through Evan. Not that I had any idea why.

"Charlie, there's a possibility this is somehow tied into Evan."

His eyes lit softly and he grinned, his ground-down teeth showing through his beard. "Now *you're* sounding a little crazy, Jay. Really, you've done all that you can, guy. Just go on home . . ."

"I will. Maybe in another day. But there could be something here, Charlie."

He was about to say something else, then simply nodded, his eyes kind of runny and sullen and his energy trailing off.

I said I'd talk to him tomorrow. His

urgency to find the truth about his son suddenly seemed to have dimmed. I thought it could be just another swing of his mood—the finality of what had taken place sinking in.

I went back and called room service and ordered an onion soup and a burger. I thought maybe I should call Kathy, but this Houvnanian thing was suddenly gnawing at me.

I was intrigued. I was pretty much just a kid back then, and I didn't know much more about him than I'd read.

I took out my computer and went online.

CHAPTER TWENTY-FIVE

Google came back with thousands of hits on the man and the horrifying events that happened on September 7, 1973. It was dizzying. I opened a link from Wikipedia.

Russell Houvnanian was thirty-four when his name became synonymous across the globe with senseless, gruesome murder.

He had been a drifter, the son of a Tennessee minister. He was kicked out of the army for psychological issues, then drifted across the country doing odd jobs, spent time in prison in Oregon for car theft and sexual battery. He moved down the coast to Northern California and took up on this commune at what became known as the Riorden Ranch, a wooded, undeveloped tract of sixty acres not far from Big Sur, which was owned by Sandy Riorden, the ex-wife of Santa Barbara real estate developer Paul Riorden.

The attached photo was the familiar one of Houvnanian being led away from the courthouse by a California marshal, leering and wild-eyed. He didn't look radically different from the image I had carried in my mind. Houvnanian was mysterious and charismatic, and he had a mesmerizing effect on rootless youths, the article read, "who flocked to Big Sur back then, attracted by drugs, music, free love, and a sense of connection, contained in his chimerical vision of evangelical prophecy and influenced by hallucinogenic drugs and rock music." He soon attracted a following. Paralleling himself with Jesus, he called his commune Gethsemane.

In Houvnanian's brain, heaven was a false paradise and had been invaded by the devil, and the earthly battle to retake it was being played out in California. The true gospel was conveyed through rock bands like the Byrds, the Doors, and the Beatles. The name he gave his brand of prophecy and social revolution—End of Days—described the battle between the forces of Truth, represented by the spiritual young, his flock, who sought out love and beauty, and the temporal agents of corruption and the devil: wealthy property owners and their local proxies, the police, who were trying to push his followers out of their "heavenly garden."

Houvnanian ultimately attracted a following of about sixty on the ranch, mostly runaway teens, musical wannabes, religious dreamers, all attracted to the environment he'd created of open sex, rock music, and LSD.

Eventually, this celebration of beauty and music gave way to a cult of fear and paranoia. In August 1973, he convinced his followers that a series of brushfires near the ranch were the work of Satan's agents trying to force them out. Some of his threats of reprisal and a few minor acts of vandalism had attracted the attention of the local police, and the Riorden clan tried to force Sandy Riorden, herself a sometime follower, to shut down the commune.

On the night of September 7, 1973, Houvnanian and four "family" members broke into Paul Riorden's Santa Barbara mountain estate, interrupting a dinner party, and ritualistically murdered him and five of his guests. They tied them up and forced them to watch as each was ultimately stabbed repeatedly or shot, the last victim, according to the police, being Cici Riorden, Paul's new, young wife, and left cryptic symbols carved into their victims' bodies.

Conjuring the image of the gaunt, chillingly reserved cohort Charlie had brought up to my father's house that day sent a tremor down my spine.

That had been him!

The bloody murders, I went on to read, convinced Houvnanian's followers that the final chapter of the conflict between good and evil had now begun. After sleeping in their van, they went to the home of George and Sally Forniciari, another wealthy Santa Barbara couple who had rebuffed Houvnanian in an earlier attempt to purchase the ranch, and murdered them in a similar fashion.

That night they had driven back to Big Sur and rounded up his clan to leave for

Arizona when police surrounded the ranch, led by tips from Riorden's sister, and arrested Houvnanian and several of his clan.

In all, Houvnanian and four of his followers, Telford Richards, Sarah Strasser, Nolan Pierce, and Carla Jean Blue, were convicted of nine counts of premeditated murder and sentenced to consecutive life sentences in California prisons.

Three others were convicted of aiding and abetting their actions and were currently serving thirty-five-year terms. One, John Redding, hung himself in his cell in 1978. Another, Alexandra Feuer, was released for medical reasons in 1998 and died shortly after from pancreatic cancer.

The third, Susan Jane Pollack, the daughter of a Wall Street executive, was set to be released in May 2010.

My eyes opened wide. *That was four months ago.*

Anticipation wound through me as I went back to Google and searched the links, finding the headline I was looking for:

SUSAN POLLACK, HOUVNANIAN ACCOMPLICE, RELEASED FROM PRISON.

It was from the *San Francisco Examiner* and was dated February 10 of this year.

I found a photo of a mousy-looking middle-aged woman being escorted from the California Women's Institution in Frontera by her lawyer. Susan Pollack didn't look like a threat to anyone these days. She looked more like a librarian or accountant, her hair cut unflatteringly short, her smile wan and resigned. She looked exhausted and her words sounded repentant. In a brief statement, she said she regretted the role she played in the horrible events of thirty-five years ago, that she renounced her past associations and was looking forward to her new chapter in life.

"I was a lost and highly impressionable young girl," Pollack said, "and, though I take all responsibility for my actions, I was easily manipulated and was under the influence of hallucinogenic drugs. For more than thirty years I've regretted the unbearable pain I've caused. I fully renounce my past. I just want to live quietly and alone and go on to the next stage of my life."

The article did not say where she was planning on living.

I closed my laptop and tried to think if there was any possibility, other than the remotest of coincidences, that Evan's death could be linked to this killer. To Russell Houvnanian.

Charlie's friend.

Could it somehow have been tied to Susan Pollack's release from prison? Could Zorn have been trying to contact Evan? Maybe for information about her? Or to possibly warn him?

Or warn Charlie?

I heard my wife's persistent complaint, how I always managed to get drawn in. This time I couldn't even disagree with her.

My brain throbbed with the memory of how I'd once been in the same room with this gruesome murderer. Houvnanian.

I went over to the bed and closed my eyes—a fourteen-year-old's distant recollection rushing back at me through the haze of time.

The blond dude in the Hawaiian shirt going on about how great Charlie was. He and Charlie, rushing out to Phil's Jag. The anger and humiliation on their faces when they returned. My father and Phil laughing at them. The curses, the pointed fingers, accusations. Russell Houvnanian's dark, laser-like eyes and, with what I now knew, that restrained yet foreboding grin. *Thank you for your time . . .*

I *was* being drawn in.

And I wasn't even trying to stop it.

So many mysteries wound into my past: Charlie. My father. Evan. It was almost as if Charlie knew it and was trying to keep me away.

But I wasn't going away.

I wrapped my arms around my chest against the chill. In a minute I was asleep.

CHAPTER TWENTY-SIX

I think I found something," I said.

Sherwood's look suggested I was becoming a nuisance fast. "You think you found something; *what* . . . ?" he replied with an edge of irritation.

I took out the papers I had folded in my jacket. "I think I found the connection between Evan and Walter Zorn."

I'd called him as soon as I had awakened the next morning. Grudgingly, he agreed to give me a couple of minutes. It came with the promise that if what I had didn't go anywhere this would be the last time I'd bother him. Along with the looser commitment that if that happened, I'd be on a plane back to New York that afternoon.

He slumped back into his squeaky chair with a glance at his watch, then back at me, impatiently. "Your meeting, doc . . ."

I pushed the papers across his desk. "Yesterday I heard on the news that Zorn had worked a couple of high-profile cases back when he was on the force in Santa Barbara. One was the Veronica Verklin murder—"

"Don't tell me your nephew Evan was a fan of sixties porn?" Sherwood clucked, rocking.

I let that pass. "The other was Russell Houvnanian."

I let *that* name settle until he gave me an almost indecipherable nod, his noncommittal gray eyes seeming to say, *Go on*.

"My brother Charlie lived on the Riorden Ranch for a while."

He furrowed his brow. "Your brother was a follower of Russell Houvnanian?"

"Not a follower. He only lived there for a while. It was the sixties . . . The early seventies, to be exact. He was rootless. A lot of people found their way there. He claims he was only there for the music and the drugs. Why, you think he prepped for his current status in life with a career at IBM?"

This time, Sherwood shot me a grin, the tiniest encouragement to go forward.

"He said he just hung out there for a couple of months. Long before anything bad happened. Charlie was a musician back then and Houvnanian was trying to raise money for a record."

"And the kicker to this is *what,* doc?" The detective leaned back in his chair. "Knock me out."

"The kicker is you were trying to find a connection between Evan and Zorn. I found one. I thought you might . . ."

"I might *what,* doc?" He rose back up, locking his meaty fingers together and dropping them on the desk. "Russell Houvnanian was attempting to arrange financing for your brother's career and you thought I'd go, *Oh, we should check this out!* You following me at all on just how this is sounding? Anyway, we're talking what here, thirty some-odd years ago?"

"Thirty-seven," I said. I heard exactly how it sounded.

"And so you're saying exactly what?" Sherwood said. "Zorn and your brother shared this six-degrees-of-separation thing, and now, half a lifetime later, the guy tries to contact his son?"

"I'm not sure what I'm saying," I said, my tone rising. "Other than it's a connection. *Something.*"

"And this *connection . . .*" He picked up the articles I had slid over to him. "It's to prove exactly what—that your nephew didn't kill himself after all? That he—let me get this straight—had some *other* motivation to climb on up there? To go off his medications. After he'd threatened to kill himself. And excuse me if I appear completely pigheaded here, but . . . isn't everyone who had an association with Houvnanian, uh . . . *in jail*? Like for the rest of their natural fucking lives?"

"No," I said. "They're not."

"They're not?"

I pointed to the *Examiner*'s article on Susan Pollack I had printed and pushed it across to him. He took out his reading glasses and scanned it, looking back up at me when he was done.

"You're saying what now? That this follower of his, this Susan Pollack, has something to do with your nephew's death?

You're a doctor. You're supposed to deal in facts. Not fantasies. It was a suicide! The kid jumped off a cliff."

I knew there was no one else here I could count on. What I'd said in that TV interview had surely taken care of that. Just people with zero interest in reversing their findings. On a case that had already been put to bed.

And now I was implying the so-called suicide was tied into a horrific, decades-old crime.

"You said you'd look into it," I said, kind of desperate.

"I said I *might* look into it. And for the record, I did."

"You did?" That took me by surprise. "And you didn't find anything?"

"Tying Walter Zorn to your nephew? *No*. At least, not anything rational," he said, sinking back in his chair. "Nothing any *sane* person would respond to . . ."

"So try *me*. What did you find?"

Sherwood gave me another grudging smile. He rubbed his jaw. Not in discomfort; more in exasperation or dismay. "There were possible markings on the victim's body that brought back something familiar . . ."

"Familiar?"

"To something related to your nephew. Something we found on him. If you chose to look at it that way."

"Now you're kind of sounding like me," I said, holding back a smile. "What kind of markings are we talking about? And familiar how?"

"I'm afraid I can't tell you. It's one of the details not released to the public yet."

"For God's sake, Sherwood, I'm a doctor. I think I understand about confidentiality. I'm not going to divulge anything."

"Just like you didn't to that reporter?"

"I know. I get it. I screwed up. Look, I'm sorry," I said, imploring, "but this is about Evan, detective, not me . . ."

He looked at me a long time. Then he said, as if against his better instincts, "There were knife wounds . . ."

"Knife wounds? I thought the cause of death was strangulation?"

"Think of this as a kind of asterisk. And if that gets out, I'll boot your ass back to Westchester so fast you won't need a plane."

"Knife wounds . . . ," I said, nodding that I got the message. "You said they were familiar. Familiar *how*?"

"You remember that plastic bag I handed back to your brother? With your nephew's personal effects in it?"

I nodded. I thought back to what was in it. A few dollars, some loose change, a key chain . . .

Then it hit me. *"That plastic hologram . . . ,"* I said. Our gazes met. *"An eye?* The markings on Zorn resembled an eye!"

Sherwood shrugged without a change in his expression. "If you wanted to see it that way."

"And how did you see it?" I stared back, suddenly feeling vindicated.

In his gray, noncommittal eyes, I could see the slightest giving in.

Sonovabitch . . . I felt a surge rush up in me. *He's beginning to have misgivings too!*

"Look," he said, pushing back, "I'm a coroner's detective, not homicide. I don't solve crimes any longer. I just see if they warrant an investigation. And this one is about as flimsy as it gets. *Beyond* flimsy! This Miguel Estrada kid says Zorn and your nephew were talking. You find something in your brother's past that connects him and Zorn. Three decades ago. There are knife marks on the victim that kind of resemble something we found on your nephew. They'd laugh me out of the squad room."

"I'm not laughing."

"Yeah." He chuckled. "I know. That's my problem."

"Can I see them?" I asked. "These knife marks."

"Not in the cards."

"I just thought it might help. To confirm what you thought you saw. So where were they?" I asked. "On the body?"

Sherwood picked up and tapped his pencil. "On the underside of the victim's tongue."

"Oh . . ." The feeling snaked through me that I had stepped in something bad. Houvnanian. His victims carved with symbols. Blood all over the walls. Zorn.

Charlie.

"You have to look into this, Sherwood."

He pushed the articles back to me. "Let's not get ahead of ourselves, doc."

"Someone, maybe this woman, Susan Pollack, may have had something to do with Evan's death."

"There's nothing tying her into anything, doc. Your nephew still went up on the rock.

Zorn."

He jumped off. Or damn well fell while attempting to." He looked at me unwaveringly.

"You told me no one would talk to me over at homicide. And maybe no one gives a shit about Evan," I said, "but they damned well might give one about Zorn."

"Look . . ." He glanced at his watch. "I got things to do. And you, you're supposed to be on a plane. *Right?*"

I looked back at him unwaveringly. "You really think I'm going anywhere until this is resolved?"

The detective stared at me a long time before he threw the pencil back on his desk and shook his head. "Anyone ever tell you, doc, you make it awfully hard for someone to like you?"

I shrugged. "My wife says it all the time."

He stood up and grabbed his jacket. "Yeah, well your wife knows what she's talking about on this one."

I said I'd call him the next day. And the day after that. Until he looked into the possibility of what those cuts meant.

And until he checked out Susan Pollack.

"I know, I know . . . ," I said with a smile. "Don't wait by the phone."

CHAPTER TWENTY-SEVEN

Kathy called when I got in the car. I had just pushed off a procedure on the daughter of a friend. Now I was pushing for a few days more. Her patience was running thin. Mine might have been too, if the situation was reversed.

"It's time to come home, Jay."

I didn't answer for a second. I wasn't exactly sure how to. "I can't, Kath. I just can't."

"What the hell is going on out there, Jay? This is beginning to scare me a little now. I'm sorry about what happened to Evan. My heart goes out to Charlie and Gabby. It really does . . . But people need you here. It's time to come back."

"I can't, Kath." I sucked in a sharp breath without explaining.

"You can't?" There was an edge to her tone.

I pulled the car over to the side of the road. "I've just found out a few things. And it's hard to explain. Especially right now."

"Well, try, Jay. *Try!* You've been there almost a week. So please, try . . ."

There was about the toughest silence I'd ever felt pass between us. Maybe twenty seconds, but it felt like an eternity.

I wanted to say, *I love you, honey. You know that. I need you. Especially right now.*

But I just can't tell you.

Until I knew for sure.

I saw something starting to open up. Something only I saw. Something only I could put together.

I flashed to Russell Houvnanian. To the time he'd been up to my dad's.

And then to Evan. The flashing "eye" they had found in his pocket. The eerie knife marks on Walter Zorn's tongue.

And finally to something I'd held back, from Charlie, from Sherwood.

And now, even from my wife.

The image of someone staring at me from their car the other night outside Charlie's apartment. Their face obscured by the darkened glass.

I didn't know for sure, but it all added up to me. Maybe only to me.

I thought I'd seen Susan Pollack.

And if I had, I knew what it meant.

It meant my nephew Evan had been murdered.

CHAPTER TWENTY-EIGHT

Charlie didn't know what to do with the photos of Sherry's gruesome murder.

He'd hidden them away—at the bottom of a drawer, with all his old music. And Evan's sneaker.

He didn't show them to Gabriella. They would only make her more distraught.

And he didn't know what to make of them anyway. Or what they meant. Why would someone want to harm her? She was someone who wouldn't hurt a fly. It was a message. After all these years. A message for him.

But what troubled him most was how they had even known where to find him.

His mind was jumbled, running wild with crazy thoughts and long-buried fears. Images he couldn't put together or stop. The unsettling feeling that the walls of the past were closing in on him.

He was tired of hiding all these years. Tired of the fears, the guilt, the shame. Of having to protect his family.

From what?

Zorn knew of Evan. The old detective had played a role in Charlie's past, more than thirty years before.

And Sherry—blond, sexy, free-as-a-butterfly Sherry—she was a part of that dark past too.

He sat there on the edge of his bed, head in his hands, afraid of where it was all going. *Poor Evan . . .* How he wished he could have him back. What hope was left for them now? Charlie knew his part would catch up with him someday. But Evan . . . Evan had been innocent. His innocent little boy.

Yet it had sucked him in too . . .

Charlie had let it.

And now the walls were closing in.

He went downstairs. Gabby was calling for the cat, putting out her food. *"Here, Juliet. Here, my baby . . ."* She noticed Charlie. "The stupid cat is missing. I haven't seen her all day. Maybe she misses Evan. Maybe she knows there's nothing here for her anymore."

"Maybe it's time we moved on," Charlie said, out of the blue.

"Move on?" His words surprised her.

"Yes." He was excited now. The thought of packing up and starting a new life seemed right. "Maybe we ought to get out of here . . . Go back to Miami. Or Vancouver. We know people there."

"Vancouver . . . ?" Gabby chortled derisively. "Are you crazy, Charlie? That was twenty years ago. We just lost our son. We live on what the state gives us. We have to be here, Charlie. That rock has killed us. There *is* nowhere to go. Go *where*?"

He sat down and put his hands to his head, afraid to contemplate what might be happening. She was right. There was nowhere to go, only to wait. Wait for it to happen.

Go where?

"I don't know."

CHAPTER TWENTY-NINE

The thing is . . . , Sherwood reflected as he parked his Gran Torino along the road in Morro Bay, in the shadow of the giant rock there:

He didn't really buy into any of this: not the thirty-year-old connection to that ritual killing case; not the meeting between Walter Zorn and Evan Erlich; not the markings on Zorn's tongue, which could be anything; not Dr. Erlich's far-fetched suspicions about the Houvnanian woman who had recently been released from jail.

Yet he was here. Spending a day in the

damp and wind when he could be working a case that actually *needed* his attention. Instead he was going over for the tenth time one he had already put to bed.

Explain that.

Since he'd gotten that stupid pastor's liver he found himself doing a lot of things he didn't fully understand.

A year back, he would've told this persistent doctor from back east to take his endovascular scope for a hike.

And hardly that nicely.

But somewhere in the closed bins of his mind, Sherwood had to acknowledge, something the guy was saying must have been making the tiniest bit of sense to him. It was the old 1 percent axiom—a detective's rule, hijacked by the previous vice president:

If there was even a 1 percent chance he was wrong, that there was something there, something he was overlooking . . . then what the hell?

He had never done much tire-kicking on Evan Erlich. Why would he? The kid was found at the base of the rock. His body signs showed he'd spent much of the night up there. Days before, he had wailed about killing himself. He had tried to buy a gun. He was off his meds.

Jesus, this isn't exactly rocket science here . . .

Sherwood hadn't even advised his boss what he was doing, wasting office time on a case he had already put to bed, when there was a pile on his credenza the size of the rock itself, and one of them a case with a family that could apply pressure.

He was fifty-six; his wife was gone; he had come back from a four-month medical leave with a brand-new lease on life. And he knew he was lucky to have this job.

Sherwood took out the police photo of Evan he had printed from his computer. He walked up to the ranger station at the entrance to the rock. A uniformed female ranger stuck her head out amiably. "Help you, sir?"

Sherwood flashed his badge and asked her, "Any chance you happened to be on last Thursday?"

"Every Thursday." The female ranger nodded.

"Any chance you happened to see this

guy?" He showed her the photo. "He was the kid who jumped off the rock."

"Oh." Her eyes lit up as she studied it closely. But she shook her head. "No. We close the station at five. Don't know what time he might have come through. Didn't it supposedly happen at night?"

"It did." Sherwood nodded. "Long shot . . ." He put the photo back in his jacket and smiled. "Thanks."

He waved and walked along the road toward the rock. Two fishermen were casting out lines in the bay along the shoals. This time of the afternoon was always a good time for rock crabs and halibut. He went up and flashed his badge. "Either of you out here last Thursday afternoon? Around the same time, maybe?"

A black man with a scruffy white beard wearing an L.A. Angels baseball cap nodded. "I came here after my doctor's appointment." He smiled at his companion, a white guy with a sunburned face in a sleeveless tee. "Caught me a three-and-a-half-pounder too."

"You happen to see this guy go by?" Sherwood brought out Evan's photo. "Maybe around six?"

The black man took the photo and scratched his head. "No, sir, can't say I did. Sorry." His partner said the same. "But you're welcome to hang around, detective." He grinned to his buddy. "Always room for the county's finest. Catch you some of those fancy Morro Bay oysters."

"Morro Bay oysters . . ." Sherwood smiled. What the locals called pelican shit. Not that there were any pelicans around here anymore. They were gone. And no one knew exactly why. "Next time."

He continued to show the photo to anyone he saw on the road, then went around the lot at the base of the rock and asked a bunch more there. Clammers. Cyclists. Joggers. Anyone who looked local. Some said they hadn't been around that afternoon. Others said they were—and had heard what had happened, how terrible it was. Everyone looked, but no one said they'd actually seen Evan.

It was getting late. Heading on six. The sun was low in the sky behind the rock, creating a beautiful orange crown. A Dodger game had started at four, and he'd like to catch the end of it with a beer.

He'd given it his best. He promised himself this was the last effing time he would get caught up in this. Sometimes no matter how hard you believe in something, you just can't make it the truth.

He headed to his car. There was a long-haired souvenir peddler in a tie-dyed T-shirt packing up his stand. Cheap, bronze-plated re-creations of the rock. T-shirts with its image on the front. Pennants. Guidebooks.

A tiny chunk of sandstone contained in a plastic dome, the inscription GUARANTEED PIECE OF THE MORRO BAY ROCK on the plastic base.

Sherwood went up to him. "You out here on Thursday afternoons?"

"Thursdays, Fridays, Saturdays . . . Sundays, Mondays, Tuesdays too," the pony-tailed peddler replied, loading a cardboard box into his SUV.

"What happens Wednesdays?" Sherwood asked him.

"Wednesdays, I'm *there*." The guy grinned, pointing to the other side of the road.

"Comedian." Sherwood pulled out Evan's photo. "Any chance you saw this kid?" The merchant continued to pack up his wares, glancing at the photo. "Last Thursday,"

Sherwood said, clarifying. "Around this time. Would've been headed toward the rock."

"He the kid who took the dive?" the man asked.

"Could be," Sherwood said, showing displeasure at the guy's choice of words.

"I seen him." The vendor nodded. He taped up a box and lugged it over to his van.

"You're sure?"

"You a cop?"

"Coroner's office," Sherwood answered. "San Luis Obispo." He took out his badge.

"No worries." The man waved him off. "The dude came by here about five twenty-five or so. Headed up that way." He sort of pointed with his chin. To the rock. "Guess the rest is history."

"You're sure it was him?"

"Sure I'm sure. He stopped here."

Sherwood felt a spark light in his chest, like a fire to kindling.

"He took a look at one of my things. *This . . .*" He picked up the piece of the rock in the dome. "Seemed fascinated with it. Here, take it; guaranteed to change your luck—that jumper dude excluded, of course.

One day I might just drop your name when someone asks to see my license."

"You say he was headed toward the rock?" Sherwood asked, stuffing the souvenir into his pocket. "Anything else?"

"One thing . . ." The peddler put down his box. "The dude wasn't alone."

Now the spark became a charge of electricity shooting through Sherwood. "What do you mean?"

"Someone was with him, that's what I mean. A woman. Older. I remembered thinking then it could be a kid and his mother, tourists. But given what took place, that doesn't seem likely."

"You sure it was a woman?" Sherwood asked.

"Damn sure." He pointed to the road. "She was standing right over there."

The jolt in Sherwood's chest had now become a jumping live wire. He reached into his jacket and came back out with the newspaper photo. The one of Susan Pollack leaving jail. "This her, by any chance? The woman you saw?"

The vendor scratched his head, pressing his lips together, foggily. "Can't be sure . . . She was in kind of a blue sweater and a cap. And she had on sunglasses. She put out a cigarette on the road." He shrugged. "Could be. I was packing up. Sorry. I don't know if that helps."

"I'm not sure either," Sherwood said. He put the photo back in his pocket.

What he did know was that his jaw had begun to throb.

CHAPTER THIRTY

I was in the motel's breakfast room the next morning. I was getting edgy, not having heard from Sherwood in a day. Charlie had gone back to acting like Charlie. Maxie was back from lacrosse camp.

Kathy was pushing hard for me to come home.

Our conversation the day before had been one of the toughest of my life. We had never kept things from each other, and for the first time in our marriage, I felt like I was. I knew I was! And I had other patients I ought to have been back for.

Since I'd arrived, it seemed like someone

had been telling me to go back home. I was wearing down and starting to feel like that was what I ought to be doing.

"This seat free?"

I looked up, recognizing the voice before I saw the face. Sherwood.

The burly detective pulled out a chair without waiting for me to reply.

I looked at him, upbeat. "Tell me this is just a coincidence and that you just happened to wander in."

"Yeah, like all your weird coincidences, doc . . ." He spun the plastic chair around and sat, facing me. "I was just wondering what you had going on tomorrow."

"Tomorrow? I know what I should be doing! Staff meeting at nine. Possible interview with a new surgical candidate at eleven. My high school senior's pushing for a new computer, so I thought I'd take him to the Apple store . . ."

"Heading home?" He grinned amusedly. "So soon?"

"Yeah." I sniffed back a wistful smile. "So soon . . ."

"Too bad," Sherwood said. "I was hoping we might take a ride."

"Since I met you, you've been telling me

to get the hell away, Sherwood. Now you want to take me sightseeing. *Where?*"

"Sonoma coast. Beautiful up there. Town of Jenner."

"The Sonoma coast? It's a nice offer. You want to have a picnic too?" I cut the sarcasm and pushed a corn muffin his way. "I've got a living to get back to. And a wife who thinks I've lost my mind . . ."

"I'm sorry about that, doc."

"'Cause I'm out here, trying to connect these dots on my nephew's death where there might not even be any frigging dots. So if you have something, Sherwood, tell me, and *please,* make it a good one, 'cause I'm really hanging by a thread right now, trying to do the right thing. Jenner, what's there?"

"Susan Pollack." The detective looked at me.

His answer hit me like a bludgeon. I waited for him to grin, like he was only screwing around. But he didn't grin. He just kept staring at me with those heavy gray eyes.

Except now there was kind of a spark lit up in them. And it looked a lot like vindication.

"You found something, didn't you?"

"Now, let's not get ahead of ourselves . . . But instead of just 'washing my hands of it,'" he said with a smirk, "I went back out to the rock—not that I was buying much of what you were selling, understand—and started asking around." He picked up the muffin and started tearing it apart on the paper plate. "Someone saw Evan there— the day it happened. Around five thirty . . . Heading to the rock."

My blood was revving, and I had the feeling he was holding something back. I waited while he made a shambles of the muffin. "And . . . ?"

"And . . ." He looked back up at me. "It seems he wasn't alone."

Those words hit me like a bus slamming into a wall at a hundred miles an hour.

First it was the possibility that maybe I wasn't so off the deep end after all—Zorn, Evan, Susan Pollack, the two sets of "eyes" leading back to Houvnanian.

Then I realized that *that,* in itself, couldn't be why Sherwood, the last person who had a reason to buy into this, was there.

"It was a woman, right?" I stared at him,

my blood surging. And then I knew! *"It was her.* Susan Pollack. *She* was with him!"

"Look, we can't be sure," Sherwood said, finally jamming a crumbled piece of muffin in his mouth. "I don't want us to be like 'buds' or anything, but a street vendor spotted them together, as Evan was heading toward the rock. I showed the guy a photo of her and he couldn't be entirely sure. She was a ways away and was wearing sunglasses and a cap. Smoking."

My mind immediately darted back to the person in the car outside Charlie's apartment. She was in a drawn-down cap. Behind a car window.

Then she tossed out her butt at me.

"But you think it's true." My blood was hard to hold back. "You must, or else you wouldn't be here."

"What I think, doc—and trust me, it's all I'm thinking—is that it's worth checking out. Just too bad you had to be heading home today, after investing all this time. Would've been nice to have the company."

My face edged into a grin, a surge of anticipation filling me up expansively. Sherwood never once changed his expression.

He only twisted his face up at the half-stale muffin. "This is what you eat every day?"

"How did you find out where she is?" I asked.

"California Department of Corrections. I have made a few buddies washing my hands of things over the past twenty-five years. While technically she's not on parole, the state requires a convicted felon to file a place of residency. Jenner's just a dot on the map. A tiny fishing village. Maybe four, four and a half hours from here."

"What are you telling your boss?" I asked him. I thought of the stack of unresolved cases on his desk.

"Less the better." He smiled at me. "What are you telling yours?"

"That maybe she was right." I smiled at him as well. "Maybe the sun out here *has* made me a little dizzy."

"What sun?" Sherwood got up, dropped the rest of the muffin back on my tray with a twist of his mouth. "How about seven A.M. then? In front of the hotel. And in case there's any doubt, I'll bring breakfast."

CHAPTER THIRTY-ONE

I took the easy way out and left a message for Kathy, saying I needed one more day.

I told Charlie and Gabby optimistically that some things were up with Evan's case. I canceled my appointments. My partners were probably starting to think I was crazy too.

I spent a lot of the rest of the day in my room, online.

I wanted to find out everything I possibly could about Russell Houvnanian. How he had gotten those people to commit the horrible acts they had. How Susan Pollack had fit in.

There was a ton of material online. Several books had been written on the case—one by an FBI investigator, Thomas Greenway, who had gone on to achieve some notoriety. Others by various journalists and criminologists, and even by a few of Houvnanian's followers. I found articles going back to the 1970s. I devoured them like the medical background to a baffling case, fascinated by how Houvnanian had been able to lure a mix of educated and sometimes affluent young women and homeless drifters onto a collision course with crime and stir them to commit such a bloody act.

He had preyed on rootless young people in the hippie culture of the sixties and early seventies—women mostly, ones estranged from their families who had found their way to his ranch near Big Sur. Most came, like Charlie, for the lure of music, fun, and free drugs. It became a refuge from the materialistic world, a haven for local musical artists. They even put together a makeshift studio there. Houvnanian deftly crafted this twisted concoction—a Garden of Eden protecting cast-off children against the encroaching evil of the outside world. Drugs were a constant, as was sex, with interchangeable partners. Houvnanian himself was said to be the father of several children by women on the ranch.

They tried to get their recordings produced—always driving down to L.A., badgering known producers. I thought of Charlie at my father's house. That was the way Houvnanian hoped to spread his message—his bizarre concept of the End of Days—to the popular culture. Houvnanian had a way of interpreting the songs of the Byrds and the Doors to back up his own apocalyptic gospel. He came to believe that the Doors' "Riders on the Storm" was written specifically for him. He looked at Jim Morrison's tragic death as a sign pointing to him, like John the Baptist paving the way for Jesus, foretelling his impending martyrdom.

In the summer of 1973, the paranoia seemed to intensify, fueled by a mixture of drugs and religion and repeated attempts by Paul Riorden and the police to get Houvnanian and his followers off the property. Several of the followers either left or were expelled. The locals around the ranch grew alarmed. People were saying there were LSD-addled orgies and blood rituals and threats against society taking place. Riorden pushed to close down the commune.

According to Greenway, Susan Pollack had spent a year at Swarthmore. Her dad was a managing director of Bache and Co., then a major Wall Street brokerage house. Another follower, Sarah Strasser, had a father who was a successful car dealership mogul from Seattle. Others, like Tel Richards of Beaumont, Texas, were simply drifters who'd had criminal records since their early teens.

In July of 1973, Houvnanian and two cronies drove down to Santa Barbara to appeal to Riorden and get him to back off his threats to pressure his ex-wife to shut down the ranch. They also went to see George Forniciari, whom one of his followers knew, to seek his help in purchasing the property. Both of them refused. Paul Riorden even called his ex-wife Sandy, Houvnanian's sometime benefactor, a "misguided slut."

Houvnanian drove back home that night in a rage, and a new sense of finality took over the ranch: The "final stage" had begun. There were three days of nonstop revelry on LSD, fueling everyone's fears that their world of "peace and harmony" was at an end. The words of the Byrds' "Turn! Turn! Turn!" were twisted into some kind of end-of-the-world prophecy: "A time to kill, a time to cast away stones." Houvnanian painted Riorden and his wealthy class as devils. He got his most ardent followers to believe that only an act of "pious bloodletting" would protect them against what was to come. They began to look at their commune as a place of impending betrayal—aptly named Gethsemane, where Judas had betrayed Jesus—and Paul Riorden and his family as the "devils," like the Romans, who would one day come for them. If Judas had not handed over Jesus, Houvnanian preached, "Jesus would have ruled the earth for two thousand years."

There were various accounts of exactly how many people set out in the commune's 1967 VW van to head back down to Santa Barbara on September 7, 1973, but in the end, the horrific acts were not in dispute: nine people brutally murdered. Five were convicted on nine counts of first-degree murder. Three more, including

Susan Pollack, were convicted of being accomplices and abetting these acts.

Houvnanian was still serving out multiple life sentences at the California state super-max penitentiary at Pelican Bay.

Head spinning, I shut the computer. I called the restaurant and ordered a meal. I set a wake-up call for six A.M. I didn't know where anyone—Zorn, Evan, Charlie, Susan Pollack—was fitting in.

My dinner came and I turned on the TV. I found a ball game on ESPN. I realized I'd now been out there for six days. I felt like my whole life had shifted on its axis and altered in just a few days.

I was a little tired, and part of me knew I should make it an early night. But my blood was pumping and I sat back down at the desk, where my computer was. This had become the only place I could feel at home.

I logged back on and did a search on "Houvnanian," feeling like I was close to something, scrolling to the third and fourth pages for additional links. I came upon a summary of the trial proceedings posted by a reporter with the *Santa Barbara Clarion*.

The trials were pretty much a slam dunk for the state. All the defendants were tried separately. The killers were amateurs and careless and had barely even made an attempt to hide their tracks. Fingerprints were left at the scenes. In blood. Articles of clothing. Most even helped convict themselves with their own rambling testimonies.

Susan Pollack pled guilty to helping to hide the murder weapons back on the ranch and washing down the inside of the van.

I'd had enough. I sat back and put my hands on the sides of my head and rubbed my temples. The lids of my eyes were so heavy. I didn't know what was in store for us tomorrow.

But someone had been with Evan just before his death.

And I was sure Susan Pollack was involved.

I was about to turn the computer off when I happened to scroll down farther ahead and noticed something. I pulled it closer to me, forcing my eyes open.

It was the transcript of a speech given by Houvnanian at the time of his sentencing. In a rambling jeremiad, he blamed the rich for their victims' deaths, their pawns the police, the lawyers who argued against him, the nonbelievers out there who doubted who he was. He ranted that it served no purpose to put him away, "no matter for how long, even for life." The social turmoil and upheaval he foretold in End of Days would come to pass.

"You can put me in the strongest prison," he declared, "in the smallest cell, let me rot for a hundred years," but one day he'd be back, he said, just like Jesus had come back, "to finish what was begun."

A moment ago I had been exhausted, but now I felt wired and breathless again.

"On that day of judgment, or even the hour," Houvnanian said to the judge, "no one will know. Not those who think they hold the power; not their pawns who enforce their will. Not even the sleeping child will know . . .

"It's like a man who goes away for a long time and puts his servants in charge of the house. He gives them tasks, duties, but they don't know when he will return. Only the master will know. Watch," the self-proclaimed messiah warned, "for no one knows when the master will choose to come back, or in what manner. It might be in the morning, or at midnight, when everyone is asleep. *Watch*," he repeated—the lawyer's account said he was grinning— "lest he come back suddenly and find you sleeping."

Suddenly the eyes on Evan and Walter Zorn flashed into my mind.

I almost heard Houvnanian saying it himself—as I'd heard him nearly forty years ago at my father's house.

"Watch!"

CHAPTER THIRTY-TWO

The night was so still, he recalled, even all these years later, *the only sound he heard was the lapping of tiny waves against the sides of the pool.*

They made their way through the ornate iron gate out front, snaking across the grounds in the dark to the sprawling house.

In back, there was the pool, kidney shaped, blue lit, a breeze blowing in from the sea. They heard laughter, the sounds of wineglasses clinking. Music playing. "Bad, bad, Leroy Brown . . ."

Through the glass doors that opened

to the back, the sight of a man and a woman dancing a bit drunkenly, two others at the long wooden table who seemed to be into themselves. Decades from now, he realized, when everything else about them was forgotten—who they were, what they did in their lives, the piles of money they had amassed—what would happen here tonight would be the one thing that would make everyone remember.

Pigs.

Grunting sounds came from nearby, from the fancy pool house off to the side. The group of them snaked around in the shadows and saw a man with long dark hair in a white cotton shirt, his jeans down at his ankles, fucking his blond cutie from behind, her palms supporting her against the pool table and her bare ass thrusting. With relish, the thought crossed his mind that he'd like to join in. Just drop the old trou and go, Surprise, kids—company! But instead he motioned to Carla and Squirrel to do what they had to do to them first and then to wait for their word.

That wasn't who they'd come for.

He and Sarah Jane and Tel went

around to the front, cutting through a row of yuccas and pines. The house was low, Spanish style, a sloping tiled roof and white stucco walls. He'd been there once before, trying to reason with the man, trying to make a proposition. Show them the way. But he wouldn't listen. Now they were only doing what they had to do. The only course that was left to them, right?

The front door was of heavy wood with black iron hardware. Like a mission door, rounded on top. Sarah Jane wore a gauzy tie-dye top with a red bandana around her hair. Tel, his hair tied into a long ponytail, wore a dark poncho. They held at the door a few moments, the sounds of merriment dancing around them. He took out a blade. Tel tucked the gun into his pants. There was no sign of wavering in anyone's eyes. He knew they loved him. They had ridden with him when it had just been fun and games, frolic and music.

And they were here with him now, when it was about to turn ugly and bad.

He always told them, nothing was evil if it came from love.

"Party time!" he said, and rang the bell.

Pig Number One came to the door—the man himself—in a floral shirt with a glass of wine, his grin evaporating as he saw who it was. "Russell?" He must've shit in his pants, knowing what they were there for and that his days were about to end. He looked so confused. "What are you doing here?"

"You told me, 'Drop in anytime, Russ.' So, guess what, Paul, we're here!"

They pushed past him into the house, Tel dragging Pauly-boy along. The sounds of merriment came to a stop.

Suddenly all eyes fixed on them. Riorden's pretty wife stopped dancing. "Who are they, Paul?"

Tel took out the gunny-gun-gun.

Suddenly everyone realized, which, he recalled, sent his dick to the moon.

Maybe one of the gals screamed. Who could recall? There was a lot of screaming later on. A shot rang out from outside, from by the pool. A woman's squeal, pitched in terror. "No, no, please, no, no . . ."

Then two more shots. Followed only by the most delicious silence.

Carla and Squirrel appeared at the back doors. Riorden's wife began to whimper.

"C'mon, everyone"—he looked around the room—"why so glum?"

"What do you want from us, Russell?" Paul Riorden asked, reaching for some kind of last authority.

He grinned. "What do I want?"

He never gave him an answer. Even now, all these years later, he really wasn't sure what he wanted that night. He put his hands behind his head and rested a leg over his knee, light from the guard's station darting off his yellow jumpsuit.

Maybe just to pay someone back. At last.

Maybe to take a piece of what he always felt was his. The good life. He'd never know it.

Maybe it was just to let the evil out. It had been in him so long.

He nodded to Sarah Jane, who went over to the stereo and turned the volume way up high.

"It's time, everyone." Party time.

Time for the devil to sprout his horns.

CHAPTER THIRTY-THREE

I think I found something last night," I said to Sherwood, who was doing seventy on Highway 101 the next morning, heading up the coast.

"What?" He glanced over from behind the wheel.

"What all the eyes are about. The ones on Zorn and Evan."

Sherwood flashed me that skeptical glower of his, taking a gulp of coffee from a paper cup. "It's a long drive, doc. I've got nowhere to go."

I told him what I had come upon last night in Houvnanian's trial transcript. The killer's psychotic rambling at his sentencing in front of the judge. I had written it down and read it out loud, pausing each time as the killer had uttered, *"Watch!"*

"That's what the eyes mean. They're warnings. They're prophesying his return."

Sherwood's face scrunched, but he kept his gaze straight ahead. "You're saying this is all about some kind of revenge? On Zorn and Evan. All these years later?"

"Zorn handled Houvnanian's case. He helped put him away."

"And your nephew?"

Evan—I admit I couldn't quite answer that yet. Other than this growing suspicion that my brother was holding something back from me.

"Look," I said, "I dug a little deeper after I read this. Zorn was only part of the police team in Santa Barbara that investigated Houvnanian. His boss on the case was someone named Joe Cooley, his lieutenant. I Googled him. Turns out he's dead too. He was killed in a car accident in Marin County back in 1991."

"That's nineteen years ago," Sherwood said.

I went on. "And one of the FBI investigators, this guy named Greenway. He even wrote a book on Houvnanian. It was sort of a bestseller back in the late seventies. Twenty-two years ago, his wife found him facedown in his pool. It went down as a suicide—by drowning."

Sherwood eyed me a couple of beats, allowing himself the slightest smile. "And all this proves *what,* doc? Blow me away . . ."

"I'm simply saying if we looked into these other cases, what are the chances we might find something in the form of an open eye on those victims too?"

He rolled his eyes at me. "You're watching too many detective shows, doc. You're starting to make me wonder about you."

"So then tell me," I asked, meeting his stare, "why are we driving all this way up to see Susan Pollack?"

He shot me a look, then shifted his gaze back to the road and drove on for a while in silence.

The traffic was light that time of the morning, so the miles flew by as we sped up the coast. We passed through the wine country around Paso Robles, where I knew a lot of great zinfandels came from. The fog lifted and it became bright and sunny.

I dozed, looking at the rolling vineyard-covered hills.

When I woke, an hour and a half in, I tried to change the subject to something personal. "Was that your wife and daughter I saw in your office?"

He looked back with a question in his gaze.

"The pictures," I said, "on your credenza."

He merely nodded at first, not offering a whole lot more. Then, after about a minute, he added: "Dorrie died a little over a year ago. Pancreatic cancer. Two months. Went like that! My daughter lives up in Washington State. She's married to an air force flight instructor up there."

"There's just her?"

He nodded. Then after another pause he said, "We had a son, Kyle, who died when he was nine. Boating accident."

"I'm sorry," I told him.

"Years ago." He shrugged, sloughing it off. "He'd be thirty now."

"I meant about your wife too."

My thoughts went to what he'd said about his liver. He'd received a transfer. He'd been handed a brand-new lease on life. But I wondered, for what?

"We had all these plans," Sherwood suddenly volunteered, his eyes ahead, "for when I retired. We were gonna spend six months and go camping down in South America. Patagonia. Bottom of the world. Supposed to be incredible down there. Some of the best fly-fishing going. Ever been there?"

"No," I said, "I haven't." Kathy and I had always talked about going to Machu Picchu. For her next significant birthday.

"Then I got sick . . ." His voice trailed off.

"Your liver?"

He eyed me, probably figuring I knew precisely what eroded a liver. And what were the signs of possible rejection, after some years.

He said, "I used to hit the bottle a bit. After Kyle died. Probably cost me a rank or two in my career. The damage was pretty far along. I was lucky to find a match. Some pastor keeled over in the middle of his sermon. Edward J. Knightly. My lucky day!"

"Funny how it works," I said.

"Yeah, funny . . . Soon as I got back from the hospital, Dorrie starts to feel discomfort in her side. Can't keep her food down. Always tired. Lotta good the damn thing's done me." He changed lanes. "Sort of a waste, if you ask me. What do *you* think?"

"I don't know." I shrugged. "Ask me again when I get on that plane."

Sherwood glanced at me, and for the first time, I think I actually saw him smile.

I asked, "Are you taking your immuno-suppressants?" I had noticed some bruising on his arms. And his eyes were a trace yellow, icteric. Signs that things might not be going along as well as they could.

"Of course I'm taking them," he replied, turning back to the road at my question.

In Gilroy, garlic capital of the world, we stopped to use the john and fill up the car. I grabbed an In-N-Out burger. It was only another hour or so to San Jose and the Bay Area. Another hour into San Francisco and then across the Bay Bridge into Marin.

"So do we have a plan?" I asked as we got back on the road.

"A plan?" He looked at me with a furrowed brow.

"For how we're going to handle Susan Pollack? What we're going to say?"

He changed lanes and flicked the AC higher. "Yeah, I have a plan."

CHAPTER THIRTY-FOUR

In Marin, we reconnected back with 101 and took it to Santa Rosa. There we turned east, on 116, through the Russian River Valley and its rows of pinot noir, heading toward the coast.

Eventually we hit the ocean again and turned north on Route 1, hugging the coastline, for another eighteen miles. The scenery grew spectacular. Winding corkscrew turns dug into the edges of steep hills, and there were intermittent turnouts that overlooked the blue sea. I was unprepared for just how impressive it was. For a while, I even forgot just why we were there.

Finally a road sign announced, JENNER. 3 MILES.

An uneasiness began to build in me. I was a doctor, not a policeman. I was used to stressful situations, but I'd never done anything like this. I realized I was only a few minutes away from meeting someone who might have had a hand in my nephew's death.

The little fishing town of Jenner was nestled in a crook along the coast. It seemed about as remote and isolated as anything could be in California. Offshore, two spectacular rock formations rose out of the ocean mist.

Sherwood's directions prompted us to turn off the main highway in town, onto a road called Pine Canyon Drive, and we took it east, climbing above the coast into the surrounding mountains. Here, the landscape became steep and forested, hills thick with tall sequoias and evergreens. The homes became trailerlike and run-down. Weather-beaten mailboxes marked dirt roads, more than actual dwellings.

A few hundred feet up, we came across a sign marking Lost Hill Road, basically a dirt road with a fallow vineyard on one side, pretty much in the middle of nowhere.

The signpost read 452.

Sherwood glanced at me and made the turn, his Gran Torino bouncing over the rutted terrain. About five hundred yards in, we came upon a red single-story farmhouse. There was a barn, separated from the main dwelling. A clothesline with some laundry draped across it. A collie came off the porch, barking.

We were there.

I took a deep breath, fought back some nerves. The place looked run-down and ramshackle and we were totally isolated.

Sherwood stopped the car. He turned to me. "The plan, doc, is you wait here until I nod that it's okay." He opened the glove compartment and took out a holstered gun. "And I do the talking, all right? We clear?"

I wasn't about to argue. "Clear."

As he strapped the holster around his chest he asked, "Did you happen to bring your cell?"

"I have it." I nodded, reaching into my pants pocket, and pulled it out.

"Doubt it even works up here, but . . ."

He opened the door, leaving the car keys in the ignition. "You hear the sound of something you don't like—say, like gunfire—be my guest and get the fuck out. Then you can tell 'em."

"Tell 'em what?" I asked, not sure I understood.

He stepped out of the car and winked. "That thing about the eyes . . . You can tell 'em you were right."

CHAPTER THIRTY-FIVE

The collie wagged its tail and went up to Sherwood. He gave the dog a friendly pat and followed it up to the house.

Sherwood looked back at me once, then knocked on the white frame door. "Susan Pollack?"

No one answered.

I noticed the rear of a car parked in the barnlike garage, the fresh wash draped on the clothesline. Not to mention the dog.

He knocked again, harder this time. "Anyone here . . . ?" I saw his hand go near his holster. "Ms. Pollack? I'm Detective Sherwood. From the San Luis Obispo police."

I felt a premonition that the next sound I was going to hear was that of a shotgun blast and Sherwood would be blown backward off the porch.

My heart kicked up a beat.

He was getting ready to knock a third time when someone came around from the side.

It was a woman. In a straw sun hat. Wearing coveralls and heavy gardening gloves. She had short dark hair; pinched, mouselike features; and a definite resemblance to the woman I'd seen in the newspaper photo. She stared at Sherwood with a hesitant reserve. "Can I help you?"

"I'm sorry to bother you," the detective said. He introduced himself again and held out his badge. "I'm with the coroner's office in San Luis Obispo. We drove all the way up here . . . We'd just like a moment of your time."

"A moment of my time about *what*?" she asked, squinting.

"Related to an incident that took place down there. A suicide. We just have a few questions we'd like to ask you, if you can give us the time."

"Ask *me*?"

"Yes, ma'am." Sherwood nodded good-naturedly.

"Am I required?" She looked past him, and her gaze fell on me in the car.

"No," Sherwood answered, "you're not required at all. But it's been a long drive, and it would save us coming all the way back here with something more official . . ."

Susan Pollack didn't seem particularly nervous or relaxed. What she seemed was *guarded,* like someone who didn't like strangers invading her world. Especially the police.

Finally she shrugged and wiped her arm across her brow. "San Luis Obispo's a long way. All right, well, you might as well come on in then. I was just in the chicken coop. They're pretty much my only friends these days. Them and Bo. Not much fun if you don't like to get your hands dirty. What did you say your name was . . . Sherwood?"

Sherwood nodded.

She stepped up on the porch. "And you might as well tell your friend, or whoever he is in the car, to come on in too."

Sherwood waved toward me, and I got out. I nodded hello and followed them in.

"This is Jay Erlich," Sherwood said.

"You a detective too?" Susan Pollack asked. She had sort of a narrow, birdlike face and barely looked at me.

"No. He's a doctor. A big-time surgeon, I hear. From New York."

"I'm from New York," Susan Pollack said. She wiped her hands. "I went to the Brayley School in the city and had a year at Swarthmore College." She looked at me. "You haven't driven up all this way to tell me that I'm sick or something, have you, Dr. Erlich?"

"No. I haven't," I said, but didn't smile.

"Dr. Erlich's nephew was killed last week in Morro Bay," Sherwood explained. "He took a fall off the famous rock there in the bay. You ever been to Morro Bay, Ms. Pollack?"

"No." She shook her head. "I haven't. There's lots of places I haven't been to. You've found me here, so you obviously know who I am. I guess you could say I've had my travel privileges curtailed the past couple of years."

She led us into the foyer. Sherwood asked, "Do you mind if we sit down?"

"Be my guest." She motioned us to a

wooden kitchen table. The kitchen had a
pleasant, well-taken-care-of feel about it.
A rack with lots of copper pots suspended
from it hung over a wooden island. An old
hand-painted olive basket hanging on the
wall. She took off her hat, revealing her
short-cropped hair. I tried to determine if
this was the face I had seen staring at me
that night from the car, but I couldn't.

She nodded, and Sherwood and I pulled
out chairs.

"I had a little money put aside from a
trust my father had set up." She shrugged.
"When I got out, I didn't really have anywhere to go. I couldn't face going back
home. And as you might imagine"—she
smiled briefly—"privacy was a selling point
of the place. I'd offer you some coffee,
but this isn't taking on the feel of a social
visit, is it? Maybe you should just get right
down to why you're here."

Sherwood nodded. "I asked Dr. Erlich to
come along because, as I said, his nephew,
Evan, was killed last week, and we're looking into his death. At first blush it was ruled
a suicide. *I* ruled it a suicide. The kid was in
a troubled state mentally and had recently
been remanded to Central Coast Medical

Center, the psych ward there. A couple of days before his death, the hospital released him to a halfway facility in Morro Bay. A day later he took a walk from the house, and the next morning he was found at the bottom of the rock."

"Sounds like a poor decision," Susan Pollack said. "His or the hospital's." She turned to me. "How old was your nephew, Dr. Erlich?"

"Twenty-one."

"Twenty-one . . ." She inhaled deeply and rubbed her hand across her brow. "And you say he was troubled?"

I nodded. "Bipolar."

She nodded, almost sympathetically. "I know something about being twenty-one and troubled. I suppose we both had to pay for it, in our own ways. I'm sorry for your loss."

I studied her reactions—a tick in her jaw, averting her eyes—trying to measure her sincerity. "Thanks."

"Nonetheless . . ." She turned back to Sherwood. "I'd still like to know just what this has to do with me."

"You say you've never been to Morro Bay?" he asked again.

"No, I haven't. I haven't left here very much at all since my release. And you still haven't answered my question."

"A number of curious matters have come up," Sherwood started in, "that might in some way connect Dr. Erlich's nephew's death to a period of your own life, Ms. Pollack. Your own past."

She smiled, more of a soft twinkling in her eyes, as if to say, *I'm not surprised.* She took out a cigarette, lit it, and tossed the match in a coffee mug on the table. "Let me hear them, please."

"Do you know the name Walter Zorn?" Sherwood asked.

She answered almost reflexively: "No." Then, blinking, her eyes lighting up with recognition, she nodded. "*Yes . . .* yes, I do."

"He was a detective who was part of the police team back in Santa Barbara that handled the Houvnanian investigation," Sherwood reminded her. "You should know the name."

"I haven't heard it in years. I was young and stoned mostly, and in a completely different world back then. And to my recollection, he didn't handle any of my depositions. But I do recall the name."

"You've not heard from him since?"

She shook her head. "Not in thirty-five years."

"Or seen him?"

"Like I said, I've been a bit preoccupied, detective." She flicked an ash in the coffee mug. "How is Detective Zorn?"

"Well, actually, he's dead," Sherwood told her.

"Hmmm." She grunted with a slight smile. "Definitely seems to be in the water lately."

"He was murdered. Three days ago. In his home. In Santa Maria. Thirty miles south of Morro Bay." Sherwood stared at her. "Any chance that you've been *there*?"

Susan Pollack met his stare and took a long drag on her cigarette. Her amiable expression shifted. "I'm not sure I like where this is going, Detective Sherwood. But I'm still interested in finding out what any of this has to do with me."

"Zorn handled the Houvnanian murders. A week or two ago, before he was killed, he was observed in conversation with Dr. Erlich's nephew, Evan. It seems the boy's father, Dr. Erlich's brother, had a connection to Houvnanian himself back then."

"Now this is getting interesting. What kind of connection?"

"Apparently he resided on the Riorden Ranch for a time. I don't suppose you might've overlapped or even remember him. Charlie Erlich . . ."

Susan's Pollack's birdlike eyes narrowed, like she was focusing back in time. "I may. Or may not, as you say. People were always moving in and out of the ranch. We may not have even been there at the same time. Anyway, we all went by different names back then. Mine was Maggie. Maggie Mae. For Magdalena, actually, not for the song.

"Anyway"—she looked back at me— "your brother's son is dead, and he had some kind of random connection to this detective, Zorn. Now *he's* dead . . ." She turned to Sherwood, the lightbulb going off. "And *I've* been recently released. I think I get it now."

Sherwood nodded. "We're trying to find out if Detective Zorn's connection to Evan was, indeed, as random as you say."

She rubbed a finger along the side of her face, knocked the ash off her cigarette. She came back with the faintest smile. "Just so you know, detective, I haven't had any direct communication with Russell Houvnanian in more than thirty years. I've taken responsibility for what I've done. What I *helped* to do. I've expressed remorse. I've paid my debt. I was a deluded twenty-year-old who was in love. I didn't kill anybody, Detective Sherwood. I didn't get in that van."

"If you don't mind me asking, ma'am—"

"I'm fifty-seven now," Susan Pollack said, cutting him off. "I've forfeited most of my life. I'd like to find some way I can make up for the pain I've caused. Counseling, animal rescue, I don't know what form. The last thing I have on my mind is the 'old days,' detective. I think you can understand that. That's the best answer I can give."

She turned to me. "I'm sorry about your nephew, doctor. I'm sorry if it's opened a bunch of wounds and old things that were better off kept closed. But I haven't been to Morro Bay. Or Santa Maria. Or seen Detective Zorn. Or knew of your nephew. Now, I know you've had a long drive up here. Is that all?"

Sherwood looked at me with an air of disappointment. As if he was saying, *Sorry, her cooperation is 100 percent voluntary at this point.* He seemed ready to get up. "We won't trouble you any longer . . ."

I fixed on her. "Both Evan and this detective Zorn had something strange on them at the times of their deaths. The image of an eye. An open eye, staring. Does that mean anything to you?"

Susan Pollack shrugged. I noticed the slightest tremor in her jaw. "No. Should it?"

Sherwood looked at me, eyes burning, but I continued on. "Do you mind if I read you something, Ms. Pollack?" I knew we were about to walk out the door with nothing and that would be the end of it. We had no proof, nothing to pin her to any of the scenes, no evidence to compel her to cooperate, and nothing on Houvnanian, who was in jail.

All we had were these unrelated pieces of the jigsaw I was trying to fit together. I needed to know for sure.

"Russell Houvnanian made a statement at the time of his sentencing. It was about him possibly coming back one day. To take revenge. Do you have any idea what this means?"

I pulled out the paper from my jacket

and tried to judge her reactions as I read. "'On that day of judgment, or even the hour, no one will know . . . Not even the sleeping child will know. Only the father. It's like a man who goes away for a long time . . .'" I glanced up, watching her watching me, the slightest veiled smile in her eyes. "'No one knows when the master will choose to come back, or in what manner . . . Watch,'" I read, "'lest he come back suddenly and find you sleeping. *Watch* . . .'"

"I think it's time for you both to go now." Susan Pollack rubbed out her cigarette and stood up. "I'm sorry you had to come up all the way here."

Sherwood stood up with her. "We appreciate your time . . ."

"Did you know my brother?" I asked, my blood heating.

She didn't answer. She just motioned us to the door. "I'm sorry for your loss, Dr. Erlich. For your brother's loss."

"Did you know him? His name was Charlie, Ms. Pollack. He had a beard and long black hair."

She waited for us to step off the porch.

I followed Sherwood down, sure I had struck a nerve, but one I'd never be able to follow up on.

Then she called back—not so much in answer to my question, but with what seemed a kind of taunt. "He was a musician, wasn't he?"

Blood rocketed in my veins.

Then she smiled, putting back on her work gloves. "I hope you have a good trip back."

Outside, we headed back to the car. I exchanged only the slightest glance with Sherwood. I was frustrated. I knew we had come away with nothing. Nothing to follow up on. Nothing to tie her to Evan's death in any way.

He went to the driver's side and eyed me, silently telling me to get in.

"Wait one second," I said, suddenly remembering something.

I went over to the garage, Susan Pollack watching me. It was more like a dilapidated barn with a rolling wooden door on tracks. The door was open. I swung it to the side just a little and peered in.

I thought back to the night outside Charlie's apartment. I brought to mind the person in the car. Flicking her cigarette. Staring at me.

A Kia wagon. Navy.

A car just like this.

I headed back over to Sherwood and got back in the car. I looked up at the house and saw Susan Pollack in the doorway, smiling at me, petting her dog.

CHAPTER THIRTY-SIX

I know it was her." I turned to Sherwood as soon as we got back on the main road.

He put on the brakes, veins popping on his neck. "What do you think you were doing in there?"

I knew I had crossed the line. "We had this one chance," I said. "I was only trying to figure out what she knew."

"Yeah, well, you leaked a confidential piece of evidence in the homicide investigation of an ex–police officer. The knife marks. Maybe in the ER, doc, you call the shots. But here you're no more than a guy who's come in off the street with no insurance. That wasn't something she needed to know."

"All right, I'm sorry," I said, taking a breath. "But she's part of it, Sherwood."

"Yeah? What did she say that made up your mind?"

I told him about the car I'd seen three nights ago outside my brother's apartment. The person in the cap watching me.

The same car I was sure I just saw in Susan Pollack's garage.

"Someone staring at you?" he said, his nostrils flaring. "Sort of like I am now."

"I couldn't tell if it was a man or a woman. I don't know how to describe it, but I know they were watching me. Or Charlie. As they drove away the window went down, and they flicked out a cigarette butt my way. It was like a warning, Sherwood. It gave me a chill."

"Well, maybe you should have listened to it, doc . . ." Sherwood stared at me. *"What* kind of car was it?"

"A compact. A Honda or a Kia or something. A wagon. Black or dark blue."

"Black or dark blue?" He rolled his eyes.

"It was night," I said.

"I know. Exactly," he replied unsympathetically. "You take note of the plates?"

"No. I didn't get them. I was talking to my wife."

"What about the car model? The year?"

"I don't know!" I snapped back. "I'm a doctor. I don't know fucking cars. I didn't even suspect that anything was going on back then. It was just a sense."

"And that's what you want me to broaden an investigation on? Some car you can't identify; a person you think you saw in the dark while you were on the phone. *A sense!* You think I can go to my boss with this and say, 'Look, all this shit is going on, none of it adds up, but my guy's got a medical degree, and he's pretty sure someone was watching him. We think we found the car. It was in Susan Pollack's garage. It was either a Honda or a Kia, either black or dark blue. It was nighttime . . . And oh, yeah, the thing that totally cinches it, Susan Pollack smokes . . . '"

"It was her!" I shouted. My gaze burned. "The eyes, the woman who was with Evan, the person in the car outside Charlie's house. It all adds up. We just have to put it together, Sherwood. She knew my brother. You heard what she said. She was taunting me. She knows why Zorn had to find Evan . . .”

“I can't keep this investigation open on taunts. I need something real! I'm a goddamn coroner's detective, not homicide. You know the score here. I have maybe, what, a year before I'm pushed aside. Six months, if the county budget cuts come down. And then what? You know the long-term prospects for a transplant at my age. You can see the color in my eyes, same as me.”

I had noticed the yellowish hue. Along with the bruise marks on his arms. Transplants at his age were always dicey. If he wasn't one of the lucky ones, two years, three years tops.

“I can't afford to mortgage the rest of my career for you!”

He glared at me with his eyes burning, then sat back and put the car in gear. We drove back down the hill toward the coast.

For a while, neither of us said a word. I wanted to say I understood. I understood everything he was saying. I knew we didn't have a single solid shred of evidence to build a case on. Other than these crazy puzzle pieces in my mind. Pieces Sherwood no longer seemed keen on putting together. We knew Zorn knew about Evan. We had the eyes on both bodies. There was a woman with Evan before he ended up dead.

We drove down to the coast and got back on the highway. The morning fog had lifted and it was now a bright and shining day.

Sherwood pulled to the side of the road. For a moment I thought he was going to tell me to get out and make my own way back to Pismo Beach.

Instead, he turned to me and shook his head. "I think you're going at this the wrong way. There's someone else you should be talking to," he said. "Who knows a lot more than he's letting on."

I didn't have to ask who he meant.

"You're gonna lose me," he said.

"I can't." I looked at him pleadingly.

"You want some answers . . ." He put the car back in gear and drove down the hill. "Quit protecting your brother and ask him."

CHAPTER THIRTY-SEVEN

It was already after eight when Sherwood dropped me off in front of the motel. I didn't feel like dealing with Charlie that night. I was exhausted and drained from the long ride. I went upstairs and ran the shower. I stood in front of the mirror and looked at my hollowed, haggard face.

I kept seeing Susan Pollack's smile. *Your brother was a musician.*

She knew him! I knew she did. Which meant Charlie was keeping something from me about his time on the ranch.

It's time for Charlie to come clean.

That's when my cell phone rang. Kathy.

This was another conversation I wasn't looking to have. How would I explain what was going on? Where I'd been today? Or why I needed more time here?

"Hey," I answered, sucking in a breath.

"Hey. You sound tired."

We tap-danced about the weather for a while, and then the kids. How Maxie had been messing around on Ryan Frantz's guitar while at lacrosse camp and wanted to take lessons.

Then she said, "Jay, I think it's time you brought me in on what the hell's going on out there."

She was right. It was time. I said, "Just promise me you won't tell me I'm crazy until you hear the whole story, okay?"

"I'd *like* to be able to promise that, Jay . . ."

"All right, here goes . . ."

I started with Walter Zorn and the things that connected him to Evan. Looking for him at the basketball courts. And then the eyes. "We all thought he was delusional, Kathy, but this friend of his confirmed he had been speaking with the police." I brought up Susan Pollack and the woman who had been spotted with Evan before he died.

Then I brought up Houvnanian. Charlie's old connection to him. How *I* had once met him.

Still she didn't say a word.

Finally I told her where I had been that day.

"Are you done?" Kathy finally asked.

I sat on the edge of the bed and waited. "Yeah, I'm done."

"Jay, are you completely out of your mind?"

"I told you, you weren't allowed to say that," I said, hoping at least for a chuckle.

There was none.

She said, "You're a doctor, Jay, not a policeman! What you're saying sounds totally crazy. Evan. This murdered detective. These sets of eyes! *Russell Houvnanian!*"

"Look, I know there's no way for you to understand, Kathy. I know that I'm onto something here. I have to see it through."

"Onto what, Jay? That your nephew wasn't sick? A few days ago you were claiming the hospital was responsible for his death. You even brought in the press. Now you're saying *what*? That he was *murdered*?"

I let out a breath. "I know how it sounds, Kathy, but yeah."

"Russell Houvnanian? Don't you see— you're scaring me now, Jay! Look, I know how tough it must be with Charlie and Gabby now. I know how Evan's death has upset them . . ."

"It has upset them, Kath, but that's not it."

"Then what is it, Jay? *Tell me.* What is it you're trying to find out there?"

"I'm just trying to find out the truth. About what happened to him. That's all."

"No. This is all going far beyond Evan. You're stepping into things you shouldn't be. Things the police ought to be handling if something's going on. You're going to get yourself hurt, Jay. *Don't you see I'm worried about you?"*

I knew I had to say something to convince her I hadn't lost my mind. "I just need you to trust me, Kathy, that's all. Like how you trusted me when you went up in the plane with me that first time. Like how you trust me every day to take care of you and Maxie and Sophie. And I've never let you down, have I?"

"No, Jay, you've never let me down."

I said, "I realized something the other day. I know this'll sound a little crazy. But how lucky we are. All of us. I tried to say it, but I couldn't. You wouldn't have understood."

"We are lucky, Jay. We are."

"I don't mean that way. What I mean is, Charlie and my father, they were the same. You know what I'm saying, right? That's why Lenny was so volatile. He just was never diagnosed. He just played it out on a different stage.

"Being out here, and watching how Charlie and Gabby loved Evan, it's made me think, maybe the only reason Charlie is where he is and I'm where I am is simply that I was lucky. That what they had didn't get passed on down to me. Charlie got it, Kathy."

"You're wrong about that, Jay. You've earned whatever you have. I've watched you. You've earned it all. And you say you're out there to find the truth . . . But the truth is never the truth, Jay, when it comes to your brother. You know that, don't you?"

"Maybe so," I said. "But I'm going to be there for them, Kathy. I'm in now. And all the way."

It was the second time in two days we had hung up with distance between us. I promised her I'd be back soon. Maybe not tomorrow, but the day after. Or the day after that.

I sat up and looked in the mirror. And while the face that stared back at me was the same—the one who scrubbed in in the OR, who laughed at *The Office* or *30 Rock,* who cheered on my son at his matches, and who drove my daughter down to college and hung her posters on the walls just right, and even cried in the car after I hugged her good-bye—I saw something different in the eyes that stared back at me.

Something *had* changed.

The phone sounded again.

I hurried to grab it, wanting to say, *Kathy, I didn't mean to scare you. I don't know what's taking hold of me. I need you too . . .*

Then I realized it wasn't my cell at all that was ringing. It was the room phone. I thought maybe Sherwood was calling me back, or more likely, the front desk—I was way, way past my original checkout date.

I reached it on the third ring. "Hello?"

"You know the one about the patient,

doc, who waits too long to find out what's wrong with him, 'cause he never wants to hear bad news?"

The voice was male, a slight southern inflection to it.

"Sorry?"

"And then it's too late. He's got cancer. And the doctor goes, 'How would you feel if I told you it was all a joke, and you just have high blood pressure now?'"

"Who is this?"

He didn't say. Instead he said, "You're a smart man, doc. Smart people like you ought to know when they put their noses where they don't belong. When they should just back off. Before they get themselves burned. Or even worse, maybe someone else, someone close to them."

"Who the hell is this?" I said, my blood instantly on fire.

"Don't you worry your little medical degree about that, doc. You worry about what you're gonna do. *Comprende?* I'm just trying to play the good citizen here and clue you in. Time to just pack up and head home, pal. Quit trying to make trouble here."

"What do you mean," I said, my temperature rising, "*someone close to me*?"

"Mine to know, doc, yours to worry about. The kid was sick, right? Why don't we just leave it at that. And speaking of sick, let me ask. You smoke, doc?"

I was about to hang up but answered, seething, "No, I don't smoke."

"That's funny then," he said, "'cause I definitely smell something burning. Don't you?"

The guy's voice had this cozy, insinuating sort of tone to it, which actually scared me a little. "Don't call me again, asshole."

"'Cause it would be easy—you don't know how easy—," he went on, "to just burn that little nose of yours right off, any time we want. Remember, doc, you're out west, not back in New York. Once a fire starts here, you never know how fast it might spread. Or to where."

I put down the phone, my heart pounding, anger pouring out of me.

I definitely smell something burning. Don't you?

I jumped up, a sudden alarm shooting through me. I ran to the door and pulled it open, stepping out into the corridor outside. I scanned in both directions, toward the lobby and the parking lot.

No one.

What the hell did he mean?

Then I looked down, my blood rushing to a stop. I saw what was on the mat.

Smell something burning?

It was a lit, half-smoked cigarette.

CHAPTER THIRTY-EIGHT

Thirty minutes later I handed the cigarette to Don Sherwood.

I had carefully picked it up—a Salem— put it out, and placed it in a bag from my Dopp kit. Then I called Sherwood, who alerted the Pismo Beach police, who arrived minutes later, lights flashing, along with a detective named Reyes.

"You wanted something real," I said, handing it to Sherwood. "Here—*this is real*! Go to town!"

The threatening call had come from an untraceable number. I had checked with the front desk before I'd even called Sherwood.

The motel had security cameras, mostly on the stairwells, but the one on my outside corridor was on the fritz. It hadn't even been turned on. The night manager said they hadn't needed to look at them in years.

"How're you doing?" Sherwood asked, taking me aside.

I was angry. Who wouldn't be? And upset. "I'm not used to receiving these kinds of threats."

"You want to file a complaint, Dr. Erlich, Detective Reyes will be happy to take it for you."

"I don't want to file a complaint!" I said. "What I want is for you to look into my nephew's death. I told you what the guy said. He was warning me to back off. He referred to someone close to me who would be put in danger. You need a scorecard to figure who he meant by that? You need to put a car outside Charlie's house. How much more 'real' does it have to get? Or maybe you just want to wait until he ends up like Evan. Or maybe next it'll be *me*."

Sherwood just looked back and shrugged. "So maybe you oughta think on that advice," he said. "There's a lotta people around here you've already managed to piss off. Let's start with the hospital. While we're at it, why not toss in the local police? See what I mean? No telling who might've done this. I can't just station a car. There wasn't even a direct threat made against your brother. In the meantime"—he held up the bag—"Detective Reyes will take this back. Not that I'm particularly hopeful they'll find anything."

"How about Susan Pollack's DNA?"

"I thought you said the caller was a man."

"So someone else is involved." I fixed on him. "You can't keep ignoring this, Sherwood. Evan's death wasn't a suicide. You know it—I know it. Please, I'm begging you, station a car . . ."

He looked at me like his hands were tied.

"At least check Cooley and Greenway. You'll find something. I know you will. Please, Sherwood, just do it. You'll see."

CHAPTER THIRTY-NINE

The hotel switched my room to one closer to the lobby, with two police cars stationed below, and I slept with the door double-locked and the chain drawn—when I actually finally made it to sleep. I watched the clock strike two.

The next morning, I headed over to Charlie's as soon as I showered.

Gabby opened the door. She was in a light green knitted tracksuit, stripes running down the sleeves. Her face seemed to have a new anxiety written all over it. "Come on in, Jay. Your brother's not doing so well.

Something happened last night. As if Evan is not enough . . .”

My alarm bells started sounding. “*What?*”

I went with her inside. Charlie was slouched over the kitchen table, his face in his hands, his hair straggly and unkempt. He barely even stirred when he saw me. “Hello, Jay . . .”

“Your brother is a wreck,” Gabby said, “and so am I. How could someone do something like this? How is it possible someone could want to hurt us in this way . . . ?”

“What happened, Gabby?” I knew already I wasn’t the only one who had been warned.

She opened the back door to their tiny fenced-in yard. There was a large plastic garbage bag set on the ground. Gabby’s face was pinched and somber. “Look, look what we found this morning . . .”

I hesitated for a second and peeked inside the bag.

“She’d been missing. We couldn’t find her for two days. I thought she had finally run off. That she had enough of us for good. I opened the front door to get the mail yesterday afternoon and this is what I found . . .”

The harsh, acrid smell told me immediately what was in there. I peered in, wincing at the charred, black shape.

"Who could do something so cruel, Jay? She didn't harm anyone. The people here are filth. Drug dealers and meth heads. I am ashamed to have to live around them. People just want to hurt, that's all! What have we done to deserve this?"

"The people here didn't do this, Gabby."

I closed the bag, my chest filling with both sadness and rage. My warning last night was suddenly clear. The butt on my front door.

I turned to my brother, his eyes dull and glazed. "There's stuff you're not telling me, Charlie."

"What do you want, Jay? What do you want me to say?"

Gabby stepped in. "Your brother is a mess," she said. "He cannot tell you anything today. He's been irrational all morning. The grief has done this to him. I tried to give him his medications to calm him down, but he won't take them. Isn't that right, Charlie? Tell him."

He had a glint in his eye. "The people here are animals, Jay."

"He says he wants to leave." Gabby went over and sat next to Charlie. "He says he wants to go to Canada or someplace." She laughed derisively. "He is really crazy today. He thinks the devil is loose here. In Pismo Beach. Have you ever heard anything so stupid in your life? I keep telling him, we can't leave. We can't go anywhere in this godforsaken world. We're stuck in this miserable, empty hole for the rest of our lives . . ."

"Gabby, please . . ." I went and sat down across from Charlie. His wild gray hair and beard were stained from the tears on his face. "The people here didn't do this, Charlie. I think you know that, and that's what's made you scared."

"Scared? Who wouldn't be scared, Jay? We're all going to hell. And you know who's the first person we'll see there? Our own son—*Evan*!"

"He thinks our son is damned and going to go to hell," Gabby said, "for killing himself. He can't accept that."

"Charlie, I got a call last night . . ." I leaned forward and put my hand on his wrist, and he tried to pull it away. "A threatening one. The caller told me to go back home. To get my nose out of where it didn't belong. You know what he was talking about, right?"

"I know my son's in hell and I'm gonna go there too . . ."

"Before he hung up, he asked me if I smoked. I couldn't figure out what he meant, but now I know. I ran to the door, and there was a lit cigarette butt burning on the mat. Now *this* . . ."

"You ought to go back home, Jay." His eyes were runny and confused. "You should listen to what they're saying to you, little brother. I don't want you here."

"Who is Susan Pollack, Charlie? Think back. You knew her, didn't you? She was with you, wasn't she, on the ranch?"

"Why does everything have to relate to the ranch? The ranch is dead, Jay. It's been dead for more than thirty years. I told you to go home too, didn't I? Before it takes you too."

"I'm not going home, Charlie. Not until you tell me. You knew Susan Pollack—*Maggie*—back then, didn't you? I need you to focus on this. I need you to tell me what she wants with you now. What she might have wanted with Evan. She was with Evan, I think. The day he died. As was Zorn. I think it wasn't about Evan, Charlie. I think by killing Evan, they were trying to hurt you."

He looked at me. One second his eyes sparked alive, as if with recall and clarity; the next they were as dim and dull as a lunar eclipse. "What does it even matter now, Jay? What if Jesus went down to hell? What if he went there and looked around and said to the devil, 'Hey, man, this ain't so bad. I sort of like it here.' What if *this* is hell, Jay? Look around. This hole. It sure looks like hell, doesn't it?

"That big fucking rock—what if it's all just a game, Jay, and everyone's trying to make their way to heaven, thinking, *This is the right way to salvation,* but what if the devil is already there—he's beaten them to it! And he's laughing at everyone, going, 'Come on in! This way, everyone . . .' What hope is there then, Jay?"

I looked at my brother, the flickering patina in his eye. The way he was acting suddenly didn't seem far from the crazed dropout ranting about Jesus and Lennon in my mother's dining room forty years ago. It scared me.

"This is how he gets," Gabby said, "when he doesn't take his medications. Isn't that right, Charlie? You know that."

"Yeah, yeah," my brother chortled dismissively. "See, Jay, this is how I get."

"He'll be better tomorrow," Gabby said. "Right?"

"Charlie . . ." I pushed my chair close to him. "Zorn tried to contact Evan and warn him about something. Maybe it was to warn you. A woman was with Evan when he went up to that rock. I'm sure it was Susan Pollack. You might be right, Charlie— about what you first said. That maybe Evan didn't jump off that rock. But I need to know what they think you know, Charlie. Or what you did back then."

"What I did? What I did was send my only son straight to hell, Jay. So what does that make me?"

"This is for Evan, Charlie." I squeezed his hand. "For him. What do these people want with you, Charlie? What did Walter Zorn know?"

"For Evan . . . ?" He turned to me. "Maybe Zorn was the devil, Jay. What do you think? That gimpy bastard, he surely walked like the devil. That's what they say,

you know, how you can tell it's him—the limp."

Gabby came over to me. "There's nothing you can do when he gets like this." She leaned over and draped her arm caringly around my brother's neck. "He's like his own son. You can talk to him all day—but he's not here . . . He's somewhere else."

He took another sip of coffee and caught my eyes. "For Evan, Jay."

I stood up and squeezed my brother softly on the shoulder as I went past him out to the narrow, fenced-in yard. I sank down in one of the cheap folding lawn chairs and looked up at the blue sky.

In my life, I'd never felt the fear of being in danger—or that I was putting others in danger. I knew the next time it might not be a warning. I thought about Evan, what he might have gotten involved in unwittingly, what might have happened up there, on the rock, and I knew I owed him something.

Two things drummed in my mind.

What if Jesus went to hell and said it ain't so bad here and just stayed, my brother had said. *What if heaven is hell?*

I realized I'd read something like that before.

From Houvnanian's ramblings. The other night, online. The End of Days.

But it was the second thing that really worried me. Not about Charlie but Zorn. The slight limp he carried.

Charlie had mentioned it. Miguel had mentioned it too.

What was worrying me was that in all the news reports and coverage, I was sure that had never come out before.

CHAPTER FORTY

Sherwood sat at his desk, cradling the phone. He looked at the number he had scribbled on his pad, conflicted. It was the number of an out-of-state detective some-one in the sheriff's department had known. He leaned back and looked at the mountain outside his window, hesitating before he dialed.

He glanced at the photograph of his wife on the credenza.

Dorrie, you'd probably say I was crazy for doing this, wouldn't you?

No. Sherwood chuckled to himself. *She would not.*

What she would say was, *God's given you a second chance, Don, so why not use it, right?*

He had this job courtesy of a friend in the sheriff's department. Mostly in recognition of what he'd put in for the past twenty-five years. And he was good at it. Usually, no one was down his back. He didn't have to solve murders anymore, just figure out if they warranted solving. And pass it along. He didn't have to beat the leather all around town—chase suspects, appear in court, buck up against the state authorities. Or put himself at risk . . .

The press didn't get on his back, making life miserable.

It was a nice, stress-free existence, a way to end his career. And he was lucky it came his way. After he'd gotten sick, the position had opened up. Perokis, his lieutenant, always gave him a lot of space. He'd earned a certain respect. He did his work; cases got disposed of; the files went down. And like clockwork, others always came.

Then this one. He didn't have to get deeper involved.

It was just that this nagging voice had

been needling him over the past week—telling him that maybe he hadn't done all he could. Maybe there was something there, these threads of doubt knitting together. Now the voice had turned into a jabbing presence in his mind.

Dorrie's voice.

And what had happened to the doctor last night only intensified the voices even more.

He stared at the mountain.

What if Erlich was right? What if Zorn's murder was connected? What if he had known something he was trying to share? Warn them. What if the "eyes" did mean something? What if Susan Pollack was the woman the street vendor had seen?

He rubbed his jaw—the joint felt like someone was sticking a needle in it. It was telling him to back off. He had already turned this case over. Let the solved cases be.

No, he knew, it wasn't saying that at all.

He glanced at Dorrie. *God gave me a second chance, huh?*

It was saying, *Use it.*

He chuckled, cradling the phone against his shoulder, and punched in the number. *So how come it feels like my last?*

After a few seconds, someone picked up on the other end.

"Meachem," the voice said. "Las Vegas Homicide."

"Detective Meachem, my name is Don Sherwood. I'm a detective with the coroner's office of San Luis Obispo County. In California."

"San Luis Obispo? I've got a sister up there. She works at the college. What can I do for you, detective?"

"I need a favor, if you can. You had a floater a while back. Name of Greenway, Thomas. He was found facedown in his pool. Ruled a suicide. It does go back a ways."

"Greenway?" Meachem seemed to be writing down the name. "How long?"

"Eighty-eight," Sherwood said.

"I didn't say how old. I meant how long ago."

"Nineteen eighty-eight," Sherwood said again, awaiting the response.

"You must be kidding," the Las Vegas detective said after a long pause.

"No, I'm not kidding," Sherwood said, turning away from his wife's gaze. "I know it's been a while, but I need to take a look at that file."

CHAPTER FORTY-ONE

Charlie's ranting earlier didn't help me with anything. I still had to find out whatever I could about how he and Zorn once fit together. When I got back to the motel, the front desk said there was a package waiting for me.

It was Greenway's book on Houvnanian. I had ordered it two nights ago online. It was fittingly titled *End of Days*.

I took it out back to the bench along the promenade. It was a clear, bright day; the surf was high. Waves crashed onto the rocks below. Pelicans danced out of the spray, searching the surf for a meal.

I opened the book. The first chapter began with a retelling of that horrible night, September 7, 1973. *"The first sign that absolute hell had arrived at Paul Riorden's doorstep was the site of three rattily clad visitors at his door . . ."*

I dove into the next few pages— Houvnanian and his cohorts barging in, taking out knives and guns, tying up the four people at the dinner party, along with a servant in the kitchen; the victims' outrage and anger shifting to premonitions of doom and fear as, one by one, they watched, whimpering, begging, as their friends were barbarously murdered, fighting against their own impending end.

I got the chills.

I flipped to the index and, on a lark, searched for my brother's name. It didn't surprise me nothing was there. He hadn't been there then. I flipped to Walter Zorn, and fittingly, his name appeared on several pages. One by one I turned back to them.

"Walter Zorn had been a decorated Santa Barbara patrolman who, at the age of thirty-one, earned his coveted detective's shield." He started out in Robbery. Violent crime in tony Santa Barbara was

rare, homicide rarer still. It mentioned how Zorn had been hit by a car while chasing after a burglary suspect as a young cop, sustaining a broken femur that never properly healed, causing him to walk with a slight limp for the rest of his life.

I wondered if Charlie had ever read this.

There were dozens of photos. Long-haired hippie types, in the dress of the times, taken on the ranch. Gardening, climbing rocks, playing music, together. Head shots of the nine victims. The grounds where the crimes were committed. Lots of photos of Houvnanian and all the perpetrators. The grisly crime scenes. I found one of Walter Zorn and Joe Cooley, his lieutenant, outside the Santa Barbara courthouse. A younger version of Zorn, his facial mark clearly visible.

I also found a photo of a large group at the ranch in happier times. Singing. A couple of them were playing guitars. It was taken in April 1973. Five months before. On a whim, I studied the faces closely, looking for Charlie. It was sort of a relief when I didn't see him there.

I began to flip around. Zorn had been recently promoted to detective and he happened to be on duty the morning following the murders when a gardener arrived at Riorden's home and discovered the grisly scene. It took most of the next two days to even process what they had found—it was so chilling and bloody even for veteran investigators. Later, they were called to the Forniciari home in neighboring Montecito when their daughter went to visit and came upon the scene.

Although his lieutenant, Cooley, was in charge, Zorn seemed to play a pivotal role in the investigation. It was he who—upon talking to Riorden's sister, Marci, about who might possibly have a motive to do this to them, and then later to his ex-wife, Sandy—first put together the possibility that people who lived on Sandy's property up near Big Sur might have been involved.

Fingerprints and articles of clothing had been left behind—prints in blood smeared into words on the victims' chests: "Judas," "betrayer," "whore"—but in the beginning they all led nowhere because they belonged to people who were not in the national criminal data bank. There was also a bandana, a black poncho, and a set of gardening gloves left at the Forniciari estate, which were ultimately matched to the perpetrators and ended up as key pieces of evidence in the case.

Suspicion quickly pointed to the Houvnanian "family," who'd had a series of disagreements with Paul Riorden and had been rebuffed by Forniciari.

But determining who had actually committed the ritual-style killings took some sorting out.

Houvnanian was first taken in on minor illegal occupancy charges, because he and his group had repeatedly ignored legal notices to vacate the property. Several of his followers were also detained on drug possession charges. Ultimately, fingerprints began to match up; several witnesses had spotted the ranch's white van not far from the Forniciari estate. The horrific picture began to be put together.

The trials were a slam dunk. The evidence was overwhelming. The state had fingerprints, clothing, in many cases the defendant's own words and bizarre confessions. None of the juries' deliberations lasted longer than four hours. The people wanted justice quickly—and they got it. Houvnanian was sentenced to nine consecutive life sentences. As were Carla Jean Blue, Sarah Strasser, Nolan Pierce, and Telford Richards.

Susan Pollack, and two others who abetted the murderers, received sentences of thirty-five years.

I put the book down.

"Hey, brother . . ."

I looked into the sunlight and saw the panhandler I had given the five to the other day. He was wearing the same torn flannel shirt and filthy work pants, and a Seattle Seahawks cap. He looked like he might have spent the night in a field somewhere. Still, he was smiling.

I said, "You already hit me up once, guy. That's all you get."

"Nah." He grinned. "I don't need anything from you, boss. Just going by and wondering how your stay was going. You know you're sitting right dab in the middle of my office, bro."

"Sorry, I didn't realize that." I smiled back, feigning an apology.

He waved. "Ah, make yourself at home.

You just let me know if I can do anything for you. I'll take good care. Chili dog? There's a stand over there where they treat me pretty good. Maybe some water . . . ?"

"No." I shrugged politely. "I'm good."

"Well, you just let me know, okay? I like to take care of my friends . . ."

"You bet," I said to him.

The guy waved, with a gap-toothed grin, and started back along the path. I opened the book again. But instead of delving in, I met his gaze. It had been almost a week now since I had talked to anyone beyond the reach of Evan's death, and a couple of words with anyone felt therapeutic. Even with this guy.

"How's business?" I asked him.

"Business?" He chuckled with amusement. "Look around, dude. This town is bone-dry. You watch the news. People out of work, the state's going belly-up. It's the trickle-down effect—even to a bottom-fisher like me, just trying to find a buck." He screwed up his eyes, trying to focus on my book. "What ya reading?"

I shrugged. "Just something I picked up." I flashed him the cover.

"End of Days, huh?" He laughed. "Now there's a book I can surely relate to. My life's resembled the End of Days for years!"

This time, I chuckled. His weathered face did look like it had witnessed its share of reversals in its time. "Bet it has."

"Well, can't stay and chat all day . . ." He winked. "There's fortunes to be made, right, man . . ."

"Take it slow." I waved.

"Always, brother. Any other way?" He started down the path again, when suddenly an idea popped into my mind.

"Hey," I called to him, "what's your name?"

"Dev." The dude grinned. "But most people call me Memphis. From Tennessee."

"Can I trust you, Dev?" I asked.

"Trust me?" The vagrant's haggard face lit up like a lamp. "Like a bank, dude. These days, probably better."

"So how'd you like to earn a fifty from me?"

"Fifty bucks?" The guy came back over and said under his breath, "Do I have to kill anyone? Can't let down my partners with any time in jail."

The idea seemed a little crazy—*I mean, look at the guy,* I thought—but if Sherwood wouldn't give me a car to watch over Charlie's, why the hell couldn't I find a set of eyes on my own?

"No, you don't have to kill anyone. All perfectly legit. Promise."

I told him I was worried about someone who was badgering my brother and how the police wouldn't help me out. I described Susan Pollack's blue Kia and gave him my brother's address. I told him I just wanted him to watch out for it.

"I guess I could do that." He shrugged. He looked at me in a strange way, then nodded. "Fifty bucks, huh?"

"Here's thirty now," I said, "the rest when you report back." I reached into my pocket and dug out a few bills, handed them to him, probably more than he saw in a good week. I shrugged. "It's not a fortune, but maybe it'll get you out of town."

"Oh, I find my way out of town from time to time," he said with kind of a smile. "Was out of town just last week."

"Oh yeah?" I said, a little surprised. "Where was that?"

The guy stuffed the bills in his pocket and said, eyeing me, "Michigan."

CHAPTER FORTY-TWO

Sherwood was making his way through an enchilada outside his favorite taqueria the next day when his cell phone rang. It was Carl Meachem, from the Las Vegas PD. "I located those records," the detective said. "That suicide you were looking for. Greenway."

Sherwood put his lunch down in its wrapper on the hood of his Torino and took out a pad. "You're my hero. Shoot."

"I'm not exactly sure what you're looking for . . . ," the Vegas detective said. "By the way, you knew he wrote a book on the

Houvnanian murders back in the seventies, didn't you?"

Sherwood purposely hadn't shared what his interest was but answered, "I knew that, yeah."

"Just making sure . . . Seems Greenway moved down here, North Las Vegas actually, in 1986. After his big book was published. I guess it did okay. They made it into a movie and he retired. We all should find a case like that, right? You remember, it had that guy who won an Oscar in it—"

"I was actually more interested in what happened the night of his death," Sherwood said, cutting him off.

"Okay, yeah, right . . ." Sherwood heard the sound of pages being turned. "Let's see, night of November 6, 1988 . . . Seems Greenway's wife was at a dinner for some women's golf committee at their club. Says here she came home and found her husband facedown in the pool. Called 911. That was nine thirty-eight P.M. The EMTs arrive, looks like, around twelve minutes later . . . Nine fifty," the detective said. "Not bad. Unable to revive him. They estimate the TOD as a couple of hours before. No sign of any foul play. The doors were all locked and the neighbors didn't see or hear anything going on. Didn't leave a note—but officers found a half-drained bottle of Absolut on the kitchen counter along with a bunch of assorted pills . . . Says here the victim had been depressed lately. His wife admitted they'd been having problems. Apparently, there'd been some financial setbacks as well . . ."

"Sounds pretty clear," Sherwood said, acknowledging it with a twinge of disappointment.

"What the autopsy seemed to confirm . . . Victim died from deprivation of oxygen to the lungs. Four point one percent blood alcohol. Along with elevated levels of barbiturates and various muscle relaxers. Though, *hmphff . . .*" Meachem grunted.

"What?" Sherwood asked.

"It seems they still kept the case open for a while, nonetheless. As suspicious. Until they checked out a couple of other angles . . ."

"What kinds of angles?" Sherwood asked. He felt a tremor of hopefulness pick up.

Meachem flipped the page. "One was that Greenway's wife apparently didn't seem to think vodka was her husband's drink of choice. She said he was always a scotch guy. 'Johnnie Walker, all the way . . .'"

"And the other?" Sherwood pressed.

"The other, it says here"—Meachem turned the page—"was something the ME discovered. In the victim's stomach. Must have been fairly recent to the time of death because it hadn't degraded . . ."

"What did he eat?"

"Not eat," the Vegas detective said, clarifying, "*swallowed*. It was half of a dollar bill. There's even a photo here . . ."

"A dollar bill?" Sherwood dug into his wallet and pulled out one. "Which half . . . ?"

But before the Vegas detective even replied, he knew.

"Which half?" Meachem replied curiously. "Let me see, the half with the pyramid on it; why? Anyway, it seems it never led anywhere. A couple of days later they called it death by suicide and let the matter drop."

Sherwood couldn't stop from grinning. He looked at his dollar. He almost felt light-headed. *"Sonovafuckingbitch!"*

The pyramid didn't mean something, in itself. Except for what was directly above it. Something he'd seen a thousand times and never thought about twice. But now it meant everything.

An open eye.

CHAPTER FORTY-THREE

Got a moment, Phil?" Sherwood knocked on the door of his lieutenant's office.

Phil Perokis pushed back from his neatly ordered desk and waved Sherwood in. "Sure. Come on in."

Sherwood shut the door behind him. He'd run it all around, from every possible angle. Slept on it. Nursed it over a Maker's Mark. A couple of Maker's Marks. He hadn't had more than a goddamn beer since the operation, but last night he just said, *What the hell!* The damn thing was eating away at him now. There was a lot that still didn't add up.

But he'd woken up this morning with the conclusion that enough of it did.

It damn well did.

"You remember that jumper I was working on? The Erlich kid. He did a back dive off the rock."

"I know, the gift that keeps on giving . . ." The lieutenant chuckled. Sherwood had told Perokis how the victim's uncle kept on pushing him to look at the case again, and everyone knew how a couple of days back, the KSLO reporter was buzzing around, trying to make some hay. "His uncle still in town?"

"He is." Sherwood sat down in front of his boss, the file on his lap. "In fact, Phil, that's kind of the thing . . ."

In a measured voice, he took his boss through the sequence of developments. Starting with Zorn—how the connection seemed to exist between him and Evan. The two, seemingly unrelated open eyes.

Then how the doc had brought his attention to this Susan Pollack character, how she might fit in. How he first felt someone watching him outside his brother's apartment. Then how it came out Zorn had a past connection to her.

"Susan Pollack?" Perokis furrowed his brow.

"She was just released from prison." Sherwood nodded. "After serving thirty-five years as an accomplice in the Houv-nanian murders—"

"Houvnanian?"

His boss's once-agreeable eyes had now grown wider and a little less patient. Perokis liked things tidy, by the book. Work processed, passed on to the right agencies. *"Go on."*

Clearing his throat, Sherwood told him how that souvenir peddler in Morro Bay had seen Evan Erlich as he was headed to the rock. Along with someone else. *"A woman."* Sherwood looked at his lieutenant.

"Susan Pollack?" Perokis wasn't smiling anymore. His look expressed his disappointment at where Sherwood seemed to be heading.

"Phil, I know what you're thinking. I was thinking the same thing too. But two nights ago, someone called Erlich at his motel, threatening him to back off."

"Back off *what*?"

"What he's been sticking his nose into. The caller mentioned something about him getting burned if he didn't. When Erlich went to the door he found a lit cigarette sitting on the mat outside."

"Could be anyone." The lieutenant chuckled. "You admit he hasn't made a whole lot of friends since coming to town."

"The next day his sister-in-law found the family cat that had been missing—*toasted.* I'm not talking about harassment, Phil. Two people are dead. Then *this* . . ."

He opened the file that was on his lap— the one on Thomas Greenway that had come in that very morning. The FBI investigator who had written a book on the Houvnanian case, he explained, whose pool drowning in Las Vegas may not have been a suicide after all.

"The doc was pushing me to look into it. He was sure it was connected somehow. What's interesting is what came up—in the autopsy." He took out the photo. "The victim swallowed something. Or, more likely, something was stuffed down his mouth."

"What?"

From his own pocket, Sherwood took out a dollar bill, folded it in half, and placed it in front of his boss. He pointed to the eye above the pyramid.

"This." Then he pushed forward the Vegas ME's snapshot from the police file—a reluctant understanding slowly forming in his lieutenant's widening eyes.

"You're trying to say this is some kind of series of murders? Zorn. The kid from Grover Beach. This guy, Greenway. Going back *what*?" He squinted. *"More than twenty years?"*

"Maybe longer," Sherwood said. He massaged his jaw joint with his thumb. "Trust me, Phil, a couple of days back I was sitting there rolling my eyes the same as you."

"And now?"

"Now I guess they're no longer rolling."

Perokis picked up the file. He stared almost dumbly at the Vegas ME's photo of the dollar bill, then paged quickly through the rest. "You have a motive?"

"I don't know the motive. Just that something's going on. And whatever it is, it somehow connects to this Erlich kid's father—who isn't exactly textbook when it comes to lucidity and isn't doing a whole lot of talking to be sure. And who insists he wasn't even there with Susan Pollack or Houvnanian at the time of the murders."

Perokis folded his fingers in front of his

face. Sherwood knew he didn't like this. He was lucky Phil had made a place for him after the transplant. Otherwise he wouldn't even have had this job. Otherwise, he'd have been on disability. Watching soaps during the day.

"So what do you want to do?" the lieutenant asked. "You want to find out if everyone *else* is crazy in this mess—or just you?"

Sherwood gave him a halfhearted smile. "Maybe that pastor's liver is getting to me more than I know.

"Let me see it through, Phil. I know what my job is here. I know I've got, what, maybe a year left before the hatchet falls my way. Call it a good-bye gift. I've earned that, haven't I? I need this."

The lieutenant's phone rang. He picked up and asked Carol out front to take a message. Sherwood knew no one in homicide would touch this thing any more than they would a pile of dog turd on the street.

This was his dog turd.

"You got three days," Perokis said. "And don't even think of putting in for mileage on this. And if it doesn't pan out by then, I don't want to hear of it ever again. *Understood?*"

"Completely." Sherwood closed the file and got up.

"So what's the next step?"

"The next step?" Sherwood headed to the door. "The next step is I want to see Houvnanian."

"Houvnanian? You must be joking, Don. You'll need a judge's order to get in to see him. If he'll even see you. And where the hell is he these days anyway?"

"Pelican Bay."

"Pelican Bay?" The lieutenant rolled his eyes. The California super-max. About as hard to get into, even for a law enforcement officer, as it was to leave.

"I think he'll see me . . . ," Sherwood said. "A wolf likes to eye his prey before he kills it. That's why I'm bringing the doc."

CHAPTER FORTY-FOUR

I spent the rest of the afternoon reading through Greenway's book, searching for any kind of connection between my brother, who wasn't anywhere in the narrative, and Zorn.

I called in to my office. Even consulted on one of my cases. Finally I went back to my room and dozed a little in the afternoon.

I had a dream—my unconscious restlessly connecting images and dots.

I saw Paul Riorden's estate in Santa Barbara. The ugly, awful crime scenes, blood on the walls. And *I* was at the dinner table—not Riorden—and my wife, Kathy, next to me. I had a fear that something truly terrible was about to take place. I kept saying to Kathy that we had to get out. Before it happened. Then there was a knock at the door. I went to open it and Russell Houvnanian stood in front of me at the door—the same chiseled face and probing eyes I had seen those years ago.

Except my brother Charlie was at his side.

And suddenly I heard my father, laughing—that same mocking tone with which he had humiliated Charlie with Phil. And I tried to warn him. *"Dad,"* I said, *"please, stop!"*

I screamed out loud: *"Stop!"*

But this time Houvnanian took out a blade.

And plunged it into my father's gut. The laughing stopped. Lenny's eyes bulged. He looked down. Blood ran into his hands.

And then Charlie was stabbing him too.

"Stop, stop!" I cried. Over and over. *"Stop!"*

My father looked at me. Helpless. Like, *Do something, Jay . . .*

"Stop!"

I woke up, and I was sweating. Blinking and disoriented.

My cell phone was ringing.

I found it on the night table and looked. Sherwood was on the line. My heart beat like a metronome on speed. It took a second for me to regain my composure. To realize in relief that it had all been just a dream.

I put the phone to my ear and answered. "Yeah, Sherwood, it's me."

He didn't even say hello. "You got a dollar on you, doc?"

"*A dollar?* You woke me up to ask me that?" I rolled over and dug into my khakis. "Is this a joke? Yeah, I have one here. Why? Things hurting that bad?"

"Flip it over," the detective said without responding. "To the back."

"Flip it over . . . ?" I said, still a little fuzzy. I stared at the familiar words, *In God We Trust.* The bold, large "ONE," spelled out. "Okay."

"Now fold it in half. What do you see?"

"*What do I see?* An eagle. The seal of the United States. What am I supposed to see?"

"No," he said, serious now. "The *other* half."

Testily I blew out a breath and did what

he asked me. "I'm really not into games like this. A pyramid," I said. "A bunch of Latin . . ."

Then I saw it. What I was staring at. The metronome came to a stop. My whole body did.

"I see an eye!"

"That's what the Vegas ME pulled out of Thomas Greenway's stomach during his autopsy in 1988. A crumpled dollar bill. Or half a dollar. Like the one you're looking at now."

"Oh my God . . ."

"You were right, doc. All along. So what do you do when everything seems to point in one direction and you want to know how it all connects?"

"I don't know. You're playing games with me again, Sherwood. Go to the source?"

"Yeah, doc, let's go to the source. Where it all connects. You're not heading home on me again, are you?"

"No." I sat up, my blood surging. "Of course not."

"Good. You wanted your case re-opened . . . I don't know how the hell it happened or where in God's name it's going to lead, but consider it reopened. I'm in now, doc. I'm all in!"

I felt alive with validation.

"And the source is *where*?" I asked, the hair rising on my arms. But I already thought I knew.

"The source? And I figured you for a smart guy, doc. The source is Russell Houvnanian. I thought maybe after all these years you'd like to renew your acquaintance with him."

PART III

CHAPTER FORTY-FIVE

The loud *thwhack-thwhack-thwhack* of the helicopter drummed in my ears as the aircraft descended over the dense redwood forest near the California-Oregon border.

Sherwood pointed out the window.

Cut into the sea of green was a patch of cleared land, with a group of interconnected white buildings, almost like an X carved out of the remote forest.

Pelican Bay.

My heart tightened from the anticipation of soon being face-to-face with the psychotic killer who had been a part of my youth.

Pelican Bay was California's most remote and secure prison, housing only Level Four offenders, the worst of the worst. To be sent there you had to either be convicted of a particularly violent crime or have earned your way through habitually violent behavior at the state's other penal facilities.

The centerpiece of Pelican Bay was the pod of four intersecting two-story halls known as the SHU, the Security Housing Unit, the giant X that I spotted from the sky. Russell Houvnanian was the SHU's most celebrated resident. It had essentially been built for him. He had been transferred there, to the isolation of the remote forest, in 1989, after spending his first fourteen years incarcerated at San Quentin.

The copter came down on a landing pad on the prison grounds. The propeller whirred loudly and came to a stop. The landing steps dropped down and we stepped out, squinting into the bright sun.

"Detective Sherwood," someone yelled. A guard in a khaki uniform came up as we stepped onto the tarmac. "Sergeant Ray Tobin. I'm supposed to escort you over to the admin center. To Assistant Warden Hutchins."

"Thanks."

We stepped into a large golf cart–like vehicle, the guard hopping in at the wheel, and it was only a short drive over to the white, two-story administration building. We went in through the main entrance, where we were directed through a law-enforcement security checkpoint and put through a metal detector.

Sherwood checked his weapon with a clerk there.

"The AW is up here," Sergeant Tobin said, leading us up a flight of stairs, past a grid of offices and the secretarial desks.

A nameplate that read ROBERT HUTCHINS, ASSISTANT WARDEN was affixed to the door.

His secretary asked us if we wanted anything; we both asked for some water. Then she took us in.

Bob Hutchins was a trim, pleasant-looking man with a long forehead and hair closely cropped around the sides. He stood up at his desk to greet us. He had a military bearing. In fact, the pictures on the wall of him with a bunch of brass confirmed that he had once been a sergeant major in the military police. He held out his hand. "Gentlemen . . .

"Good to see you again, Don," he said to Sherwood. Years back, Sherwood had been the arresting detective of a couple of high-profile inmates who had ended up there, and the two had collaborated on the convicts' parole hearings.

He introduced me.

"So you're up here for a tête-à-tête with Russ," Hutchins said. "He's like royalty up here. Our longest-running inmate. And one who's not likely to leave."

Hutchins patted what appeared to be a prisoner file. "We've got him sequestered in a holding cell for you over in SHU A. Try to keep in mind, he may not resemble exactly what you might expect. Not many requests to see him these days, and he rarely accedes to the few that come. You ought to consider yourself lucky."

Sherwood glanced my way. "I have a feeling the good doctor here should take the bow on that one. Apparently they've met."

"I was just a kid," I said. "He and my brother came up to my father's house looking to raise money to cut a record. Apparently, my brother had been living on the Riorden Ranch. This was around 1972. A year before it all happened . . ."

The warden nodded, shaking his head, then glanced back at Sherwood. "You say this is related to a string of new killings? That they may have some connection to the original case?"

"A possibility . . . ," Sherwood said. "Almost two weeks ago, Dr. Erlich's nephew was found dead at the bottom of the Morro Bay Rock, in what we first deemed to be a suicide, but are now looking into further. Last week, a retired police detective from Santa Barbara was murdered as well, who had played a role in the Houvnanian investigation."

Hutchins pursed his lips judiciously. "Anything else linking them?"

"Both bodies were found with similar items on them at the time of death," Sherwood said. "And we also found out they had recently been in touch."

"I guess it could always be some kind of copycat crime." The warden opened the file. "Houvnanian doesn't have a lot of contact with the outside world these days. Any calls, and incoming or outgoing mail, are closely monitored. Have been since he first came here. And, like I said, he may not resemble what you may recall. He's basically lived in a five-by-eight cell for the past thirty-seven years. He gets thirty minutes of exercise a day, which for him is just supervised pacing back and forth in the hall outside his cell. He's rarely even seen the sun in years. His reasoning abilities, such as they ever were"—the warden smiled—"have deteriorated over the years. We have a name for it up here—'cabin fever.'

"Mostly he just reads—the Bible, Greek philosophy, a bunch of stuff on physics, I'm told. Listens to music. He really doesn't even belong here anymore, it's just that . . ." Hutchins smiled. "Well, he's *Russell Houvnanian.* No one's about to transfer him out. He'll be fully restrained when you meet with him—standard procedure. And if you would, please refrain from handing him anything without first passing it by the guards. Ready?"

Sherwood and I both nodded.

The secretary came in with our waters.

"I wish I had something stronger to offer you, gentlemen." Hutchins stood up. "Take a breath. You're about to enter Ground Zero for the human race."

CHAPTER FORTY-SIX

We walked down two flights of stairs through a secure glass door leading to a long underground tunnel.

It was perhaps a two-hundred-yard walk to the prominent white X I had noticed from the air. The corridor forked at the end. Hutchins directed us to the left, through a door that read A BLOCK. THE SHU.

We climbed a flight of stairs and were buzzed in through another security door. This time it was manned by two khaki-clad guards, billy clubs attached to their belts along with firearms. My heart accelerated with the knowledge we had entered a very dangerous place.

"Every one of these inmates has a history of being a violent offender." Assistant Warden Hutchins took us down the hall. "And in most cases, they're already incarcerated for life, so there's nothing for them to lose except privileges for being rowdy. I've had Houvnanian brought to a holding room on the block. Rudy . . ." Hutchins waved hello to an officer. "As I said, he'll be fully restrained and there'll be two guards with you at all times. You can ask him anything you want, but again, there can be no physical contact or exchange of materials."

Sherwood nodded.

We turned down a sterile white hallway. It looked more like some futuristic genomic lab than a prison. The warden stopped at a secure door with a small glass window. Interview Room 1. A guard was stationed outside. "Warden." We stood there for a second, waiting.

"In any case, gentlemen," Hutchins said, opening the door for us, "I hope you find what it is you're here to learn."

*   *   *

Sherwood and I stepped in.

It was a tight, narrow room, no more than eight feet by eight. There was a cool, fluorescent light on the ceiling, nothing on the walls. Two guards stood off to the side, and neither nodded our way. I found myself transfixed by the slight man seated at a table in the center. A man whose iconic face rushed back to me, like a child's nightmare reappearing in his adult years.

At least, a shadow of that man.

Houvnanian was older, grayer, his cheekbones narrow and wan, his hair shaved close to his head, boot-camp style. Sunken, sad-looking eyes. His skin was sort of a parchment gray—he was more ghost than man—and he was dressed in a yellow jumpsuit. He looked up at us only briefly, his shoulders slightly hunched, palms flat on the tabletop, his wrists bound with manacles. In a million years, I would never have recognized him as the long-haired, wild-eyed beast I recalled from photos and from my youth.

Until he spoke.

His voice was calm and controlled, with a kind of friendly drawl, exactly how I remembered. He looked up, eyes bright but unthreatening, and his mouth inched into a knowing grin. "Not what you might have been expecting, huh, gentlemen?"

Sherwood motioned for me to sit. We lowered ourselves into the metal chairs, directly across the table. The convict's gaze shifted on us from side to side, almost as if he was trying to put us at ease.

Sherwood started in, "Thanks for seeing us, Mr. Houvnanian. My name is Don Sherwood and I'm a detective, senior grade, with the coroner's office down in San Luis Obispo County."

Houvnanian nodded back affably. "Detective . . ."

"This is Dr. Jay Erlich . . ."

Houvnanian fixed on me, bunching his thin lips, as if impressed. "Is the doctor with the coroner's office as well?" His voice was controlled, slightly hoarse. I didn't know what he remembered and what he didn't.

"No. Dr. Erlich is from New York. But he's the reason we've come to see you today. Nearly two weeks ago, his twenty-one-year-old nephew, Evan, was killed in Morro Bay. He either jumped or fell, but in any case was found dead at the base of the large rock in the bay there."

"Morro Bay? I've seen that rock somewhere," Houvnanian said, nodding. "I'm sorry to hear about that, doctor, but doesn't the Bible tell us, 'Go forth and stand upon the rock before the Lord, and behold a great and strong wind rent the mountains and broke them into a thousand pieces'?"

He grinned. "It may surprise you, but I spend a lot of my time reading my Bible," he said, shoulders hunched. "The trouble is, the verse goes on to say that the Lord wasn't even in that wind that rose up or in the earthquake that ripped the rock to shreds. Which begs the question—one I've been trying to answer for years now . . . Just where do you think the Lord is?" He shrugged, let out kind of a mischievous *hee-hee*. "Or you, doctor?" He looked up at me. "You're a smart man. Any ideas?"

I couldn't tell if he remembered me or even my name. I just looked him in the eye, my skin crawling.

"Well," the killer said, "I think that's part of what you came to find out. Am I wrong? Because that's what your nephew was probably looking for up there. I've found in my life that death is a strong motivator for self-enlightenment, though it's cost me some for the gain." He lifted his wrists for us and jangled his chains.

"Mr. Houvnanian, we'd like to show you a few pictures," Sherwood said, redirecting him back to the topic, "and ask you some questions, if that's okay."

"By all means, gentlemen." The convict nodded. "I've got nowhere to go."

Sherwood opened his file and glanced up at one of the guards, who inspected the contents, nodding okay. Sherwood removed a photo of Walter Zorn. "Do you recognize this man, Mr. Houvnanian?"

The convict's face edged into a thin smile. "Well, I may be the scourge of man and a lunatic, some say, but my memory's still fine. The man had the mark of the devil on his face even back then. But he was only doing his job. Root out those who would betray us. Break us apart. Jesus knew what to look for, didn't he, gentlemen? 'If you see a false prophet before you, it's only a reflection of your own sins . . .'"

"His name was Walter Zorn, correct?" Sherwood stared at him. "He was one of the detectives who prepared the case against you. And who aided in your conviction. Isn't that right?"

"If you say so, I guess he is." Houvnanian nodded uncontentiously. "And, please, call me Russ."

Sherwood took out a second photograph and laid it on the table. This was the police photographer's photo of Zorn's body: eyes bulging, face twisted in horror, strangled.

Houvnanian barely reacted. He only lifted his gaze ever so slightly to meet Sherwood's, just enough to show him a slight smile. "Well, I guess even Rome burned in the end, didn't it, so there's hope for us all. So how did the bastard die?"

"He was strangled. But the police found something very unusual on his body." Sherwood put out the next photo, from the autopsy, of the knife marks on Zorn's tongue. "I'm wondering if you can make out what that is, Mr. Houvnanian."

"What *what* is, detective?" the amused convict asked.

"Those marks. Underneath the victim's tongue. An odd place for a wound, wouldn't you agree, sir? Especially for someone who was strangled."

Houvnanian leaned forward and squinted at the photo. "Excuse me, gents, but my eyes just aren't what they were. Glaucoma. The medical plan's one of the real letdowns in here . . . But as to your question . . . they kind of look like knife marks to me, detective. *Right?* I have a familiarity with knife marks, you may remember," he said, looking up and grinning.

"They do." Sherwood kept his composure, but I was having a hard time keeping mine.

"And what would you think those knife marks resemble, Mr. Houvnanian, if you had to say?" Sherwood looked at him. "I mean, *Russ?*"

The convicted killer hunched over the photo again. He looked up and shrugged.

"To me, it sort of resembles a human eye," Sherwood said. "What do you think? One that's wide open."

I wasn't sure who was playing with whom here. Houvnanian continued to stare at the photo a while. Then suddenly he nodded, his eyes widening. "You know, I think you're right, detective. It does kind of look like an eye. If you see it in a certain way. And even the blindest man will see the truth"—he grinned—"when it's the *one* truth. The real truth! Do you know that saying, Dr. Erlich? You know, I once knew someone named Erlich back in the day. As a man of science, what's your view? To me, it's why we're all here. To see the truth. When it's exposed to us. When it's time."

I balled my hands and gritted my teeth, and said back, "Yes, I guess I believe that too."

"So then, Russ, what do you make of *this*?" Sherwood said.

He took out a plastic bag containing the plastic hologram found on Evan's body. "This was what we found on Dr. Erlich's nephew's body. At the bottom of the rock." Sherwood jiggled it in front of the killer.

One way showing the eye closed; the other way, wide open.

"I'd say, *the eyes have it*!" Houvnanian stared back at him, cackling with amusement at his own joke.

"I'd say it was all just some sort of weird coincidence myself"—Sherwood shrugged—"*if* I actually believed in coincidences. And if we hadn't come upon *this . . .*"

He brought out the Las Vegas medical

examiner's photo of the dollar bill that had been crumpled up inside Thomas Green- way's stomach at the time he was drowned. "No doubt you do remember Thomas Greenway, Mr. Houvnanian? *Russ?* He had something to do with you being here as well, no?"

Houvnanian lifted his hands, chains jan- gling. "The wind and the rain, detective, that's what I keep asking. If it can cleave a mountain into pieces, it can surely rend the heart of an evil man. Except, God *wasn't* in the wind, I'm reminded. *Was he, doctor?* I'm still trying to figure out where."

I was sure he knew who I was.

I could feel it, the sweat beading up on my back from his mesmerizing stare. I could see he was enjoying my discomfort.

I stared at him, my blood starting to sim- mer inside. "I think the eyes refer to what you told the judge at your sentencing. How it was like the owner of the home who is called away. How no one will know when it's time for him to come back. Or in what manner. How only the father knows, *right,* Mr. Houvnanian? *You.* How you told them all to *watch.* The people who had done you harm." I kept my eyes drilling into him.

"That's what Evan's death was about, wasn't it? A way for you to say, *watch*!"

"I said a lot of crazy things back then . . ." Houvnanian stretched his face into a smile. He raised his manacled hands. "Yet here I remain."

"Yes, here you remain," Sherwood said. "But not Susan Pollack. You remember *her*, don't you, Russ? She was one of three followers who served a thirty-five-year sentence for aiding you in the murders of Paul and Cici Riorden, their friends, and George and Sally Forniciari, right?"

"I never admitted to any murders, detective." The orange-clad convict shrugged with a coy smile. "Only opening the gates for judgment against those who didn't see as clearly."

"You're aware that Ms. Pollack was released from prison recently? This past May."

"I don't pay much attention to your system of time, detective. Doesn't much matter in here." He shrugged. "Anyway, she renounced me. I'm sure you know that. Like I was some blotch of ink she could just wash off. She did what she had to do."

"You mind telling us the last time the two of you were in touch?"

"Well"—Houvnanian scratched his head pensively—"that all depends on what you might mean by being 'in touch,' detective. I can see her any time I want. You know only my body is in prison. *The rest . . ."* His eyes grew dazzling. "I can walk among your streets at my will. I can take your young any time I want . . ." Finally he winked, backing down. "I guess it's been a while."

"And how long is a while," Sherwood asked, "if you don't mind me asking?"

"Years. Who even remembers? I can't even remember the last time I saw the sun, detective, never mind heard from that bitch. She wrote me a few years back. She told me she had moved away from what she had done. They stuffed her full of Xanax and mood stabilizers and they took the life right out of her. She did what she had to do. In my world here, the sun is the moon and the moon the sun. Everything meets, just not necessarily in the way you think.

"So what are you saying?" Houvnanian lit up, bright-eyed. "Ol' Russ's time has come again. *Watch!* I've barely stepped outside in the past thirty-seven years. Would probably blind me if I did. And

you're saying, *what*? I'm plotting my revenge? It's end of days time all over again!
Look, my hair's all gone. See any horns
coming through? So here's a news flash,
gentlemen. Nothing's changed. The devil,
he's never left. It's still the same ol' world I
used to be in. So if God wants to accuse
me, or any of us, for what we did back
then—bring it on! Or if he wants to forgive
us—that's fine with me too, gentlemen."

I leaned forward, unable to control myself any longer. "You knew my brother."

He didn't flinch. He just looked at me, a
sparkle in his dark eyes.

I said, "He sang and played the guitar.
You once tried to raise money for a record
he was trying to make. Do you remember
him, Mr. Houvnanian? His name was Charlie Erlich."

"Charlie, Charlie, Charlie . . . ," the killer
replied, singsong. "Sorry, all the Charlies
seem to merge into one . . . I'm sorry, doc.
I really am."

"He lived on the ranch with you. Maybe
not when everything was happening. But I
know you know him. You want to know
why I'm here, Mr. Houvnanian? I'm here
because I know that what happened to my

nephew was aimed directly at my brother. His son was a troubled, innocent kid who never really did much wrong in life, except, maybe, being his father's son. I know he went up to the spot where he jumped with someone else—*a woman,* whom I'm pretty sure was Susan Pollack. *Why? What did my brother do to you?*"

"The wind and the rain, the wind and the rain . . . ," Houvnanian started repeating again.

My chest tightened.

"I keep telling you, the wind split the rock, but you've still not answered *my* question, doc. If God wasn't in the wind, then where was he? Do you think"—his eyes bore into me—"maybe *here*?"

I threw the photos aside and hurled myself across the table, his mocking smirk digging into me like a jagged knife. The guards went to restrain me. Sherwood latched on to my arm. He pulled me back in the chair. I put up my palms, as if to say, *Okay, I know, I know . . .* My pulse raced like an engine revved above the red zone.

I said, "*I know it's you!*" my gaze direct and accusing. "I know you killed Evan."

My heart rate accelerated again. I felt

angry and out of control. And useless. He wasn't giving us anything. He was enjoying it.

I sat back down.

Houvnanian's surprised expression inched into a wiry grin, clearly having a ball. He winked, as if to say, *Gotcha!* then turned and nodded back to one of the guards, putting up his wrists, indicating that we were done now.

"I wish I could help you, doctor, I really do. But it's been mighty fine visiting with you and hearing about old times."

One of the guards stepped over and helped Houvnanian out of the chair. Sherwood and I stood. My heart was still racing and my blood was still hot. I knew when I walked out of this room I would still have nothing. It would be over. The bastard was simply toying with us, still pulling all the strings. I balled my fists and looked at Sherwood, who looked back at me, almost apologetically, sweeping up the photos into the file.

"So how'd that music career go anyway?" Houvnanian asked suddenly when he got to the door.

His gaze was trained directly at me, his

eyes wolflike now, shiny like black lacquer. Now they had that same dark glow of malice I had seen in the photos a hundred times.

"Your brother?" He winked. "He ever hit the charts?"

He knew.

I knew he knew.

He gave me a last look and a final, mocking smile. Then the guards removed him through another door, his chains jangling like scornful laughter, following me out.

CHAPTER FORTY-SEVEN

Warden Hutchins walked us back to his office.

I was so wired and frustrated at having to listen to that lunatic's ramblings it was almost ripping me apart. I was certain he knew who Charlie was. And even more certain he was connected to Evan's death.

I also knew I might've lost my final chance to prove it.

"I'm sorry that you had to come all the way up here," the warden said. "I'll notify the copter you're ready to leave. Like I said, the man's not a complete package anymore."

"Bob, you said before you monitor his outside contacts?" Sherwood asked.

Hutchins nodded. "Part of life in the SHUs . . . All calls in and out must be cleared and everyone's mail is sorted through and documented as to content and source."

"Going back how far?"

"How far do you need? Houvnanian still gets his share of activity. There's a million wackos, racists, and copycat killers out there who still regard him as some kind of god. That's why we keep a close eye on him."

I suddenly saw where Sherwood was heading. Maybe sort of a last-ditch fling, on fourth and a hundred. But we were in Hail Mary time now. He pulled up a seat across from Hutchins's desk. "Could you tell me if he's received any mail from the California Institution for Women in Frontera?"

Hutchins squinted.

Frontera was where Susan Pollack had been for the past thirty-five years.

"Guess I could." The warden shrugged. "But I would also need a court order to share it with you. We keep it for security reasons only. The information is strictly confidential."

"Bob, please, we're talking about the possibility of multiple homicides here. Homicides potentially masterminded from your own prison."

"Look, I can pretty well assure you nothing suspicious has taken place," the warden said, leaning back, "or we would have picked it up. We've got gang leaders and organized crime bosses who try to continue to run their operations while in here . . ."

"Bob," Sherwood pleaded, "do this one favor for me. Just take a look. You don't have to share what's in it—or even reply. Just let me know if there's been any correspondence from there. Even just a nod. I'll take it from there."

At first the warden looked back at Sherwood with disapproval; he was clearly a person who played things by the book. Then he gradually seemed to soften to an idea he really didn't like. He sat for a moment, rubbing his finger against his cheek. I was sure he was just looking for some way to frame his refusal.

Sherwood pressed. "Just a look, Bob, please . . ."

Finally Hutchins blew out a blast of air, then picked up the intercom and waited until his secretary came on. He glanced down at a piece of paper. "Nancy, can you bring me Inmate B-30967's Outside Communication file?"

My heart rose.

It took a minute or two for his secretary to bring it in. It was a thick accordion-style folder bound by a string. Houvnanian's name and inmate number were plainly written on it in marker. Hutchins dropped the bulky folder on his desk. "I told you, it's substantial . . . And this is only the past year." He started to look through the photocopies of letters and monitoring forms, starting with the most recent. There appeared to be a master sheet of some kind. "What did you say, the women's facility at Frontera . . . ?"

"Or maybe Mule Creek in Ione," Sherwood said. That's where two of Houvnanian's other followers were presently incarcerated. "You don't have to even say it out loud. Just give me a look and I'll know."

Hutchins put on wire-rim reading glasses and scanned down the sheet. He flipped the page—twice—his expression registering nothing. Finally he looked back up. Not even a twitch. A blank stare. "Anything else?"

"Maybe something from Susan Pollack herself?" Sherwood said. "It would have been in the past couple of months. She was released in May."

Hutchins edged into a dubious smile. "You know how many rules I'm breaking here?" He glanced back down at the sheets. Turned a page. When he finally looked up, his expression hadn't shifted.

Strike two.

"What about a phone call?" Sherwood said. "You keep records of those as well . . ."

Hutchins suddenly grew testy. "This isn't a customer service operation, Don. You can't just dial up an inmate here. There has to be prior approval and documentation." He tossed the master sheets on his desk. "I'm sorry . . ."

Sherwood looked at me, emitting a sigh. Deflated.

I looked at the warden. "Do you mind if I have a try?"

A thought had hit me; I recalled something Susan Pollack had mentioned while we were speaking to her. It was a long shot, but once we stepped back on that copter, I knew any chance of implicating Houvnanian was pretty much dead.

He frowned at me, his patience clearly thinning. I wasn't even a law enforcement officer, just someone who had lost a family member.

But maybe he saw the desperation on my face, that this was our last resort, because he picked up the sheets again. "*What?*"

I asked, "Is there anything in the file from someone named Maggie?"

That was the name Susan Pollack was known by on the Riorden Ranch. *Maggie Mae.*

"*Maggie.*" The warden sighed, clearing his throat, his expression slightly irritated.

"Yes. Or maybe even just the initial 'M.'" I nodded.

Sherwood smiled at me.

"*M . . . ?*" Hutchins repeated. He reclined back in his chair. He took the sheets in his lap and reluctantly scanned. He turned the first page—*nothing*. He pursed his lips. I was already prepared for the disappointment. He flipped the second.

That's when I saw the warden's expression change.

At first it just seemed to bore in, intensifying through the sheet like a laser. Then he looked back up at me, as if startled. His jaw parted a bit, but there was only the slightest nod, and the word that accompanied it was like the true sound of vindication for me.

"Mags."

CHAPTER FORTY-EIGHT

That's how it was done," I said to Sherwood in the copter. "That letter was a message. About Zorn. Evan. How they got back at people. It was how she let him know it was all going to begin."

On the surface, the letter Hutchins had found seemed to be perfectly benign. "These kooks are always trying to contact him," he explained. As a celebrity killer, Houvnanian always attracted his share of loonies and admirers. On his view of life. On how he had been misjudged. Or on music.

Hutchins wouldn't let us as much as

touch the letter. Or even take a copy. That would require a judge's decree. But he laid it on the table for us to have a look.

It was written in a straightforward block print on lined notebook paper:

"I watched you on TV," it began, possibly referring to a *Dateline* interview a year ago. "I know you like Guns n' Roses. Axl Rose was a kind of apostle for me too. I know the song you mentioned—'Estranged.' There's a line from that song that I sing to myself when I think I'm going out of my head: *I knew the storm was getting closer . . .*

"The storm is here!" the letter finished. *"It never has to die!"*

"The storm has never died," it ended.

It was signed, "Yours always, Mags."

The postmark on the envelope was from Richmond, California, just across the bay from San Francisco. Only an hour and a half from Jenner.

I was sure "Mags" was Susan Pollack.

"'The storm is here. It never has to die.' Don't you see, Sherwood? Zorn. Greenway. He's using his people to get back at the people who brought him down."

"And Evan?" Sherwood asked, buckling himself in.

"Evan is somehow directed at my brother." I didn't have the answer yet, but there was no more hiding it. "Maybe there were fingerprints on it. Maybe we can match the handwriting. We prove that letter was from Susan Pollack . . ."

"We prove the letter was from Susan and *what*?" The detective looked at me skeptically. "It's just song lyrics. There's nothing there. Besides, there's not a judge in the country who would grant us a court order based on that note or what we have.

"Not to mention you're forgetting one thing . . ." He kicked his briefcase under the seat. "If Greenway and Cooley *were* murdered, it all happened when Susan Pollack was behind bars. That surely wasn't her."

He was right there. I flashed to the person who had called me in the motel room. The voice was male.

"So what's the next step?" I pushed him. The propellers started to whir. In a second we'd be heading back to Pismo. "Just let it go? The guy is orchestrating murder, Sherwood. He's in jail, in chains, and he's got the upper hand. You know as well as I do what's going on here."

"I can't play this out forever, doc. I tried . . . *The next step*." He sighed as the copter started to rise. "Other than getting the truth out of your brother . . ." He turned his head toward the window. "I don't know."

CHAPTER FORTY-NINE

Susan Pollack kneeled in the coop, in her floppy hat and overalls, spreading grain into her feed bin.

"Come here, my pets . . . My little ones."

They were like family to her. Her only family now. Her one attachment of love. *Except you, Bo.* She smiled at her collie, snoozing on the porch.

"Yes, my darlings, over here . . ." They knew the nurturing rise in her tone. "It's feeding time for you, *it's time . . .*"

One by one, the chickens started to come over.

Tomorrow she would show him. That she had been loyal and true.

True to him.

All these years.

You never let me come along, did you? She smiled, conjuring up his delicate, chiseled face. *Because you knew, didn't you, that one day you would need me, my love. You told me, one day I would have to make sacrifices.*

To earn your love completely.

And when the time came, I would.

That was why.

You said I had to be ready.

The excited birds made their way into the pen. She threw a line of seed in front of Desdemona, her favorite, with her smooth white breast and feathers. The proudest and the most vain.

The bird followed her, flapping her wings and pecking at the grain.

"You are my favorite," Susan said softly, putting the feed bag down.

She grabbed the blade.

Nothing can truly be bad if it's done from love, isn't that right, Russell?

She picked the bird up and ran the knife

slowly across its neck, muffling the bird's startled squawk, blood running down its soft white feathers and through her hands.

Just as she wished she could have done all those years back then.

When you left me behind.

You said I had to sacrifice. To be ready.

For you to need me.

And I am ready.

She threw the dead bird down and looked at the others.

I will show you now.

CHAPTER FIFTY

I stopped off at Charlie's on my way back to the motel.

Gabby opened the door. They had just finished up dinner, and she was in the midst of doing the dishes.

My brother was at the kitchen table, picking on his guitar. He barely looked up, neither surprised nor particularly happy to see me. His graying beard and ground-down, toothless smile seemed beaten down.

"Hey, Jay . . ." He picked at a tune. "What's up with you, little brother?"

Gabby asked me if I wanted something

to eat, and I told her no, that I'd had something on the way.

I sat down next to him. "You wanted me to help you find out what happened to Evan, Charlie . . ."

"I know I did, Jay," he said. "At first." He strummed a familiar chord progression to a song I knew. "Let It Rain" by Eric Clapton.

"And I'm trying to, Charlie. I really am. And I'm getting close. But now it's you who has to answer some questions for me. The truth, this time."

"Let your love rain down on me . . . Hey, Jay . . ." His eyes lit up. "You remember this one?" He played a few chords, raising his guitar high in the air like an old rocker. Neil Young's "Heart of Gold." *"I've been to Hollywood, I've been to Redwood . . ."*

He banged on the strings. "And I'm getting old! I'm feeling that way, Jay." He put the guitar on his lap. "You remember that trip we took? To Montreal?" His eyes grew alive again. "When I came to visit you up at college?"

I remembered. He had swung by Cornell on one of his final sojourns back east. I think he had just been released from a psychiatric hospital. At that time, I had never spent a lot of time with my brother, just random visits where he seemed mostly off the wall to me. A bunch of my friends at school and I sat around one night basically spellbound by his tales.

"You were a senior . . . ," he said.

"A junior, I think."

"Your friends were all so smart. They must've thought I was whacked out of my mind. And you know what?" He laughed. "I probably was . . ."

"If I recall, they actually all thought you were pretty entertaining." I smiled.

"Yeah . . ." He chuckled amusedly. "I bet they did. I'm sure they'd never met anyone quite like me." He leaned the guitar against his chair. "You remember, we were walking around up there. On Sherbrooke Street. Near the college. I had my guitar with me. I was playing to a bunch of pretty little chicks there . . ."

"You were trying to pick them up, Charlie. They were college kids. And you probably would have if you hadn't had to find one for me."

"Always watching out for my younger brother!" Charlie laughed, edging into a wide grin. "You remember how that one dude came up to you? Trying to pick a fight or something . . ."

I didn't know where he was going with this, but the truth was, the whole two days up there were like a fog. We'd had some beers. Charlie got me stoned. I spent the night on a narrow bed in a Marriott while he screwed some street gal across the room. Most of it had long slipped away in my mind. "I sort of remember you were the one picking the fight, Charlie, but who can recall?"

"This guy—he didn't like how you were talking to someone. About hockey, right? It was during the Olympics or something. He wanted to beat the shit out of you. Right there on Sherbrooke Street. You were pretty zonked out."

"I was with *you,* Charlie." I couldn't believe with all the brain cell loss he could even bring that to mind. I hadn't since.

"You remember how I got right in his face for you? The guy outweighed me by a hundred pounds!"

I recalled now. "We had to make a dash for it in the snow. You were about to whale him with the guitar. Then you thought better of it."

"Of course. It was the only thing I owned!"

I shook my head at him. "How do you even remember that, Charlie?"

"Because I never wanted to put you in any danger, Jay. Not from me. That was about all I could ever do for you; the rest you had all figured out on your own. And I still don't want to. Put you in any danger. I wish we could've been friends, Jay. Not just brothers, but friends . . ."

Maybe I should've said that I wished that too. That we could have been friends. But instead I drew my chair in and leaned close to him.

"Why don't you tell me about Russell Houvnanian, Charlie?"

CHAPTER FIFTY-ONE

Russell?" Charlie acted surprised. "What do you want to know?"

"About what happened back there on the ranch. About what connection it all has to you. I know you were part of it, Charlie."

He scratched his gray-flecked beard and shrugged. "I've told you everything, Jay. I lived there for a while, that's all. It kept me from having to sleep under a bridge somewhere . . . Russell tried to interest some record people in me."

"Why did he want to push your music, Charlie? That day when you came up with him to Dad's."

"Who knows? That's how he did stuff. Maybe he thought I had talent. He said he had connections. People trying to cut records were always coming in and out of the ranch."

I looked at him. "I think that was how he was trying to push his message, Charlie."

"His message?"

"The End of Days. This crazy philosophy of his. Up is down, heaven is hell. Through the music, right?"

My brother smiled, pushing back his hair. "I think you're reading too much into this, Jay. All that was, was his way of bringing in the chicks."

"No. I saw how you reacted. That day up at the house . . . You wanted to kill somebody, Charlie. Dad even."

"I always wanted to kill someone back then. And I was mad at my shit-ass father for turning against me again. He knew why I was up there. Just once, I wanted something from him. Damn right I wanted to kill him, Jay."

"No." I looked at him closely. "There's more. Why would Houvnanian want to get back at you, Charlie? Through Evan?"

Saying the name of his son was like

thrusting a knife into his gut. He recoiled. The color changed in his face. I knew then there was a lot he wasn't telling me. And that it wasn't the haze of drugs or schizophrenia clouding it.

I said, "I saw him today."

"Who?"

"Houvnanian. I went up there. With Detective Sherwood. We talked with him in prison."

Charlie's eyes grew agitated. *"You saw Russell?"* Alarm spread across his face. "What are you getting yourself involved in, Jay?"

"No, what are *you* hiding, Charlie? I'm trying to help you, but you've got to tell me everything. Evan's dead. And I think you might be right, maybe he didn't jump off that rock on his own after all. Maybe someone else had a hand in it. Wouldn't you want to know that, Charlie? A few days back you wanted to. When you were using me.

"Why don't you start with Susan Pollack, Charlie? You knew her. I know you did now. Zorn. Greenway. I know you're tied to all of them somehow." I reached out and put my hand on his arm. "What happened there, Charlie, please . . . ?"

He pulled away from me and suddenly jumped up, his guitar rattling to the floor. He was never one to show fear when he felt cornered. He just got angry. Like my father. He lost control. Fought his way out.

And I could see he felt cornered now.

"I want you to leave now, Jay. Before I really lose it. You're getting into things you have no business in."

"For God's sake, Charlie, they killed your son." I stood up too and grabbed him by the arm. "Don't you see? They killed Evan."

It was like a switch suddenly triggered in him. He wrenched his arm away, and blood rushed into his face. "You don't know what you're talking about, Jay!" Suddenly he lunged at me with a strength I never expected from his smallish frame.

He pushed me back into my chair, dinner plates and a vase clattering, and suddenly I swung at him—my anger coming from I don't know where—and we crashed into a side table, toppling a lamp to the floor.

We both fell against the wall—his arms wrapped around my throat, me just trying to fend him off. "I told you to stop all this, Jay. I told you to go home!"

A canvas painted by his mother came crashing down.

"I didn't kill my son." He glared savagely into my eyes. His hands squeezed around my throat. *"I didn't!"*

He reared his fist back at me, an animal intensity blazing in his eyes. I knew what was fueling it—that mixture of anger, grief, and guilt.

"I know you didn't, Charlie." I looked back at him. *"I know!"*

"Evan didn't have anything to do with that. *You hear?* I want you to get out of here, Jay. I want you to go back home."

"I saw him, Charlie!" A warm ooze trickled down my chin, blood from somewhere. "I know he's behind what happened to Evan. He and Susan Pollack. I saw a letter she wrote to him in jail. It was her way of telling him it had begun. *What's* begun, Charlie? Five people have died." My eyes locked onto his. *"Evan died . . ."*

My brother's eyes filled up with tears and he cocked his fist again. I was certain he was about to let it go and hit me.

And I would have let him—if that's what it took to bring to the surface what it was he needed to say.

Gabriella ran over—"*Charlie, Charlie . . .*"—and grabbed his drawn-back arm. He fought against her for a second. "*It's Jay,* Charlie," she screamed, "it's your brother! He's only trying to help us, Charlie. What are you doing?"

I recalled the image of Evan squeezing the life out of my son. I also saw our father's own unforgivable temper massed too.

Charlie glared, his eyes filled with ire. Whoever it was aimed at, I knew it wasn't me.

Gabby's frantic protestations finally seemed to get to him, and he blinked himself back to consciousness and put down his arm. He took a series of shuddering breaths and bowed his head, and rolled off me onto his back.

We both lay next to each other for a few seconds, breathing heavily.

"I'm sorry," he said. His eyes were glistening and his cheeks moist. "I'm so sorry, Jay . . ."

"It's okay. It's okay." I lay next to him and reached over and put my hand on his chest.

"*Look!*" Gabriella shouted, staring around the room. "Look at what you've done!"

She pointed to his guitar. It was completely broken. The neck separated from the body, the wood splintered.

He'd had it as long as I could remember. He rolled over and picked it up, the broken neck coming apart in his hands.

All that he had ever done in his life seemed to fade there.

Gabby cried too. "Look at what you've done!"

"It doesn't matter. It doesn't really matter, Gabby." Charlie turned to me, like an empty weight. "You have to go back home, Jay." He dropped the broken shaft and it lay on the floor. "There's nothing to do here anymore. Please. Just let us be."

I sat up and we stared at each other on the floor. I shook my head. "I can't, Charlie. It's too late. Not now."

Gabby and I cleaned up the mess. Afterward she brought me a damp rag, and I dabbed my mouth. There was blood all over it. Charlie was back at the kitchen table, his hair wild and covering his face. He had picked up one of his other instruments, an old blue Fender Stratocaster that hadn't worked in years, strumming at the silent strings.

Just when you say your last good-bye
Just when you calm my fears . . .

"He loves you, Jay," Gabby said to me. She took the rag and wiped my face, blotting the blood. "But for your brother the past is a locked place. Even I cannot be let in. What's happened has happened, Jay. Nothing is going to bring Evan back. I have to salvage something here. Maybe he's right. You tried to help. You always help us, Jay. Now go back to your wife and kids. They need you there. That's where you belong."

"What's happened *has* happened," I said in agreement, "but even if I go, Gabby, it's not going away."

Charlie continued on the guitar:

Just when the dawn is breaking,
There's always one last thing . . .

"Then let happen whatever will." Gabby's blue eyes fixed on me. "That's what he wants. You can see that now. Now that Evan is gone, what is there for us, any-way?"

I took her hand and squeezed it warmly. But I shook my head. "It's not just about him anymore, Gabby."

I listened to my brother's distant voice. The lyrics to his one recorded song.

Oooh, girl, it's always one last thing . . .

"I've got to go." I picked up my jacket and gave Gabby a hug, heading toward the door.

I turned a final time to look at Charlie, playing. He didn't even look up at me.

**The wind and the rain knocking at my
  door,
Don't you know, girl, the dawn will be
  here soon . . .**

I stopped, the words to my brother's song knocking me back.

The wind and the rain . . . That refrain. I suddenly realized I'd never heard the whole thing through before, only pieces:

**The storm's outside, but in here how do
    we tell,**
The morning sun from the dying moon?

The hairs stood up on my arms.

Those were Houvnanian's words: *The
wind and the rain . . . The moon is the sun
and the sun the moon.*

I'd assumed it was just all gibberish.

But it wasn't gibberish.

Houvnanian knew.

I brought back his face, that last mocking grin as they led him away. And suddenly it dawned on me that he hadn't even
been talking to me at all in there.

But to Charlie through me.

He'd been pulling the strings all along.

The room suddenly turned cold, and I
looked back at my brother as he silently
strummed the guitar.

Houvnanian's ramblings about where
God was, it was all from the lyrics to Charlie's song.

CHAPTER FIFTY-TWO

Now I knew. I knew for sure.

And it left me feeling like I had to vomit. Dread creeping up inside me.

Charlie *was* a target.

Houvnanian had simply been toying with Sherwood and me all along. Greenway. Zorn. Evan. Whatever my brother had done, whatever role he played in what took place more than thirty years ago, they were massing around him. Torturing him slowly.

Piece by piece, slowly cutting him up.

The wind and the rain were at his door.

Charlie was next.

As soon as I got back to my hotel room,

I called Sherwood. "My brother's in trouble," I said, my heart pounding off my sides from what I'd just learned.

"Take it easy, doc," the detective said, trying to calm me. The agitation in my voice was clear. "*How?*"

"Houvnanian. All that gibberish about 'the wind and the rain'? That he didn't even remember Charlie? Oh, he remembered him, Sherwood! Those were all lyrics. They were straight out of my brother's song."

"What lyrics?"

"From a song he recorded back then. I heard him playing it tonight. What we heard in that prison, it was all basically just a threat! He was warning him. Through me!"

"A threat of what?" The detective snorted skeptically.

"Please, Sherwood," I begged him, "don't play the skeptical cop shit with me. Not now. *You know!* I know you know. Maybe I can't prove it. Maybe it all sounds crazy when you try and put it together. But Houvnanian made a vow at his sentencing to get back at the people who had harmed him. Who put him and his followers away. And now he's doing it. One by one. He's been doing it! Greenway. Cooley. Zorn. *Evan*. And now they've got my brother in their sights."

"You've still never told me how your brother is involved. *Why him?*"

"I don't know why him!" My brain throbbed. "He won't come clean with me. I think he's too scared to admit he had a hand in his son's death. But that's what Evan's death was about. And their cat. And that cigarette butt left on my doorstep. They're warnings. Warnings that were meant for him! Don't you see, Sherwood? Charlie's next!"

"Listen, doc," the detective said, clearing his throat, "I've done everything short of ruining what's left of my career trying to tie the strands together for you. But they're just not tying. Because that's just what they are, *strands*. There ain't no bow. Now you're talking about lyrics to your brother's song. From more than three decades ago? It's been a long day, doc. Just what is it you want me to do?"

"I want you to put someone on Susan Pollack. I want you to station a car outside my brother's apartment. Unless you're ready to wake up and find him dead too."

"I told you, I can't just take personnel off the street. I'm a coroner's detective. There hasn't even been a direct threat made against anybody. There's not even a case open against anyone."

"Then make one!" I realized if I'd lost Sherwood for good, I was completely alone out here and I couldn't just walk away. Not now. Too much had happened. With Zorn. Susan Pollack. Evan. Sherwood was all I had.

In my life, there had been only a handful of moments when I felt like everything was at stake. One of them was rushing my son, gasping, to the ER. Whatever the outcome, good or bad, I always felt I had this cushion to protect me. A beautiful wife who loved me. Kids who were healthy and made me proud. A position in life that gave me stature and money. Even when things got bad and we had to negotiate a new deal with the hospital or when my father died, I knew I'd make it through.

This was one of those moments.

"Don, please . . . it's time to risk it," I said to him. "To pay it back."

"Risk what, doc?" he replied a little testily.

"Whatever it was they gave you that new liver for."

He remained silent for a while. I knew this was my last chance, and without him, I might as well just go back home and leave my brother to his fate. He and Gabby meant nothing to anyone there. Other than to Sherwood and me. And it all meant nothing if he sent me packing.

"All right," he finally said, exhaling, "I'll find you a car."

"How?" I asked. I wanted to hear. Charlie's life was in the balance.

"It doesn't matter how." His voice had a resigned quality to it. "So tell me," he said with a laugh, "you ever gonna go back to practicing medicine again, doc, or are you just gonna move out here so you can become a permanent pain in my ass?"

"I sure hope so," I said, and exhaled. "About going back."

"Well, let me know, 'cause I want to be first in line to drive you to that plane."

CHAPTER FIFTY-THREE

An hour later, darkness setting in, Sherwood drove his car down Grand Avenue, past the empty fast food storefronts and closed-up auto supply stores, toward Grover Beach.

The clock read eight forty-five. Only a few cars were on the road. The small beach town shut up like a cell block after dark. One or two of the Latino bars still had some life, field hands and out-of-work construction workers drunkenly staggering out.

In another lifetime, he might've stopped and checked them out as they headed for their cars.

He made a left on Fourth, and then Division, heading farther down the hill along the tracks. They used to find bodies dumped in the woods around there. He could still have told you every clearing in the brush where you could score weed or crack. The only time he'd ever fired his gun was on a bust down there back when his hair was still dark and he was still in a uniform.

You've got to risk it all, the doc had said.

Funny, he thought as he drove. He thought he had risked all he had twenty years before.

He thought of Kyle.

He drove his Torino up to the run-down apartment complex. He had been there twice before in the days after Evan had been killed. He stopped the car and put it in park in a dark spot out of the glare of the streetlamp, maybe thirty yards from the entrance. From there, he had a good view of the courtyard and the first-floor apartment. He saw a light glowing behind the drapes. He sank deeper into the car seat and made himself comfortable. He hadn't done this sort of thing in more than a decade. In a way it felt good.

Dorrie would laugh, he thought. He turned off the ignition. *No, she wouldn't.*

She would smile.

Erlich was wrong. He knew *everything* about risking it. About losing it all too.

It had been a family camping trip. On the Clackamas River, up in Oregon. He, Dorrie, and Merry, their twelve-year-old daughter.

And Kyle.

They went rafting. It was the week of the initial spring release. The rapids were mostly level threes and fours. They'd taken pictures. The whole family smiling. Having the time of their lives.

Later, they coasted downstream. The river grew wide and the current smooth. The group pulled over to the shore for a basket lunch, part of the outing. The guide broke out the single-person kayaks that the rafting company had towed there. Everyone took a shot at it. It was fun. The current was easy. Kyle was a little scared to get in, but some other kid not much older tried it and had a blast.

Maybe if he hadn't pushed him, Sherwood always thought when the dark moments came.

Maybe if he hadn't pushed Dorrie: "C'mon, he's a big kid. He can handle it."

He was nine.

Kyle was paddling a few yards behind the main raft when the current, more like a series of small eddies, intensified.

Still not enough to make anyone alarmed, only enough to keep an eye out. Kyle suddenly seemed to be having a little trouble steering. No one paid much attention. There was no danger. Sherwood had been telling his war stories to one of the other couples, a stockbroker and his wife from Seattle. The guide even broke out the cold drinks.

Then Kyle called out.

"Donny," Dorrie shouted, noticing the gulf between them had widened.

For the first time Sherwood saw that his son was afraid.

"Mom," he called out, struggling. "Dad!"

"Right side, right side," one of the guides yelled out to him, doing his best to slow the main raft.

"Keep it steady, son!" Sherwood called.

If the boy had just been twelve, even a little larger, it would have been nothing. The current was barely more than a trickle.

But a hundred yards downstream, the

river divided. There was a sliver of an island in the middle separating the two sides. No more than a couple of hundred yards long. Everyone watched with elevating concern as Kyle got himself caught in a midstream current and was drawn, against his increasing attempts to right himself, to the other side.

Dorrie became alarmed. *"Don!"*

That was when Sherwood took off his sneaks and went to jump in. But the guide held him back. They were too far along.

"He'll be okay," the guide said, trying to reassure him. "There's nothing dangerous over there." He signaled to the other raft. "We'll meet up with him on the other side."

Sherwood yelled out. "You'll be okay! Just paddle, son!"

But his heart told him something entirely different.

Back outside Charlie's apartment, Sherwood gazed out at the darkened courtyard. He turned on the radio. Something easy and soothing. Country. Annoyed at himself.

Why did he have to go through this now?

It was called a strainer—a thatch of branches just below the surface.

And the sound of that word still brought him anguish and pain, though it had been almost twenty years.

They steered the main raft to the far end of the island and waited for Kyle to make his way out.

Everyone was shouting, *"Kyle! Kyle!"* Even the other rafters.

He never did.

Sherwood finally jumped in. Panicked. Running ahead of the guide. Thrashing against the current upstream. The river was no more than thigh high and seemingly smooth, but after running hard a hundred yards Sherwood's thighs began to tire and feel like concrete, a steady stream of water pushing against them. *"Kyle! Kyle!"* His heart suddenly accelerating in a way he had never felt on the job.

"Kyle!"

The second hundred yards lasted a lifetime. All the power in his legs simply gave way. They turned to fire and then to rubber, and he had to stop, the guide running past him.

Where are you, Kyle?

Up ahead, he saw the guide kneel in the water, freeing his boy from the brambles that had caught on his life jacket, under the surface. He gazed back with a look Sherwood would never forget, crying out, *"Oh, man, oh, man, oh, man . . ."*

It's time to risk it, Sherwood . . .

Really? He had already lost it all!

He snuggled in the car seat in a comfortable position and took out a burrito from a bag and settled in. He turned up the volume.

Thank you, the doc had said. And it made Sherwood smile.

Don't thank me. Thank that damn pastor. Knightly.

Behind the shades in the apartment, the light had gone off.

CHAPTER FIFTY-FOUR

That night, I fell asleep while paging through Greenway's book.

I woke up a couple of hours later. The digital clock read 2:17 A.M. I climbed out of bed, poured myself a glass of water. I checked my e-mails, flicked on the TV. *Criminal Minds* was on.

My brain seemed to be repeating the same question over and over.

How is my brother involved?

I lay on the bed, suddenly hearing noises everywhere: a car passing by. Two late-night guests returning to their room. The low drone of the TV. I turned on the light again and picked up my book. Skimmed through a few pages at random, through the photos of the major participants, the ranch as it was back then, the police shots of the gruesome crime scene and evidence. I was hoping Greenway's painstaking detail of the investigation would lull me back to sleep.

It didn't take long after Riorden's sister, Marci, was informed of her brother's murder for attention to fall on his ex-wife, Sandy, and the "bunch of loonies" she was tied to.

Some of the threats Houvnanian had made against Riorden had found their way to the Santa Barbara police. A local gas station attendant remembered seeing "a van full of hippies" similar in appearance to Houvnanian and his group filling up at his station, only a couple of miles from the Riordens' house earlier that day.

Houvnanian was brought in for questioning by local police. He was held on minor trespassing charges while police searched the premises. A few of his followers were brought in on misdemeanor narcotics possession, as small amounts of marijuana and hash were discovered.

While their leader was in custody, several other inhabitants of the ranch seemed eager to talk, and a picture began to emerge of the hallucinogenic frenzy that had stoked up their leader's rage and paranoia.

My eyes began to feel heavy, but I pushed on.

Walter Zorn had handled a bunch of the early interviews with some of the ranch's residents. I flipped ahead, ready to put the book down, as the clock neared three.

One of the people Zorn interviewed was a blond twenty-year-old runaway known as Katya. It wasn't her real name.

Described as blond, pretty, with an affable, upbeat demeanor, it was Katya, Greenway claimed, who first gave up the names of the others who had abetted the perpetrators, among them Alex Fever and Susan Pollack, and she told the police that five others, Telford Richards, Sarah Strasser, Nolan Pierce, Carla Jean Blue, and Houvnanian "had gotten into the van early on the morning of the murders and didn't come back until noon the next day." She said, "It was clear to all of us something bad had happened."

Another one who talked was Katya's boyfriend, identified only as Chase, a nervous, long-haired musician who had dropped out of college back east.

Zorn suggested it was Chase who first led him and Joe Cooley to a marshy pond on the property where a bandana and a bloody poncho that were eventually tied to the killings were found.

And a day later, two knives with matching blood residue on them.

As the evidence tying Houvnanian, Richards, Blue, Pierce, and Strasser directly to the murder scene mounted, the identities of these early informants were withheld from the public records and their testimonies were never needed at trial.

A sudden tingling came over me.

Katya. Chase.

I sat up and read the pages over a second time, my blood picking up with adrenaline. Susan Pollack said they all had different names back then. I got up and opened the sliding door. Stepped out on the balcony. A cool breeze hit me off the ocean.

Could it be?

The breeze took my thoughts, and I pictured a man who owned a large home, who had been away on a journey for a long time. No one knew the moment when the owner might one day return.

Only the father will know . . .

Watch, Houvnanian had warned. I shivered.

For no one knows when the master will choose to come back. Or in what manner.

In my dream, the owner of the house was Russell Houvnanian. As I had remembered him from back then. Dark and intense and scary.

And the servant . . .

The servant who was waiting sent a chill down my spine.

He was my brother.

A sheen of sweat came over me. I saw it all, as if for the very first time.

Watch, Houvnanian had warned.

Chase, watch!

CHAPTER FIFTY-FIVE

That morning I drove Gabby to the market to pick up a few groceries. She had asked me to dinner again that night and was making a Greek stew called *stifado*.

As we left, I noticed a white police car stationed along the tracks down from their apartment. I thanked Sherwood silently and felt better about leaving Charlie in the house alone.

While Gabby shopped, I got a cup of coffee and followed her around with the cart while she went to the meat department and bought inexpensive cuts on sale, and then went through produce, checking the onions for ripeness and examining the peppers for color and price.

I wanted to be alone with her, and after we went through checkout, with a small tussle over allowing me to pay, we rolled the cart over to the coffee bar and I bought a latte for her.

"Thank you for the coffee, Jay," she said, "and for the groceries. This is a real treat for me." She sipped her frothy latte with a smile. She wore a red knit shirt over a skirt, her blond hair in a ponytail. "Usually we bring our own cups here because they charge us fifty cents less."

"I'm sorry for the way you have to live, Gabby . . ."

"This is our fate to bear, Jay, not yours. We are who we are. The way your brother is. You're nice, but there's nothing you can do."

I shifted my stool around and looked at her. "I need you to help me, Gabby. I need you to tell Charlie to unlock the past. I need you to help me help you both."

She smiled at me, a little fatalistically. "After Evan there is no life for us."

"I know, but if someone conspired to kill your son, Gabby, wouldn't you want to know? Wouldn't you want that person brought to justice? Especially if it put the two of you in danger?"

"Danger? I've thought about that." Gabby put down her cup. "Believe me, I have nothing but hate in my heart for that person if it is the case. But maybe the feeling I have most is, in the end, what does it matter? My son is dead, Jay, and if in some way Charlie was involved, with things from his past . . ." She looked at me. "I don't want to lose my son and lose my husband too. That is the true danger. Can you understand that? I've never seen him quite like this, Jay. He's losing his mind."

"Gabby, whatever's in his past is no longer buried. It's *here.* It's taken Evan, and it will take him too if you don't help me. Get him to talk about his time on the ranch. *Please.* I need him to tell me what he did there. I already have some idea . . ."

She nodded, a little tentatively. Then she pushed a hair in place on top of her head and finished her coffee with a smile. "I will do my best, Jay. For you. Now, come on, we have to go to the bakery. Do you like sourdough bread?"

She waved good-bye to her friend behind

the counter, and I wheeled the grocery cart outside through the sliding doors.

I had parked the Lincoln in an open area around the side. All the spaces around us had filled in. I got to the car and popped the trunk. Gabby went to load up the bags.

"Let me help you . . . ," I said, reaching for two of the heavier ones.

"No." She laughed, her eyes blue and light. "I am old, but I am able to do this, Jay."

"Okay, okay . . ." I hoisted a bulky bag containing milk and juice cartons into the trunk and went around and opened the driver's-side door. I smelled the acrid scent of oil coming from somewhere. I looked but didn't see anything. "I'll take back the cart."

I wheeled it toward the lineup of carts in the front, and a pretty Latino woman happily took it from me.

Heading back, I watched Gabby close up the trunk. Though she was probably sixty, she still looked trim and attractive. Her smile, however brief, always lit her face, and I thought to myself that this was a woman who would have really enjoyed her life if things had been different. I felt sorry for the look of anguish that had replaced her quick smile, and all the pain. She had tried hard to be a good mother to Evan, whatever the outcome. How loyal she had been to Charlie all these years.

She caught sight of me staring at her and briefly smiled.

The same moment I realized something was horribly wrong.

Walking toward her, I caught that smell again, and my gaze fixed on a slick black river of flame traveling toward us on the pavement, one car away.

No . . .

I ran to try to put it out, but it sped quickly under the blue Ford truck parked in the space adjacent to us, a dangerous stream of fire picking up speed.

That's when I realized that the smell under my car wasn't engine oil at all, but *gasoline*!

My eyes were now drawn to the widening black circle pooled underneath the Lincoln.

No!

I stopped, knowing I was too late, and turned back to my Lincoln in panic.

"Gabby, no . . . !"

She had climbed back in the car and

shut the door. Still a picture of that same happy smile glancing my way.

My own gaze unraveling into horror.

I ran toward her, shouting out her name, a passerby turning, just as the stream of flame met the pool of gasoline underneath my car—suddenly engulfing it in a bright whoosh of scalding yellow heat.

"Gabby!"

I stared, helpless, as a burst of heat shot at me as if the car was an enormous gas grill overloaded with propane. Scalded, I turned away for a second, blinded. When I looked back Gabby had her arm covering her face, a twisted expression of horror on it, frantically tugging at the door, the vehicle erupting around her in flames.

"Gabby!"

I darted over, ripping off my jacket as I went for the already scalding door handle, swatting the flames away from my face.

All around me, people screamed.

The door was jammed. Gabby's mask of helplessness and fear inside whipped the quickening drumbeat of my own exploding heart.

"I'll get you out!" I screamed, tugging with my jacket over the fiery handle.

Goddamnit, open, please!

I pulled and pulled, but I couldn't get my fingers around the handle. Smoke began to rise, starting to fill up the inside of the car. Gabby's fear intensified and I realized that at any moment the whole thing might explode.

I flung down my jacket and squeezed, and finally the door mercifully released. I threw it open, grabbing on to Gabby's arm, ripped her out of the seat, as onlookers rushed from the market, pointing and screaming all around.

I picked her up in my arms and carried her over my shoulder, twenty feet away, just as I heard this chilling, enveloping whoosh from behind me and my rented Lincoln erupted into an orange ball of flames.

"Jay! Jay!" Gabby was screaming.

Then it blew.

The blast knocked me down, and we hit the pavement, hurled up against another parked car. Gabby clung to me, shaking, coughing smoke out of her lungs, unable to look back, guttural sobs coming out of her, from both relief and fear.

"Oh, Jay, oh, Jay, oh, Jay . . ."

I turned around. My car was engulfed in

smoke and flame. A stomach-turning, fuel-like stench was all around. Shocked shoppers ran out of the stores, eyes stretched wide.

"It's okay, Gabby, it's okay." I stroked her, my own heart slamming against the walls of my chest, as I squeezed her close. *"It's okay . . ."*

But no matter how many times I said it, I looked back at the smoking carcass of my car and knew it wasn't okay.

The truth came over me. As inescapable as the wall of flames I now watched in disbelief.

This was my car.

I was supposed to be inside. *If I hadn't wheeled the cart back . . .*

The blazing fireball, a bonfire of burning oil and smoke, melting metal and leather . . .

It was meant for me.

CHAPTER FIFTY-SIX

The police arrived. Two black and white sheriff's cars and a white county vehicle, lights and sirens blaring. They pushed back the surging crowd, some of whom had helped us.

"I'm a doctor," I said. "I'm okay."

A minute later the EMTs came.

No matter how I stared at the melted, smoking chassis, I still couldn't believe what had taken place.

I was okay. Just some slight burns on my fingers and a scrape on my arm from the tumble. Gabby had some first-degree burns on her face and legs. But she was completely in shock.

I muttered to one of the EMTs that I was a doctor.

They took her off to the ER in Arroyo Grande. I declined any treatment and stayed, taking the police officers through what had happened. I traced the black river of smoking fuel from beneath my own vehicle to a Dumpster around the back of the market where the fire, and whoever had set it, had originated.

Two local detectives came on the scene and took my story. The lead one was a young Latino with a shaved head. He asked if I knew anyone who might want to hurt me.

I didn't even know where to begin.

I told him I had to speak with Sherwood.

"Detective Sherwood's with the coroner's office in San Luis Obispo," the detective replied. "We're here to help you. This isn't his terrain."

"Find Detective Sherwood," I said, not backing down.

It took a few minutes to locate him.

"I just heard what happened," he said when I finally got him on the phone. "Are you all right?"

"I know what it's all about," I said, my blood racing, ignoring his concern.

He didn't answer. Maybe he thought I was raving. Or a little wacky, from the shock.

"Sherwood, I know what my brother did back then. Why they want to hurt him. You can meet me at Charlie's later. I'll get him to talk." I exhaled a breath, grateful Gabby and I were both alive. "We're going to bust this wide open now, Sherwood."

CHAPTER FIFTY-SEVEN

I called Kathy on the way to check out Gabby at the hospital.

I knew she would freak out over what had happened. I'd been keeping so much hidden from her: the phone warning I had received before. My visit with Russell Houvnanian.

I started by saying it was all just some random accident. My car blew up, some kind of crazy oil leak. That Gabby that been in the car, but we were all right. Just a little shaken.

That was all I could say.

"Oh, my God, Jay!" Her first reaction was one of shock, horror. She'd clearly figured out it was bigger than what I'd made it sound. "How did it happen? I'm just so glad you're alive!"

I felt like I was cheating on her, concealing the truth.

I didn't know if she even believed me, but it didn't matter. I just needed to hear her voice. "I'm okay," I told her over and over. "I promise. I am."

But something must have made her think I wasn't being entirely truthful. Maybe my shakiness.

"You say Gabby was in the car?" she asked after a protracted pause.

"She's going to be okay too. Look, everything's finally all out in the open now anyway. I'll be back soon."

"What's in the open, Jay?" Worry turned to frustration. "This wasn't an accident, was it?"

I didn't answer.

"Jay, I don't even know if I know you anymore. What happened out there? What have you been keeping from me?"

"I'll tell you soon, Kathy. I promise. I

know I've been acting crazy to you." I didn't know how to explain it now. I felt like a fool hanging up.

I felt a lot of things slipping away right then and didn't do much to stop it. One of them was Kathy's trust.

One of the sheriff's cars drove me to the hospital. Inside the ER, Gabby was behind a partition receiving oxygen.

I introduced myself to the attending physician, a red-haired guy named Paulson, and he briefed me on how she was. Smoke inhalation. First-degree burns along her arms and neck. Lucky it was nothing more. Shock.

Charlie was already there. He was basically sobbing, resting his head on the gurney.

I said, "They're going to keep her overnight, just to be sure." I put my hand on his shoulder. "They've given her something for the shock."

He nodded, wiping his tears on the sheet. Pretty much all I saw was the back of his long gray hair.

I leaned down and brushed my hand

against Gabby's cheek. "How're you doing?"

She blinked at me, her eyes a little glazed. "I was really scared, Jay. Really scared. I said my prayers. I thought this was it."

"You ought to sleep," I told her. "They're going to admit you and get you in a room, just for observation."

"Thank you, Jay." She reached out and took hold of my hand. Her dull eyes brightened. "Thank you for saving my life."

I winked, smiling at her. "*No problema, señora.*"

Gabby smiled back, but weakly. She petted her husband's head. "Charlie, you go home. You have to talk to your brother now. You have to tell him. Everything. Do you understand? Everything you have not told me. Our son, Charlie . . . our son's soul will never rest. He has to sleep in peace."

Charlie nodded, wiping his nose with the back of his hand, and lifted his head.

"You go home with Jay. You tell him. I don't blame you for anything, my husband. Not one thing."

Charlie pushed himself up. "I'll come and get you tomorrow," he said.

"Good," she said, her voice a little hazy from the medication. "Now I'll get some sleep."

I drove Charlie's clunky Taurus. We didn't say a word for most of the trip. He pretty much just sat there staring straight ahead. Something he had bottled up inside him for decades was slowly rising to the surface. We turned off Fourth down the less traveled road that led to the tracks. I knew I didn't have to say anything—Gabriella already had.

On Division, I slowed before turning into his carport.

"Stop here, Jay," Charlie told me.

I pulled up on the side of the street.

He was silent a moment, puffing out his cheeks. Worry etched into his eyes. "I can't live knowing I hurt her." He turned to me. "She's all I have left. It's hard enough to bear to think of Evan . . ."

Tears streamed down into his beard. He mashed his palms up against his face.

And then it came. Like a flood. Everything I'd been waiting for.

"I had nothing to do with it, Jay—the murders. Nothing." His eyes were swollen and contrite. "I swear. I was a lost soul back then. You know that. I was crazy. I felt at home there. All I ever wanted was to make music. It's all I ever did well. I felt I had a chance there . . ."

"Why did they want to make your record, Charlie?"

"Because it was Russell's way." He avoided my eyes. "It was his crazy way of getting everything out. Russell had his own songs. He felt if he could get a record made, the world had to listen. It was his way of reaching people. His stupid fucking message. The guy was insane, Jay. We were all insane . . ."

"When did you really leave there, Charlie?"

He pressed his hands on the top of his forehead and pushed, like he was forcing the demons out. "After it all took place. Everything started to get crazy there, Jay. Russell was ratcheting up all this fear. Tightening the screws he had on people. Everyone was freaked out on the fear that the storm troopers were coming to raid the ranch. The drugs didn't help. They only fed the paranoia. The music was going to die forever. The music was love, Jay. I know you don't see it that way, but it was.

But I was never part of what took place. Not for a second. That was all his people. His inner circle. The ones closest to him."

"Why would Houvnanian want to hurt you, Charlie?"

He just kept staring straight ahead and put his hands over his face.

I reached across and touched his shoulder. "You're Chase, aren't you?"

He didn't answer. He only turned. A kind of light flickered in his eyes, as if he was relieved to finally hear me. "How did you know about that?"

"You turned them in," I said. "Russell, Susan, all the rest. To Zorn and Cooley. You led the police to their bloody clothes in the marsh. And then the weapons . . . They think you betrayed them."

He didn't have to say a thing. The answer was etched on his tearstained face. He smiled. As if a lifelong weight was finally lifted from him.

"I've hid out for more than thirty years . . . More than half my life, Jay. Thirty-seven years of telling myself I didn't matter anymore. Afraid that one day they would find me. Or Gabby or Evan. I was afraid to even let Evan play ball. To let him have a life. To ever leave this shit hole. I knew one day they would find me. Russell promised they would and they did. That's what Zorn told Evan. That they knew we were here . . . That's what my son came and told me."

He put his arm across his face and started to sob.

I drew him to me. "It's okay, Charlie." I knew he felt responsible for Evan. "You couldn't have known."

"No." He turned and looked at me. "It's not okay, Jay. *There's more . . .*"

His eyes grew sunken and shadowed, like a moon crossing the sun in an eclipse. "You wanted in, Jay, now there's no turning back. Park the car. There's something I need to show you inside, little brother. Come on in."

CHAPTER FIFTY-EIGHT

I parked the Taurus underneath the carport and followed Charlie in.

He went into the living room and knelt beside the chest that contained his old keepsakes. The old pictures of his family back in Miami. His medical diagnoses, kept like grade school report cards. The *Billboard* Top 40 sheet he had shown me.

He pulled out a thick folder and leafed through dog-eared sheets of music and lyrics until he came upon a manila envelope. He took it out and handed it to me, barely looking me in the eye.

"I got this about a week ago," he said, shrugging. "A couple of days after Evan died . . . I can't remember exactly when. I didn't know what to do with it, so I hid it. I didn't even tell Gabby. I was scared. I knew they had found me. I didn't want to believe they had anything to do with my son."

The envelope was addressed to Charlie. No return address.

"You have to believe me, Jay, if I knew this could have ever hurt anyone . . . Evan, Gabby . . ." Tears glistened in Charlie's slate-gray eyes. "*You.* I would never have kept it to myself . . ."

The envelope was torn open at the top. I slid out the contents and stared in shock at what I was now looking at, reacting as if I'd been punched and recoiling.

There were photos of a dead woman.

Not just dead, it became clear to me, mutilated. My mouth went dry. She was naked, her face and torso cut up. Red slits and bloody lacerations disfiguring her all over.

The woman was blond, kind of pretty in a way, I could still detect. Her hair was strewn to the side in long braids. Maybe in her fifties. I leafed through the shots one by one, my stomach clenching. Only someone who wanted to cause terrible suffering to someone could have done something this cold-blooded.

They'd tortured her.

"Who is she?" I asked, but something made me think I knew.

"Her name was Sherry." Charlie let out a deep, pained exhale. "I hadn't seen her in over thirty years. I knew her back then—on the ranch . . . She's—"

"I know who she was." I looked up at him. "It's Katya."

He just stood there staring at me, his eyes wide. Then he sank onto the couch and ran his hand through his ponytailed hair. *"Katya . . ."* He smiled fondly and gave me a slight nod of confirmation. "She didn't deserve something like this, Jay."

"Both of you pointed the finger at Houvnanian. And the ones who went with him down to Santa Barbara. You helped the police in their investigation?"

Again, he gave me the slightest nod. Then he looked up, befuddled. "How do you possibly know all about this?"

"It doesn't matter how I know. What mat-

ters is what we do about it now. You're
who they want, Charlie. Greenway. Zorn.
Evan. Sherry . . . This has all been leading up to you. For what you did. They're
torturing you, just like they did to this
woman. By killing off the things you love."

Charlie rubbed his brow in anguish. He
leaned forward and picked up the photos,
leafed through them again, pressing his
lips in sadness and a held-in anger. "She
was a beautiful person, Jay. She wouldn't
have hurt a fly. Look at her. The kind of
people who could do this . . ."

"You already know the kind of people,
Charlie. We were with one the other day.
But now you have to step back. Out of the
prison you've been in. You have to help
me bring them down."

Charlie nodded, exhaling a breath that
might have been in him thirty years.
"There's something else . . ."

He went over to the chest and dug
around in the back of a drawer. He came
back with something wrapped in a blue
towel and handed it to me.

"How long have you known?" I asked as
I took away the towel and stared at what
was inside.

"That first week. After you came to dinner. It was in the trash."

"You could have told me," I said, and Charlie simply nodded, sorry.

I was staring at a black Nike sneaker.

CHAPTER FIFTY-NINE

Susan Pollack watched from the woods, smoking. Her car was hidden safely around the block from the apartment house.

At around one P.M., she saw Charlie and his brother pull up.

Chase.

The two of them stayed in the car and talked for a while before going in. Though far away, something in Chase's hanging head and tormented expression gave her a feeling of delight. It was too bad that his nosy brother and his whore of a wife had escaped the little present at the market earlier.

It had made her giddy, watching the two of them fighting for their lives in the flaming car. As it was, just hearing the bitch's screams, seeing the shell-shocked looks of panic and fear on their terrified faces, had almost been enough. She knew there would be other times for them. And soon.

Soon, my darling. Mags smiled from the woods.

Her blood stirred with an exhilaration she had not felt for many years. Susan, that shell of a dried-up woman, who had dutifully done what was asked of her, was dead now.

But Mags was very much alive.

You never left me, all these years. Not for a single second. Our thoughts have always been entwined. I know it was me all along who nurtured you. The one you truly wanted. The others were just the playthings who threw themselves at you. They were candy to make you smile. But it was me, your Maggie Mae, your Mags, who was your music. Who gave you the will to do what had to be done.

Who was your true music!

She saw movement coming from the

car. Charlie and his brother got out and went inside.

Well, wait till you see what the music has in store for you now, Charlie.

Her thighs felt alive, moist for the first time in years. *Isn't that what you said, my love? That nothing could ever be evil, not if it comes from love.*

And what greater love could I have shown for you? This is my gift. I am yours whenever you want me. I always have been.

I know you can hear me, Russell. There are walls, but what is between us cannot be kept out. It knows no walls.

"No one knows when the master will choose to come back, or in what manner."

I have never forsaken you for a second, my love. You gave me the gift of love back then. You protected me.

You left me behind.

Now I give it back to you. In full.

CHAPTER SIXTY

A short while later, Sherwood knocked on the apartment door and I spotted him through the blinds.

I was glad he had come alone. Charlie had barely moved in twenty minutes, sunk into the couch, his head in his hands, staring into space.

I let him in.

"You all right?" he asked, giving me a look that was different from any I had seen from him before.

"Yeah. Thanks." I nodded grimly, blowing out my cheeks.

"And Gabriella? I checked at the hospital."

"She's doing okay too. Take a seat."

He glanced at Charlie, lowering himself on the threadbare ottoman. "You said you had something important for me to see?"

"I think you'll think so, Sherwood." I handed him the photos Charlie had shown me of the woman named Sherry. He leafed through them, stoically and detached at first, then wincing once or twice as he grew increasingly somber. "Who is she?"

I looked at Charlie to reply, but he just stared straight ahead.

"Her name was Sherry," I answered. "She was a friend of my brother's from a long time ago. They were together back then. On the Riorden Ranch."

"Oh." Sherwood nodded, putting together what these photos, sent to Charlie, meant. "How did you get these?"

"In the mail," Charlie said from behind his hands. "Just after Evan was killed."

"You know who sent them?" Sherwood inspected the envelope. The postmark was local. No identifiable markings. No return address.

He shook his head. "No."

"You must have some idea." He glanced through them again, waiting for Charlie to answer. "When was the last time you were in touch with her?" he asked after a stretch of silence.

Charlie shrugged. "Over thirty years ago. We stayed together for a couple of months after we moved on from the ranch. We hitchhiked across California. To Arizona. Sedona, if I remember."

"If you remember?"

"We were only together for a couple of months. I hitched around everywhere back then. We hung around for a while in the desert. Did a lot of drugs. Then I moved on."

"You moved on?"

"Picked up." My brother shrugged. "With someone else. I never knew what happened to her."

"So only someone who knew you from back then—from the ranch," Sherwood said, "could have put the two of you together?"

Charlie nodded weakly. "Yes."

"And how would that same person know where to send these to you now?"

This time Charlie looked up. His face was a beaten blank. "I don't know the answer to that question, detective. These past days, I've asked myself that a hundred times."

"But you now know *why . . .*?" he pressed, and glanced at me. "*Why* they would have sent this to you?"

"Yes," Charlie said, moistening his lips. "I know why."

"Her name was Sherry," I said, picking up the photos, "but she went by the name Katya back then. You remember how Susan Pollack said everyone had their own names on the ranch? Susan was Maggie, short for Magdalena. Houvnanian was what?" I looked at my brother.

"Paul," he said softly.

"Paul," Sherwood said. "You mean like from the Gospels?"

"No." Charlie sniffed with a slight smile. "McCartney. He thought he wrote directly to him."

Sherwood smiled drily too. "So who is this woman?" The detective looked at Charlie and then at me.

"Initially, the police were led to Houvnanian by the threats he had made against Riorden," I answered. "And by Riorden's sister. Also, the ranch's white van was spotted in the vicinity of the crime scenes.

He and a few of his inner circle were picked up and held in the local jail on trespassing and minor drug possession charges. Walter Zorn and his team went around the ranch and questioned people there. Some of them closed ranks. Others apparently decided to talk. It's all in Greenway's book. Katya—*Sherry*," I said, correcting myself, "was one of them."

Sherwood fixed on Charlie, the truth starting to settle on him. "I guess what I'm about to hear is that you were another, huh, Mr. Erlich?"

"Yes." Charlie rubbed his beard. "I was."

"And what was your name back then?"

"Chase."

"Chase . . ." Sherwood let out a breath. "So what was it you told them, Charlie?"

"It's all detailed in the book," I said. "Walter Zorn and Joe Cooley conducted the initial interviews. Katya first revealed the identities of those who went along with Houvnanian to Santa Barbara. Charlie led them to a pond on the property where some of the evidence had been buried. A bandana. A poncho. Articles of clothing worn during the murders. Ultimately they found the murder weapons there too."

"So you testified against them, Mr. Erlich. You were part of the trial?"

"No. Once the evidence against Houvnanian and the others became overwhelming—they had prints, the murder weapons, their own incriminating confessions—the names of those followers who talked were concealed. Their testimonies weren't needed at trial."

Charlie looked up. "We were only there for the damn music. And the drugs. Russell had this ring around him. People gave him whatever he wanted. He made it feel like you were blessed to be in his graces. We weren't into what took place down there. When it happened, we just wanted to get out."

"You and Katya," Sherwood said to him. "Sherry."

Charlie nodded.

"You see it now, don't you?" I asked Sherwood. "How it all fits. Susan Pollack was with Evan when he went up to that rock. And I have the proof."

"*The proof?*" Sherwood said, furrowing his brow.

I showed him the sneaker. Evan's sneaker. Sherwood's gray eyes widened.

He knew exactly what it was, because he had seen the other one, on Evan's body.

"When did you get this?" He stared at Charlie.

"Last week. It was left in the trash." He sat there with his elbows on his knees, ashen.

"This is all about Charlie," I said. "They're torturing him. Just like they did to that woman. They tried to kill Gabby today. And me. They're trying to make him bleed for what he did. Zorn knew they had found him and tried to warn them. That's why he reached out to Evan."

"So you knew about this?" Sherwood fixed on Charlie.

"Evan said the police had been talking to him. He said they wanted him to help us. To make us safe." Charlie cradled his forehead in his hands. "My son was off his rocker—just like me, right? It sounded like more of his ramblings . . ."

"It probably was ramblings by that point," I said. "He probably didn't know what was real and what wasn't."

"Instead I let them kill him," Charlie said. "I let them take him away . . ."

I placed a hand on my brother's back as he sobbed, forcefully, into his beard.

Sherwood picked up the top photo. "Can you give me any information about her? Where she might have been living lately? Her family? Even a last name?"

"Myers. Sherry Ann Myers." Charlie looked up glassily. "At least that was her maiden name. She was from Lansing, I think. In Michigan."

Sherwood fit the photos back in the envelope. He wrapped the sneaker up in the towel and stood up, meeting my gaze in a corroborating stare.

He went over to the door. "I don't think you could have helped your son, Mr. Erlich, if that's what's on your mind. We still don't know what happened to him up there. But you damned well could've helped the investigation. By sharing this earlier."

He gave a final look to me and left.

Charlie waited awhile until we heard his car start up outside. "You can go now, Jay," he said, still hunched over.

Gabby was still in the hospital. I didn't want to leave him. "Maybe I should stay."

He lifted his head and looked at me with

swollen, bloodshot eyes. "No, I mean tomorrow. It's all out now. You can go back home."

I squeezed his shoulder and said, "We'll see."

At that moment, I thought he was simply caring for me. For the time I had spent there, away from my family. Now that the truth had come out.

A day later, I wished I'd heard him more clearly.

CHAPTER SIXTY-ONE

Russell Houvnanian's five-by-ten cell was dark and dim at night, but he was still able to conjure Charlie Erlich's face.

Chase.

Though he hadn't seen him in thirty-five years, he'd memorized every line: the slant of his chin, his ground-down teeth, the bad-boy glimmer in his eye. He also saw the image of his younger brother—at their father's fancy home in the Hollywood Hills. It was no surprise to see him again the other day after all these years. In fact, it was damn well the highlight of his month!

He'd seen him dozens of times over the years in his dreams.

With a smile, he also brought to mind the face of their father.

"Mags," Houvnanian whispered in the night, "my beautiful Maggie Mae. I could touch you as if I was with you now. You can feel me, can't you? I told you, didn't I, that what was done from love could never ever be bad or evil? Only twisted that way. I told you to trust me over time and I would give myself to you in a way I have not to any others.

"And now it's time.

"You will do this, and I will come to you, my Mags, like I've always come to you. Like I have always traveled from these walls and been with you in the night.

"You were always my little sweetness, you know. My muse."

On his cot, Houvnanian raised up his knee, a smile etched onto his face.

Even behind these walls I can fly. I can walk your streets. I can be among your children. I can fuck your daughters.

He'd waited thirty-seven years; what was another day or two?

Enjoy what's left, Charlie boy.

I always told you the master would one day be home.

And now I've come a-knockin'!

CHAPTER SIXTY-TWO

The next afternoon, Sherwood sat in his office, staring at a file.

A gradual transformation had taken place. He no longer believed that Evan Erlich had climbed up that ledge and jumped off on his own.

The shoe proved that.

He still didn't know what happened up there. In truth, he still had nothing—nothing even a twelve-year-old might consider evidence: no proof, no witnesses, nothing directly linking Susan Pollack or anyone else with any criminal actions. Other than these horrible pictures Charlie had given to him.

And the file on his desk that had come back a short while ago. Inching him closer to the realization that from his cell, possibly starting years ago, Russell Houvnanian was engaged in a process of deadly revenge.

That Greenway's and Zorn's deaths had been part of it. That Susan Pollack might have been aiding him.

That Evan was the way they got to Charlie.

And now, thanks to the doc, he also knew why.

Sherwood thought back to the remote house up in Jenner. The navy Kia the doc said matched one he had seen outside his brother's house. The testimony of the street vendor at the rock. They all began to fit in, into some shifting puzzle that was starting to take shape. He knew how skeptical he had been, how simple it had all seemed only a week ago.

A flashing eye—no more than a Cracker Jack prize, found in a boy's pocket at the bottom of the rock.

Sherwood now accepted that Susan Pollack might be involved, but she surely wasn't alone.

Thomas Greenway was killed in Las Vegas back in 1988. Susan Pollack was still at the Frontera Women's Correctional Institution then. Walter Zorn might have been getting on in years, but he still weighed more than two hundred pounds and had fought for his life while being strangled. The doc was sure that it had been a man on the phone threatening him.

Sherwood looked at the open file. This cinched it.

Now it was only a question of what he would do.

It had come in an hour ago, from the FBI's ViCAP system, a data bank of details on most violent crimes.

He had run the details from the photos Charlie Erlich had given him.

Her name was Sherry Ann Frazier. She lived in Redmond, Michigan. A small resort town on the UP. She was fifty-two years old and had been found beaten and murdered in her home by her daughter eight days before.

There was a local police contact on the file. Some young detective named Arlen Douglas. Sherwood had rung him up. The kid seemed a bit green. What kind of things

even happened up there on the Upper
Peninsula anyway? A moose wandering
into town? Geese sightings? Sherry Ann
Frazier lived alone. She was recently separated. She ran a bakery in town. No one
had any clue who'd killed her. There were
no prints or fibers left behind. Nothing was
taken from the house. They clearly didn't
have many homicides in Redmond. The
case had gotten nowhere.

"I want you to take a look at the files,"
Sherwood told the young detective, "and
tell me if you can find something for me."

"Sure," the kid had replied, empty in the
biggest case of his career. "What?"

"An eye," Sherwood had told him.

"An eye?"

"That's right, or anything else that resembles one. On the body. Or maybe left
around the scene."

Ten minutes later he called back. A little
confused. They *had* found something actually. Not quite an eye, Douglas had said.
But *something . . .* Something they hadn't
been able to figure out.

Something weird.

He said, "The coroner found a contact
lens. In her right eye . . ."

"Only the *right* eye?" Sherwood asked, his heart rate picking up.

"Just the one," Arlen Douglas confirmed. "But that's not even the point. According to the ex-husband and daughter, Sherry Ann Frazier didn't even wear contacts. Or glasses. She didn't need them. Her vision was fine. Pretty weird, huh?"

"Crazy fucking weird," Sherwood said.

Through the door, Sherwood saw his boss, Phil Perokis, come back into the office. He said good-bye, got up, grabbed his files, along with the incident report on the car fire yesterday and all that Charlie had told him.

He was about to head after Perokis when his desk phone rang. He grabbed it, answering sharply, "Detective Sherwood here."

"Detective, it's Roland Martinez," the caller said. "From up in Jenner."

Earlier in the day, Sherwood had called up there as well. Martinez was the detective who had happened to pick up his call. He had asked Martinez to ride up to Susan Pollack's spread on Lost Hill and check on her whereabouts.

"Thanks for getting back to me, detective." Sherwood sat back down. "So what'd you find?"

"What'd I find? You ready?" He sounded almost annoyed. "There was a gate up across the driveway. Newspapers scattered on the road. Two days' mail. I went in anyway. No car in the garage. No sign of anyone around. Even the front door was bolted shut."

Sherwood didn't like the sound of it. "Thanks."

"Something else though . . ." the detective went on. "I smelled something coming from the back. And I'm talking wretched. Thought it might have been a body. So I went around the side."

Sherwood waited. "What did you find?"

"A bunch of fucking chickens, detective. All with their throats cut. Blood everywhere. You know whose place it is, don't you? I checked. The county has it registered to a Susan Pollack. You know who that is, don't you? This doesn't exactly sit well up here. Anything I should know?"

"If there is," Sherwood said, "I promise I'll let you know . . ."

He hung up. He knew what it all meant. She had said those chickens were her only friends these days . . . He felt the hairs raise on his arms.

She wasn't going back there.

Sherwood saw the lieutenant's door open. He took his jacket and stood up again; then something stopped him and he put back down his files.

Whatever it was you got that second chance for, he heard a voice say, *this is it.*

He sat back down. He felt a pain throb in his abdomen. He said a thank-you to Edward J. Knightly. For all the good work he had done.

He lit up a cigarette he'd been saving in his drawer, then wheeled his seat around and sat there staring out at the hills.

CHAPTER SIXTY-THREE

Charlie took an extra Xanax along with his usual pills that morning. He felt totally wound up, his heart racing at twice its normal speed.

First, he went and brought Gabby home from the hospital. She was still a little woozy and in shock; she'd been prescribed four milligrams a day of Klonopin, just like himself. Otherwise, thank God, she was fine. She walked into the house, looking a little perturbed at the mess Charlie had let accumulate—his papers and old music strewn all over the couch, dirty plates thrown in the sink—and she snapped at him for always being in his own world, especially with what had happened.

He sat her down at the table. "Gabby, we have to talk."

He could no longer hide the past from her. Or pretend it had not caught up to them. He had put her in danger now.

She could see his anxiety, how he couldn't sit still. "What's wrong, Charlie?"

"It's all coming apart, Gabby."

"What is coming apart?"

As calmly as he could manage, he told her about the photos he had received days before. The ones he had hidden from her. And the horrible things that had been done. How Sherwood had taken them, but he still described them one by one, what his old friend's killer had done to her.

"Who is this person?" Gabby looked at him, befuddled, recoiling as he described Sherry's terrible wounds. "Who would do this to somebody? Like some dog." The more he told her, the less she could even believe it.

"Gabby, there are things I haven't told you. Things about me, before we met."

"This is what your brother has been saying, Charlie." A deepening apprehension robbed the color from her face. "This is what he wanted you to admit. He—"

"Listen to me, Gabby." He clasped her hands and slowly, his mind remarkably clear for once, told her of his time on the Riorden Ranch.

Who Sherry was. And Russell Houvnanian—a name Gabby had never heard him utter in all their years but, it now became clear to her, had influenced every day of their lives together, even how they had raised their own son, and how they had hidden like fugitives, shrunk from any chance to raise themselves up.

And finally, he told her who Zorn was. How their paths had crossed years and years before.

Gabby saw it all now. A fog opening up. And the cruelest part was Evan.

"Why, why wouldn't you ever let him leave, Charlie? When your brother invited him? You said it was because we needed the state support for us all to continue to live. Otherwise we would die. But I see it now . . . That was a lie. You never wanted him to leave. You never wanted him to have a chance. *Why, Charlie . . . ?*"

"I was scared, Gabby. It was the only way I could protect him."

She pulled back, a sudden judgment flashing in her eyes. "You did this to Evan? All these years. To your own son. You kept him from being someone. And *why*? Because you feared they would find you? That they would do these things to you too? You said it was out of love, but it was *this*? You took this out on our son, Charlie?"

"No. No." He shook his head, but the answer was on his face. In his guilt he felt that it was true.

"You held him here. For what? For the money he received from the state. So we could continue to hide? All these years. Because without him, we had nothing? Your brother begged him to come to New York. When he had a chance, Charlie—to give his life a chance. Things we couldn't give to him." Tears shone in her eyes. "When he was not so ill . . ." She grabbed him by the collar. "You stole our son's chance in life, Charlie . . ."

Then she put her face in her hands and started to cry.

"Gabby, you're not seeing it. What happened yesterday to you was part of it too.

They found us! They're trying to hurt me for what I did back then. That's all that Zorn was trying to tell us. We have to get out of here."

"Get out of here?" Her face grew taut with rage, and she laughed, a scornful, challenging retort, staring back in his eyes. *"To where?* To where, Charlie? We have no money. Our car can barely make it around town. There is no place to go. The past is here? Then it has found us both, because you have sucked me in too. We are in the same prison as this man who wants to hurt you, Charlie. And we have been for years!"

"I'm not going to let them hurt you, Gabby."

"You've already let them hurt me, Charlie! They cannot hurt me any *more*."

She wept, seeing it all for the first time. Their twisted, pathetic fate. Charlie just sat there, his hands spread, unable to comfort her. He tried to think what to do.

"Where are these pictures?" Gabby asked, looking up and wiping her eyes.

"Sherwood has them."

"Why?"

"To find out who Sherry is now. And to find out who killed her."

"And Jay? Has your brother seen them too?"

He nodded. "Yesterday."

Anger swept onto Gabby's face. "So you knew this man? Walter Zorn. And you knew that our son was trying to tell us something. The truth. This is something I just cannot believe."

Charlie shook his head and wiped away a tear. "No, that's not the way it is."

"Yes. Yes, it is the way it is. You struck a deal, years before. A deal with the devil! And now that devil has taken our son."

"And it may take us too, Gabby."

"For me, there is nothing left to take, Charlie. It's all gone."

"No, there is something else." A knot tightened in Charlie's stomach. He felt like his world had fallen apart. "There's one more thing. Last week, I found something else too, Gabby."

CHAPTER SIXTY-FOUR

He told her about the sneaker.

Evan's sneaker. The one he had found in the trash a week before.

The one that proved that Evan hadn't killed himself. That he hadn't been alone up there.

"You found his sneaker?" Gabby looked at him, confusion spreading over her face.

Charlie hung his head. "Yes."

"And you didn't show it to me. For a whole week. You let me think all along our son had killed himself?"

"I couldn't, Gabby. I was scared to. It would have brought everything out."

"Everything? Everything that is more important than our son?" Her eyes became bright with anger. She slapped him. Charlie didn't make a move to defend himself. She hit him again, a flood of emotion rushing into her cheeks. *"How, Charlie?* How could you have held such a thing from me?"

"I'm sorry, Gabby. I was scared. Scared for what it meant. I would give everything to take it back."

"Where is this sneaker? What did you do with it, Charlie?"

"I had to give it to Sherwood. It's evidence. But you know what it proves, don't you? This proves he wasn't alone up there."

"I know," Gabby said, raising her fist to strike him again. "I know . . ." Then, lowering it, tears staining her cheeks: "Our *son,* Charlie . . . Our poor son."

She fell into his arms, sobbing, her tiny fists coiled against him, and he clutched her, tighter than he had ever held a thing in his life.

"Don't hate me," he said. "Don't hate me." He couldn't bear to lose her too.

"I don't," she said into him, her tears on his shirt. "I don't." She lifted her head, eyes shining. "Our son is here. I can feel him, Charlie. I can feel him in this room."

"I can feel him too," Charlie said. Then he choked up, realizing that whatever had befallen Evan—his innocent, only son— had been aimed at him. Had been meant to hurt *him.* "I'm so sorry. I'm so sorry, Evan . . ."

He sat down at the table, like a mound of broken bones. He was sobbing too.

"There was a note," he said, drawing in a breath. "In Evan's shoe. I didn't give it to them." He ran over to the chest. He dug through one of the folders in the bottom drawer and came out with it, and brought it to her.

She read it. Then put it down on the table.

The handwritten scrawl read: *"Music's over now, Charlie. Want to know how it all ends?"*

Gabby's eyes shook with ire. "Who would do this to us, Charlie? I want to kill these people."

"I need to show this to Sherwood," he said. "And to Jay."

"No, no," Gabby said, holding his arm. "They don't have to see this."

"They do. It's possible that—"

"No." Her tone was adamant, but there was a gentleness to it too. She placed her hand on top of his and gave him a soft smile. "What is left for us, Charlie? You know this as well as me. It's over for us. Your brother has everything. Everything we have not. Yesterday, he could have died as well. For *this*? For whatever *we* have brought him? No. This is our business, Charlie, these people. Our fate. Let him be free of this."

It took a moment for him to completely understand. And it scared him. "No, it's *my* fate, Gabby. You have to get out of here too."

"No." Her hand was still on his and she squeezed. "We both know there's nowhere for me to go." She brushed his hair away and put her hand on his face. "I'm sorry, Charlie, what I just did. You are my husband and I stay with you, whatever fate has in store. You ask me what I want? Okay. What I want is to know the truth, Charlie. To hear it from them. The real truth about my son. What I want is the one chance to look the person who did this to him in the eye. Who made me feel like my

boy was crazy. Who sent this to you—our son's shoe—as a trophy, to torture us. I want to show them that we are not animals, Charlie. To make us suffer this way. This is all I want now. Nothing more. You see? What else is left for us?"

Charlie's hair fell around his face like a shroud. He knew she was right. Their time was up. He wouldn't put Jay at risk. It was *their* fate. He squeezed her hand. It was trembling, but at the same time, it was strong too—like the light in her eyes. *You are wrong, Gabby,* he was thinking, *there is something else we have left, one thing no one can take from us.*

"My whole life." He gazed at her. "Has been a tale of wrong choices. All the drugs and my time on the road. How I threw away the one chance I had. All of them wrong. All but *one* . . ."

Tenderly, he wrapped his palm around her hand.

He kissed her. It had been years since they really kissed. Felt in their hearts the charge of what had brought them together.

"You couldn't help it," Gabby said, placing her head gently on his chest. "You were sick, Charlie. Evan was sick."

"No, I *could* help it," Charlie said. "I could."

He pulled away and picked up the note. He read it again, and for the first time in a long time, years maybe, he felt perfectly clear. He said, "I can never make it right, not now. But I know what I can do to make it end."

CHAPTER SIXTY-FIVE

Sherwood's call caught me just as I was coming back from a late-afternoon jog along the shore.

His tone sounded peremptory. "I have a few things . . ."

I sat down on a bench near my hotel. "I'm listening."

"I got some word back on your brother's old girlfriend. Her full name was Sherry Ann Frazier. She did live in Michigan. In a town called Redmond. On the Upper Peninsula."

"Michigan." Charlie was right!

"Apparently, she was killed eight days

ago. Her body was found in her home by her daughter when she arrived for a visit. She ran a small bakery in town and was separated from her husband. She lived out in the boonies by herself so no one caught a glimpse of anything suspicious. Nor was there any knowledge of anyone who would want to do her harm."

"So they don't even know if it was committed by a man or a woman?" I asked, wondering if Susan Pollack had done it or someone else.

"No." Sherwood exhaled. "They don't. But something did come up you might find interesting."

"Okay . . ."

"I asked a Detective Douglas up there if there were any distinguishing signatures that might fit into our own case profiles. Like with Zorn or Greenway or Evan, if you know what I mean."

I said, "You're talking *eyes,* I assume, right?"

He didn't respond right away, but his silence suggested I was on the mark. "At first he had no clue what I might be talking about. Then, ten minutes later, he called back. It seems the coroner there *had* found something worth mentioning."

My heart rate picked back up. "And what was that?"

"The victim was wearing a single contact lens. In her right eye."

"Only her *right* eye?" I asked. I wasn't sure what sounded so strange about that. The woman was beaten and repeatedly stabbed. She'd probably fought for her life. The other lens could've fallen out at any time.

"That's right," Sherwood said. "Just the right. But that's not what was interesting . . . According to everyone there, Sherry Ann Frazier didn't wear contact lenses. They even checked with a doctor in town. Her vision was fine. She didn't even wear glasses . . ."

My heart came to a stop. One lens. An eye! *Watch!* "Jesus, Sherwood, you know what this means . . . ?"

"Before you tell me what I already know, doc, I asked another detective up in Jenner to check in on Susan Pollack for me." The gravity began to deepen in his voice. "Just to make sure she was still there."

"And was she?"

"No. The gate was up blocking the driveway. A couple of days' worth of mail and newspapers was in the mailbox."

"You know why, Sherwood, don't you?" My blood began to rush like rapids. "Because she's *here*! She's here, and she's not alone. You know that, right?"

"Yeah, I know that, doc," Sherwood said resignedly. "Look, I worked it out with a few friends to keep a heads-up out there for her car. I can't have her arrested—you understand that, right? So far we can't prove she's done anything wrong. But I can damn well have her brought in. And let her know that we're onto her."

"Thanks. And what about Charlie and Gabby, Sherwood?" They were exposed. I felt a drumming of alarm.

He sighed. "Don't worry about them. I have a car watching their apartment. Twenty-four/seven. I'm actually handling the late shift on that. I'm heading home now."

"Okay, *thanks,* Sherwood. Thanks."

"One last thing . . . ," the detective said, and took a long pause. "You know those chickens Susan Pollack was raising behind the house?"

"Yeah," I replied, wondering why he would bring them up. "Her buddies . . ."

"The detective I sent up there said he found them. Apparently they're all dead. Throats cut. You know what that means, don't you, doc?"

"Yeah." I felt a shiver travel through me. "I know what it means."

It meant whatever Susan Pollack was planning, she wasn't planning on going back there again.

CHAPTER SIXTY-SIX

After we hung up, I remained on the bench, staring out over the cliffs, sure that something terrible was about to happen.

Cooley. Greenway. Charlie's old girlfriend in Michigan. Zorn.

Evan.

It was like this whole thing had been some kind of long, orchestrated countdown leading directly to Charlie. And if Susan Pollack was there—an "if," but one I felt sure about—it meant whatever the countdown was leading to was happening now.

I had to warn Charlie and Gabby about this.

"Dude!"

I looked up, shaken from my thoughts, and saw Dev, the panhandler.

He was in his usual worn Seahawks cap, the same old woolen plaid shirt over his straggly carpenter's pants, with beat-up sneakers. "How's it going, Jay?" He lit up a smoke.

This time, his overly familiar use of my name rubbed me the wrong way. And anyway, he was about the last person I needed to deal with right then. I realized how foolish it had been to make him a part of what was going on. I shrugged, barely meeting his gaze. "Just watching the birds."

"The birds are gone, I hear. Cleared out everywhere. Used to be all over the damn place . . . Now look at them. Like every-thing around here. Gone. Maybe they got a sixth sense or something . . . So, hey, I was wondering, you ever find that dude?"

I shook my head. "No, I didn't." Then I remembered I still owed him some money. I reached in my pocket. I wasn't even sure if he had followed through or not.

"Nah . . ." He waved me off. "Save it, man." He took a drag off his cigarette. "You gave me enough already. I didn't do much for it. Anyway, I'm cutting town."

The guy was just being friendly, but he was the last thing I needed right now. Anyway, I'd brought it on myself. "Leaving?" I tried to act surprised and looked around. "All this?"

"Yeah." He laughed. "Paradise, huh? Isn't that what they say? Look around, Jay. Nothing but busted dreams around here. Anyway, my reasons for relocation here are coming to an end."

Reasons for his relocation. I tried to read the smile upon his face. "Where you heading?"

"East." He shrugged. "Who knows, maybe New York."

That surprised me. "I'm from New York," I said.

"That right?" Dev grinned, one as wrinkled as his trousers. This gave me the uneasy feeling that I was telling him something he already knew. "Maybe I'll look you up there." He smiled.

Something in his slate-colored eyes locked on mine. He was making me uncomfortable, and what I needed to think about was what Sherwood had just told me, not him. "Maybe you will."

The guy just stood there for a while, like a bent stick, his clothes ripped and way too big for him, and took another drag on his butt. The conversation had gone on about as long as it was meant to.

"Well, adios," I said. "I have to get back. I wish you luck."

I was about to put out my hand; then I hesitated. He didn't seem to want it anyway. He just smiled at me with an odd steadiness, which at first I thought was just the sum of the million differences between us but later realized was something far more.

He took a final drag off the cigarette and tossed it on the path. He rubbed it out with his sneaker.

"See you around, doc."

CHAPTER SIXTY-SEVEN

He backed down the pathway with a wave. I watched him go, his hands in his pockets, stopping a couple along the way to hit them up for a little cash. He pocketed some change and, pleased, seemed to look my way once more. Then he disappeared around the bend.

That remark about back east—*Maybe I'll look you up there*—didn't sit well with me at all.

I'd let things go way beyond where they should've.

I glanced at my watch—it was going on seven P.M. I thought about calling home but didn't want to worry anyone. I figured I'd shower and change and head over to Charlie's. Check out the protection Sherwood had arranged for them.

A nervousness ground in my stomach, and it took maybe thirty seconds until it hit me just what it was.

What Dev had said as he walked away. *See you around, doc.*

My head suddenly throbbed. I wasn't sure, but I couldn't recall ever telling him I was a doctor.

I sat there, going back over my three interactions with him. The first time we met, in my first few days of being there, he had come up to me, asking for a handout. For Veterans Day. *Every day is Veterans Day when you're looking for something to eat! You're in my office, brother.*

"Brother," "doc" . . . Maybe they were both just similar expressions of familiarity.

The next time he'd been cozier, asked what I was reading. End of Days, *huh? Now there's a book I can surely relate to. My life's resembled the End of Days for years!*

Or had *I* asked him how things were going? I couldn't recall.

But if he had wanted to find me, I wasn't hard to spot.

If he'd been somehow interested in Charlie.

I was taking my brother around, getting involved with the police. I'd even accompanied Sherwood when we went to see Susan Pollack.

And then to Pelican Bay!

Suddenly my heart started racing. I ramped back to all the things Dev had said to me. One in particular hit home: Days ago, when I gave him the thirty bucks and joked about his getting out of town, he'd come back that he had been recently.

Out of town.

This time my heart jumped like a needle indicating a seismic tremor.

Michigan. That was where he said he'd been. Seeing an old friend.

In Michigan.

Where Sherry Ann Frazier had been killed.

Suddenly that tremor rocketed around inside me like an 8.0!

I put my hands to the sides of my head, desperately trying to recall the voice I had heard on the phone in my hotel room, the man who had threatened me. The one who had left the lit cigarette outside my door. My heart was pounding now. *Yes, it could be.* I'd never even thought in that direction. Why would I have? But there was a similar sort of accent. It was possible.

Oh my God. It was all right there in front of me.

I was leaning forward, elbows on my knees, my head throbbing, and I realized I was looking directly at the walk path.

At the butt Dev had just put out.

I scanned down the pathway, searching for him, but there were only a few stray pedestrians in sight, not him.

I bent down and picked it up between my fingers.

My stomach started to climb its way up my throat.

Salem. Salem was the same brand as the one left outside my door!

I started to feel the sweats come over me, recalling those horrible images of Sherry Ann Frazier in Michigan. The police pictures of Walter Zorn strangled. The eye carved gruesomely into his tongue.

Could Dev be the one who had called me? Allied with Susan Pollack?

With Houvnanian.

Jesus, I told myself, *calm down. This could all just be your own crazy paranoia, Jay. Dev could have just as easily bummed that butt from someone down the road.* I stood up and looked down the path again. I almost felt him watching me, observing me coming to the conclusion. Enjoying this! I wasn't quite sure what to do next. Call Sherwood?

It would just be another of those count- less uncorroborated fears: Susan Pollack at the rock with Evan; the black or dark blue Kia outside Charlie's apartment; my brother's thirty-year-old lyrics echoed by Houvnanian.

This time I needed something more. Something real.

And suddenly I realized that I might have something more. Something that could pin Dev to this.

I wrapped the butt in some paper and headed back to my room.

I hurried, my heart beating rapidly now. I looked back around, like he was watch- ing me out there. Toying with me.

I got to my wing of the motel and bounded up the outside flight of stairs. I hurried down the hall and jammed the card key into the lock. It took a couple of times for it to open and I let the door shut behind me, switching the metal bolt, just to be sure.

I went over to the bed and took the book off my night table.

Greenway's book.

I flipped it open, skimming to where I wanted to go. My blood certain that this was it.

I located the insert of photographs. All the shots of Houvnanian and his other conspirators. The evidence photos: the guns, the knives, bloody clothing. Their VW van.

I'd been through them all before.

I searched until I found the photos taken on the ranch. There were two or three of the "family" all gathered around—drifters, hippies, outcasts, as they were in their days there. Making music. Working the farm. Gethsemane. Their paradise, before their world collapsed.

One shot was of a group sitting out on boulders they had cleared from a field. The same one I had searched for my brother's face only days before.

I recognized a younger Susan Pollack. She was there.

As were Sarah Strasser and Carla Jean Blue, who had participated in the killings.

And some other names I recognized.

But no Dev. He wasn't there!

I skipped a few photos ahead. There was another group shot of them, this time clearing brush for their vegetable garden. I'd read that there was always a lot of work that had to be done there. Two of the gals were raking soil. Carla Jean again. And Tel. And another guy in a long ponytail, planting, who looked vaguely familiar. But when I checked, his name was Scott Oulette.

It wasn't him.

Three or four others were standing around holding tools. None of them even resembled Dev.

Damn.

I was about to give up when behind them I noticed someone perched on a small, dilapidated tractor.

My breath stopped. It was like a hand had put its icy fingers around my heart— and squeezed. I bore in on the face.

And I felt my blood about to explode.

It was the same person, except his hair was long then, a thin dark beard on his chin, wearing a bandana. He was grinning innocently, one arm on the wheel, but I could see it, as clearly as I could see the faces of my own kids when they were young.

I looked among the credits for a name.

And I read it twice, just to make sure I had seen it correctly.

Devin Dietz (on tractor).

I put down the book and just sat there for a while, everything slowly sinking in. I knew I had to call. I fumbled in my pocket for my phone. I located my previous call—to Sherwood—and pressed *Redial*.

He answered on the second ring, sighing when he saw who it was from. "What's going on there, doc?"

"Susan Pollack's accomplice," I said, trying to hold my voice together. "*I know who it is!*"

CHAPTER SIXTY-EIGHT

Sherwood grabbed his gun off the kitchen counter and strapped on his holster. He'd made a vow, a few days back, he wasn't sure precisely when. Maybe it was after Pelican Bay. Or when he'd heard about the lyrics to Charlie's song. Or maybe it went all the way back to that dollar bill in Thomas Greenway's stomach.

Or maybe back to the doc asking what that new liver had been for . . .

If it was going to end in a fight, he'd be the one to end it.

He put on his jacket and touched the picture of Dorrie good-bye, pressing his fingers to her smile, just as he did every time he went out on the job.

"The guy's a panhandler," the doc had said, excited. "Near my hotel. He's pushed his way into my life. I didn't realize it—but for the past few days, I think he's been stalking me."

"Stay where you are," Sherwood had instructed him. "Whatever you do, don't leave. I'll be right there."

It was time to end this thing—and now.

He headed out the kitchen door. His Camry was parked in the drive outside. He had about a fifteen-minute ride from where he lived to the Cliffside Suites motel. He needed to warn the patrol car he had stationed outside Charlie's apartment to be on alert, but he decided he might as well do it from the car, on his way.

He crossed around to the driver's side, this weird sensation flashing through him: how Jay Erlich had wormed his way into his life, past his defenses. It had been a long time since he had let anyone in. One day there would be very little he would miss in this life. His friends had all moved on, down to San Diego or Arizona. The people he really loved were gone. But this past week . . . He chuckled. Something had awakened inside him. Something he hadn't felt in a long while. Something vital. Over people he had never even heard of or given a rat's ass about just a week before.

Funny, he thought to himself, *how these things go. You never know what's really important to you, until—*

As he reached for the door handle, he heard a rustle from behind him.

Then he felt the most excruciating shock of pain cleave deep into his back.

The next thing he knew he felt the pavement, cold and firm against his face. Something sharp and body-splitting deep in his back. The air rushed out of him. He didn't know what had happened, only that he couldn't move and that it was bad. He tried to inhale, but it was like there was a hole in his air sac, his breaths leaking out of his back.

Turn over.

Before he could, he heard a loud grunt and felt another bone-splitting blow bury into his upper back. The pain almost sheared him in two. He tried to reach for it. He tried to power his brain through the pain—What had happened? What was there to do?—with whatever clarity he still possessed.

He had to warn the doc. He was in trouble too.

That was all.

But he couldn't move. A warm, coppery taste was on his tongue and he saw blood trickle down the driveway past his face into a growing pool. *Damn.* He tried to force himself up, like an animal fighting for one last breath—one last rush—but then another cracking jolt cleaved through him, his spine splitting in two.

"*Ahh . . . ,*" he groaned deeply. He reared back around and saw, almost with a glint of amusement, what appeared to be the wooden handle of an ax.

Chickens, he thought, and lay his head back down. *Damn.*

"*Don't . . .*" He heard a woman's voice. It was more of a plea than a command. His mind was fuzzy. "Please, don't. We told you to stay out, you dumb bastard. If you had . . ."

There was another, spine-splitting blow. No longer pain, just numbness and cold. All the air sucked out of his body from his back.

He felt sad to have let the doc down. Not to have finished what he vowed to complete.

He knew it was time to let go, but as he did, something else came into his drifting mind.

He struggled forward, like a snake cut in half continuing to slide on his belly. His fingers gripped the pavement, now like sand. Each small measure forward consuming most of what was left of his strength.

And he crawled, down the driveway, every inch labored and life-emptying, like a strong current fighting against him, keeping him away.

No, not this time, it wouldn't . . .

He looked up to the shining, sunlit sight. He could almost touch it. Just a few more feet.

Please . . .

Sherwood opened his eyes. The driveway was gone, and instead of asphalt, soft leaves and moss brushed against his face. Green and cool now. The soothing tide of the river felt good against him.

Just stay with me, son. I'll be there.

Through the haze he saw the blue craft up ahead. He kept forcing himself, pushing against the current, against the dissipation of everything inside him. To get there. "Please, please, please, son, please . . ."

He reached out, desperation in his voice.

He made it. He felt the smooth, slick exterior of the fiberglass hull. The bright white stripe. His heart in panic, he turned it over and looked inside.

There he was. Kyle, all huddled up inside. Smiling at him. In his helmet. In the River Tours T-shirt they had bought him at the check-in station. The greatest joy he had ever felt coursing through him. Welcoming him.

"It's okay, Dad," Kyle said, reaching to hug him. "I'm okay. I'm here."

CHAPTER SIXTY-NINE

I hung up and waited, sitting on the bed, my right leg bobbing crazily. I didn't know what to do.

I'd be a liar if I said I wasn't afraid. The guy was stalking me. Mocking me, in the same way Houvnanian had. He was saying good-bye. *My reasons for relocation here are coming to an end.* What reasons? With Susan Pollack unaccounted for, it could only mean that whatever they had planned for Charlie and Gabby was going to happen soon.

I grabbed my phone again and punched

in my brother's number. I let it ring six or seven times—*C'mon, Charlie, Gabby, pick up!*—but no one answered. Finally the message recording came on. Gabby. "Please leave a number . . . We will get back to you." *Shit.*

I didn't know if they even checked these things.

"Listen, Charlie . . . ," I blurted after the beep. "It's Jay. I need to talk to you about what's going on! It's vitally important you call me back. *Please . . ."*

I hung up, not feeling good at all. Thirty seconds went by, and it felt to me like ten minutes. I must've glanced at my watch three times. They wanted me out. They wanted to face this alone. Something could already have happened! It was driving me crazy. I didn't know what to do.

Only that, in that moment, I knew I couldn't wait for Sherwood another second. I had to do something. Why wouldn't they answer? It was possible, even likely, that while I sat there, something was going down right then.

I threw on my jeans and a shirt and grabbed my car keys off the desk. I opened the door and headed out, phone in hand. I figured I'd let Sherwood know what I was doing on the way.

I never saw a thing, only felt the impact of a two-handed swing from the side, as if a baseball bat had slammed into the side of my head.

I fell against the wall.

"Jeez, doc, where you headed so fast? You and I still have some things to talk about, no?"

The next blow struck me solidly in the face, the butt end of a large gun. I staggered backward through the half-closed door, attempting to catch my balance.

"You eastern folk . . ." The voice was like a faraway echo in my brain. "Always in such a big rush to go everywhere . . ."

The third shot almost knocked me down.

I was pushed back into my room, my head completely dazed, my legs rubber.

"Sorry, doc."

He hit me in the stomach, sending me to a knee, and when I looked up, it was as if every bit of air had left my lungs and I heaved in desperation to draw a breath.

Dev was in the doorway. He let the door

close tight behind him with a loud and very foreboding click.

This was bad.

Through my haze, Dev was grinning at me. "Maybe I'll just take you up on that invitation a little earlier than you planned. That fine with you, doc?"

I could make out the gun in his hands, heavy and oversize, sending a tremor of fear shooting through me. My car keys were on the floor and he bent down and picked them up, catching them once in his palm. "I don't know, I feel like we still have a few things to hash out. No reason to rush out now."

I put a hand to my face. Warm blood streamed down the side. My brain was numb and clouded, but not so clouded that I didn't realize I was in real trouble here. I flashed to Zorn and Greenway. And that woman from Michigan, her body all cut up. A chill shot through me. "What are you doing, Dev?"

"C'mon, Jay." He laughed. "I may not have the fancy degree and all, but don't play me for a complete fool." He went over to the bed and picked up the copy of

Greenway's book I'd left there, opened to the photo of him on the tractor. "Man, I was a handsome bugger back then. A little lost, perhaps, but, hey, we all were. They called me Mal . . ." He tossed the book back on the bed and shook his head at me sympathetically. "Jeez, I couldn't have laid it out for you any prettier, could I, Jay?"

I pushed up onto my feet and tried to run at him—all I could think to do—but he caught me on the side of the head with the gun butt, a blast ringing out this time and something thudding into the wall above the bed, creating a quarter-size hole.

I crumpled onto the floor, my head exploding.

"Damn, doc." He chuckled, wide-eyed. "This thing really works. You know, it's been a while."

I flashed to Sherwood. He was on his way. "You don't need to do this, Dev. I just called the police. They'll be here any second."

"The police . . ." He didn't exactly seem worried. "If by 'police' you mean your ol' buddy Sherwood . . . *Hmmph,* I'm afraid I have to inform you, doc . . . He's just a shade under the weather at the moment."

Sherwood. He was my only hope.

That's when my fear really began to escalate. I knew now there was no one coming to the rescue. I was going to have to fight for my life.

Now.

I wasn't a small guy. I'd played lacrosse in college. I kept in shape—*forty-year-old shape.* Like eighteen holes of golf or thirty minutes on the treadmill. Not fight-for-your-life kind of shape. Dev wasn't exactly Rambo, but I knew the things he had done.

And my head was bursting.

"What are you going to do to me?" I asked, scanning around the room for something I could use.

"What am I gonna do? That's a really good question, doc. One you probably should've worried about a little earlier in the game. Like when I asked you nicely to get back on that plane and go on home. Or before you had to visit Russell. Now it's just a little late for asking me that, don't you think? Now you're, like, part of the music. Know what I mean?"

He stepped back, drawing the curtains closed. The room became dark and a chill shot through me.

My gaze swung to the night table and I grabbed a lamp there and lunged at him with everything I had.

It was a desperate act, and the electrical cord caught in the wall. Dev easily fended it off. With a backhanded swing, he drove the gun butt across my face and sent me reeling again, blood filling up my mouth.

Like an animal, he took the same lamp, yanking it free from the wall, and cracked it into the side of my head. I felt my eyes roll back. *No, Jay, you can't let him win. If you do, you're dead,* echoed in my brain. I tried to get up again, thinking I could bull-rush him and take him down to the floor, but I was like a bloodied, beaten animal about to be put out of its misery, everything reeling and slipping away.

I suddenly found myself on my knees.

"What to do . . . ?" He shook his head and chirped. "Just what to do . . . ?" He spun around the desk chair and sat, facing me.

My brain struggled to clear.

He picked up the remote from the desk and turned on the TV. It was *Everybody Loves Raymond.* It was bizarre. I recognized it instantly. The one when Ray and

Robert go out golfing when Deborah thinks he's working on his novel . . .

He turned the volume up high.

He sat there and shrugged, his steely eyes glinting with this remote, mirthless smile. "Oh, who needs *this*," he said, and tucked the gun into his belt and came back out with a six-inch blade. "I think you already know, doc, there are people who seem to think I'm quite the artist with this thing."

I tried to stagger up one last time and he just pushed me with his boot, sending me down to the floor.

"I truly wish you'd just kept that cute little nose of yours out of things, doc . . . I kinda like you, I really do." He kicked me over, faceup. I tried to push my way up one more time, but he pressed his foot onto my chest. My strength was gone. There was a look of inevitability in his coal-black eyes. "But I guess it's a little late for the big show of affection now."

I saw the blade dance before me and felt a pain across my cheek, blood trickling into my hands.

"Whoops!" he crowed.

Then with a gleam in his eye, he dug the blade into the nape of my neck, under my chin. A spasm of absolute terror sped down my spine. My eyes shook with tears, tears of just how very stupid I had been. How I'd stepped into something I had no business in. And now I was about to pay for it with my life.

"You killed them," I said, glaring with whatever strength I still had. "Zorn. Greenway."

"Ancient history, doc. What we oughta be a bit more focused on is what's going to happen to you."

"And Evan," I said, glaring into his dull, animal eyes.

At that, he sort of chuckled and shrugged impassively. "Let's face it, doc, it wasn't like we were robbing the world of a future Nobel Prize winner, don't you think? But we did think it might get a rise out of his old man."

A last wave of anger went off in me, and I lunged for his throat. He hit me in the face with the blunt end of the blade and his fist, darkness rolling in front of my eyes. When I opened them again, he had the blade under my chin.

"You know the score here . . . I give this blade a little twist into your carotid artery, you last what, ten, fifteen seconds, before

irreversible brain damage begins to oc-
cur? Thirty, maybe, at the most, before
you bleed out."

Yes, those were about the numbers.

"Now this may hurt a little, doc . . ." He
laughed. "You know, I bet you've probably
said that to people a thousand times."

He seized me by the collar. I was listing
in and out of consciousness, trying to will
myself not to give in.

"Your brother and his wife are going to
be dead soon."

His words reverberated through my
brain like far-off echoes, echoes that filled
me with remorse that I couldn't do anything about it. And dread.

And sadness. For Kathy and Maxie and
Sophie. Knowing I would never see any of
them again. Thinking of the agonizing way
they were going to hear of how I died. Probably believing I'd lost my mind out here.

"Oh, and one last thing. You better listen closely, doc . . ." He raised my face, so
close to his I could almost feel his smile,
the intensity of his eyes.

And as I passed out, he said the words
that turned my last nightmare into an even
greater hell.

CHAPTER SEVENTY

Officer Tim Riesdorfer had been on the job only a little more than a year now, but that was long enough to know he hadn't been handed the plum assignment that night.

He sat in his patrol car down the block from 609 Division Street, watching the ground floor apartment on the other side of the courtyard.

Maybe he'd pissed off his sarge by being a little overzealous with that tourist in town the other night, catching him making an illegal turn and not liking the guy's attitude and all—and showing him who was boss by slapping on the cuffs and threatening to throw his ass in jail.

Okay, he knew he got a little jumpy now and then. I mean, he'd spent eighteen months in 'Stan, and if that didn't make you jumpy, nothing would. But being pulled off his regular assignment and told to sit here all night by the tracks and watch over this rat trap . . . As what? A favor for some coroner's detective. Not even a real cop.

All he was told to do was watch out for this car—and if he saw it, to radio in.

Not even go for the arrest!

He glanced at the two APBs on the passenger seat. One was for the car: navy Kia wagon with the license plate 657 E4G.

The other was for a woman, Susan Jane Pollack. A photo from DMV. She looked like she was around fifty. Short, light brown hair. Not pretty. So far he hadn't seen anyone down here but two teenagers, winding their way into the woods, most likely on their way to get high.

By all means, light one up on me!

Suddenly something caught his attention. A vehicle turning into the building, into the carport.

He rolled down the window, focusing on

the model and the plates. Nah, it was a Honda. A person stepped out. One motherfucking, heavyset Latino, not a woman at all, who went around the car and opened the hatch. He watched the dude head into the courtyard with an armful of groceries, climb the outside stairs to his second-floor apartment.

Hot shit, Timmy boy.

He heard Dispatch send out a call for an officer to be sent to 407 Hilltop. A domestic dispute. He was only a couple of blocks away. He could be on the scene in seconds.

Anything was better than this.

He went to ask permission to investigate when suddenly there was a rapping on his passenger window.

It was a woman. Dark glasses and a kind of baseball cap down over her eyes. Her short hair barely peeking through. She was trying to ask him something, indicating for him to lower his window.

He did, just slightly, leaning forward. "Sorry, I'm off duty, ma'am . . ."

She asked, "Do you know where 730 Division would be?"

That was just down the street, in the other

direction, which Tim Riesdorfer was about to tell her when his eye went from her face to the photo on the seat, and he felt his whole body jolt like when his convoy was ambushed as he noticed the slightest resemblance in her eyes.

Instinctively he reached for his gun, leaning toward her, but the only thing that came out of his mouth was *"Hey . . ."*

The initial shot burst through his jaw and out the side of his neck, blood suddenly all over his chest. No pain, no panic, just this sense that he was really, really confused, and he turned toward his lowered window in the direction of the shooter . . .

The second shot was only a bright yellow spark that made his world colorless forever.

CHAPTER SEVENTY-ONE

I blinked.

My eyes opened.

I tried to turn, my head seemingly held in a restraint. My arms and legs were numb. My thoughts completely blurred. I ratcheted my eyes from side to side.

As I tried to get my bearings, I heard a voice:

"We'll be arriving at the hospital in five minutes."

How was I alive?

There was a mask pressed over my face, oxygen flowing. I stretched my eyes and saw a green-clad EMT, a woman. Red hair tied back in a ponytail. I felt an IV tube coming out of my arm. My vitals beeping back on a monitor. The EKG needle going crazy.

"You were attacked," the med tech said. "You're on the way to the hospital. Just hold on . . ."

Through the haze, I strained to recall what had happened.

I remembered running back to my room, looking frantically for something. A book? After that, everything was a complete blank. I felt a stinging pain on my neck and a throbbing on my palm. I lifted it slightly to look. It was wrapped in gauze.

Then it hit me, there was something I needed to say . . .

Something important.

"I just want to prepare you," the EMT said. "When we get to the hospital, we're going to wheel you into the ER. They may want to ask you some questions there, if you can concentrate. About what happened, who did this to you."

I know, I said to myself. *I know all this*.

I suddenly remembered. *I'm a doctor . . .*

My brain was buzzing. I tried to focus. There was something I needed to tell them.

Andrew Gross

Was that it?

No, it was something much more vital, but my mind was totally clouded and whatever it was bobbed farther and farther away on a wave of unconsciousness, drifting out to sea . . .

I could hear by the beep that my heart rate was slow and my blood pressure was falling. *You can't let me die.*

I heard the siren and the ambulance swerved into a turn. I tried to speak and latched on to the tech's arm.

"Don't worry," she said, "we'll be there in a minute. You're a lucky man your door was left open and people found you when they did . . ."

Door left open . . . ?

I suddenly saw Dev, the knife at my throat. Saying good-bye to Kathy and the kids. Knowing I was about to die.

And then the words he had said as I slipped into darkness.

Words that jarred me all over again—my mind sliding backward; my pulse starting to dive; the beeps growing louder and louder as I conjured up Dev's face, his chilling smile, and his knife dancing before my eyes:

"We've got your son."

CHAPTER SEVENTY-TWO

I woke again just as we arrived at the hospital. My head was still in a daze, and woozy.

The EMTs briefed the ER doctor and a nurse they had radioed ahead to. "Patient's name is Erlich, Jay . . . Lacerations on his hand and arm. Cranial trauma. Blood pressure one sixty over eighty. Heart rate one thirty . . . He's been drifting in and out of consciousness . . ."

"Okay, sir," the Latino ER nurse said confidently to me, "we're going to take care of you now . . ."

They eased me out of the ambulance

and onto a gurney. I grabbed the ER doctor by the arm. Even my own voice was a reeling echo. "I'm a doctor. I need a policeman."

"We're all aware of that. You can be sure a detective will be here shortly. In the meantime we're just gonna check you out."

They wheeled me inside the ER, a nurse stabilizing the IV line alongside. I knew my brain was still swollen from being beaten, and most likely, I had a concussion. And multiple lacerations. Even dazed, I knew they'd be sending in an investigative team when they checked me out. That was standard procedure.

I still didn't even know what I was doing alive.

Suddenly I flashed to what Dev had said as I blacked out.

About Max.

I had to let Kathy know.

I tried to force myself up, tugging against the binds. "Hold on there, sir." The ER nurse restrained me. "We'll have a room set up for you as soon as we can check you out."

"No, no, you don't understand . . ."

I was seized by an onrush of panic. My

mind was still in a haze. I had no idea how much time had elapsed since Dev had attacked me. He had told me Charlie and Gabby were next. They might even be dead by now. Or any minute, as I lay there.

I grabbed the nurse's wrist and tried to force myself up. Even words were difficult. *"My brother, I need to call him . . ."*

"Someone from the detective's unit is on his way," the nurse answered me. "They'll be here soon."

Soon? Soon wouldn't work. I need someone now!

I fell back, still numb, and they wheeled me into a hallway in what appeared to be the triage area. "We're just going to leave you here for a moment while a station opens up. It'll only be a minute. Then we'll check you out . . ."

Slowly, I felt my wits beginning to come back to me. My head throbbed and my recollection of the beating was a blur, but I knew I couldn't wait around for some detective to arrive. And then have to explain the whole thing to him. Dev had said my brother and Gabby were in danger. And I needed to find out about my son. Fear and worry seemed to cut through the haze.

I needed to do something—*now*.

I saw that I was alone outside a line of curtained treatment rooms. The two EMTs were no longer around. The ER nurse had gone to get an admitting form. A few patients were crowded around the admitting station, clamoring to see a doctor.

I had to get to a phone.

I raised myself up. My head felt about twice its normal size. I was still wearing the clothes I had on when I was beaten, and there was blood dried all over me. Every minute I waited was a minute Charlie and Gabby might be in trouble. My thoughts suddenly flashed to Sherwood—what had happened to him?

But my first priority was to call Kathy about Max.

I pulled myself up to a sitting position, steadying myself on the gurney rails, trying to determine how I was going to explain everything to a new detective.

That was when I knew I had to leave.

Impaired or not, I had to find out about Max. And I had to go to Charlie's.

I looked around and, for that second, couldn't spot any of the medical team who had wheeled me in. Or the EMTs. I disengaged the IV, slipping the needle out of my forearm with a sharp sting; grabbed a sheet off the gurney; and dabbed away a spot of blood. A Hispanic mother and son who'd been injured seemed to be occupying the attention of the front desk.

I pushed off the gurney and headed in the direction I had come from, fully expecting to hear someone shouting, "*Stop! Stop!*" any second, but no one did. I thought about going to the front desk and calling the police, but whether my reasoning was rational or flawed, the voice inside my head kept on telling me I had to get out of there now.

I ran toward the exit.

CHAPTER SEVENTY-THREE

I can still see the police car out there," Charlie said, peeking through the curtains at the vehicle in the shadows across the street.

He and Gabby had sat around all afternoon and into the night, looking through old photos of their families and Evan as a kid. They hadn't told anyone about what they had found. Evan's sneaker. They had decided that this was *their* fate to bear. How they wanted this to end. They'd decided not to put anyone else at risk. Especially Jay. This was where all the reversals of their ruined lives had led them. Charlie strummed a few of his songs on the busted Stratocaster. The splintered neck to his acoustic guitar sat on the mantel above the fireplace. The broken body leaned against the wall, like a boat without a mast, a reminder of all his busted dreams.

Periodically he stirred and jumped up to the window, whenever they heard a noise outside.

"It's just someone passing by," Gabby would say.

"He's still just sitting out there," Charlie said, parting the curtains.

"Look," Gabby said. She went to show him the album. "Do you remember this?"

The photo was of Evan, Charlie, and her at Hearst Castle, sixty miles up the coast. Evan was sixteen then, already more than six feet and fully grown. That was the last time they had left their town. He still had that innocent, freckled face. The truth was, even at that time, he was already taking his anger out on them, beating up on them, using slurs and ugly names. Threatening to kill them one day. Yet there they were—smiling, a family. The same day they had watched a colony of sea lions on the rocks.

Gabby smiled tenderly. "We had some good times, didn't we, Charlie? We did."

"Something weird is going on out there." He was ignoring her. "The passenger window, it's been down for a while. I can't see anyone in the car. What if something's happened, Gabby? What if something's gone wrong?"

He was ranting, Gabby knew. But this time he actually had something to fear. She went over to the window and looked out too. "Of course, it's dark. The streetlamps are out, this godforsaken place . . . Come back over here and sit with—"

They saw it at the same time. Both their eyes grew wide. They gasped in unison.

A woman. Outside. In a cap pulled down, with her hair barely showing through. Standing there, staring directly at them. Like a ghost had suddenly appeared.

Gabby, whose imagination ran to things like that, screamed.

The woman stood there in the cone of yellow lamplight, smiling at them.

Then, in the next instant, she headed toward the front door.

"Charlie, quick!" Gabby shouted. "She's trying to get in."

Charlie darted to the door just as the woman got there, twisting forcefully on the handle.

"Charlie, make sure it's locked!" Gabby instructed him, her heart flailing.

They heard the handle rattle as she kept tugging on it. Frantically, Charlie clung on to the other end. This wasn't right. They were supposed to wait for instructions. Not here. Even locked, it felt like she might tear the handle off the door.

He looked back at Gabby, his eyes white with fear.

"Who is it, Charlie? Who is that woman?" Gabby screamed.

She had changed. She was only a shadow of what she looked like back then, Charlie thought fearfully. A grotesque shadow. He hadn't seen her in thirty-five years.

But he knew. He knew who she was. And he knew why she was here.

"Gabby, call the police!" Charlie said.

She backed away, immobilized with fear. "I can't, Charlie, I can't! I'm scared."

"It's locked!" he said, trying to reassure her. "She can't get in. *Just call!*"

Suddenly from behind them they heard the clinking sound of glass splintering.

His heart almost climbed through his chest.

Someone was coming in.

Charlie ran around to the kitchen almost like someone reacting to multiple leaks on a sinking ship. He grabbed a chef's knife he had left out on the counter.

A hand had already smashed through the pane and was reaching in, twisting the inside lock.

It opened. *It was too late.*

Charlie lunged at the hand with his knife, but the door thrust open, smacking into him like a linebacker powering him to the floor, the knife clattering off to his side.

A man entered. He and Gabby stared at him in fear, Charlie from the floor. The intruder wore a torn flannel shirt and soiled baggy pants, his hair receding under his cap, with long sideburns and a thick mustache.

"Who are you?" Gabby looked at him with terror. "What are you doing in my house?"

"Get on up, Charlie," the man said, his grin suggesting any resistance was useless. He shut the door behind him. There was a gun in his hand. "Don't go for the knife, guy. You'll ruin all the fun."

Charlie sat there on the floor, transfixed by the blade. He would do it, he thought, *go for it,* try to end it here. But who would protect Gabby? And there were things the man knew that he and Gabby needed to hear.

So he just sat there staring, at what he knew was the end of his life. "Hello, Dev."

CHAPTER SEVENTY-FOUR

I headed out the same doors I had entered—my head still throbbing, my steps
unsure.

I spotted the medical van that had brought
me there parked in front of the entrance. I
looked around for a policeman, at the same
time wondering just how I was going to explain things. A bloodied man, staggering
about, barely coherent. Going on about how
his son was in danger back east. And how
the only detective who could corroborate
his story was possibly dead. How he had to
save his brother and sister-in-law.

How would that go over? It sounded

insane. They would probably just escort me back inside and order a sedative.

I had to do something.

I ran out of the drop-off area and made my way, disoriented, onto the street. I spotted a taxi parked in front of the hospital. I headed toward it, shaking out the cobwebs in my head, trying to remember Charlie's address and what the hell I was going to do when I got there.

I climbed into the back.

"Six-oh-nine Division Street," I told the cabbie. "In Grover Beach."

The driver, a Pakistani, barely even looked at me, putting the car in gear. "Okay, sir . . ."

He pulled a U-ey and headed in the opposite direction. I sank back into the seat. Within seconds, I was clear of the hospital. The craziness of what I was doing was starting to sink in.

I leaned forward. "Do you have a cell phone?" I asked.

"Yes." The driver nodded. "I do."

"Can I borrow it? It's an emergency. I'm a doctor . . ."

The driver turned and actually eyed me for the first time, and warily. Who could blame him? I was disheveled, bloody, and barely coherent. He hesitated, probably wondering if he should pull over and tell me to get the hell out.

"Please, it's a police emergency," I said again. "My son's in danger. I'm a doctor. I need to call my wife."

Something must have convinced him, because after thinking a second, he pulled his phone off the seat next to him and handed it back to me.

"Thank you," I said, grateful, meeting his concerned eyes.

The first call was to Kathy. I could barely punch in the number, I was so nervous and disoriented. Dev had said they had Max. I could barely hold on as I heard it ring.

"Hello?"

"Kath," I shouted as she answered. I saw the clock on the taxi's dashboard. It was eleven P.M. back home.

She heard the disturbance in my voice right away. "Jay, what's wrong?"

"Kath—where's Maxie?" I asked. "Is he okay?"

"Max? I don't know, Jay. He's out at a friend's. He said he was studying. What's wrong?"

"When was the last time you heard from him?" I asked her.

"The last time? I don't know. A couple of hours ago. He said he'd be home by eleven. Why?"

"Kathy, you need to call him," I said to her, "*now.*" My heart was leaping around like a cod in a catch bin. "He could be in trouble. Do it for me, Kathy. *Now.*"

"Jay, you're scaring me. What's going on?"

"I can't tell you right now, but *please,* please, Kathy, just do it. Call him. While I'm on the phone. *Now!*"

"Okay . . . ," she answered tremulously.

I figured she was in bed. Reading. She got up and ran to her phone. The next seconds seemed like an hour to me. My hands were shaking. Like most doctors, I was a guy who didn't rush to assumptions, who always waited for the facts to determine a course of action.

But my mind was rushing to the worst now.

Finally she came back on the line. "There's no answer. Jay, tell me what the hell is going on."

"Kath, I just need you to listen. Call the

police. Tell them to look for him. Tell them where he was. Give them his license plate numbers."

"*Jay!* You're sounding crazy. I don't know the plate numbers. You're scaring me!"

"Kathy, please, just do it, okay! Someone here said they had taken him."

"*Taken him?*" She became apoplectic. "Jay, tell me what's going on!"

"I can't. Kathy, I can't. I'm sorry. Just do it for me. Please. I'm on my way to Charlie's. They could be in danger too. I know how this all sounds. I know it's crazy. But just call the police. Call the house where he was at." I looked at the clock. "You can call me at Charlie's when you know something. Okay? And, Kathy . . ."

I knew I sounded crazy. I also knew I had no idea how the next minutes might turn out. I couldn't say it before, but now I could. And I did. "I love you, honey. And the kids . . ."

All she could say back was, "I love you too, Jay."

I hung up. The driver must have thought I was crazy. "*How long?*"

"Long?" He turned around.

"How much longer until we're there?"

He shook his head; his eyes went wide. "Five, six minutes . . ."

The palm of my right hand was throbbing. I hadn't even noticed it since I left the hospital in such haste. I bit off the end of the tape and began to peel away the gauze, not sure what I would find.

It was covered in antiseptic cream.

I rubbed it on my pants and my heart almost climbed through my throat.

The ugliest cuts were there. Four slash marks dug in the skin—from Dev's blade. Each a kind of a half semicircle.

I had seen them before, but now they were staring back at me. As a gruesome reminder. On my own hand.

An eye!

A feeling of nausea rose up through the waves of pain. My next call was to Sherwood. His cell number was embedded in my head. Dev had made me believe he was in trouble, or even dead, but how could I be sure?

The call went through, his phone rang— two, three times. No one picked up. My pulse buzzed like a bass guitar. *Come on, answer, Sherwood. Please . . .* Now it was five rings! To my dismay, it transferred into voice mail. "You've reached Detective Don Sherwood . . . Please leave your name, a message, and your number. I'll . . ."

My body was flooded by a sensation of dread. He wasn't picking up. Which wasn't good. Dev's mocking smile came into my mind. *If by "police" you mean your ol' buddy Sherwood . . .* He *had* become a friend. And I was both nervous and scared for him.

I struggled through some kind of hurried, rambling message. "Sherwood, it's me. Jay. I've been beaten. By the guy I mentioned. It's after eight. I'm heading to Charlie's now. If you get this message send someone there. *Please, Don . . .* And God, I hope you're all right."

I hung up, pushing back the most horrible feeling something terrible had befallen him. He had said he was on his way. If he had been he would have found me at the motel. The EMTs would have mentioned it.

"I have to make one more call," I told the driver.

This time to Charlie.

His number rang. I let the line ring and ring. Each was like a sharp blade cutting into my heart, taking a piece of me with each unanswered tone.

Where could they be?

No one picked up.

I was starting to get really scared now. And I wasn't sure what to do. I handed the phone back to the driver. The neighborhood began to look familiar. We were on Costa Verde Drive now, only a few blocks from their place. The driver stopped at a light. Each second was like an eternity. He turned on Fourth and started to go up the hill.

"Call the police," I said. "As soon as you drop me off. Tell them to come to that address. Six-oh-nine Division. Apartment two. Tell them there's a possible homicide in progress."

The driver looked at me, scared.

"Just do it," I said. "And I'm sorry. I can't pay you now. I'm staying at the Cliffside Suites. You know it?"

He nodded. I don't think he cared about being paid now.

"My name is Erlich. Ask for me there. I'll leave money. I promise."

We were only a block away, but Division was a one-way street and he'd have to wrap around the block, which I couldn't wait for. I actually saw Charlie's building. It would be shorter if I ran.

"I'm getting out!" I said. "Thank you for the phone. *Now call . . ."* I put my hands on his shoulders and squeezed. "Please . . ."

I jumped out and headed down the darkened street. One side bordered a thicket of trees, the train tracks. I glanced behind me and saw the taxi drive away. I prayed he would follow through. My pace was erratic, my balance off, my brain still woozy. But I had regained my wits now and I prayed I wasn't too late. That Dev hadn't already gotten there.

Your brother and his wife are going to be dead soon . . .

I got to the carport of his building. The dimly lit courtyard.

I glanced across the street and what I saw there made my spirits soar.

A police car. Stationed outside. Like Sherwood had said. Parked in the shadows.

Thank God!

I hurried over. The car's lights were off. The driver's window appeared to be down. I could see a huddled shape behind the dash.

"Officer, officer!" I yelled as I ran up. My

heart was ricocheting off my ribs. "I need some help."

I got to the car, put my hands on the window. "Officer, my brother's inside that house and—"

My stomach almost came up my throat at what I saw.

The cop inside, his cap off, head slumped to the side, blood all over the top of his neck.

And a bright red circle dotting the center of his forehead.

CHAPTER SEVENTY-FIVE

So many things to go over, Charlie. So many years . . ."

Dev had let in Susan Pollack, the woman Charlie knew as Maggie, and they had their guns out, grinning. "And the little woman. So nice to finally meet you. So where to start?" He picked up the splintered neck of Charlie's guitar that sat on the mantel. He whistled sympathetically. "Man, that must've put a dent in the ol' music career . . ."

"What do you want with us, Dev?"

"What do I want? What could we possibly want, Charlie? When it comes to you. *Hey!*" He placed the guitar neck back on

the hearth. "How'd you like the pictures? I made 'em up just for you."

His eyes grew wide, flashes of relish and enjoyment in them. "I'm thinking definitely some of my best work, don't you agree? As I remember, you two were kinda cozy back then. Man, it was sure a bitch to find her. She'd really lived quite the regular life since she left you . . ."

"You didn't have to kill her, Dev. She was just a kid back then. She wouldn't have hurt a fly."

"Of course we had to kill her, Charlie. I mean, you see that, don't you? That it wasn't even about *her,* anyway. Not about her at all." He sat across from him, spreading his knees. His gun bobbed against his thigh. "That was about *you,* mate. We had to kill her because we wanted to make the point to *you*. You get it now?"

"Yeah, I get it, Dev."

"I mean, you knew what the score was, Charlie. *Chase*. Buckaroo. You knew even back then. When you brought those pigs into the garden, the rest of us had to do *what*? Clean up the mess. Right? It's like with the Bible, Charlie. Ain't no statute of limitations on betrayal."

"That was all more than thirty years ago, Dev. We've lived out our lives."

"Thirty years . . ." The words had a certain importance to them. Dev looked over to Susan. "He wants to know what thirty years is, Maggie."

"Thirty years is what I gave up," she said to him. "Over ten thousand days, Charlie. Each one spent counting the hours. Marking them off in my head. Until I could do what I was spared to do. What Russell wanted me to do. He knew part of his flock was weak. That they would betray him. That was why some got to go with him and others had to wait behind. So they would be here one day . . ."

"Russell was crazy, Maggie! He murdered all those people. Now you're as guilty as him. What you've done is evil."

"Evil?" Susan Pollack chuckled and dangled her gun. Her smile was mirthless. "Don't you remember nothing is evil if it's done from love, Charlie? And your son . . . That was done from the greatest love I knew."

"Evan?"

The woman he knew as Mags's eyes bore in on him. "I gave up my life for him. For

Russell. What did you give up? You gave up nothing, Charlie. So you had to pay."

"What did you do to my son?" Gabby said, glaring at her.

"What did I do to your son?" Susan laughed and looked as if she was talking about a dying insect. "Your son was a confused little child who didn't know whether he was alive or dead."

"No, he was innocent," Gabby said, standing up. "He was sick."

"He was crazy, you stupid bitch. I learned more of what was in his heart in an hour than the two of you knew about him your whole lives. He wanted to kill himself out of spite just for the pain it would cause you. He hated the two of you—*you both*! But he was afraid, just like you were always afraid, Charlie. The little coward didn't have the guts to do what had to be done."

"What did you do to him?" Gabby's face became twisted with horror and rage. She took a step toward her, and Maggie raised the gun to her face, aiming it at her with two hands.

"Gabby, please . . ." Charlie tried to stand and go to her, but Dev lifted his foot and kicked him back onto the couch.

"You'll have your own turn, Charlie boy."

Gabby stared into Susan Pollack's impassive face. Tears suddenly glistened in her eyes, the moistness slowly trickling down her cheeks. *"What did you do to him?"* she pressed.

Susan Pollack merely smiled.

"Please. You were there with him. Tell me. I need to know. Do what you want to me, I don't care. But I need to know. It's all that matters to me now." She took another step toward Susan, not menacingly, more like imploring her. "Somewhere in your heart you are a woman too. Can't you see? Our lives are over. They were over the day he died. So tell me, I beg you, please. It's all that matters now. What happened to my son?"

Susan Pollack raised the gun and aimed it at Gabby's face.

Charlie's chest flooded with fear. *"Gabby, no!"*

Susan gave her a smile. Then she lowered the gun, eyes bright with delight. "You really want to know? He said I was his angel. So I did what an angel does." She grinned. "I showed him the way."

CHAPTER SEVENTY-SIX

He stepped out on the ledge once again, trembling. He gazed at the million lit candles far below, heard the whoosh of the surf crashing onto the rocks.

"Just fly, Evan . . ."

"You mean like this?" He spread out his arms.

"Yes," his angel said, "just like that."

He wanted to, he told himself. He really did. He wanted to end it, end the pain and hurt; end the confusion and the voice and all the disappointment that he knew he caused. His mom and dad had turned him over to the police.

They had abandoned him. Put him away. How can people who love you betray you? This was the way . . .

He took another step, leaning forward.

But he couldn't. He just stared out at the lights and started to cry. He realized how mistaken he had been. The things he'd done. His part in the hurt he had caused. He flashed to his mother and father. He imagined what it would be like, their hearing the news, and instead of relief and joy, he saw how devastated they would be. How, through it all, they still loved him. Through the cursing and the anger and the fights, that's what he saw there.

They loved him.

And he loved them.

This wasn't the way.

"I can't," he said, stepping back from the edge. "I can't."

"Just let God take you, Evan. I'm your angel. You know that, don't you?"

"No." He shook his head. Tears streamed down his cheeks. "I want to go home."

"You cowardly little shit," the voice

said, her tone hardening. "Do what you're fucking up here for. Do what you have to do."

"No!" He turned and stared, and suddenly saw an ugly, foreign face, a woman he had never seen before. Not his angel. Not his inner voice. "Who are you?"

"I'm not your little angel, you ignorant shit." The woman's face was now twisted in disgust. "I'm your hell, boy! And your hell is here. Now do it! You want to die? Well, I'm here to bring you to the promised land. There's no turning back. Your parents don't give a shit. They hate you just the way you hate them. Now do what you came here to do."

"No—I see it now," he said, the moon illuminating his face, slick with tears. "I came up here to see God. And now I've seen him." He turned to the panoply of lights, the millions of candles assembled before him. "Look, I understand it now. I see—"

"You see nothing, you stupid, drugged-out worm! You wouldn't know God if he was with you now."

"He is," he said, ignoring the taunts. "I can feel him. He's—"

"Then let him save you," the woman said. She threw her weight against him, forcing him toward the edge. His heart started to race. He tried to gain his balance, stumbling over a rock, his right foot coming out of his shoe.

"Dad!"

"Your daddy isn't up here," the woman said. "Just me. That's all." She pushed him again. This time he tried to grab on to her and spun his arms, teetering.

"You want your parents, little boy? You'll be with them soon enough. Tell him that, Evan. When you see God. Tell him Mommy and Daddy are on the way."

She taunted him again. He tried to latch onto her, the angel he had trusted, but found only air.

He stared down at the bottom, terrified. "Mom!"

She pushed him one last time, and he spun, seeing clearly now that the lights weren't candles at all, but streets, homes, cars, and that the choir below wasn't angelic voices, but waves crashing, hitting the rocks.

Yet, instead of fear, something else

entered his heart as his arms fluttered, unable to stop his fall.

Something welcoming. For the first time, a kind of attachment.

Everything seemed to reach out to him in a friendly way.

Mom, Dad . . .

He reached out, trying to grab on to them.

But it was only the night he held, the endless starry night.

CHAPTER SEVENTY-SEVEN

You killed him!" Gabby stared uncompre-hendingly at Susan, tears streaming down her cheeks. "You killed my son."

"I merely did what the gutless little shit didn't have the balls to do himself," Susan Pollack replied. "I showed him the way."

I heard this, pressed against the front door, having crossed the courtyard to Charlie's apartment. Susan Pollack's spiteful re-creation of Evan's death, and Gabby's heartbroken reply.

I had the dead officer's gun with me.

The curtains were drawn, but the door was still slightly ajar, and I could hear what was happening inside. I prayed that the cabbie had done what I'd begged him to and called the police. Through a slit in the curtains, I saw Dev and Susan Pollack holding guns on Charlie and Gabby.

I was the only one who could help them now.

"You're not an angel," Gabby said, her gaze blazing like a furnace bursting with hate. "You're a monster. You killed him. You're the one who should die. This monster killed our son, Charlie . . ." She was starting to lose control. "I cannot live with that."

"Dev, please!" Charlie turned to him. "You've got what you came for. Here I am. Can't you see she's suffered enough? She's done nothing to you. Let her go."

"Let her go?" Dev cockily wagged his gun. "That's where you're wrong, old friend. She's done everything to me. She's your wife, Charlie. She's the mother of your son."

Helpless tears ran into Charlie's gray beard. *"Please."*

Dev just shook his head. "Sorry, mate. No can do."

"I waited thirty years," Susan Pollack said

with a gleam in her eye. She raised the gun to Gabby's face. "You want your little boy so bad . . ." She cocked it with both thumbs. "Be sure and tell him hello from me."

I couldn't wait any longer. I burst through the door.

Susan Pollack spun, surprised.

I trained my gun on Dev, who sat there with neither shock nor real concern on his face. More like amusement.

In front of the hearth, Susan Pollack's gun had fixed on me, her hands shaking.

My problem was, I couldn't just start shooting.

They had Maxie.

"Drop the gun," I said to her, the dead policeman's gun trained on Dev.

Dev just sat there, his gun dangling nonchalantly against his thigh, actually facing Charlie. *"Gonna kill me, doc?* Bad policy, wouldn't you say, all things considered . . . ?"

"Get out of here, Jay," Charlie said. "Please. Get out now. This is our fight."

"It *is* my fight, Charlie. They've got Maxie. The police are on their way." I looked at Susan, not knowing if she would respond to reason. "There's no way out. You shoot me, I shoot him."

"Loosey-goosey, huh, doc?" Dev grinned. "That's how you want to play it? Well . . ." I saw him firm up his grip on the gun. "Just the way I like it, I guess . . ." He shifted toward me. "Though I was thinking, surely a guy with such a fancy degree would be smart enough to have been a long ways from here by now . . ."

There was a kind of chuckling, almost fatalistic quality to his tone, and it made me worry. Almost as if he sensed he had the upper hand.

We both knew I couldn't shoot him dead.

That was when Gabby turned to Charlie, her cheeks tearstained, a kind of finality on her face. "I am sorry, my husband . . ."

Fear in his eyes, he suddenly realized what she was thinking.

"I am sorry . . ." She shook her head. "But I cannot live in this hell anymore."

"Gabby, no, no!"

She lunged, surprising Susan Pollack, who brought her gun back in a defensive gesture. Gabby barreled into her, driving her back into the stone mantel with the fierceness of an enraged animal.

Susan uttered a horrific, garbled scream

as she went backward. Her mouth parted in a frieze of disbelief and horror.

Her throat impaled on the jagged neck of Charlie's guitar.

I heard the muffled blast of a gun firing, Susan's gun, but not before Gabby wrapped her hands around Susan's throat, forcing her harder and harder against the hearth, the splintered wood ripping through her larynx like a sharpened lance.

The gun fell to the floor amid her twitching, guttural rattles.

"You killed my Evan!" Gabby kept her hands on Susan, her eyes ablaze, squeezing the remaining life out of her, looking directly into her face.

We all just stood there frozen.

Gabby finally let go, Susan remaining upright for another second or two against the fireplace. Then she slid, her rattles ending, to the floor.

Gabby turned, holding her abdomen, blood on her fingers.

That's when everything went crazy.

Dev whirled and the next thing I knew, his gun went off, and I felt a scorching pain in my abdomen.

I looked at a bloody, jagged hole in my shirt.

I spun against the wall, my gun seeming to fire on its own. *Three times.*

One bullet tore into Dev's shoulder. Another found its way into his thigh, causing him to double over and cry out. The last shot shattered the mirror behind him.

He looked at the hole in his thigh, blood seeping through. His wounds seemed only to make him madder. He looked back up at me, his eyes ablaze. *"You fucking son-ovabitch!"*

He raised his gun toward me.

I heard Charlie yell out, *"No . . ."*

He threw himself into Dev, Dev's gun firing off wildly, Charlie's eyes widening.

They struggled for a few seconds, the gun kicked away, my brother's face twisted with pain and rage. I pointed my gun, tried to tear them apart, but I couldn't get a clear shot at Dev and I was fearful my next shot might kill him before he told me where Maxie was. There was blood around, but I couldn't tell from whom.

I tried to pull my brother off and get my gun on Dev, but Dev grabbed an iron poker from the fireplace, hurling me against the wall, and swung it against Charlie's head. Then he pulled himself to his feet, turning his gaze on me. "I gave you every fucking chance in the world." He swung the poker at me and I dodged it, my ribs on fire. I wanted to kill him more than anything I'd ever felt, but I couldn't.

Not until he told me what I needed to know.

He was like some savage animal made even stronger by being wounded. He charged at me, grimacing. Then he hurled himself on top of me. He grabbed my arms, trying to wrestle my gun away.

I knew my life was only as good as my strength to hold on. But he was lit up by some animal fury, his hands tightly wrapping around mine, my fingers pressed against the trigger guard. I began to feel the gun inexorably make its way toward my chest—my strength eroding, my side feeling like it had been scorched by flame—and I fought with whatever strength I still had to fend him off.

But I was losing.

"I don't know, I thought you were a smart

guy, doc." Dev grunted, eyes ablaze, his blood smeared across his shirt and mine.

"Where's my son?" I said, straining.

My chest tightened and my eyes grew wide as the muzzle kept shifting toward me.

I no longer had any certainty whose fingers were on the trigger. I was terrified that it would go off and that my son might never be found. I had already been about to die once today. Now it was happening all over again.

Dev's large hands seemed to envelop mine, my life, *Maxie's life,* in the balance. I felt with rising alarm his thighs shift over mine, his fingers about to squeeze, my breath held back in panic for what I was sure was the inevitable explosion in my chest.

Please, Jay, please, you can't let him win.

Then I heard it go off.

I screamed—braced for the sensation of the bullet tearing through me.

I didn't feel it.

Then I heard another shot.

Dev groaned, his viselike grip on me beginning to relax.

I looked up and saw my brother, one hand pressing a red hole in his own stomach, the other holding Dev's own gun.

Dev reached for his back, grasping at it like he was trying to pull a knife out of himself.

"Move away, Jay," Charlie said, his eyes like a furnace. "Just get away."

"Charlie, no. Don't!" I begged him to stop. "He has Maxie!"

Dev's face twisted, his flannel shirt matted with blood, and he let out a groan and fell off me.

I looked around. Susan Pollack was sitting on the floor with a shard of wood through her throat, a hand stuck to each side.

And Gabby . . . *Poor Gabby* . . . My sad gaze fixed on the sight of her slumped against Susan Pollack's legs, her eyes completely still and wide.

Charlie sat holding the gun. "I'm sorry, Jay, get away. He killed Evan. I want him dead."

"Where's my son?" I yelled at Dev.

His eyes rolled toward me, gloatingly.

"Where's my fucking son!" I said. "Tell me, or I'll let him kill you, so help me God."

Dev smirked and spat a glob of blood out of his mouth. Wobbly, he pushed himself up to a knee and grinned. "Tell your brother to take his shot, doc. Then we'll see where it goes, huh? We'll see who wins."

Pressing his thigh and reaching around to his back, Dev winced in pain and staggered toward the open door.

Charlie raised the gun again, and I could see him trying to summon the strength to squeeze off one final round, his aim wavering.

I begged him, "Charlie, please, no . . ."

He trained the gun on Dev's midsection. He strained in anguish to find the power. His eyes lit up with hate.

Then he just silently set it down.

Dev grinned and turned to me. "Enjoy the ride, doc."

Coughing blood, his hand reaching for his back, he slipped through the door.

I went over and took the gun out of my brother's hand. I saw a hole in his chest that was bleeding badly. He needed attention fast. I checked the wound on my side. It was ugly and red, but I was pretty certain nothing vital had been hit. Charlie looked toward Gabby, who was slumped against the wall next to Susan Pollack with an open, lifeless gaze.

I said, "I have to go after him, Charlie. Just hang in there, *please . . .*" He stared back blankly at me. "Keep pressure on your wound. Here . . ." I put his hand there. "I'll be back as soon as I can. Don't die . . ."

He nodded, eyes sagging behind his wild hair.

I ran out the door. It was dark, the courtyard erratically lit. Some people had come out of their apartments. *"Call 911!"* I shouted. "There's people dead in there. My brother's barely alive. *Help him!*"

My abdomen was on fire and when I pressed my hand to it; blood leaked out.

Don't let me bleed to death.

Twenty yards ahead, I caught the sight of a figure staggering into the darkness. I followed, spotting dots of blood on the pavement. He was probably headed for the woods across the street along the tracks, but I knew there wasn't far he could go. My biggest fear was that he would die—that I would find him rolled on his back, glassy eyed—without telling me what he knew about Maxie. I headed after him onto Division Street. I saw him up ahead, one arm hanging limply, dragging his leg.

I pointed the gun in his direction and squeezed off a shot above his head. "*Stop, Dev. It's over. There's nowhere to go.*"

He took two or three more steps, unsteadily. Then he did stop, at last. He turned slowly, blood oozing from his mouth. He had a crazed look in his wolflike eyes, a mixture of fury and defeat.

Suddenly I heard the wail of sirens. From all directions.

Dev whirled, almost losing his balance, and faced two police cars that had turned onto Division Street. Flashing lights everywhere.

I set the gun down on the pavement and raised my hands. Police leaped out of their vehicles, weapons drawn, shouting at both of us, "*Hands in the air! Get down to the ground!*"

"*Don't shoot!*" I yelled. "Whatever you do, don't shoot. He's got my son."

One of them knelt behind their car door and pointed his gun at us. "*I said put your hands in the air and get onto the ground!*"

Nervously, I crouched down, lowering my knees to the surface of the road, hands raised.

Dev just stood there, ignoring their commands. He shifted back toward me. "Want to know why you're still alive, doc?" he said, almost smiling.

My hands were in the air, an eye on the approaching officers. "Yes, I do."

He winked. "Because you still have work to do. Things yet to find out."

"Tell me what you did with Max, Dev! Please!"

More police arrived on the scene. Six or seven had now basically encircled us, barking for Dev to get down.

"Don't shoot!" I hollered, raising my palms. A couple of them were approaching, weapons drawn. "He has my son captive." Then I turned to him again. "What do you mean, Dev, things to find out?"

"Ever play cards, doc?" the bleeding killer asked.

"No." I shook my head. "Not since college."

"You oughta." He stretched a smile.

A heavyset black policeman came up, pointing his weapon directly at him. He shouted, scaring the wits out of me, "Put your hands above your head and get your ass down. *Now!*"

"You know the jack of hearts?" he said, turning away from him.

I nodded.

"You should. I think you might learn something from it. That card just might have your future in it."

The jack of hearts. I had no idea what he was talking about.

The officer bellowed one last time. "*Get on the fucking ground!*"

Dev seemed to smile, glancing at them, then back at me. "*Me*—my future's run out." He finally raised one hand high in the air, as if complying—but with the other, kind of in slow motion, reached under his shirt and came out with a knife. The same one he had waved in my face at the motel. That he had used to cut me.

I pleaded, "*Dev, don't.*"

"I think you remember." He grinned in my direction. "Some people feel I can do just about anything with this thing . . . The jack of hearts, doc. Don't forget. One day it's gonna give you a real smile. The day the devil sprouts horns."

He started to come toward me, the knife in his fist, raised high.

"Don't do it," I said, almost helpless, "please."

His pace picked up.

Now the police were really pointing their weapons at him and screaming.

"*Don't shoot,*" I hollered, "*please don't shoot!*" getting up and putting out my hands to push them back.

Suddenly, a couple of them trained their weapons on me. I was almost crying. "Don't shoot. He's got my son. *Please!*"

Dev got about five paces away. I never budged. I saw only Maxie's fate in his mad eyes, slipping into darkness.

"*Don't!*" I screamed. "*Don't! Please!*"

The next thing I heard was a deafening barrage of shots—maybe six, eight, ten echoing pops. Bullets tearing into him, ripping into his clothes with flashes of yellow and orange, the stench of cordite everywhere.

Dev was blown onto his back, the knife clattering against the pavement. From there, he just sort of raised his head and grinned at me. *You still have work to do, doc. Things yet to find out.*

That was all.

Panicked, I scrambled up to him, against shouted commands to stay where I was. He was making wheezing, guttural noises. Blood seeped out of his mouth.

"Please, Dev, please. Where's Maxie?"

"Damn" was all he said. "I thought I would see him."

"*See who?*" I asked. "*See who?*" The cops were pulling me away.

His eyes rolled back and what he grunted last explained it all.

"Russ."

CHAPTER SEVENTY-EIGHT

A moment later I was surrounded by cops, their weapons still drawn, barking commands I didn't hear.

As they pulled me away, it hurt like hell. I told them my brother was dying back inside the apartment and two additional bodies were in there.

After a quick explanation, they let me go back to the apartment.

Poor Gabby was slumped at the feet of Susan Pollack, dead. Charlie was resting where I had left him propped up against the wall.

"Charlie," I said, kneeling down next to

him. There was blood all over his palm and a lot more congealed on his shirt.

"Where's Gabby?" he asked in a hushed voice, staring glassily.

"She's here, Charlie, she's here." I didn't want him to see her. I didn't want that to be his last sight.

"She's dead, isn't she, Jay? I know she's dead."

"Yes," I said, even as the life slipped away from him. "She is."

"Evan didn't do it, Jay." His eyes showed a sparkle of vindication. "He didn't jump. She pushed him. He said he wanted to come back down. To be with us. It was just as I said all along, right?" He smiled. "I'm sorry, little brother, for dragging you into all this."

"You didn't drag me, Charlie." Tears in my eyes, I squeezed his bloody hand. "I just wanted to help."

"Help?" He smiled affectionately. "How could you possibly help me?"

"I know."

"I want to touch her, Jay." His hand fell to the floor and reached toward her body. "I need to feel her one more time. Please . . ."

I pulled Gabby's arm toward him and he

was able to press his fingers over her cold palm.

"She's all I have. She's the only thing in my life I didn't manage to destroy. Because she loved me, Jay. And Evan too."

"I know she did, Charlie. I know."

"I hope your boy is okay, Jay. I really do. You know that Evan always liked him . . . He really—"

The sound of the phone ringing pierced the room. Suddenly I remembered I had told Kathy to call here. About Max. My heart picked up.

"I'll be right back." Holding my side, I went over to the table where the phone was. Nervously I picked it up. I was so scared, I could barely get a sound out of my mouth. "Kath?"

"I have him, Jay!"

"You what?"

"I have him. Maxie's okay!"

"You do?" My eyes immediately flooded with grateful tears. The words soared through me like the happiest thing I had ever heard, just as they had on my wedding day when Kathy said, "I do," or when the doctor who delivered Max said, "Dr. Erlich, you've got a great-looking boy!"

"He's here. He was just on his way back home. From Chris's. I don't know what you thought, honey, but Max's safe. You want to hear his voice?"

"Yes," I said tearfully. "*Yes*. Put him on." *He's safe.*

"Hey, Dad." I heard my boy's uncomprehending tone, about as droning and impassive as if I had just stuck my head in his room and asked if he had a good day. "What's going on?"

"I don't know, Max, I just—" I put my hand to my face and the tears started to come unchecked. Some were from absolute joy, at knowing everything was somehow going to be okay, at making it through it all alive. And some were from grief. For Evan and Gabby. How it had cost people I loved their lives.

For Charlie.

"Dad, you okay?"

"Yeah, I'm okay," I said. I caught myself and sniffed against the sobs. "I love you, Max."

"I love you too, Dad," he said, unsure.

"Put Mom back on."

I waited a few seconds, trying to regain my composure.

"Jay?"

"Some things have happened here, Kathy. Bad things. And I want you to be protected. Call the police. I'll be in touch. I promise. *Soon*."

Kathy pressed, scared. "What kinds of things, Jay?"

I didn't know why Dev had said what he did, about my son, if he didn't have him. Or why he had let me live with just a mark on my hand when everyone else had died.

Or what he meant by *You still have work to do, doc. Things yet to find out.* The jack of hearts.

I still felt fear.

"I love you, honey," was all I said. "I gotta go. I'll call you, I promise."

I hung up and went back to see Charlie. "He's safe!" I said, kneeling back down. "Max is okay . . ."

But Charlie's eyes were fixed and still, strands of long, graying hair covering his face, a peaceful stare.

Peaceful, maybe for the first time ever. His fingers curled warmly around Gabby's.

I started to cry.

"Oh, Charlie . . ." I sat down next to him

and put my arm around his shoulders. I drew his bearded face gently down to me.

One of the policemen came over. He stood above me and looked at me, as if trying to sort it out. "Your brother?"

"Yeah." I nodded. I stroked his face gently and spread the hair out of his eyes. "And my friend."

PART IV

CHAPTER SEVENTY-NINE

I spent the next two days in the hospital, re-gaining my strength. That and undergoing about a dozen interviews with the police.

The bullet Dev had put in my side had gone clean through. Nothing vital dam-aged, like I'd thought. I had a grade-four concussion from the beating he'd given me and a bone was fractured in my jaw, which had to be wired. My hand required twenty stitches.

Other than that I was okay.

The rest of my time there was taken up with the police. Five people had died, and I was the only one who'd survived. I was deposed by the local detectives maybe a dozen times. Even the FBI.

I was very sad to learn what had happened to Don Sherwood. Over the past week, I had grown to look at him as a friend, and who knows, maybe he felt the same about me. I realized that if I hadn't drawn him in against his will, he would still be alive. Of course, that would have been true for any of us—even Charlie, if he had gone early on to the police and told them all he knew. I allowed myself to feel some solace in the suspicion that the detective's transplanted liver wasn't altogether holding up and that he had, in the end, felt he was doing something right in being part of all this. I truly wished he was there to see how it all ended and to tell me, for the umpteenth time, that I could head home. In my thoughts, though I am not much of a believer in such things, I imagined maybe he'd been rewarded and had joined his wife and son. Maybe they were a part of his last thoughts—if they weren't spent cursing me. I pictured that might have made him shake his head just a bit and smile.

Kathy flew out that next day, after I finally told her about Charlie and Gabby and everything that had happened. She kept Max safe with her parents, under the watch of a private security agent. When she stepped in the room I was in bed, still a little woozy from all the sedatives.

"Oh, Jay," she uttered sadly, looking at my puffed-up face, all black and blue and swollen. She came up to the bed with tears in her eyes and brushed her hand softly against my face.

"The side hurts more." I tried to smile.

"Don't," she said. "Don't say a word. I know." She sat down on the side of the bed.

"I'd take you through it all, but my jaw's been wired shut."

She didn't answer. She didn't even smile. I just saw the tears well lovingly and the sorrow on her face and I reached out my hand to hers and wrapped her fingers in mine.

"I'm sorry," I said.

She took a breath and nodded. "I'm sorry too."

"For what?"

"Because I judged them." She meant Charlie and Gabby. "And because I guess I judged you too. I wasn't there for you, honey, and it almost cost you your life."

I squeezed her. I tried to say in my look

that it didn't matter. That I was just glad she was there. "I thought they were different, Kath . . . But they weren't. They were the same. They loved Evan just as we love Max and Sophie. And it killed them, the same as it would kill us if we lost one of them."

"I know." She reached into her purse and took out a small frame. "I didn't know what to bring, so I just brought this."

In it was a picture of the four of us, on the deck of our place in Amagansett, the kids sitting on the railing of the deck, Maxie's cap turned backward, Sophie in a Coldplay T-shirt, the sun on their faces.

"I would have brought the Bob Seger CD, but I figured it wasn't exactly a lucky charm . . ."

I laughed. *"Don't,"* I said, pointing to my jaw. There were a lot of things that rushed into my heart at that moment, but only one made it to my lips.

"Yes, it was."

Kathy rested her head against my stomach and I stroked her hair.

Damn lucky.

Thursday, they let me leave. I wanted to hop on a plane as fast as I could—be back in my own house, my own world, with the kids.

But there was one last thing I had to do.

I had Charlie's and Gabby's remains cremated at the same mortuary where we had visited Evan only a few days before.

Charlie and I had always been different. Different roots sprung from the same tree. I had had love and support, and I guess I wasn't bipolar, and things just worked out for me.

Charlie had been contentious from the start, and life didn't treat him well.

Yet in the end we were the same. And it had been Charlie who saved me. I meant what I said to that cop: I hadn't just lost my brother; I'd also lost my friend.

I knew exactly what the two of them would have wanted. Seeing their hands joined at the end told me so even more.

It was only a matter of where.

That was *my* decision.

The morning of our flight home, we drove back out to Morro Bay.

"It's huge!" Kathy said as we got within sight, driving down to Embarcadero. I saw her eyes widen behind her sunglasses. "And it's beautiful."

"I know. There's a legend that when God created the valley here this was where he stopped to sit. Apparently, there used to be pelicans all around here. And peregrines. The shallow bay was kind of a feeding ground for them. But something's driven them away."

"What?" Kathy asked.

I shook my head. "I don't know."

We drove down the inlet and parked near the same spot I had parked with Charlie and Gabby. From the backseat, I took out the three cardboard boxes we had brought. Each contained a few ounces of gray, silty ash.

I pointed. "This way."

We walked out into the shadow of the gigantic mound, past the handful of tourists and fishermen who were gathered there. Past the chain-link fence. Kathy looked at me, unsure. "You sure this is okay?"

I nodded. "Yes."

We made our way onto the tiny, gray cove of beach and the large, jagged rocks. I looked for the narrow path that went up the slope. The sun was shining. The surf was up and occasionally a wave crashed over the outer rocks, sending spray into the breeze.

"You need some help?" Kathy asked, navigating her way across the rocks.

"No, I'm okay." I knew my gait was a bit unsteady. But I also knew where I wanted to go. I looked up and saw the promontory halfway up the cliff and pointed. "Here it is . . ."

We looked at the jigsaw of boulders at the bottom of the rock.

This was where they had found him.

We stood, staring up at the enormous wall, waves spraying spectacularly.

I thought of Charlie and Gabby climbing over the same rocks just a few days ago, and a burning sensation rose up at the back of my eyes.

"It feels like a good place, Jay. It really does." Kathy smiled, seeing my eyes well up. "I think they'd be happy here . . ."

"Okay."

We took out a container the mortuary had provided us and opened each of the cardboard boxes containing Charlie, Gabby, and Evan's remains. We poured a slow stream at first, then steadier, letting the flow of ashes all merge into one.

My brother, his wife, and their son.

When we were done, we just stood there.

Kathy shrugged. "You ought to say something."

I hadn't thought about saying anything. So much had happened. All that seemed to come to mind was "Here's to Charlie and Gabby and Evan. Your lives all took a different path. It wasn't a straight one, but you all ended up in the same place. *The right place.* With each other."

"Rest in peace, guys," Kathy said. "At last." She looked at me. The spray from an incoming wave shot over the rocks.

It seemed like the right time.

We both took hold of the container and, with a nod, threw some of the ashes over the rocks.

A wave crashed over them, battering them with spray. We threw out more as the next wave barreled in, the ashes merging with foam and sand. I liked that. I watched them squeeze through the maze of rocks and head back out to sea.

"Look!" Kathy pointed.

Out on one of the sandbars was a pelican. Just one. It stood there, all spindly legs and beak, seeming to observe us, like some solitary mourner at a funeral. Then its gaze drifted back out toward the bay, scanning the tiny whitecaps for a meal.

Kathy grinned that beautiful blue-eyed smile of hers. "See, they're back."

"Kathy, I love you," I said.

It seemed to startle her. She covered her eyes with her hand, staring back into the sun. Then she smiled. "I love you, too, Jay."

Suddenly the pelican flapped its wings and took off across the shallow shoals. We watched as it dove into the ripples, snapping something up in its beak, and rose—graceful, almost majestic—and flew over the bay.

I smiled.

The foam and the surf turned to spray again on the rocks and sand and then, as if pulled by an angel's hand, slid back out to sea.

I nodded to Kathy and lifted the container. "One more."

CHAPTER EIGHTY

We flew back to New York. Max and Sophie, who had come up from school, were waiting at the house with Kathy's folks. Tons of hugs and grateful tears as we came through the doors.

Still, Dev's final words rarely left my brain.

And why had he let me live, when everyone else had died?

You still have work to do, doc. Things yet to find out.

I spent the next couple of weeks recovering. I went into the office a couple of times and checked up on my cases. I didn't know exactly when I would begin to practice again. Some of that related to my hand, which was slowly healing.

Some was related to my mind.

You know the jack of hearts? You should. I think you might learn something from it.

It was like he was continuing to taunt me from the grave.

Gradually, things got back to normal. Sophie stayed a few days and went back to Penn. Max started up in school. Dev's threat seemed to pass.

"It's over, it's over," Kathy would say, trying to calm me. No matter how many times I woke up in the night in a sweat.

Haunted by the same recurring dreams.

Coming to in the ambulance, Dev's words chilling me: *"We've got your son!"* Susan Pollack's gruesome death. Or Dev, coming at me with that knife. Getting closer.

But this time, no shots brought him down.

Each time, Kathy would wrap her arms around me and pull me back down, brush my sweaty cheeks with her hand, saying, "It's over, baby. It is."

But I knew it wasn't over.

They'd let me live, for some reason.

You still have work to do, doc. Things yet to find out.

The jack of hearts. One day it's gonna give you a smile.

I knew I'd never be able to fully rest, or put it behind me, until I figured out why.

After about a month, I woke up with a start one night. The clock read 3:17 A.M. I was breathing heavily. My heart felt like it had been given a jolt of epinephrine. Damp sweat drenched my back and sheets.

Kathy shot up next to me. Since we'd gotten back, she'd been telling me that I ought to talk with someone, and I'd begun to think that maybe I should. She reached across the bed and put her hand on my shoulder. "Another dream, honey?"

"Yeah. A crazy one." I sat up in the bed and tried to clear my head.

This one had been about my father. That incident at the house in California, when Charlie, the producer dude, and Houvnanian had come up to see him.

The same dream I'd had out west.

Except this time, the "music producer dude" was Dev. His ratty clothes and wolf-like eyes.

And it really wasn't a record they were talking about but somehow "making him pay." *My dad.* For all the crap he had done to Charlie.

And instead of just smiling that creepy, probing smile of his and simply leaving, Houvnanian nodded to Dev, who took out this blade.

And suddenly everyone was screaming blazing, angry taunts, accusing my father of betraying them. And then they started to stab him. Like what I had read in Greenway's book. But it wasn't Riorden, it was my father. They were hacking away at him. Writing words in his blood. "Pig." "Betrayer."

And I was outside the glass window watching it all take place. Unable to do a thing. Or scared to. The three of them cursing and stabbing, until in shame and grief I had to turn away . . .

And that's when I woke.

Kathy tried to calm me. "It was a dream, honey, only a dream." She lowered me back to the covers. "Try to go back to sleep. It's okay."

I closed my eyes again. "I'll try."

But I couldn't get back to sleep. My heart was racing. I couldn't clear my father from my mind. I almost felt like Houvnanian's icy grip had me by the bones.

Like he was mocking me. Thousands of miles away. Taking his revenge.

Whatever the jack of hearts was about.

His revenge on me.

I waited until Kathy's breathing told me she was back asleep.

Suddenly I couldn't lie there anymore.

I crawled out of bed and went down to the basement in my T-shirt and shorts.

I wasn't sure what drew me there, just something urgent and incomplete related to my father.

There was a cabinet underneath the built-in bookshelves where we stored boxes full of old things. Albums, folders stuffed with items from when the kids were young, at camp and at school. My old papers from med school.

My father's artifacts.

His old photos that ended up with us—from when he dated models and was in the navy. At the beach. Playing tennis. His military records. Newspaper articles. A bunch of worthless old stock certificates from one of his business ventures that was long defunct.

There was also a box of things from the night he drove his car into the bay.

I'd never fully made my peace with what had happened. He always drank at night. Half a bottle of Cutty was his usual routine. Generally he was in front of a TV with a chicken he'd pulled apart. And sometimes in his favorite pubs. No matter how drunk, he always managed to find his way home.

He could do it with his eyes closed.

A new business venture he was gearing up to launch had fallen apart. The partners pulled out—this time, Russian Jews from Brooklyn who'd been implicated in insurance schemes. For someone who used to run with the glamour crowd, truly the bottom of the barrel.

He pretty much kept to himself in those last days. He'd driven out to the beach and had a couple of Rob Roys at one of his haunts there. I was told he'd tried to dazzle some woman at the bar without much success. He threw a twenty down as a tip for his guy behind the bar and waved, and made his way home.

I opened the box containing his things.

There was his death certificate, from the

Suffolk County coroner. *Cause of Death: Accidental drowning*.

A copy of the police investigation related to the event. It mentioned the tire marks heading into the bay. On a road he had driven a thousand times. A high level of alcohol in his system.

My father's adage was that you kept on turning corners. No matter what life dealt you. You never gave up.

I guess he'd turned one too many that night.

I sat on the floor piecing through his old effects. I'd never really looked through them. My dad had hurt so many people in his life. At the end, there were only a handful of people who even came to the funeral. I had just wanted to put it behind me then.

One of the photos I came across was of him and Charlie at my dad's beach house, taken in happier times.

At the bottom of the box, I found a thick manila envelope. From the Quogue Police Department.

It contained whatever he'd had on him at the time of the accident.

I recalled looking through it once, just after it happened. My dad's possessions at the end were minor. I'd given his Cartier money clip to my son as a keepsake. All we got were worthless paintings and penny stock certificates. I remembered being pissed off, even a little ashamed, at how his life had declined.

But now I was suddenly interested. I untied the envelope clasp and poured out the contents.

His oily, worn wallet, crammed with his stuff. His driver's license; I noted, laughing—*typical*—that it had expired the year before. His credit cards—what he'd been living on in those last days. Around sixty dollars in cash, dried out from the bay. Dozens of meaningless receipts—why he kept them I never knew. Probably so he could phony them up for his taxes, I surmised.

I was about to toss the wallet back when I noticed something.

Suddenly my whole body shook to a stop.

I was staring at something, but it didn't make sense. But more than not making sense, it made me rethink everything. In a flash.

Charlie. My father.

Houvnanian.

My life.

A thousand different memories. *Forty-five years.*

It was a card. A playing card. Hidden among a stack of business cards, in the inside flap of his wallet.

I knew exactly which one before I even turned it around.

The jack of hearts.

The single eye—a circle had been drawn around it, just so there was no doubt.

And it was winking.

Winking, as if to remind me just how foolish and blind I had been.

He'd left the restaurant pretty sober, the bartender had claimed. Yes, it had been a little foggy. But his was the only accident that night. The tire tracks suggested a moderate rate of speed. He'd made the same drive a hundred times. In far more drunken states.

My father could have driven to Canada after two Rob Roys!

You still have work to do, doc. Things yet to find out.

Winking, just as Russell Houvnanian had winked at me.

Because he knew the truth.

As if to say, all these years later, *No one*

knows when the master will choose to come back, or in what manner.

Only the master will know.

Me.

I stared, a desperate plea of *No, no, it can't be,* clawing up inside me, as a word, a single, haunting word, formed in my brain.

Watch.

EPILOGUE

On the first weekend of the fall, Max Erlich bounded down the steps of the music shop onto Greenwich Avenue, lugging his guitar. He had found it on Craigslist, an old Gibson—for all of sixty bucks—and he was learning how to play. His dad had bought him a series of lessons on Saturday mornings at ten.

Down the hill, his mom was grabbing a latte at Starbucks or window-shopping at Richards while she waited for him.

Since what had happened, they never let him get too far away.

Outside the store, a guy was playing on

the street. Kind of a grungy, older dude. Max checked him out—one suffering from a severe wardrobe malfunction. An old green army jacket and a crumpled cowboy hat.

Ever since he'd started messing around on Ryan Frantz's guitar at lacrosse camp, learning to play had become Max's new passion in life. He played in his room at night, on his bed, teaching himself little riffs from his favorite artists, Daughtry and Coldplay. He wasn't exactly musical—neither of his parents played anything or even pushed him in that direction. His sister used to take dance; that was about the extent of it.

But he liked how it made him feel, surprising himself with some new riffs. His teacher, Rick, claimed he had a knack for it. And besides, Samantha Schall thought it was kinda cool, and she was certainly texting him a lot more now.

The guy on the bench seemed like he was waiting for a lesson. But as Max listened, he was actually sounding pretty good.

He picked away at it—a vintage Martin—with nimble, worn-down fingers. It seemed to come naturally—he muttered some lyrics under his breath, not even looking at the instrument. It sounded a bit like country, Max thought. He recognized the tune.

The dude could play!

The guy finished, finally looking up from under his hat. His face was wrinkled, and he had a scar on his cheek. A couple of other people who had stopped uttered a few words of praise and moved on down the street. He didn't have his hat out and didn't seem to be looking for money, and truth was, on Greenwich Avenue, that wouldn't go over big.

Max grinned at him, impressed. "*Sweet!*"

The guy nodded back in appreciation, with yellowed, ground teeth and a mustache on his weathered face. He noticed Max's guitar. "You play?"

Max shrugged. "Learning. But I like what you were doing there. Neil Young?"

"Fogelberg . . ." The man shook his head. Then he smiled. "Maybe a bit before your time." He strummed a few more chords. "I could show you, though."

For a moment Max thought, *Sure, awesome!* He'd kill to learn how to pick like that. Then he remembered his mom, down the avenue.

"Sorry, wish I could," he said. "I gotta go."

"Responsibilities, eh?" The guitar player grinned. "I getcha." He rested the guitar on his knee. "Listen, you seem a good soul. I could meet you here sometime. Maybe next Saturday. Show you a few things. Just you and me. How's that sound?"

It sounded good, actually. But then Max hesitated. "I don't know . . ." The guy seemed cool and all. Maybe a little old. Not much of a threat.

"I tell you what . . ." The guy dug into his pocket and came out with a scrap of paper. A matchbook, actually. And a worn-down pencil. "You can give me a call, when you're around. I'll meet you here. Nothing fancy. I'll have you picking like a pro in no time . . ."

He slowly printed out his name and his number in a shaky hand. He handed it to Max. "How's that?"

"Cool!" Max glanced at it, then looked around, suddenly a little wary. "Sorry, I gotta go."

"No worries. I'm Vance, by the way," the man said.

"I'm Max." He folded up the matchbook, about to put it in his pocket.

"Nice to meet you, Max. You remember, next Saturday maybe? You let me know."

"Okay." Max put the matchbook in his pocket and had started down the hill when the guy called after him. *"Hey, Max!"*

He turned.

"Stays our little secret, right? No reason to involve anyone else." He winked. "You know how parents are."

Max grinned. "Yeah, I know."

He headed down the hill, not sure if he would keep the guy's number or toss it into a bin. It all seemed a little weird.

Still, he'd sure like to be able to play like that.

At the bottom of the block, Max took a look at the matchbook, at what he'd written. The shaky letters, *Vance.*

On the cover, there was a logo he was familiar with.

CBS, the television company. He'd seen it a million times. He stared, wondering where a guy like that would have come in contact with it.

That big wide eye. Staring at him.

He'd keep it, he decided. Max folded it up and put it in his pocket.

Samantha Schall's smile was the kicker.

Man, he said to himself, *I'd give anything to play like that.*

575 | Author's Note
When Evan first fell "in love" with the girl in the

AUTHOR'S NOTE

This much is true: On the morning of July 26, 2009, my twenty-five-year-old nephew Alex—bipolar and severely troubled for most of his brief life—was found on the jagged rocks at the bottom of the six-hundred-foot-high Morro Bay Rock. He'd either jumped or fallen some time during the night.

The day before, Alex had been released from a hospital mental health ward into the care of a small halfway facility, just like the character Evan in this book. Only three days earlier Alex had been taken into custody after a violent episode at his home, which, truth be told, was not the calmest of environments. Alex's body was found with no identification on it; he was processed by the local police and the morgue as a John Doe for almost two days until his parents were notified of his death. And wrenchingly, as in the book, they did hear the story of the then-unidentified youth who jumped off the rock on the news, only to learn a day later that it was their own son. And like Evan, my nephew's left Nike hightop sneaker was never found.

While questions still remain about what happened to Alex, such as issues related to his care, whether he jumped or fell, what was in his mind when he left the halfway house, instead of answers, all I have at my disposal is fiction. If you want to learn more of the background or information related to the real story of what happened to my nephew, including photos, family blogs, etc., I hope you will go to alexwemissyou. com.

This book is for Michael and Suzanne, but it is also for anyone who has suffered the loss of a child. As a father myself, I wince every time I relive this true family story during the writing—and still do every time it comes to mind. This book is my brief anthem of remembrance to a life that didn't turn out as anyone had hoped. And having been present at Alex's birth, having seen him that first day in all the beautiful promise that any new life holds, I am also reminded that, like a lot of us, I could have done more.

To the people who had a hand in its writing: Dr. Greg Zorman and Dr. Elizabeth Frost for medical advice; Roy Grossman, Brooke Martinez, and my wife, Lynn, early readers of the drafts; Henry Ferris and David Highfill, my editors at William Morrow, whose dual efforts made this tale come to life so much more compellingly; and to the rest of the team who took it from there; and to Simon Lipskar, for his usual insights and council, I give you my deepest thanks.

This book was a totally different kind of story for me to write, and all of you have made it easier and far better.